RETURN OF THE CONVICT

A Novel of 97,500 words

WILLIAM ALAN

THOMAS

ISBN: 151925508X
ISBN 13: 9781519255082

For Rob Thomas. (1947-2004)

ACKNOWLEDGEMENTS

Return of the Convict was not done in a vacuum. Sylvia Taylor, past president of the Federation of B.C. Writers and author of The Fisher Queen, looked over the manuscript at an early stage, and encouraged me to reexamine the plans for the novel's structure.

As the project evolved, I sought feedback from members of the Editors' Association of Canada. I'd worked with Marg Gilks before. Susan Mayse took an interest also. I contacted Eva van Emden originally for her strong science background, but her advice on other aspects of the story was sound as well. These editors approached the script from different angles, and their insights went deep.

Eventually things fell into place, and another draft was completed. At this point I turned to Garth Pettersen, a retired teacher and member of the Chilliwack Writers, who is also interested in science fiction. Garth made a thorough reading of the manuscript and sent me comments, chapter by chapter. His help was crucial, and I remain grateful.

Michael Hiebert did the final copy edit. A brilliant and dynamic younger man who's won prizes for his short stories and literary suspense novels, Michael improved the book immensely.

My last acknowledgement is to Charles Dickens. The basic setup of Return of the Convict was taken from Dickens's masterpiece, Great Expectations, and his influence remains throughout. Borrowing from the classics seems out of fashion these days, but in my opinion it's well worth doing.

CHAPTER 1

Dec. 16, 2143

There were forty-five of us transports crammed into the space bus, and even though everyone was sedated, the two and a half day trip was arduous.

After we docked there was a slight shaking. Our capsule shot backward, and stopped. With a hissing of air, the door slid open. "Welcome to Mir," a man's voice said. "Everybody out."

The artificial gravity here was less than the moon's; I got up without much difficulty. Two uniformed guards checked us off as we came out. "You're Dominic Tessier," one said crisply, when she touched my ID tag with a scanner.

My legs uncertain, I stepped onto a moving sidewalk that took us through a tunnel. In a few minutes the passageway curved, and the main terminus area of the space station came into view. I held tight to the railing and stared. The people here arrived and departed from all over the solar system: personnel from the space ships, businessmen, and new-world workers. Some, while roughly dressed, had a special swagger. I thought they might be prospectors. Then a group of T-men walked through in unisex suits and skull caps. Although silent, their expressions and gestures showed communication. Thanks to their brain implants, they were telepathic.

Only a few months earlier, I'd been a student at the Space Training Academy. My brain was being transformed through implants, and I looked forward myself, to a career in space as a T-man administrator. An awful injustice had been done to me, and my dreams were trashed.

Yet I felt no regret, resentment, or any emotion at all. A silver bracelet around my wrist created a chemically-induced docility, more powerful than chains.

Our guards took us along a walkway above a large, brightly lit loading dock. Through the side-mesh I could see the *Stellar Blossom*. The ship's blue hull seemed to stretch on forever; it dwarfed the men gathered to service her.

Ahead was a short, balding man I remembered from my time in jail. "Phil," I called, catching up to him.

He turned to me without surprise. "Hello, Dom," he said in the slow speech of the bracelet wearers. He pointed up the dock to a line of people entering the ship under a bright yellow canopy. "Did you notice? Some are women."

"Passengers," I said. "A different world."

Inside the ship, Asian men in yellow jumpsuits put me through another scanner. They directed me to a corridor where Phil was walking up ahead.

The interior of the ship was light brown. There were no sharp corners, only curves. The walls and floors yielded to the touch, and there were hand-holds throughout. Music came from some of the rooms.

The music stopped when we entered the prison section. I was hit immediately by the smell of vomit. In here, everything was a drab gray.

At Compartment Six, Phil and I parted. "I'll see you soon, Dom," he said. "We'll play some cards."

"I'll look forward to it," I said.

Compartment Seven was a long, windowless room, with double bunk beds on either side. My bed was on the bottom, and it had a small dresser at the end. Inside the drawers, I found a change of clothes and some toilet things. I sat down on the bed, put my feet up and lay back. More men kept coming in.

After about half an hour, a young, dark haired man claimed the bottom bunk across the aisle from me. I reached over to shake his hand. "It's good to see you, Nevil."

Later that night the ship moved, and we were in weightless conditions.

Chimes sounded, early in the morning. "Everybody up," a voice said. "Report to the dining area for breakfast and orientation."

Moving in zero gravity is difficult at first, and men were drifting around. My space cadet training helped a lot. Using the hand-holds, I went out into the hallway and followed lighted signs to a bright, clean room where rows of chairs with attached trays were fastened to the floor.

There was little laughter amongst us, and no loud talk. Everyone here wore the silver bracelet.

Large windows let us see outside. Not far away was the space station we'd been docked at the night before. It was slowly spinning. The great globe, Earth, loomed beyond. There was no view of the space elevator, but our ship was being loaded on all sides by small, slow moving craft that carried huge container modules.

After breakfast the windows darkened, and the room lights dimmed. With a blast of music a large video screen lit up.

A stocky, middle aged Asian man in a dark blue uniform looked at us from behind a desk. "Welcome, convicts," he said in clear, unaccented English. "I'm Captain Lee, commander of the *Stellar Blossom*. You're embarking on a voyage of almost six months, destination Mars. Use the exercise facilities at least an hour a day; don't let your muscles atrophy. Also, I urge everyone to stretch your minds. Seize every opportunity to prepare for the new world ahead."

The captain's image was replaced by a black, starry sky. A thrilling violin solo began, followed by the rolling of drums. Then a panoramic view of the Martian terrain showed endless plains, enormous mountains, and deep canyons. "We who live here love this land," a woman said. Excavators gouged holes in the side of a mountain, and loaded giant trucks. The scene shifted to the inside of a smelter, and rivers of molten metal.

"The strong ones do best here," the woman said. Dressed in a skin-tight black suit, she was young and slim, standing outside a busy entrance-way to a glittering glass building. "Mars can be difficult for the dreamer or the aesthete, but those of purpose and energy will carve a place. One main law prevails: work or die. Make your living, because nothing will be handed to you."

When the lights came back on, we began a series of interest and aptitude tests which were to help us choose the type of work we'd do on Mars. Around four that afternoon, I discussed my results with a counselor.

My interview was in a small booth in the library. The image on the screen was of a vivacious, older woman. She was enthusiastic about the results of my tests, and said that lots of opportunities were open to me.

In the course of the interview, I learned there was a shortage of entertainers on Mars. My first career choice, musician, might be viable.

Despite the silver bracelet, my spirits lifted as I returned to the prison area. Cadets at the Space Training Academy were encouraged to take arts electives, and I'd picked music. This chance selection became more than a hobby to me; music was something I loved.

Doubt arose within me. Was musician a job for a real man?

This feeling was so strong, I stopped to think. These concerns were alien to me. I revered musicians. Music explores the vast range of spiritual possibilities, and provides harmony, and outright joy, even in darkest times.

After this, I was blasted by pure scorn.

Then I continued on, but not as a person unused to weightless conditions. No, I moved like a mature wolf in its native forest. The slightest pulls and twists propelled me with speed and power. I arrived at Compartment Seven in almost no time.

Although several other prisoners were here, the room was quiet and peaceful. Lying back on my bed, I closed my eyes. For a moment I'd lost control of my own body.

This demonstration on how to get around without gravity was helpful, and perhaps needed. To my sorrow, Lucas Rivera, the man who ruined my life, was the only possible source.

A convict and Martian transport himself, Lucas was my parent clone. An aged dissolute, he suffered many health problems, and the brain implants I'd received as a space cadet provided him the opportunity to reclaim his youth. Then a setback in his health led to a desperate attempt to force a merger. I fought back and killed Lucas, but the information about his self was sent to my implants.

This invasion of privacy was monstrous for me. My brain is my only castle, and I'd never doubted that I was autonomous and in charge.

Lucas claimed descent from Genghis Khan, one of the worst men who ever lived. Homer describes the warrior Achilles as a sacker of cities, and a breaker of men. The conquests of Genghis Khan went beyond anything that Achilles could have dreamed of.

The Lucas I'd met was no Genghis Khan or Achilles. Still he did not hesitate to breach my defenses, and force himself on me. Lucas was a wily and powerful opponent, who'd established himself in my brain. There'd be further attempts to gain control.

He must not enjoy the slightest influence over my actions. Knowing that he disliked musicians made me determined to consider music as my new career.

Luckily I enjoyed many advantages over him. My health, youth, superior education, and training in mental strength and rational thought were all in my favor. I'd build him a dungeon, deep in the depths of my mind, and keep the brutish lout locked up forever.

My success depended on understanding him thoroughly, and I had access to all his memories.

It was time to sort through them systematically, just as I'd learned to do at the academy . . .

CHAPTER 2

Three weeks in the recovery spa at the bottom of the space elevator could not overcome the effects of thirty years off-world, but Lucas Rivera was anxious and had to get going. He took a flight to New York City, stayed overnight in a hotel near the airport and, in the morning, boarded Continental's airship to Seattle.

A lanky man in his fifties, he had a blond brush cut and wore casual, loose-fitting clothes, distinguished only by a homemade bead belt with a red buckle. His seat was on the topmost of the three passenger decks. Thankfully, his section was not crowded and he was able to relax.

At Chicago, more people got on and a large, older woman sat beside him. Sturdy looking in her long-sleeved gray dress, she had alert blue eyes and a mass of curly, orange-blonde hair. Almost immediately she started fussing with some presents. She looked up at Lucas. "For my grandchildren," she said.

A diminutive stewardess brought around an extensive drink menu. After consulting with the grandmother, Lucas decided on a vegetable juice cocktail with a touch of Bliss, guaranteed to add "enjoyment at being high."

When the drinks arrived, the woman took the stewardess's hand and looked closely at a silver band that held a sparkling, blue-tinged stone. "Is this a space diamond?"

"It's from a mine off of Greenland. My boyfriend's an undersea geologist."

The juice cocktail failed to lift Lucas's enervating drowsiness. After excusing himself to the grandmother, he took the escalator to an observation room on the under deck. Here he viewed the mammoth work project on the plains below.

"Eighteen years after the Yellowstone eruption, reclamation is still ongoing," the interactive map-tutor said. Huge worker robots secured mats composed of native plants and grasses, ramming root nodes deep into the cleared ground. Far in the distance, mountains of ash were bulldozed into a deep chasm.

This was his homeland, and he longed to aid in the struggle. As a returned transport though, he would not be welcome. The bitterness swept over him anew, the shame and sorrow at being sent away forever by the court. "Traitor," they called him. "Hard core gangster." "An arrogant, selfish criminal." It was not true and it was not fair.

It was a huge gamble to come back here, but there was no choice. He was terribly ill, and the Martian doctors had run out of options. Vancouver's Grace Hospital had technology that might save him, and one of the owners, Dr. Johansen, owed Lucas a big favor.

"You have two messages from Mars," Tomi said.

The small octopod clinging to his back was a Martian robotics product that used the movements and energy field of the human body as its power source. An implant in Lucas's brain allowed him to communicate with Tomi by thought.

"The first one's from your wife."

Lucas caught a scent of lavender and saw a white envelope stamped Universal Post. Then Lena appeared. "I'm thinking of you," she smiled. Dressed in a white robe, her light brown hair falling loosely to her shoulders, she was on the couch in the solarium of their Marsport apartment. A well-known musician and composer, Lena came from one of Mars's first families. "I trust the trip went well, and you're receiving this message on Earth. Things are about the same here. I'm working hard, preparing for the concert. I miss you. I love you."

Lucas's eyes moistened. Their marriage saved his life; all he'd achieved he owed to her. Despite her affairs with other women, she never shut him out.

He imagined the two of them holding hands and let his love for her well up. "Hello my darling," he said. "As you can see, I'm here on Earth, passing over the Great Plains. The trip went well and soon I'll be at the hospital. I love you forever."

"The next message was sent by Rosie," Tomi said.

"All right, give it to me."

His partner looked up from her desk in the upstairs office of their bar, The Two Moons. A dark-haired, slender woman, she wore a red top and satiny white slacks. Music and laughter drifted up; business was good. "Hello, Lucas. It's busy tonight. I wish you were here."

He met Rosie when she first arrived in Marsport. Nineteen years old, transported on some trumped-up charge, she'd arrived scared, with no idea what to expect. He showed her around and helped her get a job. Now in her early thirties, Rosie was endlessly resilient and energetic. Shrewd and sometimes ruthless in business, she was perfect for The Two Moons. All types of people came to their bar but nothing fazed Rosie.

"Oh Lucas, if anyone can do it, you can. My prayers are with you, and I live for the day when you walk into The Two Moons once more. Good fortune, my dear spaceman."

"Rosie it's wonderful to hear from you," Lucas replied. "Yes I'm on Earth, and at this moment I'm in an airship heading west. It won't be long till I see the boy. Go ahead and contact the lawyers, and make sure my apartment's ready. Also you can notify Dr. Johansen that the Ferryman is on his way."

The contact with Mars cheered Lucas up considerably. "Lena and Rosie love you too," he told Tomi. "Aren't you grateful to have me as your master?"

"You've often told me that you're of noble birth, a descendant of the conqueror Genghis Khan," Tomi replied. "Serving you is an honor for me."

"Well, never mind that now. You did a good job getting those messages through and I'm glad to have you with me."

Lucas drifted off, and when Tomi woke him, they were above Montana. Ash was heavy on the ground; he might have been looking at the sands of Mars, except that this desert was a whitish-gray.

"We've entered a void spot," Tomi said. "The ship's lost contact with the outside world."

A long, black form moved slowly past their window. Over large for taxi service and smaller than a freighter, the smooth, cigar-shaped craft had wings which looked retractable. This type of ship was sometimes used by Earth-based prospectors.

A horn blasted repeatedly. "All passengers sit down," a deep voice said. "There's been an unforeseen emergency and we have to land." Forward motion stopped, lights flashed, and the ship descended rapidly.

Lucas was glued to the window, shocked to have his carefully planned trip disrupted by random chaos. They landed on a patch of flat plain.

The hijackers came from a thick stand of leafless trees. Masked from head to foot in black, they rode their four-legged robots horseback style in a way seldom seen on Mars. The side walls of the dromies were translucent, and more men sat in the inside compartments. The riders wore clown masks. They were Resisters Lucas realized: the surviving North American Federation fighters, still waging guerrilla warfare against the United World States.

The horn blasted again. "This is your captain speaking. The ship is now in the command of insurgents and they are boarding this vessel. Do what they say and we'll be on our way again shortly. I repeat: cooperate with the brigands and make no attempt to fight back."

Shouted curses and harsh laughter rang throughout the ship.

The crew was outside, watched by two Resisters who carried ray guns. The taller one seized Lucas's stewardess and took her ring. She protested vehemently, but nobody else moved. The sweep of a boop gun would give the crew an excruciating death.

Three of the raiders entered the observation room. "It's tax time," one yelled. "Get ready! The North American Federation needs your money and any valuables."

A heavy-set man with a huge red smile painted on his mask confronted Lucas. "Thought you could hide from the tax man, did you? Well I found you."

"I'll gladly donate to the NAF," Lucas said politely. He opened his money folder, showing the bills. "Here's everything I have."

The Resister took the folder and shoved it in his bag. "Much appreciated. Now I'll ask you to stand up." He ran his black-gloved hands over

Lucas's body. "You older ones can be tricky, always trying to hide things." When he felt Tomi plastered against the upper back, he stopped. "Let me see it." Lucas pulled off his shirt, and the man snickered. "Look at the thing, holding on for dear life." Then he stiffened and stepped back. "The lumitoo on your shoulder, are you one of them? The boss has to see this. If you're faking he'll kill you."

Outside, the sky was clear and the wind was strong and warm. Seeing a ramp set up to the ship's open cargo hold, Lucas gave a low whistle. "Something big is happening."

"Shut up," the Resister snarled. They went inside the hold, where a man with a red "C" on his back watched four others wrestle a metallic gray case, marked with the UWS government insignia, onto a hovercart. "Colonel. This passenger has the same mark as you on the right shoulder."

The man turned and his fierce blue gaze softened. "For God's sake, it's Lucas. You're coming with me, brother."

CHAPTER 3

<u>March 9, 2143, Vancouver</u>
Early Saturday morning our dormitory building shook and I woke up. Everything was very still. "Did you feel it?" I asked my roommate, Wang Yu.

"Earthquake," he said. "Charles, are you tracking this?"

"Yes, Master Wang." As always, our school's voice was perfectly calm. "According to the initial reports, a hundred and twenty kilometer stretch of northern Vancouver Island has dropped about three meters."

Jumping out of bed, Wang went to look outside. He wore only the bottom of his pajamas, and the rocket lumitoo glowed faintly on his chest. Most of us space cadets bore the same mark.

"Stand back from the window," Charles said sharply.

Wang reacted immediately, and made it to his bed just as the building moved again. "Don't do that," he shouted to the Earth.

Things calmed down after this, so I lay back and closed my eyes.

"Dom, are you asleep?" Wang asked.

"Trying to," I said. "There's an important meeting in the morning."

"You'll survive," he said. "Good night."

"Good night."

Around nine-thirty that morning, I left for my psychology appointment. It was pouring with rain, and the wind was blowing hard. The Space Training Academy is on Point Grey, a peninsula that juts into the Strait of Georgia. STA's parent, the University of British Columbia, is to the northwest; it took about twenty minutes to walk over.

I kept an earphone in to hear about the tsunami. There'd been considerable damage on Vancouver Island, but here we were protected.

Inside the hospital, the high ceilings and wide halls had a hushed, timeless quality. UBC is a world leader in brain transformation, and the west wing is given over to this field. My psychologist had an office on the third floor.

The waiting room was decorated in cream, pink and chocolate, with curved walls and soft, conforming chairs. The womb-like surroundings were meant to relax, not cause anxiety. Yet I was aware of being nervous.

The side door opened, and Dr. Penner came in. A tall, thin woman wearing a light green smock, she was a full Tee professional, with huge knowledge and powers. The repeating floral pattern on her beige skullcap indicated she'd budded out, and mothered clones. "You're looking well, Dominic," she said.

"It's good to be here." I followed her into the transition room. All four walls were lit up; images of me were everywhere, outside running on the track, swimming in the pool, giving a presentation in history class, and relaxing in the lounge at the dorm. Interspersed throughout was my name, DOMINIC TESSIER, in different fonts and sizes. I'd never seen so much of me.

She turned off the pictures. "According to my information, you're well accepted and respected by the majority of freshmen, your fellow middies, and the seniors. Not many students enjoy your kind of regard."

Embarrassed, I avoided the compliment. "The Lupine scholarship was a tremendous opportunity."

I lay back on the couch, and the scanner moved in and fit itself around my head. The face piece was transparent, allowing me to watch Dr. Penner at the controls.

She started off asking me simple arithmetic questions and detoured to vocabulary and basic science before venturing into deeper waters of history and philosophy. In all, it took a couple of hours. At the end she brought out some of my earliest memories. A feather drawn over the bottom of my foot made me shriek, and Dr. Penner and I giggled uncontrollably.

"That's it," she said.

Once freed from the scanner, I went up to where she was sitting and looked at the picture of my brain on the wide screen. "New pathways opening up?"

"Thirty percent improvement, which is very good. The implants continue to extend, and they're well accepted." She gave me a greatly enlarged view on the screen, and I saw the filaments, chains of tiny nodules, winding through the dendrites and the axons. "Notice the neurons forming synapses with the nodules. They're connecting with the implant more readily than they connect with each other."

"Does this mean I pass?"

"There was never any doubt." Going to the side of the room, she took a small silvery package from a chute in the corner. "You'll use this telecap for the coming year. When you're close to graduation we'll insert the thought transmitter. The crest is fitted into the skull, and you'll be fully telepathic."

The gray material was soft and silky and slid on easily. Dr. Penner smoothed it behind my ears, and above my eyebrows. *"How does it feel?"*

"Good," I said. Then I realized she'd used her thought voice. *"Good like peaches," I said, seeing them heavy on the tree, and then a knife slicing the yellow flesh, and the experiencing the first taste of the summer's fruit.*

"Whoa," she replied firmly. "If you think too fast it gets garbled and your receiver won't understand."

"Slow, slow," I said, drawing the word out while seeing a small boy lagging far behind his playmates.

"Let's stop here," she said.

I pulled the cap off my head, grinning with the wonder of it. "This is fun."

"Thought communication can be difficult. The aspiring T-man needs to establish a calm mind, free from background noise. Practice clear and logical forms of thought and you'll get there."

Outside it was still raining hard, but the interview with Dr. Penner left me with a feeling the weather couldn't touch. Success was especially sweet for me, as I did not come from a wealthy background. Somebody's love child, brought up in the crèche, I never even knew why they chose me for the scholarship. My guardian was a lawyer, and, while there was never a problem with fees or my monthly allowance, he was very close-mouthed about the Lupine fund.

The dormitory, a ten-story cylindrical building, loomed out of the mist. Inside, pleasant odors from the cafeteria indicated dinner was being prepared. Eager to try the telecap again, I ran up six flights of stairs to my room.

Wang Yu was sitting in front of his easel by the window, working on a painting of Serena, the cadet he was fixated on. Here she was sitting on a swing, dressed in a high necked, tightly fitted orange dress. He'd given her long, straight black hair; in real life her head was shaved, as were all STA cadets.

The paintbrush looked clumsy in his big hand but there was no denying his talent or his yearning for beauty. "It's good," I said.

"There's something missing. Sculpture might do her more justice."

"That'll work well! A statue of Serena, riding on a dolphin or a salmon or something. If you need a mold I can give you a hand putting on the cast." Expressionless, Wang gathered up his paints. "Dr. Penner says in another year I should be ready," I told him.

"My fellow T-men," Wang said, raising his fist. "Prepare to read my thoughts. I want to give you shit." He frowned. "Oh I don't know. It might be all right--when you grow up with four other clones, it gives a different perspective on individualism and privacy."

"Try living in the crèche." I sat on the bed and slipped on the telecap. Wang had his own cap on and was perched on his desk, eyes tightly closed.

There was a blaring of brass, and a low-pitched "chuck, chuck, chuck."

A curtain opened on a small stage, and at the side a chicken appeared. Wearing a white Stetson, a sequined vest that barely covered its wide breast, a short skirt of white feathers, and high, white boots, the bird glanced around with shiny black eyes. A drum beat a swift tattoo and settled into a simple rhythm. The chicken strutted forward, did a pirouette in the middle of the stage, and bowed low. "Are you coming to the lecture tonight?" it asked in a high-pitched squawk.

Laughing helplessly, I tore the cap off. "Seriously," Wang said. "The speaker, Felicia Semper, just retired from space administration. She graduated from our school."

"I'll be there."

After Wang left, I looked at the pair of intake receivers hanging from a peg on the side of my desk. These elephant ears had served well up to now, but the telecap promised to be much better. Along with the telepathy applications, I'd be able to access intakes anywhere around the campus.

The intakes opened up new ways of learning, not dependent on reading or listening. Information was sent direct to the brain implants. Right now I was doing a course in off-world power systems. Today's intake would put me into an artificial reality created by people who actually worked in space. I'd see through their eyes and feel what they felt.

Slipping on the telecap, I registered with Charles. Then I was on a small base in a remote area of our moon, putting on a spacesuit. An asteroid had smashed into the solar panels, and it was my job to go outside with a helper and repair the damage.

When it was time to do the report I took the telecap off, but the sense remained that this was all very real. When it was my turn to go out there, this type of situation would be second nature to me.

Felicia Semper's lecture was a must, because she was the type of person we hoped to become. When Wang and I arrived the seats were all taken, and we joined the crowd standing at the back.

Wang elbowed me. "Serena came down. She said she might."

The uniformed cadets all faced the front, yet I soon spotted Serena in the second row. Her shaved scalp glistened under the light, and it was amusing to think of Wang's painting, where she had long black hair. I knew the woman beside her, Astra Allison, from Blackberry Hill Elementary School. We lost contact during high school years because I went to St. David's in Toronto. It was good to see her at STA, except that she was going with George Damon, not my favorite person.

Everyone clapped as our principal came to the edge of the stage. Mr. Rossiter, a tall slender man who kept his enthusiasm strictly under control, hushed us with a wave of the hand. "There's a special treat in store tonight," he said in his dry, matter-of-fact way. "We don't get near enough returning veterans. Felicia's served at Lunaport, Mars, and Ganymede. She's a valid role model for all of us here at STA. Let's welcome Felicia!"

We applauded wildly as she strode onto the stage and embraced Mr. Rossiter. Of medium height, she wore a close-fitting, black suit over her athletic-looking body, and seemed dynamic.

"She must have seen a lot in her years of service," I said to Wang.

"Space didn't hurt her looks any."

"A little over twenty years ago I was where you are," she began in a low-pitched, vibrant voice. "If you asked me would I do it over again--the answer is definitely yes." From the side of the stage Mr. Rossiter applauded and we all joined in. "In my talk tonight I want to focus on my own specialty, space station supply. It's likely some of you will also enter this field."

"Very likely," Wang said.

"I should warn you that once we leave there are few trips back to Earth. When we do return, we appreciate the paradise for what it is. Walking through the forest today, my body drank in the impressions through every pore. Each nerve was alive, and all my senses open. The bird songs and the smells of trees were pure ecstasy. You never appreciate the homeland fully till you've been off-world.

"For years now there's been talk of the supposed terraforming of Mars. You'll be shocked to find how far short of that goal we still are. Ganymede's a more congenial place, but hardly earthlike. Then the smaller sites scattered about the solar system--well, some are not much different from a spaceship. We have to do better."

After the talk we stood around the back, waiting for Serena and Astra to come out. When she saw us, Serena bubbled over with laughter and seized Wang's hand. "Mind if I steal your roommate?" she asked me over her shoulder.

16

Quelling an impulse to jump up and down and do somersaults, I fell in step with Astra. Her major field was engineering, and I knew she wanted to build off-world structures. "Felicia Semper is quite the speaker, isn't she?" I asked. Then I stopped short. Astra's left eye was partly swollen shut and encircled by a purplish bruise. "What happened?"

Covering it, Astra gave a little laugh. "This is what comes of walking around in the dark and bumping into things--not to worry, it'll heal soon."

With her hand up to her eye I noticed George's ring was gone. This was a hopeful sign. "We should get together. Have a coffee or something."

"Sure, sometime. Right now I'm tied up with schoolwork." She touched my arm and joined some women standing by the EXIT door.

CHAPTER 4

The line of dromies moved swiftly through the dead forest. Lucas and the Resister chief, Eddie McCool, rode at the end, keeping an eye on the metallic gray UWS cases being pulled along ahead of them.

Meeting up with the hijackers was extremely bad luck for Lucas, but at least he was not cramped up like the ones inside the compartments. Their voices drifted up, indecipherable sounds of mingled curses and shouts of laughter.

"How do you like this dromy?" McCool asked, turning back to him. "Does it remind you of Mars?"

His stiff, patronizing tone grated on Lucas's nerves. Lucas remembered when their gang, the Rogers, brought in a scrawny, hapless youngster who was living out on the street. Given the choice of anything, the boy pigged out on ice cream. "We don't usually ride horseback style on Mars, Ice Cream," Lucas said. "The planet lacks air, so people ride inside."

"People don't call me Ice Cream any more. Not for years."

"If they call you Ice Cream do you give them a licking?"

McCool grabbed hold of Lucas's cheeks. "Do you think I'm talking for the fun of it?" He delivered a sharp rap to Lucas's nose with his forehead.

"Ow!" Lucas touched his nostrils, and there was blood. "It must be thirty-five years since you did that to me. After I beat you at horseshoes, wasn't it?"

"Welcome back," McCool said with a chuckle.

Lucas managed a hearty laugh. "It's good to be home. Are there many of us Rogers still left?"

McCool shook his head. "Kenny Summers, out on the coast, is the only one I know of."

The forest trail ended in a small clearing where vehicles were parked. Lucas and McCool climbed down from the dromy, and Lucas helped his old comrade out of his body armor. McCool had aged; tall and big boned, he was softer looking and had a paunch. His longish blond hair was turning white. Hearing him called colonel was a shocker. Lucas remembered McCool enlisting in the US Army at eighteen, and never imagined he'd get that far.

Most of the other Resisters had already changed and were starting to leave. A youth with a sparse dark beard came around with a compressor bag, and McCool tossed in his suit. "You did good work today, Donny."

"Thanks, Colonel. We're working for our country."

"God willing, we'll win back our land one day. Get going, now. No need to wait around."

A van pulled away loaded with Resisters, some saluting McCool with clenched fists.

A short man in a broad-brimmed slouch hat eyed Lucas. "He needs to cover that yellow flat-top. They'll be on the lookout for their missing passenger."

"It's a disguise. I've taken the identity of a dead man."

The short man spat on the ground. McCool lifted off his hat and put it on Lucas. "All right, Hank?"

Without the hat, Hank was bald on top, with graying, light-brown fringes. He turned and spat again. "It's a little better but the clothes stand out."

Lucas rolled up his homemade bead belt, and put it in his pocket.

They took the dromies through the trees to a paved area adjoining a large industrial center. An older Quick Deliveries truck was parked at the edge, beside a multi-trailer Interstate rig. The men sent off the dromies with the Quick truck, then took the hovercart up a side ramp into the Interstate's middle trailer. The container was already half-loaded. Maneuvering the hovercart between some large crates, they threw a cover over the cases and locked up.

Getting into a blue van, they followed the trucks out to the highway, where the Quick truck turned east. They followed the Interstate truck as it headed west toward the mountains, staying about half a mile back.

Surprisingly soon, three small planes screamed by in tight formation. Ahead, a black line appeared on the horizon; police airships came in rapidly, hovered for a moment, and fanned out over the land.

The traffic slowed to a crawl. Across the divide, the eastbound lanes stopped altogether. Then a huge explosion sounded in the distance, rocking the van.

"They found the Quick truck," McCool said. "We need to hide our passenger for the checkpoint."

Climbing into the back, Hank rearranged the seats and uncovered a shallow compartment. "Get in. Make one sound when those inspectors come, you're dead."

"Relax," Lucas said. "I won't cause you problems." He scrunched down and closed his eyes as the seat snapped into place above him. The van moved only occasionally now; the wait seemed interminable.

Loud banging sounds came from overhead. "You could pack a lot into this van," a man said.

McCool chuckled. "I hire real human beings for my farm, even if they take more maintenance."

"I'm with you," the inspector said. "To hell with the robots." Doors slammed, and they drove on.

The men were silent, and Lucas slipped into a semiconscious state. Finally they stopped. *"How long has it been?"* he asked Tomi.

"Three hours and twenty-five minutes. We're in the foothills of the Rocky Mountains, in Northern Montana."

McCool opened his compartment. "Stay there for now," he said, handing Lucas a bottle of water. "We're inside a warehouse, moving the cargo to a different truck." Lucas lay back, and the seat clicked into place above him.

When the van stopped again they were in the midst of a forest, at the side of a narrow road. It was early evening, just getting dark. Hank helped Lucas get up, and gave him a hard stare. "Keep that freaking lid on."

"Well, damn," Lucas drawled, reaching for the hat.

In a few minutes they came to a wide valley, with extensive fields. After passing over a creek, they turned off on a side road, and stopped in front of a closed mesh gate. From here a five foot high wire fence extended around the property, held up by slender orange posts. DANGER, ELECTRIC FENCE, a sign read.

To the right was a little booth, where another sign said CALL FOR ADMITTANCE. "It looks like a nice place," Lucas said, gazing at some cattle in the fields.

"Our plan was just to be self-sufficient, but it got to where we sell some of our produce in town," McCool said.

"You never got dumped on by the volcanic ash?"

Hank gave a scornful hoot. "Where you been, Mars? The whole world got dumped on. Three years, no summer."

"Yellowstone's close by, and we got hit hard," McCool said. "The prevailing winds were strongly from the west and spared us from the worst of it. Folks around here pulled together for the cleanup; everyone knows we got saved for a purpose."

McCool pointed a little white rod at the gate. It opened, and after they went through, he used the rod to close it again.

"Good security," Lucas said.

"My wife runs a tight ship when I'm away," McCool said.

As the van continued on there was a loud yipping, and two dog robots loped up. About four feet tall, they had slim bodies and long legs, and reminded Lucas of greyhounds. One was pale, with black spots, while the other was reddish brown. The spotted one let its mouth sag open, and Lucas glimpsed shiny fangs.

They drove past a large white barn, some smaller maintenance buildings, and stopped in front of a rambling two-story house surrounded by lawns and flower beds.

A middle aged woman with short blonde hair, wearing black shorts and top, rushed out and threw her arms around McCool. "I was getting worried."

"I went to town and got feed for the animals. What's this worry talk for?"

"Sorry," she sighed. "You know how silly I am."

The two dog robots stared at Lucas. They had unwavering red eyes, elevated on stalks. McCool bent down to them, and patted their heads. "A new friend, Lucas, is staying for a while," he told them. He grinned to Lucas. "We call them both Rover."

"I'm glad to meet you, Rovers," Lucas said, holding out his hand to the spotted one.

The two came close and sniffed him. "Welcome, Master Lucas," they chorused.

"It seems we have company," the woman said.

"This is my wife, Gloria," McCool said to Lucas. "She'll show you the guest room. Get cleaned up, and come downstairs for a drink."

"This way," she told Lucas, heading for the house.

"Find him some clothes, too," McCool hollered. He and Hank went back toward the maintenance area.

Walking quickly, Gloria led Lucas through a mirrored foyer, up some stairs, and down a long white passageway which smelled of cinnamon. It was very quiet, and Lucas sensed the area was seldom used. "You're in here," she said, opening the door to a bedroom. She checked for soap and towels in the adjoining bathroom, and opened the bedroom window.

Lucas hung up his jacket and went to the window, looking out on a wide lawn and a row of small trees with white blossoms. Beyond was the forest. The other buildings were not visible.

"You'd be advised to keep that thing on your back hidden," Gloria said. "We're all natural here; nobody has artificial enhancements."

"Whatever you say." Lucas brought Tomi out to show her. "A varlet is a real help with an illness--Tomi monitors my system and regulates the dosage from the drug implants." Gloria touched the octopod gingerly, and shrieked as a little arm reached up and adhered to her finger. "Don't worry," Lucas said. "He'll stay in one of the dresser drawers for now, all right?"

She nodded. "I kept dinner warm, there's lots if you're hungry. It's veal cutlets."

"I've often dreamed of such a meal. I've been gone for years."

Gloria narrowed her eyes, and turned to leave. "Go ahead and get washed up," she said tonelessly. "I'll find you something to wear."

"That woman doesn't like me," Tomi said.

"Don't worry, she'll come around. To know you is to love you. Let's have a bath."

The blue tile shower was large, almost a room in itself. When Lucas turned the water on, water jets blasted from all sides. He held Tomi up to the spray, and washed the varlet's body while all eight arms twisted and squirmed. Although slender, Tomi's arms provided ample mobility and were quite strong. The suction cups on the underside were handy too.

"I've never seen a shower like this on Mars," Tomi said. "Is this usual for Earth?"

"No, it's wasteful here too. Our host is a show off."

It was McCool's way, Lucas thought. As youngsters they were both orphans, while Kenny Summers, the son of the gang's president, was destined for important things. In reaction, McCool turned everyday events into occasions for glory. It was like he was watching himself perform, an audience of one that never failed to appreciate his star quality.

When Lucas and McCool were young, they spent a lot of time in the shooting range under the house. Instead of just concentrating on hitting the target like they were supposed to do, McCool did tricks, often tossing his gun high into the air, end over end. He was full of himself.

After the shower, Lucas dressed in some gray work clothes that Gloria had left on the bed. He went downstairs to the living room, where McCool and his wife were sitting on the couch. McCool pointed to a small cabinet across the room. "I got a deal on a truckload, so don't be shy."

Taking a tumbler from the nearby rack, Lucas poured from an open bottle of whiskey, and added ice water. The Rogers always considered Wild Grouse their premium bourbon, and Lucas was pleased. He held up his glass. "To old friends."

"Show Gloria your mark," McCool said, getting up and stripping off his shirt. "Look at this, sweetie. Two of us Rogers." Lucas pulled down his shirt and stood so their shoulders were together.

"The dagger in the rose," Gloria said, looking at the glowing lumi-toos. "They are definitely the same."

"Don't be comparing guts now," McCool said. He put a hand on Lucas's abdomen. "You don't have an inch of flab. How do you do it?"

"The cancer helps," Lucas said.

"Sorry, I didn't know." McCool went back to his chair.

"What happened to all the other Rogers?"

"Those who survived the Yellowstone eruption and the epidemics died fighting against the conquest. And for me, the war is not over. Kenny Summers managed to adjust, he's doing really well."

"Kenny set me up," Lucas said.

"I never knew that."

"I've had thirty years to figure things out. It keeps coming back to Kenny."

The next morning Lucas slept late. When he opened his eyes the octopod was on the other pillow. *"Good morning,"* Lucas said.

"Good morning. How long will we be trapped here?"

"I don't know yet." He went into the washroom. His bowel movement came easily, but he noticed the same black blood he'd seen on Mars. Not good. Like the doctors said, if they started cutting there'd be no end to it.

When he came out, he put Tomi on some towels in the top dresser drawer. *"I'll find out what's happening. McCool has to realize that we need to get going."*

A rich contralto filled the stairwell as he came down. Gloria, dressed in a black leotard, was mopping out a ground floor bathroom. He watched from the hallway as she swung around the room, singing at the top of her lungs. When she noticed him she stopped, and her face reddened.

Lucas smiled. "You really meant it about doing things the natural way."

Gloria stuck the mop in a bucket and washed her hands. "This is a place of deep connections. We are tied to the land, to this house, to the food we eat, and most of all to one another."

He followed her to the kitchen, which was filled with the aroma of baking bread. When Lucas took a place at the table, Gloria folded her arms and scrutinized him. "You told me last night you've spent thirty years hating a man, you also said that you have cancer. Do you think there is no connection?"

"Hold on," he said. "That's quite a statement to make about someone you only met yesterday."

A bell rang, and she opened the oven door. "Tell me about these Rogers you and my husband ran with," she said, pouring him a cup of coffee.

He smiled noncommittally, and took a bun from a platter on the table. "Are these homemade?"

"Yes, of course. Is that all right?"

"They look delicious." Lucas poured thick yellow cream into his coffee and added a teaspoon of sugar.

A door slammed and McCool came in, his fine hair mussed. He pulled up a chair, and Gloria got him a cup of coffee. "I've been running around. Took the cows down to the lower pasture, and a couple of them wanted to go exploring."

Smearing an opened whole wheat bun with butter and strawberry jam, Lucas crammed it into his mouth. "This is the real thing," he said.

"I'll show you around when you're ready," McCool said.

They paused in the entrance foyer, and McCool gave Lucas a pair of orange coveralls to wear with the slouch hat. "You are the only passenger we took from the airship, and your picture is on all the newscasts. That blond brush cut really stands out."

The information was chilling. "I'm using the name Bart Peters. He was a prospector who had an accident on Phobos. After he died, the Martians hushed it up to let me use his identity and get to hospital here on Earth."

"Let me think on this," McCool mumbled. "We'll straighten things out."

His response raised Lucas's spirits considerably. "I'd appreciate that."

Outside the sky was clear, and a stiff breeze blew over the moist fields. Lucas filled his lungs, and spread his arms. "Good morning, Earth."

McCool chuckled. "Just think, if we hadn't hit your airship you'd probably never know about our place here."

"Since I'm terminal, every minute is precious. I needed to see you again; to meet your wife and know you are doing so well."

McCool's eyes watered, and he pulled Lucas to him in a tight hug, rocking back and forth. "The doctors around here are first rate, maybe someone can help. The main thing is to get you a new identity."

McCool's casual take on things was not what Lucas had hoped for but he remained calm. He gestured to the white barn and maintenance buildings. "If I can help out in the meantime, let me know."

As they approached one of the smaller buildings, an older man in orange coveralls brought out a hovercart loaded with rolls of fencing. It was Hank. Lucas nodded, but the man remained expressionless. As he and McCool stopped to talk, Lucas went through an open door to a garage, and watched two mechanics change the bucket on an earth mover.

McCool joined him. "I have to give you a shackle belt, it's standard for newcomers."

This came out of nowhere for Lucas, and he was furious. "You don't put that on a Roger. I'm your brother."

"Sorry," McCool said, not meeting his eyes. "We can't risk you leaving, you'd get caught for sure." Hank was there now, and the two mechanics came over. They took Lucas to the far end of the garage and got his shirt off. His lumitoo was glowing strongly, and McCool put a hand on Lucas's shoulder. "It's only temporary."

"You think this'll help anything?"

They cut the belt from a length of two inches wide black fabric that adhered easily to the skin. Hank and one of the mechanics passed it around Lucas's back and brought the ends forward, so they touched. The other mechanic took a slender white rod from a wall cabinet. He ran the tip over the front of Lucas's belt, until the ends of the fabric seamlessly coalesced.

Taking the rod, McCool pointed it at Lucas. "Can you feel it?"

"A slight buzz, is that all you've got?" A powerful shock ran through him and he fell to his knees, his body wracked with spasms. "Turn it off!" he yelled.

"Never try to leave this farm," McCool said. "You'll die in horrible pain, right there beside the fence."

Lucas stared into his eyes. "What are you saying, I'm a prisoner here? Or some kind of slave?"

"God no," McCool said, helping him stand up. "It's just that we can't take any chances. You're a wanted man, the only lead anyone has to the hijacking. When you get a new identity it won't be so risky if you decide to leave."

"I understand," Lucas said coolly. McCool was now the chief, and shouldered a lot of responsibility. He'd not forget the insult, though.

Back in his room, Lucas used Tomi to message his partner Rosie on Mars. He explained his new situation and asked her to get advice on what to do. Afterward he lay on the bed, with Tomi on his chest.

"This delay is life threatening," Tomi said.

Lucas pressed the octopod tight to him. *"You and I have been through a lot together. We'll beat this too."*

CHAPTER 5

The bugler sounded reveille. Our drapes parted, and the dawn's light poured in on Wang, who was intaking at his desk. Going to the window, I looked down at the courtyard where the color guard was assembled. We all took turns in this duty, and there was an element of humor watching my four classmates in dress uniform, as they marched toward the flagpole. A swelling of strings began the anthem of the North American Nation, and I stood at attention as our banner ascended, whipping in the strong wind.

Wang took off his elephant ears, and got up. He looked pale, and seemed unsteady.

"Did you cram it again?" I asked.

"I was running late on the history presentation," he said wearily.

"If you spent less time painting pictures of Serena." Making no response, he left to go to the washroom.

I was getting worried. Wang used fast time more and more, and intakes are not meant to be rushed. While information goes directly to implants, the purpose is assimilation by the wider brain. Course material carries sensory lures and dramatic hooks for this reason.

Fourteen of us were taking the advanced history option. I arrived a few minutes early, and took my usual spot beside Zack, our star wrestler, weightlifter and body builder. He nodded and gave me a little smile. "What does Wang have for a presentation?"

"I don't know. He was still working on it this morning."

Mr. Beebe came in. A graduate student who taught classes on the side, he gave an otherworldly impression, as if he'd just left his research to be here with us.

The horn sounded, and we all stood at attention. "Good morning to each of you on this lovely day," the principal's voice said over the public address system.

Our voices chimed in. "I pledge allegiance to the United World States and our world president, Ranjit Kumar. I promise to obey the laws of the North American Nation and to accept my fellow citizens wholeheartedly, as one family under God."

"Sin and you're out," Mr. Beebe intoned.

"Amen," we replied.

"Amen," Wang said, appearing ninja-like beside me.

When we sat down, everyone looked at my roommate. He just sat there, his arms folded, face expressionless. Not at all sure he was ready to do his presentation I fought off the impulse to giggle.

"You're up," Mr. Beebe told him.

"Yes sir," Wang said, suddenly coming to life. He looked around the table with a smile. "I've stated before my strong reservations about viewing human history as separate from the history of the overall biosphere. We need to get away from the distortions of the past, and see the story of life on this planet as it really is."

In a rapid-fire way that was highly impressive considering he'd in-taken much of the information in fast time only an hour or so ago, Wang gave a concise, abbreviated account of the ubiquity of symbiosis, from lichen fungus relying on algae photosynthesis, to interdependent soil bacteria, to the animal reliance on bacteria for digestive process-es. The development of agriculture, and downright slavery practiced by the ants was his springboard into human history. Beatific expres-sions around the room showed that people's brains were lighting up, as Wang's presentation led them into unfamiliar ways of thinking about colonialism and economics.

"The aim of life is to survive, by whatever means. Peoples' ability to cooperate allowed them to populate the entire planet, but once materialism was accepted by the East things became unsustainable. As we see today it led to Earth's sixth great extinction, in which not just the animal and plant species, but most of humanity, were wiped out."

Wang glanced at the clock and spoke even faster. "In my remaining time I'd like to put the human race in the context of them no longer being the dominant species. They had their chance and failed miserably. They've been a cancer in nature's bosom, finding beauty and abundance and leaving it ravaged, diseased and dying. There's a new dominant species in the world today which is the Great One, Raina. Although she hasn't been around very long she's already established herself as a clearly superior being.

"Here at STA we're all hoping to become T-men, and we look forward to working closely with the Great One in bringing health back to Earth's biosphere. I say that our behavior is like that of animals that allowed themselves to be domesticated by the humans. And it paid off for them. Look at our pet dogs and cats, and the horses, cows, pigs, and sheep. For the most part they live in a way that's far superior to what's available out in the wild." Here Wang grinned widely. "Mr. Beebe, that's my basic presentation and I welcome any comments and feedback."

Toward the end I'd sensed the atmosphere in the room become dismal and disapproving, and now there was dead silence. I raised my hand. "The Great One is basically a quantum computer. I don't see how you can talk of a new species in a biological sense. Especially if there's only one."

"Look at how far she's gone in her brief life span," Wang said. "I argue it's a waste of time discussing what a species is. We should admit that mankind has lost its position of dominance, and readjust our thinking."

Mr. Beebe smiled. "We don't know if the Great One will ever reproduce, or even if she'll remain with us. She's still very young."

"What about the starship program?" I asked.

"It's definitely an issue," Mr. Beebe said. "She's expressed a desire to go with each ship. How it'll happen is uncertain."

The buzzer rang and people started to leave. Zack held Wang back. "What's your basic point? Human history is no longer relevant?"

"Overall it's slipped, just as Neanderthal history slipped once the Cro-Magnons came on the scene."

Zack gave him a hard look. "Are you trying to imply something?"

"I know who I am--do you?"

There was an hour before my next class, and I went over to the Polaris. A three-story building designed with sweeping curves, the Polaris is where cadets take their arts electives. Some study dance, theater, video, design, or sculpting. I'd picked music.

I found an empty practice room, and took a seat behind the multivox. Shoes and socks off, I touched the percussion center with my toes and began a steady drum beat, easing into a syncopated, polyrhythmic pattern. Pulling the mouthpiece down, I trumpeted a martial salute, while my fingers drifted up and down the keyboard. I began "The Cosmic Song."

The composer Andre Pares was one of mankind's first space babies, born on Ganymede to a couple of geologists. While the Song's first movement is renowned for its grand depiction of space, the second movement, devoted to Earth, has inspired the most love. Pares arrived on our planet at the age of twenty. The squirrels, crows, goldfish in a pond, and even the common houseflies were new to him, and he studied the creatures endlessly. The result was his unique perspective on the rhythms and harmonies of life.

Some describe Pares as being in the same vein as the Romantic poets and artists of the nineteenth century, especially Tchaikovsky, but the music of the twentieth and twenty-first centuries gave him a huge boost. Only thirty-two when he died, he's one of the immortals.

These practice rooms are not private; it was not unusual when the door opened. Astra and Serena came in with three other women, and I stopped playing. "Please keep going," Serena said.

"We heard you down the hall," Astra said. "It's lovely."

I began the second movement, and was soon immersed in the music. The women slipped off their wraps, revealing skintight leotards. Stretching athletically, they made some turns and spins. Then they started dancing.

Their style was modern freeform; they drew on everything, from classical ballet to Brazilian street dancing. Judging from the unity with which they moved, they'd been practicing together a lot. While their intent was to express the music, individual responses did emerge, which the group then responded to and elaborated on.

Playing "The Cosmic Song" on the multivox was godlike enough. Having Astra and her friends become part of it was pure bliss, and when it ended, there was the sense we'd been lifted to a higher plane. The women were all laughing. Her eyes shining, Astra kissed me on the cheek.

The inner glow I experienced lasted all day long. I felt that the music and dancing had burned away the separation of our high school years, and we'd gotten back to the trust and understanding of childhood. The only course I took with Astra, physical education, was my last class, and I could hardly wait to see her again.

Today's PE class was an introduction to the strength-enhancing pro suit. To my chagrin, George Damon was the attending senior. A tall, dark, hulking man, George was often sullen, had a mean streak, and was not much liked by us middies. I loathed thinking of him with Astra, and hoped with all my heart their relationship was over.

It was sunny on the playing field, with just a light wind. We prepared by touching our toes and stretching our limbs. Our group was a diverse bunch, all different colors, shapes, and sizes. No one was fat or overly thin. We were fed well, and the relentless physical training kept us very fit.

Someone whistled. I looked down the field to see the Old Lace women running toward us, dressed in their mauve sweats. Astra was in the second row. One of the tallest there, she ran with an easy flow that pleased me deeply.

"Eyes front," George shouted. "Jumping jacks, one, two, let's go!"

The women came in at a right angle to our group. Their senior, a petite, dark-eyed woman who was a nationally ranked judoka, shook hands with George.

"I never told you to stop," George barked, looking back at us. We resumed our jumping jacks and now the women were doing them too.

Hideo Yashido, the school's martial arts and weapons instructor, strolled toward us. In his early sixties, the short, muscular man could be nimble as a deer, but he was never known to hurry. On seeing him, our concentration became intense.

Coming into the space between our two wings, Hideo nodded to the seniors and looked around at us intently. We kept on with our exercises, very aware of him standing there with his arms folded, the sun shining on his wide forehead. When he held his hands up we stopped immediately. "As technocrat administrators you're the proud carriers of authority and power, and your word will be the law on many occasions." He motioned to Astra, and she went over to the case where the suits were stored.

"Pro suits can be an important survival tool when faced with projectile and directed energy attacks. Bacterial and chemical agents are also screened out. Your strength is magnified about three times, as the suit coordinates with your intentions."

Astra walked slowly back toward the group. The whitish, one-piece suit seemed to impart a judicious, impersonal air. The blue-tinted eyepiece was wide and deep. The ribbed breathing section was rectangular, and gave no hint of her delicate nostrils, or the lovely curve of the lips underneath.

Hideo smiled to her. "Remember it's not only your muscles, you'll use the senses in the skin itself. It's a new power you'll learn to trust." He nodded to George.

George walked up to Astra and stared down at her intimidatingly. She dropped her shoulders slightly, and waited for his move. Sliding behind her, George draped his arms around her.

She reacted spasmodically, sending George flying backward a good ten feet where he sprawled on the grass laughing.

Hideo split us into small groups so everyone could try the suits. Zack and I watched George throw one of our best athletes, Chico, off to the side. Then George gestured to Zack. "Come and kill me, wrestler boy," his distorted voice said through the ribbed mouthpiece. A couple of inches taller than Zack, George stood straight and relaxed, hands on his hips.

Zack was slightly crouched, the muscles in his thighs bulging. "I'm going to take him," he said. George made a perfunctory swat, and Zack grappled with him. Suddenly stepping back George ripped out of Zack's grasp and came in with a straight punch to the gut. Zack fell to his knees, gasping for air.

Hideo bent down to Zack. "Are you all right?"

"Winded," he groaned.

"Remember to control your strength," Hideo told George. "Don't hurt someone."

George nodded, and beckoned to me. "Come on."

Having swallowed a lot of anger toward George, I was determined to make the most of this chance. When I got within range, I faked a couple of times and exploded in a fast combination of kicks and punches, not connecting, but stopping very close to him. Finally I stepped in and caught him with an uppercut to the jaw. It was like hitting a wall. He'd been rocked though, and when I swept his legs he went down.

When he got back up, George came after me like a bull. I danced away and hit him a couple of times, each contact jarring my arms. Then he got his hands on my shoulders, and he pushed me to the grass with overwhelming power.

"Enough," Hideo said sharply. George gave me one last squeeze and backed off. "That was very interesting," Hideo said as I got to my feet.

George was scowling when he got the suit off. More than willing to continue the fight, I gave him a grin, but he looked away.

"You'll learn from that," Hideo told him. "If you become confused you can be overwhelmed. The key is control of your inner self." He nodded to me. "Your turn."

The suit slid on with ease, conforming to my skin. Inside the hood the air was pure and fresh. My vision was clear, and there was a sense of detachment.

I walked slowly back to the others, getting used to the sensations. It was marvelous to walk in, my soles were coming alive. I tried a short jump, and went up about four feet. "This is going to be fun," Zack called.

"Let's go, then."

Zack came at me with a half crouch. Grabbing me quickly, he tried to twist me to the side. Although he outweighed me by a good thirty pounds, he had no force. Swiftly bending down, I put an arm behind his knees and stood up, cradling him like a child. He kept struggling, trying to get purchase on me. I started spinning faster and faster until he stopped fighting and lay still. Then I put him down on the grass.

When I put the suit away Wang was nearby with Serena and Astra.

"I threw Wang around like he was a little kitten," Serena laughed.

"You and I should wear pro suits to the Grand Ball," Astra said to her.

Wang lifted Serena by the waist. "I won't need a pro suit to do this," he said, twirling her around.

"How about us?" I asked Astra. "Will you go with me?"

She bit her lip and tilted her head slightly so she was looking at me in a lopsided way. "You should call me," she said, and turned away.

Astra's answer left me in a state of total uncertainty. Did she mean we'd go out together? Anything was possible.

CHAPTER 6

Despite his health problems, Lucas slowly adjusted to Earth's gravity. He ate well, and used McCool's exercise equipment every night. The expert who was supposed to provide a new identity was still in Europe. In the meantime, Gloria shaved his scalp and dyed his beard dark brown. She'd also found brown lenses for his eyes.

McCool had Lucas operating a trencher on a pipe-laying job in the bottom pasture. On the third day, his machine hit a soft spot in the ditch and lurched sideways. When he went in for lunch, he reported a pain in his back.

McCool looked up from his soup. "Gloria handles the doctoring around here."

"Do you have a medical background?" Lucas asked her.

"She has veterinary experience," McCool said. "There's not much difference."

After lunch, Gloria took him to a small room off the kitchen. Despite his pain Lucas was not immune to her attractiveness, and being alone with her always woke him up. Sensing that years of being taken for granted by McCool had eroded Gloria's self-esteem, he never lost an opportunity to compliment her. She'd be an invaluable ally if he could turn her.

Gloria had him take off his shirt and sit down on an examination table. He felt no numbness or tingling, or any sensations radiating to his extremities. Probing under the shackle belt that encircled his lower back, her fingers found some tenderness to the right of the spine. "I think it's muscular. Lie down, I'll ice it for a while."

As the cooling penetrated the fabric, Lucas sighed with contentment. "It's strange, but the disease heightens my senses, so I feel extremes of pleasure as well as pain. My appreciation for beauty is also strengthened. I'm seeing your real angelic self."

Gloria narrowed her eyes. "I think you're ready to get this little butt of yours back to the job. Be more careful--you don't want serious back problems."

Lucas chuckled to himself as he left for work. He was being as nice to her as he knew how to be. Gloria seemed to like it, but the little bitch showed no regret or guilt over his wearing the shackle belt. It probably made her feel superior. One way or another, he'd escape from this farm. He'd never accept dying here in slavery.

That evening, the three went out. The van took them about twenty miles down the road, through the town of Indian Falls. It was getting dusk.

Turning down a tree-lined driveway, they parked behind some other vehicles. From here they walked to a huge house with a pillared entrance. Gloria had put on a chic black dress and a string of pearls for the occasion, and Lucas could tell she enjoyed being away from the farm.

Inside a vestibule, two older women were behind a reception table, a round-faced man in a worn brown suit standing beside them. "You're looking well, Colonel," the man exclaimed. "It's a pleasure to see you, Mrs. McCool."

McCool brought Lucas forward. "Dr. James, meet another friend. Up on Mars they like the T-men about as much as we do."

Dr. James took Lucas's hand in a firm grip. "Welcome. The cause always needs good men."

Downstairs was a large room where chairs were lined up in front of a podium, behind which huge United States and NAF flags hung from the wall. The old colors brought back heady memories for Lucas; there'd been fervor throughout the United States when the northlands opened up for their people. Unlike McCool, he never joined the service. For him, doing away with the Canadian border meant the Rogers could expand their operations into Vancouver. Those were good times.

Joining the crowd clustered around a refreshment table at the back, Lucas chided McCool for introducing him as a Martian. McCool only shrugged. "Your personal history is nothing much, folks here are concerned about the cause."

A woman filled their mugs with steaming coffee. Then ecstatic cries came from upstairs. "President Andrews is here," a man announced. "He can't stay long, so take your seats."

They sat beside Gloria in the second row. "It's over a year since his last visit," she gushed. "This is thrilling!"

Palpable excitement coursed through the room. Lucas jumped to his feet with the others, applauding as Dr. James brought a broad-shouldered man with a full black beard to the front. The bearded man stood to the side, arms folded, as Dr. James took the speaker's stand and motioned for quiet. "My friends, it's wonderful to see you here on such short notice. Although Indian Falls is a small community, this is one place where the love of liberty will never die. It's over fifteen years since the World States proclaimed their takeover of North America to be complete. And yet, they have never conquered the people of Indian Falls, and, with God's help, they never will. Please welcome President Andrews! A true son of North America, President Andrews was elected fairly by voters throughout the land and he commands our loyalty as our only legitimate head of government. President Andrews!"

The president shook hands with Dr. James, and stepped onto the podium. He stood a moment and looked around the crowd. "My fellow Americans, thanks for inviting me," he said in a resonant baritone. "Lately I've been visiting communities large and small all over this land, and it's a sobering experience. From the Atlantic to the Pacific, people are sick of being ruled by foreigners. We want our land back.

"Often I think back on history, and remember the pioneers who first colonized the eastern shores. While some were defeated by the harsh conditions, others survived and put down roots. Their descendants began the long push westward. Not minding the hardships and the endless sacrifices, these American heroes created our nation.

"Casting off the shackles of the British Empire, our ancestors rose up strong and proud. They stood for the rights of men, and our Statue of Liberty cast a beacon to the entire world. America's principles were not empty words; this land of freedom offered opportunity to all. Not only the wealthy and high-born, but the offspring of peasants, serfs, and slaves became innovators and entrepreneurs whose enterprises prospered, and created immense wealth.

"This is the land of peace. After defeating the Nazis, and then the forces of Communism, America became a giant. The world has never witnessed such power, and there is no questioning her dominance. The union with Canada gave increased access to fresh water and other resources of the Northlands, and opened up even more possibilities for our people."

Pausing, President Andrews gazed out at the silent crowd. "Let us contemplate the loss of our autonomy in context. Our adversaries took full advantage of the Yellowstone tragedy, striking in our moment of weakness. The space-based weaponry, which we'd come to rely on, they wiped out almost instantly with their diabolical new weapon, the Shiva ray. The enemy was helped by American traitors. Many of our scientists collaborated with their comrades from the United World States. And today they remain among us, as our overlords, the so-called T-men, or transformed ones.

"My friends, hear me now.

"The Conquest is not complete. This war is not over. When the time is right, the American people will again rise as one, and will again be overwhelming. Until then, we must keep faith, remain strong, and most of all do not lose hope. I'm here to meet you face-to-face, and I didn't come to do all the talking. I want to get to know you, and that means listening to what you have to say. Everybody has a voice. Everyone should be heard. Speak freely about your concerns. What's uppermost on your mind." He turned to Dr. James. "You know them all, will you handle the questions?"

"Yes sir, I'm delighted to," Dr. James said. He pointed to a brown-haired woman in the back. "Nora?"

The woman stood up. "President Andrews, I have two teenaged boys and soon they'll need to go to college. I despise the thought of them with brain implants, but it seems implants are the way to get ahead."

President Andrews nodded. "Our representatives are strong advocates of implant-free universities, and negotiations are under way to ensure that a percentage of our schools are reserved for the fully human. Never forget that in many fields the fully human perform as well if not better than the T-men."

Dr. James pointed to a man across the room. "Harry?"

"Stay strong on this, Nora. Those brain implants are a form of mind control. You'll lose your sons forever once they put them in."

The room erupted with applause. "God made us fine the way we are," a gray-haired woman shouted.

"Mankind rules the animals and the machines too," a man in work clothes said loudly. "To hell with the Tees."

"Quiet down, President Andrews doesn't have a lot of time," Dr. James said. He nodded to a large blonde woman in the first row. "Judy?"

"Thank you," she said, getting to her feet. "President Andrews, I'd like to ask about the Hindu computer, known as the Great One. According to reports it gives instructions to the T-men, and it's worshipped as a god in India. Are we losing our Christian heritage when the world's rulers bow down to this?"

"No, no. Never fear of losing your Christian heritage. Keep Jesus in your heart and God will keep faith with you." The president checked his watch. "The Tees are telepathic, and they communicate with the Great One, Raina, in the same way. I'm not aware of them taking instructions, or bowing down, but there is some overall guidance. I don't think it was a wise decision to create a fully autonomous artificial intelligence. The Indians did it though, and we have to adapt to the situation. Apparently a sect has sprung up which worships Raina as a manifestation of divinity. Hopefully this will not become widespread." The president spread his hands, and turned to Dr. James. "Sorry, I'm on a tight schedule."

Dr. James pointed to McCool. "Before President Andrews leaves, I believe there's news about Mars from our visitor?"

"Tell them something," McCool whispered to Lucas.

Lucas stood up, and the room went totally quiet. "This meeting's an eye-opener for me. On Mars there's much less conformity, or mind control. We're building a world in harsh conditions, and there's a big demand for individual initiative. People need to be strong and independent. Despite our advances, Mars remains a colony under Earth control. We're gouged with huge taxes on whatever enters or leaves the planet. The average Martian is not too fond of the Tees."

President Andrews looked at him thoughtfully. "Interesting information. I'll certainly think this over."

Lucas nodded, sat down, and McCool patted him on the back. Then everyone sang "America the Beautiful." Afterward it was time to go.

As everyone left the basement, McCool stayed to chat, while Gloria and Lucas went out and walked back to the van. It was dark now, and the departing vehicles had their headlights on. "Is your back recovering from the strain?" Gloria asked Lucas.

"Yes, thanks to your care."

When they came to the van, Lucas took his place in the second row, while Gloria sat in front of him. "Has anyone told you how pretty the back of your neck is?" Lucas asked.

"No, the back of the neck is an unknown area for most people." Lucas stroked it lightly with his forefinger and she shuddered. "Don't, it gives me goose bumps."

The three of them were quiet on the drive back. While Lucas sympathized with the people at the gathering, the evening made him realize his deepest love and loyalties were for the Martians.

Back home in the living room, Gloria poured large whiskies. "People are giving up," McCool said. Gloria settled next to him on the couch and he put an arm around her. "The struggle seems futile--it's hard to get any leverage, even with the best lobbyists. The head Hindus care as much about the Chinese and the Africans as they do about us."

"I wish you luck but my fighting days are over," Lucas said.

"There's different ways of fighting," McCool said. "It's a help to me just having you here."

"You look a lot better than when you first arrived," Gloria said. "With all your nerves on edge, and carrying that awful thing on your back. Today you're more relaxed, and I think you're gaining weight."

"Fresh air, the best of food and exercise," McCool said. "The movement has some first-rate doctors, I'd like you to consult with Dr. James."

"Good idea." Lucas stood up and stretched. "Well it's bedtime for me."

McCool raised his glass. "Pleasant dreams."

"Sleep well, Lucas," Gloria said. She put her head on McCool's shoulder, and closed her eyes.

Up in his room, Lucas put the octopod on his head and took a chair by the open window. *Any news yet?* he asked Tomi.

"Rosie sent the address of a safe house in Helena. We're to go there if possible."

"All right. Get to work and find out the different ways of reaching Helena."

CHAPTER 7

Vancouver Island was still struggling with earthquake damage, and Wang, Zack and I were given a community service assignment at a commune in Cedar River. Friday and Saturday we'd fill in at their large cleanup project. Saturday evening they needed a multivox player for a benefit concert; that would fall to me.

On Wednesday evening I used my telecap to intake the information about the remediation site. The superintendent's avatar led me through a layout of the area, and explained my duties. Then it taught me how to use the hazard suit. We'd used similar gear before.

After the intake I got a cup of hot chocolate from the cafeteria and went to the lounge. Wang and Zack were in there playing chess, and I watched their game.

"Take a look at the video, there's another unfencing," said one of the seniors sitting across the room.

Recently there'd been several of these unfencings as part of the reclamation of vast areas hit by the Yellowstone eruption. The screen showed a prairie landscape divided by a long, straight road. On one side of the road was a fenced-off field of grasses. On the other side, a translucent barrier held back a herd of buffalo.

A slim blonde woman wearing an Indian feather headdress and a close-fitting, patterned deerskin robe stood beside an airship. "Three hundred years ago there was a massacre here," the woman said, smiling serenely as the wind played through her feathers. "The plains ran red with blood as these magnificent creatures were wantonly butchered."

As the woman spoke, a gap appeared in the barrier. We laughed and applauded as the animals found the opening and spread out into the grass-lands. "They love it," someone shouted. "Go buffalo, go!"

"Put the NAN farmers out of work, and make more business for the plantations in Siberia," my freshman charge said in a loud, clear voice. "Why do they never show unfencings from overseas?"

His remarks brought groans throughout the room. "Give it a rest," Zack said. He and Wang turned back to their chess game.

Caplin Hanson was now established as a well-known character. Stocky, with thick, dark eyebrows and blue eyes that crackled with energy, he was fearless and outspoken. His obsession with politics was not well received however.

As Cap's mentor it was my duty to help guide him through first year, and seeing him stride toward the door I got up and joined him. "You're missing part of the program," I told him. "At STA we care for the interests of the whole world, not just our own section."

Cap gave a harsh laugh. "Nanny gets the short end every time. It happens too often to be coincidence."

His attitude was worrisome, but it was not a mentor's job to argue. "Once we become T-men we'll work together with the Great One," I said as we went up the staircase. "It's for the good of all."

"Sure thing," Cap said. He opened the door to his floor. "I know you mean well," he said quietly, and went through.

One more failed encounter with Cap! It became clear long ago that my mentorship with him was floundering. In describing the program, the school assumed that because incoming freshmen were inexperienced, they would welcome guidance from the upper classmen. Cap never fit the expected freshman mold; from the moment of his arrival he was as cocky as anyone I'd ever met. He was a real contrarian, always railing against our established order.

My own life experience provided some detachment from the situation. When I first came to STA as a freshman they assigned me a mentor who was gay, and he developed feelings for me. Being with him was sometimes difficult, but things worked out and we became good friends.

My plan with Cap was to remain consistent, and always be available to him. If he disregarded my well-meant advice, it was not worth losing sleep over it.

Back at my room I started working on a set of engineering problems, and hardly noticed when Wang came in. Untroubled by the lack of response, he sat on my desk until I looked up.

"There's about five men for every woman at STA," he said. "Astra won't wait forever."

He hit a nerve; I'd put off making the call. "Hello, Charles. Contact Astra Allison in her room at Old Lace."

Music filled our room, and a cool, female voice said, "You've reached Ms. Allison's abode. Unfortunately she's not available. Would you like to leave a message?"

"Tell her Dom called."

The music died away and Wang laughed. "It's Wednesday night, maybe she's starting the weekend early. Parties, dances . . . "

"If she's already at home she's probably working her head off." Who was I trying to convince?

CHAPTER 8

Shortly before two in the afternoon, McCool took a dromy out to where Lucas was working and called him down from the machine. "Something's come up, and I have to go out of town. You'll be working on your own for a while."

Lucas glanced back at the pipeline. "We should do all right."

"I'll leave you Rufus to get around on." McCool slapped the tan colored dromy on the side and turned to the two laborers in the ditch. Lean, with weathered faces, the men had stopped working and were leaning on their shovels. "I'm leaving for a couple of days," he told them. "Lucas is in charge."

The shorter one spat to the side. "Hank won't take orders from a Martian."

McCool flushed. "Hank's coming with me." He went to the edge of the ditch. "No more of that Martian talk--Lucas is a good friend, and a brother."

Going back to Rufus, McCool introduced Lucas as its boss in his absence. The dromy's large blue eyes rose on their stalks, surveying Lucas. It shortened its forelegs to make an obeisance. Lucas stroked the dromy's head and its nostrils expanded, snuffling to take the new master's scent.

"I'll leave you a pass key for the farm buildings," McCool said. He opened the dromy's passenger compartment, and showed Lucas a narrow piece of white plastic lying in a niche on the front wall. "At nighttime, you and Gloria will be pretty much alone. Hank and his wife have a cottage up in the northwest corner, in the trees, but the woman keeps to herself."

Before leaving, McCool grasped both Lucas's hands in his. As he gazed into McCool's eyes, Lucas understood that something serious was going to happen. It was like the old days. When the Rogers went out riding, there were times when not everyone came back.

Rufus took McCool to the house and the dromy returned by itself an hour later. Seeing the dromy gave Lucas a huge lift. It was a symbol of freedom. His new ride had a rakish look; it wasn't some ordinary farm drudge.

Up on Mars the enclosed living spaces could become claustrophobic, and it was joyous to get out in a dromy and race across the desert sands. The four legged robots were well suited to the low gravity. Lucas had scaled huge mountains and jumped deep chasms with them.

At quitting time Rufus came over to the ditch, and the three men got into the inside compartment. Lucas took the back seat, and the two laborers sat in front, facing him. Rufus's seats adjusted to fit its passengers, which made for a comfortable ride. "Are you a sporting model?" Lucas asked as they started off.

"Yes, I'm rated as such," Rufus said.

"I thought so. You're out of place in this farm situation." Grinning to the other men, Lucas advised them to hold on. Then he swung himself out of the compartment, and climbed onto the dromy's back.

They were traveling up a path between two fenced fields, and the way ahead was clear. Deciding to put the dromy through its paces, Lucas first tested the limits of its speed then brought it to a quick stop. "You're good," he laughed, giving Rufus a playful slap. Then they jumped the fences on either side. "Do you have fighting capabilities?" he asked afterward.

"Not that I know of," Rufus said.

"That's when you go up on your hind legs. You use your front legs for striking." Lucas held tight to the dromy's neck as it reared up. "You're first rate," he said. "You and I could go places."

They stopped at the maintenance area, and let the other men out beside their van. "I'll see you here tomorrow morning," Lucas told them.

John, the shorter man, spat to the side. "Any more of this and I'll walk to the ditch."

His partner Fritz, who was usually taciturn, nodded vehemently. "We didn't sign up to be thrown around while you do stunts."

"Sorry," Lucas said. "It'll be different tomorrow."

Dinner that evening was subdued without McCool. Gloria served up some leftover stew, and talked non-stop on the videophone with a woman friend who lived down the road.

Lucas finished as soon as possible and went up to his room. *Any progress?* he asked Tomi.

"There are several ways to reach Helena once we escape. The longer we stay here, the lower our chances of reaching the goal."

"Don't worry. I didn't travel all this way to die on a farm."

The next day when Lucas went in for lunch, the kitchen table was bare. Hearing the video in the living room, he found Gloria in a white bathrobe, holding a tumbler of whiskey. Her attention remained on the screen. Lucas took a chair beside her.

On a barren hillside, a fenced-off transmission tower was collapsed in a jumbled heap. "Stations were hit in New York, Pennsylvania and Georgia," an announcer said. "Apparently the sabotage was meant to disrupt the government's communications. We take you now to Albany, where Governor Levitz is meeting some reporters."

The governor, a thin man with long, white hair, stood on a platform that swung over a map of his state where markers showed several sites attended by emergency crews. "The Resistance attacks are a sign of desperation," Governor Levitz said. "The state of New York remains calm and orderly."

"Is the government still operating normally?" a reporter asked.

Levitz turned on her. "Don't worry about that. Most of our networks were not disrupted, and everything continues as usual."

Gloria shut down the video. "It's been like this all morning. Come to the kitchen, I'll fix something."

Lucas sat down at the table and Gloria brought him some bread, cold meat, and a slab of cheese. He drank some juice and ate hungrily.

"It said on the news the Resisters have a smaller version of the Shiva ray, the United World States used in the conquest," Gloria said.

"Did McCool say anything about it?"

She shook her head. "He never tells me anything."

On his way back to the job, Lucas realized the talk of the new weapons fit with what he'd seen when the airship was hijacked. The two gray cases were probably around here somewhere, and they might well hold the key to his freedom.

From what he understood, the Shiva was a major advancement on previous ray guns, as it could penetrate and destroy most materials, including concrete and metals. It transformed ordinary matter into dark matter, which was composed of minute particles not held together by any force. The thought of so much power in his hands made him laugh aloud.

After work he found Gloria in the living room again, still wearing her white bathrobe. "Is it dinner time already?" she asked in a slurred voice.

"It's getting on to six," he said, going to the bar. He took his drink to the couch. "Did you hear any more news?"

Gloria gave him a bright smile. "The Resisters attacked more sites. All around the country." She held her glass up to him. "Do you mind?"

"It's a good thing McCool bought that truckload of whiskey," he said, making her another drink.

"Well he acquired it," Gloria said, giggling. "I'm not sure he paid anything." Then tears rolled down her cheeks. "It's six o'clock and I'm not even up yet. I'm going to have a bath and get dressed. Are you hungry?"

"Don't worry about it. I'm going to have a shower myself. There's plenty of food in the fridge, I can easily grab something later."

Lucas took Tomi into the shower with him and had the octopod on his shoulder when he came out. Then Gloria appeared. He covered himself with the towel and put the varlet on the dresser.

Gloria still wore the white bathrobe and had another big glass of whiskey in her hand. "That lumitoo," she said, staring at his shoulder. "It's meant a lot to me, over the years. In the quietest hours of the darkest nights I'd see it glowing beside me. It was a sign that we were alive, and we'd make it through."

"It's a mark from a different era," he said, reaching for his pants.

Suddenly he was hit by a severe shock. Helpless, he lost control of both the pants and his towel. "You little bitch," he said in disbelief, realizing Gloria had done it.

"Oh, I'm only playing." Laughing, she sat on the bed. "McCool told me about the parties you Rogers had. You shared the women."

"Those days are gone, I'm out of commission."

Gloria frowned and raised the control rod again. "Don't mess with me, I'm not in the mood."

Lucas shot his casting ring and snatched it from her grasp. "No more," he said. He pulled his pants back on and stuck the rod in his pocket. "I'll give this back in the morning when you sober up."

"Don't fight," Tomi said. "She can be an important ally."

"She just zapped me! You're right, though."

"Damn, Lucas, how did you do that?" Gloria asked.

He showed her his ring. "In zero gravity, these things help you move from place to place, and save you from drifting away. Mine's modified, to make it handier."

Gloria gulped some whiskey. Then she began to cry. "I'm sorry," she sobbed.

Lucas disliked drunks, and was not moved by her tears. But he needed to advance this situation. Sitting next to her, he put his arm around her. "Come on now, try and settle down."

Gloria blushed deeply. "My husband thinks you'll be a big advantage to us. Kenny Summers offered a lot of money to have you killed and Eddie absolutely refused."

Lucas tightened his embrace. "There's a ton of stress on you right now. We need to talk, but not here. How about if I cook dinner tonight? After a bite to eat the world always looks more normal."

She caught her breath, and smiled through her tears. "You know how to cook?" she asked, looking up at him. "Amazing. I'm glad to find this out. All right, mister, let's try it."

Lucas sensed more freedom between them when they left the bedroom and went down the hall. While they'd stepped back from the brink, a sense of intimacy still remained. "I can't believe you zapped me," he said, giving her a playful slap on the butt. "Do you have any idea what that feels like?"

"I'm sorry," Gloria replied. "Maybe I wanted some attention."

"Roger women are a breed apart. And you're one of them."

Downstairs in the kitchen, Gloria sat at the table while Lucas opened a bottle of Canadian Red and poured them each a glass. They'd promised to get off the bourbon that evening, and wine with food was a proven way to start.

"Cheers," Gloria said, holding up her glass to Lucas. "Thank you for understanding. It's difficult for me. I'm no weakling, but my husband is gone so often, committed to these endless missions. I worry and fret, all the time. Nights are the worst."

"Does whiskey help you sleep?" Lucas asked.

Tears welled again in Gloria's eyes. "I think drinking makes things worse. Dr. James gave me some sleeping pills. I plan to go back on them, starting tonight."

"That'll be better," Lucas said.

Dinner that evening was standard for the farm: onions, potatoes, carrots and greens from their own garden, and warmed up roast beef. Having Lucas prepare it was a welcome change for Gloria, and she praised his culinary skills.

Gloria's comment about the Rogers sharing their women made Lucas realize that she held misconceptions about his and McCool's early life, so while they ate he told her how things really were. "In Tacoma back then, the police were useless. The Rogers protected local businesses and the ordinary people from attacks by outside gangs. As youngsters living in the clubhouse, McCool and I were raised to be soldiers. One day I came home from school and invaders had gotten in. Nobody else was around. It was up to me to defend our home, and so I ended up shooting all three of them.

"After that the Rogers moved me up the ranks. At fourteen I was too young to become a full-fledged member, but they held a party for me." Lucas looked to Gloria and laughed. "This is where the sharing women story might have come from. McCool and I were only kids, though. Did he tell you about this?"

Gloria narrowed her eyes. "I can't remember exactly what he said. Please continue."

"Different women came around the place, girlfriends, wives or whatever, but McCool and I never had much to do with them. After the party something amazing occurred. Two sisters, maybe fifteen or sixteen years old, were assigned to me. I had them for a whole month.

"McCool's room was in the basement next to mine, and the walls were thin. He wasn't too happy about the situation. Then an emergency happened over in Seattle, and McCool shot somebody. After that, he demanded to share my girlfriends, and got his way. It only lasted for a couple of weeks, because the girls left."

"What a terrible upbringing," Gloria said, shaking her head. She poured more wine for Lucas.

"The two of us were orphans, and without the Rogers we might not have survived. At eighteen McCool joined the US Army and made a career out of it. I respect him a lot."

After dinner Gloria made some hot chocolate, and she and Lucas brought their cups to the living room. They were determined to keep the news videos turned off, and the bar closed.

Gloria sat on the end of the couch. Lucas was in an arm chair, across from her. The room was very quiet. "I love it here in the country," Lucas said. "McCool did a fine job with this farm."

"He gets what he wants."

"Did he design the place originally?"

"Of course."

"The two of us lost touch over the years. How did he move up so far?"

"The main thing he did was before the Conquest. Did you hear about the swarming up on Mars?"

"I heard," Lucas said. "Millions of people went on the move, looking for somewhere to live."

"There was no such place! The world had run out of room, especially in North America. There was barely enough living space as it was, and the swarm threatened to drag us all down. My husband was one of the angels of mercy, they called Johnny Appleseeds. It was God's will. The plague came so humanity could survive."

The information was disturbing, but Lucas kept his feelings to himself. Gloria turned on some music, and he kept her company until shortly before midnight, when she announced her intention to take one of the sleeping pills and go to bed.

He went upstairs with her. As they were about to separate, she asked him to give back her control rod. Lucas was hesitant. "So I'll be a slave again?"

"You're the least of my worries," Gloria said. "I use the rod for our fence, and other things too." She held out her hand, and he gave it to her.

Back in his room, Lucas lay down on his bed with Tomi on his chest. *"I need a couple of hours rest, but no more."*

It was close to three in the morning. Creeping along the hallway, Lucas passed the stairwell and entered the far wing of the house. Somewhere along here, was Gloria's bedroom. Working as quietly as possible, he tried each door. He found a closet with cleaning supplies, and another small room where the shelves were piled with sheets, pillows, and blankets. The next three rooms were empty. Then he found a locked door he thought was probably Gloria's.

Farther down the hallway, he came to a room with an illuminated fish tank. Lights came on when he entered, displaying a life-sized picture of a much younger McCool in uniform. One wall was all windows; he pulled the drapes over it. A large video screen and a stationary bicycle made him feel McCool could spend a lot of time in this room.

The contoured gray desk had no visible drawers. Lucas pulled out the chair and sat down. *"How do I get in?"* he asked Tomi.

"You're being scanned. Since you are not authorized, the room is not responding."

Lucas slapped his hand on the top of the desk and leaned back in the chair. "Hello," he said loudly. "My name is Lucas. Mrs. McCool sent me in here to make a call."

"Welcome, Master Lucas," a voice said. A video screen rose from the top of the desk.

Lucas examined the edge of the screen, and looked around the back. Then he put Tomi on the desk beside the screen. *"Fix it so we can access McCool's site plans,"* Lucas said. *"On the back it says SENSEI, and there's a model number here too."*

"I'm receiving the service override."

A screen on the left wall danced with light; the front of the house appeared. "Welcome to the Mountain Valley School," McCool's voice said. "Here in this idyllic setting, children will live a healthy, normal life and follow educational paths tailored to their unique interests and aptitudes. At the end of their stay here, each child will step into the larger world strong and self-reliant, fully capable and living proof that the implant-free human being made in God's own image is still the highest form of life on this planet."

Lucas shook his head. Like him, McCool started off as an abandoned orphan taken in by the Rogers. Now he planned to surround himself with children in a residential school. It probably never entered his head that a mass murderer was not the best role model for young people. *"Skip the school,"* he told Tomi. *"Get me the plans for the work buildings."*

Scanning through the drawings, he learned the farm was run by solar power, with a backup fuel cell system. The fence around the property included breakers; it should be possible to shut it down. Farther on, Lucas discovered a half-basement sketched in underneath the garage, with the staircase clearly outlined. He'd never noticed a staircase there before. Feeling strongly that he'd found an important piece of the puzzle, he closed down the screen.

Back in his own room, Lucas put on his clothes from the airship and left the farm duds in the closet. Rolling up the bead belt with the red buckle, he shoved it in his pocket. If all went well, he planned to leave tonight.

Outside it was still dark, and Rufus was waiting by the door. The two Rovers were there too. He stroked their heads, and told them he was going to the shop.

The garage was quiet and dark, no machines were in for servicing. Lucas smiled at the sight of the two full bays, high ceilings, and extensive racks of tools. Once again, McCool had built for a future vision. This went far beyond his present needs.

According to the drawing, the stairs were at the back on the right hand side. But, no stairs were there. Lucas went outside, where he was immediately met by the Rovers. The robot-dogs accompanied him on his walk around the building.

Finding nothing, Lucas went back inside the shop. He looked carefully along the left wall, again to no avail. He slapped it in frustration, looked back the other way, and noticed a control panel on the right wall.

The panel had an array of buttons; he pushed the one marked South Door and the main entrance door rose up. Quickly, he pushed the button again and the door closed. Next he tried the one marked North Door. With a wrenching screech, the back wall on the left hand side began to rise. "Naturally," Lucas sighed.

Inside were pipes and a large tank; to the right was a staircase. The door at the bottom was securely locked. Lucas put Tomi next to the small red light on the wall. *"Can you sense anything?"*

"Asking for identification . . . confirmed."

The door swung open, and lights came on inside the basement room. In the middle of the floor were two silvery-gray cases.

When he threw off the lid of the first case, the black sacks the hijackers had used for their loot were right on top. *"This looks promising."* He opened one of the sacks and found some jewelry. Grabbing a handful of rings and necklaces, he let them spill back into the sack. Sticking up from the side was his money folder. He put it in his pocket. Rummaging farther down, he came to a gray cloth belt. Feeling metal as he brought it out, he opened one of the sections and removed a silver-white wafer inscribed with foreign writing. He whooped with joy. *"It's platinum. This will take us anywhere."* Shoving the sacks to the side, he searched deeper into the case, and found stacks of what looked like short, fat-bodied rifles. The weapons were dark gray.

Suddenly hit by a severe shock, he shrieked in agony and went sprawling to the floor.

"Were you looking for something?" McCool asked, putting the white control rod back in his breast pocket.

His teeth bared, Lucas pulled himself into a sitting position. "I'm keeping an eye on things. It's good to see you back." He noticed McCool was holding one of the new guns and his grin faded.

"I should have known better than to trust you," McCool said. "You made a big mistake. You could have been happy here for the rest of your life."

"You're right, I am happy. Nothing's changed."

"I'm going to take Kenny's contract after all," McCool said. "Did you ever see how a Shiva gun works?" He pointed the weapon at a length of pipe jutting out from the wall. Blackness covered the end of the pipe; it collapsed and sagged. With the same show off stance as when they were teens, McCool tossed the gun in the air so it flipped end over end.

Immediately shooting his casting ring, Lucas snatched McCool's gun. It bounced along the floor, and then he had it.

"No!" McCool roared, charging at him.

Lucas pointed the gun, his index finger searching for a firing mechanism at the top of the pistol grip. Finding a trigger button, he squeezed. The blackness covered McCool's legs.

"Agh!" McCool screamed, rolling around on the floor.

"Ice Cream, you're melting away."

McCool's right hand was at his breast pocket for the control rod. "You're dead!"

Lucas pressed the button. The blackness covered McCool's elbow and lower abdomen, and his arm sagged helplessly. "Are you going to give me a licking?"

Cautiously approaching, Lucas took the white rod from McCool's pocket. McCool's eyes were closed, and he did not appear to be breathing, but there was hardly any blood. Did the Shiva ray cauterize as it destroyed? Lucas held down the trigger and McCool was reduced to a crumpled mound.

His legs quivering, Lucas sat down on the closed gray case. *"Tomi, I feel sick. I'm too old for this."*

"Your Excellence, you saved us both."

"Yes, it had to be done."

Growing up with the Rogers, Lucas became familiar with all the latest weapons. Ray guns were introduced shortly before he was transported. With a boop gun it was impossible to miss at short range, and any hit caused extreme pain. The Shiva's ability to dissolve matter was a major improvement.

With the gun on his knees, the range finger was on top of the sight, set for close combat; when he moved the dial, the barrel extended. It showed a maximum range of one hundred meters, but he wouldn't trust it that far. Ray guns typically had power switches. He found it on the underside of the frame, and the range finder eye went dark.

"The boop gun power pack is in the grip. What about this thing?"

"The entire butt is the power pack," Tomi said. *"Two cartridges behind the pistol grip, one box shaped and one cylindrical, contain materials which create the rays."*

Lucas gave the gun a twist, and pulled it apart. *"You're right."* He opened the second case, and found it packed with Shiva guns. Going back to the first case, he put the sacks of loot on the floor and searched through the remaining guns until he found the power packs and boxes of cartridges at the bottom. He put six cartridge boxes in his pocket and took an extra power pack. He stared at the cases. *"I'm tempted to make those weapons disappear."*

"The weapons will help the Resistance in their fight against the T-men. They could also be used to kill you."

Lucas's nausea grew worse. *"They'll both be after me now. The two most powerful forces on Earth. Oh, to hell with it. They can only kill me once, and I'm almost dead already."*

He tossed the sacks of loot against the wall for Gloria. Standing far back, he held the Shiva gun on the weapons cases until nothing was left but a twisted mass. Then he made McCool's remains disappear altogether. Afterward he put fresh cartridges in his gun.

When Lucas looked through the folder he'd brought from Mars, his cash was still there, along with the Bart Peters identification. Bart's ID was compromised; the Resisters and the police would both be watching for it. He had to keep it, though. If the authorities questioned him, he'd tell the truth: the Resisters had kidnapped him from the airship, and he managed to escape.

The money belt looked like a huge asset. Squeezing it he could feel four more of the platinum wafers nestled in the cloth. *"This will help."*

Lucas went back upstairs to the garage. Morning light was coming through the windows. Time was running short; no one must see him leave.

As he'd hoped, there was an old tool box in one of the cupboards. The Shiva gun, the extra power pack and the cartridges all fit, along with the money belt. He looked for the shop's control rod, but couldn't find it. McCool had arrived at the right time.

Outside, the dromy was still waiting. Lucas slapped it on the side. "Open up, Rufus, we're going for a ride."

Inside the compartment, he and Tomi looked closely at McCool's control rod. *"There must be a way to choose different functions," Lucas said.*

One of the rod's surfaces was slightly curved, and when Tomi stroked it, they saw a small screen. The rod seemed to govern three main operations: the gate, fence, and shackle belts.

Lucas told the dromy to go to the southwest corner of the farm, where he'd be close to the forest. He'd seen a breaker there on McCool's plans. Hopefully the control rod would shut down the fence from a safe distance.

They set off at a brisk trot. After a few minutes, a shrill yipping told him that the Rovers were still with him. Then one soared past his compartment window, barking loudly.

"Why are they jumping and barking like this?" he asked Rufus.

"The electric fence is dangerous, and the Rovers are warning us away."

Stopping the dromy, Lucas opened the compartment door and spoke to the Rovers. "I'm going to do some work on the fence, so the power will be disconnected for a while," he said. "You need to check for possible intruders, especially at the gate."

"Yes, Master Lucas," they chorused. The Rovers loped away in the direction of the gate.

The fence was now in view. Lucas shut it down with the control rod, and Rufus jumped it like a Martian.

CHAPTER 9

The earthquake relief assignment was exciting for me; I'd never been to Vancouver Island before. On Thursday we attended morning classes as usual. After a quick shower and some lunch, Wang, Zack and I took our bags out to the transit loop.

Our bus was already there, so we ran for it. When we boarded, the seats were filled. We had to stand all the way downtown.

Nearing our stop we pushed through the tightly packed passengers to the exit door. "Coming through," Zack said in a booming voice from behind me. "Don't leave, driver, we're getting out."

"I don't have all day," came the swift reply. "Next time think ahead."

We made it out, and the bus sped away. "These robot drivers are getting rude," Wang said. "Who teaches them to talk like that?"

"Smash the robots," Zack said.

Directly ahead was the Landmark Hotel, where the airport limo stopped. Two young women with long black hair and short, tight dresses strolled by as we got there. "Amazing," I said, watching them go into the hotel. Wang and Zack stared too. We adored our sister cadets' shaved heads and uniforms, and believed with them that character outweighs the outward show, but the other types of women could be highly alluring.

A horn blared, and the red and gray limousine pulled up. It was operated by a middle aged man with an amiable smile and strong looking hands. Feeling that we'd stepped up considerably from the bus, we settled into plush, high-backed seats right behind the driver.

The Landmark Hotel was our last scheduled stop in Vancouver. Once we were seated, the limo pulled out into traffic. Then everything slowed down. Ahead was nothing but gridlock.

A uniformed policeman waved us down a side street; from there we turned left. When we came parallel to the main road, everyone gasped. The far side of the roadway was a large crater, and buses and transport trucks were toppled over. Floating above the debris was a pale balloon in the image of bare buttocks. "Resisters," Wang spat out.

"Let's stop and help," I said.

"We can't do that," the driver said. "Emergency crews are on the way, they'll look after things." Once past the accident, we got back onto the main road and soon came to the bridge over the Fraser River.

"Resisters are slime," Wang said.

"Well, they probably feel they're doing the right thing," the driver said.

I shook my head. "They're never going to win." My conviction was mirrored in Zack and Wang's set faces. The insurgents claimed they were waging a just war against United World States rule. In fact, there was no chance the world would ever return to the divisions and chaos of the past. The Resister actions were senseless crimes, committed out of malice. Soon the last of them would be tracked down, and they'd be eradicated.

The limo arrived at the airport right on schedule. With no luggage but our bags, we went straight to the departure area and spoke to the reception clerk. "Three for the Coaster," he said, examining our tickets. "It'll be loading in a couple of minutes."

We went to the window and looked out at the landing area. Off in the distance, a white airship was slowly descending. The embodiment of power, beauty, and romance, it would be an international or intercontinental flight.

Our own ship was right outside. Rust colored, with a cap on top for passengers, and a wide base for the freight, it served routes where speed was not a main priority. A doorway was open in the hull. "The Coaster is now loading," a voice said. We grabbed our bags and started down the narrow hallway that led to the ship.

The passenger compartment resembled a big lounge, where everyone relaxed. People sat every which way, while children ran back and forth, seemingly in high spirits.

Taking the outside aisle, we found seats against the window. The order came for passengers to sit down, and the ship slowly left the ground. It turned while ascending, and we got a panoramic view of the city, the ocean, the mountains, and Vancouver Island in the distance. When it stabilized we were in the rear, looking backward. Point Grey was visible, and we saw the STA buildings and our dorm.

Shortly after take-off, a tall, long-haired woman in a rust-colored Coaster smock came around with a food cart. "There's no kitchen on this flight but our coffee's hot and the sandwiches are fresh made."

"They promised to feed us when we get there," Wang said, taking a bottle of orange juice.

"I see you're STA men. Years ago I thought of going into space myself."

"What happened?" Zack asked with a grin.

"Oh, life got in the way." She nodded, and moved on.

Wang downed his juice and sighed deeply. "There's an old Chinese proverb," he said, reaching for his bag. "Use wise management of your minutes and hours. The years will take care of themselves." He took out his telecap.

Zack and I looked at each other. "I never knew that proverb was Chinese," he said.

"It's a good chance to get some work done." We put our telecaps on too.

STA men often say it's impossible to really know someone until you meet their mind in telepathy. When the food lady returned for the empties, the way Zack watched her breasts was a revelation. *Soon he embraced her from behind, and had his hands on them.* Zack's facial expression was as calm as ever. She left with her cart, unaware of the stir she'd created in his brain.

Wang sent a picture of Zack posing with weights, all his muscles standing out but with a head like a pea and a penis to match.

Zack projected a vision of Wang walking along with long hair and a tight dress that did not quite cover the buttocks. "Slow down, bitch," he sneered.

The two clones soon escalated their war, battering each other with erections that looked about four feet long. And I was in the middle! Feeling there should be at least one adult in the room, I adopted the manner of our principal, Mr. Rossiter. *"Ahem," I said sharply.* The disappearance of the amazing erections was a minor victory, but it made things more comfortable for me.

The first stop was the provincial capital, Victoria. The airport was inland, and seemed to be functioning normally. Port Alberni, a smaller city at the head of a long inlet, came next. We noticed considerable damage around the waterfront area; the tsunami had destroyed docks, ripped yachts from moorings, and flattened buildings. The Coaster stayed here about three quarters of an hour, unloading supplies and equipment.

On leaving Port Alberni, our ship soared high above the nearby mountains and went north along the coastline. Soon we tracked another inlet to our destination, Cedar River. The town was about ten kilometers from the water and well above sea level.

When we disembarked, a middle aged man with a dark, lined face was waiting at the terminal entrance. "Community service? I'm your host, Paul Lozano." We followed him through the waiting room, and out the other exit, to a brown van with CEDAR RIVER CO-OP on its side.

After driving past a cluster of small stores and restaurants, we took a narrow bridge across a rushing stream, continuing on toward some closely grouped houses, all painted brown. "This section is owned by the cooperative," Paul told us. "Our laws hold precedence."

The van stopped in front of a narrow, three story house that was set back from the road. As we got out, some dogs rushed up, barking furiously. Wang put his hand on the first one's head, and the others crowded around and climbed up until Paul chased them away.

Passing through a yard of fruit trees and long grass, we climbed some stairs to an enclosed front porch. A large, round-faced woman with short gray hair, wearing a long, faded green dress, was standing in the midst of potted plants, and piles of empty jars.

"I got the workers," Paul said.

"Good," she said, putting down a jar which was half-filled with water. She smiled, looking us over carefully with calm dark eyes. "I'm Nora, Paul's wife. We're happy to have you here, and hope you'll enjoy your stay." She showed us inside to a bright, reddish-brown room that had four bunk beds. "Your bathroom's in the back. Dinner's almost ready, come upstairs when you're cleaned up." She left, closing the door.

We looked at each other and grinned. Zack flopped into one of the bottom bunks. "Not bad," he said.

"Don't get too comfortable," Wang said. "You're sleeping up top."

"I'm sleeping here," Zack said, turning onto his stomach.

"This constant bickering gets on my nerves," I told them. Stepping onto the little ladder at the end of the bed, I climbed into the upper bunk. "Being on top is more natural for me."

"Farts rise," Wang said. "All night long."

"Piss flows downward."

They made no reply, but the brooding silence was short-lived. "I'm going to have a quick shower," Wang said.

"Me first," Zack said, jumping out of bed. He went into a half crouch. "Come on, I'll fight you for it."

"You'll need whatever strength you've got for community service," Wang said. He stepped past, and, at the last instant, threw his arm around Zack's neck, bearing him over backward. Laughing merrily, he went into the bathroom.

Zack twisted onto his hands and knees. "Come back here!" he roared. The bathroom door clicked shut, and the shower started.

There was a knock on the bedroom door, and Paul Lozano looked in. He stood with his head slightly bowed. "They're wondering--I know you didn't plan on doing any work till the morning, but we are very short-handed."

"That's why they sent us," I said.

His face lit up with a smile. "As soon as you're ready, come upstairs for dinner."

As the three of us went out, we passed an open door to a bedroom. "Hello, there," said a tall, gray-haired woman. She sat at a small table, working a bright orange pattern into a black blouse with needle and thread. "I hope you're hungry, Nora made a big meal."

"We can handle it," Wang said. "Are you coming up?"

"As soon as I finish here."

An aroma of cooking meat came down the staircase, and Zack stopped us. "I'm off vegan for the weekend."

Wang and I looked at each other, and nodded. "There's not much choice in community service," Wang said. "We're not here to starve to death."

On the next floor, a door was open to a long room where Paul sat at the head of a wooden table, carving slices from a roast. "You're just in time," he said.

"Take a seat," Nora said from the kitchen. She put some dishes filled with vegetables on the table. "Go ahead, start in. I know you must be hungry." I put potatoes on my plate, and gave the dish to Wang. Zack passed me the green beans.

"Here's Nora's sister," Paul said as the woman from downstairs came in. "You'd better get something in your stomach, Dorothy. You're looking kind of peaked."

Not deigning to reply, Dorothy sat beside me, and Paul passed her the platter of meat. "Deer come through the village all the time," she told us. "They don't mind if we take one once in a while."

"This one nibbled on everything it could," Nora said. "One day it stayed around a bit too long, and Dorothy bagged it." She went around the table with a large teapot, filling our cups. "It's good you came, we need the help."

At first it felt strange to try the venison, as deer were everywhere around our school and only wolves or poachers would think of eating them. It tasted good, though. The meat was rich and filling; this food would give energy for hours to come.

After dinner, Paul drove us to a small park overlooking the inlet. There was debris everywhere from the tsunami; benches were torn away, and the park's small buildings crushed. Continuing south along the water's edge we found more devastation, especially at the dock area where boats were smashed, and some tossed up far onto the shore. Crews were working all around, salvaging what they could from the wreckage.

We followed the road farther south, to the co-op's aquaculture processing center. The section built out over the water was collapsed, with a large crane half-submerged.

Paul parked the van beside a nearby boat ramp, where a dark-haired youth had a white barge pulled up. "Johnny," Paul called. "Is everything ready?"

"Yes, we're done," Johnny replied, coming to join us.

Paul took us inside the main building. The five of us loaded two hovercarts with bales of kelp, boxes of cabbage, and tubs of fresh fish from the cooler, making several deliveries down to the barge.

When the barge held enough, we headed for the north end of the bay, where the co-op had some holding ponds. The tsunami had wrecked them too, and it was an all day job for Johnny and his crew to set them up again.

We were just finishing unloading the supplies onto the float, when a sleek black and white cabin cruiser approached very slowly, guided by a woman in a yellow jumpsuit. The water around her craft was in a frenzy, with orcas breaching and smaller dolphins rushing all around. The bay resounded with their high-pitched cries.

The boat stopped for a minute before coming in. It was followed by a group of other animals, swimming with their dark backs and small heads above the water. When the woman leaned out of the boat and patted one, they all turned to her.

"Steller's sea cows," Zack said. "I heard they had them out here."

Paul grabbed hold of the cabin cruiser as it came alongside, and Zack and I kept it in place while he secured it. "Any trouble?" Paul asked the woman.

"Not since the tsunami," she said, stepping out. In her late twenties, she was very slim, and wore a light brown skullcap embroidered with the shape of an orca. "Hello there," she said, smiling to us.

"Lisa Hays is our top biologist and also an oceanographer, one of the few who really understands how things fit together," Paul said.

Her smile broadened, and I sensed the high-powered energy and vibrant spirit common to the Tees. Something splashed behind us. One of the orcas was up against the float, looking at Lisa. A ridge was prominent on its head. "Our friends are hungry," Lisa said.

Johnny and Paul tossed out some fish and the water creatures went wild.

Lisa and the crested orca looked steadily at each other; clearly, they were together in thought. Wang went over and lay on the edge of the float, leaning out to the orca. "Her name's Celene," Lisa told him.

The sea cows approached now, and Paul and Johnny fed them. Mostly it was kelp, and the animals seemed to like that, rubbing against the side of the float and chewing complacently. Then Paul offered one of them a hunk of red cabbage. The animal raised its head, accepting the treat in its mouth, and Paul drew it inside a pen as Johnny held the door open. A good twenty-five feet in length, with a rotund belly, it was an awesome sight. Sea cows could weigh in excess of ten thousand kilograms.

The orcas went to work, collecting the rest of the herd. The sea cows whimpered but made no resistance as the orcas sped around, nipping and nudging them toward the gateways. There was plenty of food inside, and the animals seemed to relax there.

Lisa came back to town in the barge with Paul, Wang, Zack and me. Johnny remained at the float with the cabin cruiser, as they did not want to leave the herd untended.

"Did you ever try sea cow milk?" Paul asked, taking a clear jug from under his seat. He poured us each a small glass of white liquid.

I tasted mine, and smiled at the extraordinary richness and sweetness.

"Now you know what our world president drinks at bedtime," Paul said. "This milk gives power."

"The early Europeans were crazy to kill them all off," Wang said.

Everybody knew the story. The last sea cows were hunted down around 1768; they weren't seen again until three hundred years later, during the melting of the polar ice caps. Tissue was taken from thawing carcasses, and with the help of living relatives, the manatee and dugong, a resurrection was achieved.

"None of this would be possible without the orcas," Lisa told us. "The sea cows are very gentle, but not normally submissive to humans. The orcas are brilliant at keeping order and enforcing discipline. Working with them, we're able to do real ocean ranching."

"Is it difficult to train the orcas?" Zack asked.

"Not when the dominant female is transformed," Lisa laughed. "The main thing is to keep the herd moving, so the kelp can replenish itself. The orcas understand all that as well as anyone."

Back at the house, Paul had everyone take a laxative, as we'd be wearing hazard suits in the morning. I soaked under a hot shower for a long time, and was happy to climb up to my bunk. For once there was little bickering between my roommates, and I soon drifted off to sleep.

Hours later something woke me up. Wang was on the phone, talking excitedly in Chinese. I heard him say "Celene." The conversation was outside my standard Mandarin; Wang was holding out on me. Contemplating an intake of further Chinese dialects, I went back to sleep.

CHAPTER 10

It was starting to get light now. Desperate to get far away before his disappearance was discovered, Lucas kept to the forest trails, urging Rufus to travel ever faster. The inner compartment rocked violently, as the dromy leapt over small streams, jumped fallen logs, and charged through bushes and around trees. They burst through a clearing that overlooked the road, and regained the shelter of the trees.

"Indian Falls is about two miles from here," Tomi said.

Helena was over a hundred miles, up in the mountains. He'd never make it with the dromy; the farm would track it.

Speeding down a hill, they crossed the road where it made a wide curve, and got back in the trees. Nearing the town, Lucas took out the Shiva gun. "Stop and let me out," he told Rufus. "Wipe this trip from your memory."

"Yes, Master Lucas." The side door opened.

Lucas stepped out and turned the gun on the dromy. Shame gripped him as it sank to the forest floor. "Sorry for this," Lucas said, continuing to squeeze the trigger. A vision of McCool's legs disappearing in the same way came to him strongly, and he shuddered.

The large blue eyes looked right at him. "This incident is wiped from my memory."

Lucas held the gun on until the robot shrank to nothing, and the ground was clear.

The main problem now was the shackle belt. With his torso bared, he set the Shiva gun to cutting mode, making sure of the depth on the bark of a nearby tree. Going down on his hands and knees, he helped Tomi balance the gun on his back. He grasped the belt at his stomach. *"It'll try to kill me when you cut it. Be sure and fast."*

"One, two, three . . . now."

Lucas tore it off even while flattened by a last jolt. He was free! Jumping up, he turned the gun on the hated black fabric until the last of it disappeared.

Up ahead was a wire fence, overgrown by bushes. He climbed through and started down a narrow road that led past some houses. Despite the dangers all around, it was marvelous to be free. The money belt and the Shiva gun would give him the power to overcome most obstacles.

The modest residences were well kept up, many of them with small gardens. He thought the community would be mainly working folk. With his tool box, slouch hat, beard, and casual clothes, he'd pass for someone's relative, here on a visit.

Lucas waved off a city bus that slowed for him, and crossed a bridge over some railway tracks. This marked the edge of the residential area. On the other side, container trucks were lined up in front of low-lying warehouses. He went through here at a leisurely pace. Was there a chance for him to hitch a ride, or sneak unnoticed into the back of one of these trucks?

After walking a few more blocks, a smile came to his lips. Music! He'd stumbled on the town's entertainment district: a street lined with bars, casinos and sex joints. He was the lone pedestrian this time of the morning, but, as he approached, a man and two women stumbled out of a bar and got into a waiting robocab. The familiar scene impressed Lucas deeply. Nobody bothered much with drunks.

Adopting the overly careful manner of someone who was half-bombed, he entered a place with blacked-out windows, the Puppies Playground. The bar was deserted, except for a man sleeping at a corner table. Hearing whistles and loud cheering, Lucas went into an adjoining room where people were watching the mog races on a large video screen.

He took a table close to the screen, where mogs leapt a four-foot fence before plunging into a wave-filled pool. Part man, part dog! Along with millions of others, Lucas was a huge fan of their races. When a uniformed waitress came over he ordered a tall Trapeze, a mixture of stimulant, euphoriant, and alcohol, often favored by all-night drinkers.

The people in the lounge cried out in dismay as a straggler missed the leap and impaled himself on a spike. Lucas too was sickened by the blood, and deeply moved by the agony in the mog's eyes. It was Black Beauty. Up in Marsport, Lucas had followed this mog for years, celebrating his many victories, his life of luxury, and triumphs with the bitches. He could hardly watch as the track veterinarians carried him to the ambulance.

As the waitress arrived with Lucas's drink, she read his face and her fixed smile vanished. "Sorry," she said, putting the glass down. Then she started to cry. "I'm so sorry," she said again. "I really loved Black Beauty."

"Me too."

They were getting ready for the next race. Lucas knew the favorite well. Catherine the Great's exceptionally tall greyhound body provided surpassing speed, and she also had extraordinary muscular power. She was ruthless and very smart. Her innumerable victories over mainly male opponents had developed an arrogant, autocratic streak. She intimidated her rivals from the beginning, and this gave her a big edge.

"Have a look at Thor," Tomi said. "He's only raced on the minor circuits, and his times are exceptional. I consider him a ringer."

Gray in color, Thor had the long, lithe body of a tundra wolf. While the others stalked around, getting warmed up and glaring at their opponents, Thor sat quietly at the side. He looked explosive. The odds were fifty to one against him.

Lucas was sorely tempted to bet on Thor, but could not afford to cause a stir. He put four hundred units on Catherine to win.

The waitress made a wry face when she brought his next drink. "Almost everyone picked her."

"My luck's bound to turn," Lucas said. As she walked away he noticed two hard-looking men in dark suits standing off to the side. *"Those pissants don't look too happy. They wouldn't last long on Mars."*

"As you say, your honor. Be discreet."

Lucas had another drink and made two more losing bets. It was after seven now; his fellow pipeline workers John and Fritz would be getting ready for the day. They lived on a neighboring farm, and McCool only called on them for special jobs.

Lucas pictured them showing up for work at eight and waiting at the maintenance area to be picked up. It was unlikely they'd raise the alarm right away. Someone might notice McCool's absence, but there was no real reason to be concerned. If they went into the room below the garage there was no corpse, but they'd discover the ruined Shiva guns. Did anyone beside McCool have a key to that room? Whichever way things played out, sometime after eight o'clock people would begin to notice that he, McCool and Rufus were all missing.

Deciding it was time to leave, Lucas asked the waitress to call him a robocab. He tipped her well, and she came outside with him. "Sure you're all right?" she asked as he got into the back seat.

"Everything's fine," he said in a slurred voice. He told the cab to take him to Helena, and paid the fare in advance. Then he made himself as comfortable as possible, and fell asleep.

CHAPTER 11

Paul had us up well before six. Upstairs, Nora served hash and eggs, with mugs of strong tea. When we went out to the van, it was just getting light.

It was misty at the bay. Boats lined the replacement dock, and a group was standing at the end. A woman called to Paul as we approached. "Did you get some new recruits?"

"They sent us space cadets," Paul said. There was a low ripple of laughter.

"Red Sky Island is a long way from outer space," a man said in a resonant voice. Shorter than average, he was broad in the shoulders and chest.

A crew boat emerged from the fog, and everybody got on board. I had an aisle seat next to the man who'd spoken. Paul was across from me, and soon after we pulled away from the dock, he pointed out a tall, straight figure in a small boat. "Dorothy's going after some rock cod," he said. Our crew boat operator tooted his horn, and she waved at us.

"Did they tell you what to expect?" my seatmate asked. "We're dismantling a military research site left by the old people, and those chemical and biological agents are still dangerous."

"We're prepared for it," I said. "My name's Dom, what's yours?"

He shook my hand. "I'm Ronny. If you run into any problems, let me know."

Once out of the inlet, we ran north for about half an hour. The sun was well up now, and the sky was clear.

Directly ahead were the towering white cliffs of Red Sky Island. The old people sculpted several of these super islands, taking rock from neighbors destined to disappear, but Red Sky was the only one on the northwest coast.

The crew boat went down the eastern side, and we approached a long breakwater. Toward the middle, a tall pillar flashed ENTER. Our boat went through a narrow opening and we entered a wide bay.

"In a few years this'll be a part of our university, a real school of the ocean where our students can mingle with the other species," Paul said.

"The Nuu-chah-nulth are involved too," Ronny told me. "This place is part of our ancestral homelands, and we're back stronger than ever."

The boat pulled alongside a platform built out from the steep stone wall. Everyone got out, and we went up a staircase that was cut in the cliff.

"This harbor doesn't seem hurt much by the tsunami," Zack said.

Ronny pointed to the piles of debris lodged in the breakwater. "Can you imagine if the earth shifted like it did up north? They were crazy to build a germ factory here."

At the top, we went to the guard post, and got temporary passes. Then a site bus took us in through a flat landscape where the pavement and buildings had been stripped away, and the ground roughly plowed. Patches of grass and wild flowers intermingled with the sparse growth of bushes and small trees.

Ahead was a complex of buildings, including a garage with huge machines parked around it. When we left the bus, the regular workers went into a cafeteria entrance, while Paul took Wang, Zack, and me to meet Chief Victor, the head superintendent.

Inside the cavernous garage, we joined a group examining a new excavator. I recognized Chief Victor, a tall man with graying dark hair, from the avatar on the intake program. After a minute he turned to us. "I understand you're already rated, is that so?"

"Yes, sir," Zack said. "It was for a cleanup project by our school."

Chief Victor nodded. "Well, I can definitely use your help. Don't forget, safety first. We have the building plans, but the old people destroyed their work records before the conquest. Because of this, each new building we enter is a mystery. In case of any problems or accidents, be sure and call for help. This is not the place to take chances or cover anything up."

Paul took us into a locker room, where an attendant fitted us with cream-colored biohazard suits with built-in breathing units. We'd remain in the suits for the entire ten hour shift. The suits had three tubes for nourishment: a savory, jellylike substance that was supposed to be nutritious, a sweet tea to maintain alertness, and ordinary drinking water.

Wang and Zack were assigned to excavator machines, while I was the ground-based supervisor for our little team. Wang gave me a lift to the job site. The cab was a bubble with only one seat, so I stood hunched over.

"Let's go," I said. With a sharp beeping sound the excavator backed out of its slot, and fell in line with the other machines leaving the parking lot. We started down a narrow road through a flat, barren landscape, heading for a line of buildings partly obscured by a cloud of dust.

On the outskirts, earth movers were exposing structures from deep underground. Our job site was closer in. Far to the side was the low gray dome of the thorium reactor, which was to be left standing. It was safe and clean, and would meet the island's needs indefinitely.

Around us, elegant buildings rose in swirls, and spread like petals, while fragile looking skywalks went everywhere. This space age style of architecture, often called modern triumphalism, began with the building of the space elevator and the opening up of the solar system. New materials, super-strong and ultra-light, allowed architects to seemingly defy Earth's gravity and express a surging optimism that saw no limit to man's reach.

"Trucks are here," Zack said on the radio.

Our office tower had been down for a couple of days, imploded by carefully placed explosives. The building material was highly sought after, and this batch was already sold to a contractor on the mainland. A line of automated trucks stood waiting.

Wang and Zack's experience was limited, and despite skills gained from intakes, they had problems grabbing with the excavator jaws. They needed my guidance from the ground.

In a couple of hours they caught on, and after break I got shifted to a different job, working with Ronny. The two of us took a van to another section scheduled to be demolished soon. Our job was to make a survey, take photographs, and do a rough inventory of the contents. This was for the database. Eventually everything would be known about who lived here, and what they did.

The buildings looked well kept up, thanks to systems that watered and trimmed the grass and cleaned the windows. The complex's relaxed, subdued atmosphere struck me as attractive and livable, in contrast to the old people's more extreme works.

As we approached the first entranceway, I pointed out its little peaked roof. "Cute."

"It rains a lot here." Cutting a seal from the door, Ronny stuck it in his shoulder bag. "There's no pilfering."

"Of course not. Do you think I'm a thief?"

"Sometimes people are tempted. Here on Red Sky security is really strict." He unlocked the door and we went inside.

The top floor had two large apartments. Before going in, we went and looked out the window at the end of the hallway. Below us was a little park with benches and a fountain. On the far side was a low-lying clubhouse with a tennis court. I thought of banquets, dances . . . then something moved. "An animal?"

Ronny laughed. "Try not to imagine things; this job can get to you."

The home we entered first was impressively spacious, with high ceilings and open rooms. We started the survey with me filming, while Ronny gave an audio account of the contents. Deeper into the apartment we exchanged roles, as it was faster for me to assess the things we came across.

We got to know the former occupants fairly well. Peter Smith was a chemist; his wife, Margaret, a microbiologist. They'd married in their early twenties, and their two children were grown, and on their own. The Smiths had strong cultural and artistic interests, which were reflected everywhere in the apartment. We came across nothing deviant or extraordinary, nothing that explained them helping develop the weapons that wiped out so much of humanity.

After going through three floors, it was time for lunch. "Most will never enjoy the life style of these old people," I said to Ronny as we went out to the van. "Murder paid well."

"Why not join us? Connect with living nature; you'll have the best life there is."

"It's attractive, but I've dreamed of space since childhood." As we drove away I noticed the clubhouse again. "I'd like to see that place before it's torn down."

"We'll ask about it."

The clubhouse was rated low priority, and Chief Victor had to rummage through his file cabinet for the key. "It's not a bad idea to look it over," he said. "Our buyers are on the lookout for a variety of high quality goods."

The wind was up when we went back out, and it blew pink petals from the ornamental cherry trees lining the walkway to the clubhouse. Ronny wiped away a spider's web from the front door. "We don't get much of this on Red Sky. Birds don't like the place either." I pointed out a broken window at the side; he photographed it.

Inside an old time waltz was playing, and Ronny shuffled around to the music, his arms outstretched to an imaginary partner. He maintained such a serious expression I burst out laughing.

A large silver trophy cup was mounted on the wall, next to pictures of lean, suntanned players in white, posing with their racquets. Tennis was not played much anymore; the game was out of fashion. I'd seen it in videos though. It was easy to imagine the old people unleashing powerful serves and volleying at the net, and relaxing afterward with drinks inside the clubhouse.

Ronny went spinning down the hallway while I lagged behind, trying to match faces from pictures in the apartments with the players on the walls. Then a loud curse shattered the peace.

"Get in here," Ronny cried, motioning frantically from a doorway. I joined him in a dining room of the dead. The banquet guests were all skeletons.

Ronny called Chief Victor and reported the bad news. He turned to me. "Security will be here soon, so we'd better complete our survey. Remember, no pilfering."

There was no point replying to his baseless insinuation. The background music had changed to a Gershwin medley, played by a small jazz ensemble. I'd intaken the Gershwin repertoire months ago, and now the different parts played through me as if I was on the multivox.

Ronny started filming. I began my audio, reporting that the dining room was of modest size, with dark brown walls and wine drapes. Glittering chandeliers lent a festive air, and the white-draped tables were set for a substantial banquet. About half the skeletons were dressed in suits; the rest had on feminine attire, including jewelry. Altogether I counted forty-eight deceased.

A loud crashing noise came from the back, and we both jumped. "What in hell!" Ronny exclaimed.

We went down the passageway that led to the kitchen, and found a partly-opened door to a storage room. A man with no hazard suit was on the floor, propped up against a chair. His long brown hair and beard were matted, his clothes smeared with dirt. The little room was filled with the odor from his body, mixed with the scent of spilled wine.

"Welcome to the party," he muttered, squinting up at us with blue eyes. He held up a bottle of wine. "There's stronger stuff if you prefer."

"You're inside a secure area with no authorization," Ronny said. "Who are you? Why did you come?"

"The name's Gern," he replied. "I'm a freeman, and have as much regard for your laws and territorial boundaries as a squirrel or a crow."

Ronny grabbed a piece of fine rose chain dangling from Gern's shirt pocket, and pulled out a heart-shaped pendant. "Pilfering. You're dead, Gern."

Despite loud protests, we helped Gern up into his chair. Gern told us he'd come to Red Sky Island by accident, thrown upon the cliffs by the tsunami. Before this he'd lived alone on his boat, and found work wherever he could.

In a few minutes Chief Victor came in with two security men. Gern was not capable of standing on his own, and they took him away on a stretcher.

On the way out, Chief Victor paused in the banquet room for a long look at the skeletons. "It's lucky you found this. There's no way of knowing what the old people died from, and having Gern increases the risk."

"Do you doubt they ingested poison?" I asked.

Chief Victor frowned. "We'll wait for the investigation."

Ronny and I drove back to the other building in silence. "Chief Victor must think I'm an idiot for jumping to conclusions," I said finally.

"He's just teaching you." We parked in the turnaround, and sat for a minute. "Doing these building surveys, it's easy to imagine the old people were similar to us. But that's wrong. They hated us, and wanted to destroy a world they couldn't rule. Anywhere you go on Red Sky there's a chance of a trap, set to release more plagues."

I grimaced. "It's not a good idea to drink their wine."

Ronny laughed. "The medics will soon have Gern vomiting it up."

"Will he get charged?"

"I don't know. They'll have to quarantine him for a while, keep him under observation--for someone who loves freedom as much as Gern, it won't be pleasant."

The crew boat was quiet coming back from work. Beside me, Ronny was asleep, while I remained upright, staring out at the water. Each wave bore the same message. One day we would be gone, just like the buildings on Red Sky Island.

A bleak, depressed feeling had come over me after leaving the site. It was not usual and I connected it with the death banquet. While no poison, bacteria or virus could penetrate my hazard suit, the despair surrounding this awful act may have been communicated.

Back at Paul's house my spirits lifted. Dorothy's rock cod were baking in the oven, and smelled delicious. When we went upstairs for dinner, Nora told us Lisa Hays was invited too.

There was laughter from the stairs. "Is somebody talking about us?" Lisa called. We all stood up as the ocean expert came in with her eight-year-old daughter Dana. "Thanks for having us," Lisa said. "I didn't have anything prepared this evening."

"You're welcome any time," Nora said.

As radiant as her mother, Dana looked around at us with considerable enjoyment; we were probably the first space cadets she'd ever seen. Lisa explained they'd been with the orcas almost all day, as one was close to giving birth. "Our pod is so excited."

"It's her first baby," Dana said.

"The orcas have the longest gestation period of any mammal," Wang said. "Seventeen months."

Nora and Dorothy put the food on the table, and everyone sat down. "You had some excitement today on Red Sky?" Lisa asked Paul.

"Dom handled it," he said.

"It wasn't exactly excitement," I said. "Ronny and I went around filming stuff."

"There'll be excitement in the morning," Zack said. "It's Dom's turn to operate the excavator."

"We're truly grateful you came," Lisa said. "STA has a stellar reputation, and you three certainly live up to it. I understand one of you is going to perform at our benefit concert tomorrow evening?" Wang and Zack pointed to me. "We need your talents in the worst way. Milly Tall is arriving tomorrow, but her group can't attend. Our usual multivox lady is up north; her mother was hurt in the earthquake. So we're very pleased to have an accompanist."

Milly Tall was a well-established star, everyone knew her music. "I'll try my best," I said. "It's my first time performing in public."

"She wants you to enhance her vocals with subtle harmony and restrained embellishments. The multivox should not take over. You can intake the repertoire after dinner, at our place. We're just down the road."

Like the co-op houses, the Cedar River town hall was made of wood. It was spacious inside and had a comfortable, relaxed atmosphere. According to Lisa, it was used for political rallies, badminton, dances, banquets, and whatever else it pleased the locals to do.

Saturday evening the purple curtains in front of the stage were closed, and I pulled a crack open to see the audience. People were dressed up, and seemed in high spirits. Prominent in their uniforms, Wang and Zack stood at the back, chatting with some workers from Red Sky Island.

The multivox was placed far back, on the right side of the small stage. I'd had a chance to practice for an hour or so. This was fortunate, as unlike the school's it had tremendous power, and easily filled the hall with sound.

There was laughter at the left side of the stage, and a small group came out. Lisa brought Milly Tall to meet me and she immediately gave me a hug and a kiss on the cheek, as if we were longtime friends. An erect, dark-haired woman, she felt very light in my arms. "I'm told you're a volunteer," she said in a husky voice. "I love volunteers." Everybody laughed. Then she introduced an older woman in a long white gown. "Susan will stay in case you need a cue." She touched my sleeve. "I like your uniform."

Lisa and Milly went off to the dressing room. I sat at the multivox and Susan took a chair beside me. "Are you a musician too?" I asked.

"I used to play the viola in the London Symphony," she said. "Today I teach, and travel with Milly." I showed her my copy of the night's program, and she started humming through the list of songs while I joined in tapping and humming the instrumental parts.

When Lisa reappeared with Milly, they were both dressed up in black slacks and tops. "I told Milly you're very familiar with her songs, though intakes," Lisa said.

"No worries," Susan said. "He's nailed it."

"Good luck then," Lisa said with a grin. She slipped through the curtain, and there was loud applause.

Lisa told the audience about the orca's new baby, and invited everyone to visit. "Be part of the family." She explained that Milly Tall had interrupted her European tour to be here. "Milly is from this area, and never forgets her roots. She'll always be one of us."

Susan signed to Milly. "This is our cue," she told me.

I started the first piece with a steady drum beat and overlaid a simple keyboard pattern lifted from early twentieth century boogie-woogie. The curtain opened to the darkened auditorium, and Milly Tall began to sing.

The early twenty-second century has seen awesome events, with one disaster after another, and then the conquest. Our music reflects that: spirituals that express mourning for the overwhelming loss, hard-driving, gritty numbers from the reconstruction period, and the strong self-assurance of today's generation. Milly had lived through it, and this night she sang it all.

Many have commented on the power and range of Milly's voice, but the experience of being at her concert can never be fully captured in words. As her voice soared in haunting loveliness, her movements and facial expressions heightened the effect.

Afterward several people complimented me on what I'd done. In my opinion, as Milly Tall's accompanist I was there to frame the picture. I never tried to imitate her group's usual accompaniment with the multivox; instead I used a minimalist approach. My aim was to enable her performance, and avoid getting in the way.

The adage, "less is more," seemed to fit the night. Apparently Susan agreed; at least she never stopped me.

CHAPTER 12

When Lucas awoke, the robocab was navigating a steep curve, through mountainous terrain. "How much longer?" he asked the driver.

"We're almost there."

Lucas had visited Helena in the old days, when it was known as a fun city, and it was horrible to think of the Yellowstone disaster hitting here. He expected to find the city still struggling.

He was wrong. A basin amongst the mountain peaks, Helena's land would always be limited, but the elegant new towers at the city's core radiated prosperity. The streets were crowded with a cosmopolitan mix of well dressed, attractive people who appeared to be having a good time.

The safe house was in the north end, in a mainly residential area. A couple of blocks from the address, Lucas left the cab and walked. It was pleasant out, with sunny skies and a light breeze. The low-rise apartments on either side had well-trimmed lawns, shrubbery, and small trees. The younger women pushing baby carriages made him smile; on Mars childbirth was welcomed but difficult.

He and Tomi kept track of the residential numbers, and on approaching their cross street, felt considerable anticipation. This turned to bitter disappointment when they arrived; nothing was there but a construction site. Lucas went up to the fence that closed off the sidewalk, and stared down at a deep excavation. *Are you sure this is the right address?*

"There's no mistake," Tomi replied.

A large dragonfly was hovering about two feet from Lucas's face. *"What is this thing?"*

"The bot is part of the safe house. Follow it."

The dragonfly led them back through the residential area to a small park where children soared on swings and splashed in a wading pool that encircled a sparkling fountain. Lucas sat on a bench in the sunshine, and the dragonfly left.

Hearing the music of an approaching food truck, Lucas realized he was ravenous. He lined up behind some boisterous youngsters and got a cup of coffee, a hot dog with mustard, and a box of chips. The hot dog, his first in over thirty years, was even better than he remembered. The coffee was real too; he relished every sip.

A striking young couple entered the playground and came his way. The man looked close to seven feet tall, with broad shoulders, a narrow waist, and blond hair that fell to his shoulders. After registering his stature, Lucas's eyes went to the woman, who was not at all dwarfed by her companion. Her dark hair was pulled back severely from her spare face. Her walk held freedom and a certainty.

"Are you Uncle Bud?" she asked as they came up.

Lucas rose to his feet. "Charlene," he said carefully, following the safe house script. "I haven't seen you for seventeen years."

"I'm Mia," she murmured. Her voice had something of an accent, possibly Iranian.

"Boris," the man said. He definitely sounded Slavic.

Lucas looked from one to the other, struggling with something. Then it burst out. "Shanghai Surprise!"

They laughed, and applauded. "You're very sharp," Mia said.

They left together, Lucas declining Boris's offer to take the tool kit. "I remember that movie like it was yesterday," he said as they got into the waiting robocab. "The whole world was in love with Mia Zadora back then. And grateful to Boris for protecting her."

"The Outfit knows Helena well; you're in good hands," Mia said as the cab took them through the business district. "Of course I'm not the real Mia Zadora, just a daughter clone."

They passed some large casinos and stopped at a hotel, THE BLACK PEARL, which towered above its neighbors. The Chinese characters in the sign were larger than the English.

"No one will question us," Mia said. When they went up to the reception desk she introduced Lucas as her uncle, from the Yukon. He paid cash in advance for three nights, and scrawled a signature.

Lucas had the Mountain Suite, and the living room wall was decorated in a scene from earlier times. Rolling to the horizon, fields of ice shimmered in the sun, split by chasms and burst by rocky peaks that thrust high into a cloudless sky.

Mia showed him a small, windowless room at the side. "Your sauna."

"They offer an extensive bar list," Boris said from the kitchen section. "There's a dumbwaiter, do you want something?"

"A bottle of Wild Grouse."

"Are there things you'd like to do?" Mia asked.

"I'd like to get cleaned up, and have a nap. Get some clothes. The identity problem is the main thing."

"The problem is fixed. You were sentenced a long time ago, by a government which no longer exists. Rather than create a new identity for you, the Outfit thought it best to lift the original out of Deep Freeze, and delete your criminal files. You'll go on with your life, using your biometrics under your own name, Lucas Rivera."

Lucas sat down. "What if somebody spots me?"

"Age and sickness have altered your appearance. Also, exile to Mars is considered final, and escape believed to be impossible. It's unthinkable anyone will connect you with that long forgotten, minor case. And things have changed so much. Bringing in immigrants is not criminal in today's world; you deserve a medal for saving those people." She nodded emphatically. "Your birth certificate arrives tomorrow. Afterward you'll get your international driver's license, here in Helena."

"I'll be happy to get my own name back," Lucas said. "There's some loose ends with the Bart Peters identity though. Right now the kidnapped passenger remains a wanted man, and I need to deal with that situation, otherwise I'll always be looking over my shoulder. Maybe they can leave it active for a while longer? Have them create a search block, so no one will find the connection."

"I'll ask about it," Mia said.

"Whiskey's here," Boris said, holding up a bottle. Lucas joined him, and took some glasses from the cupboard.

"Do you want the hotel barber?" Mia asked, following. "The masseuse? The tailor?"

"Yes to all, but later." Although in good spirits, he was desperately tired, and unable to finish his drink. Mia and Boris left, promising to return in the morning.

Alone in his suite, Lucas's thoughts went first to security. Opening the safe in the bedroom closet, he set it to his fingerprints and put the money belt inside. On closing the safe, it locked with a satisfying click. The tool box with the Shiva gun went on the closet floor; he wanted easy access. Too tired to have a bath, he collapsed on the bed.

When he woke up, music and traffic sounds were drifting in. The bedside clock said 11:40. He went to the living room window and looked down on a street clogged with vehicles. A big casino across the road had come to life; crowds of revelers were going in and out. It looked like fun, but not tonight.

The realization of his good fortune came anew; his record was wiped clean. The nastiness of being a transported convict had festered in him for years, warping his life. Now he'd walk freely in any circles.

Startled by the ringing of the phone, he jerked around and saw its small screen flashing. It was on the counter that separated the kitchen unit from the living area. Could it be Mia?

He pressed the talk button and an old friend, Fred Chan, appeared on the screen. About the same age as Lucas, Fred had put on a lot of weight but his eyes were still clear, and sparkling with good humor. "It's good to see you," he said, his voice as strong as ever. "Do you like Helena?"

"It's good to see you too," Lucas said. "Yes, everything's fine here. Where are you?"

"Shanghai, otherwise I'd come. Sorry for the nonsense about the safe house. When Rosie got in touch it was short notice, and this is the best I dreamed up."

Lucas grinned. "I feel safe here. It's comfortable."

"You mentioned Mia Zadora in the old days--I prefer Boris, more muscle."

Lucas laughed loudly. "Some things never change."

Lucas met Fred Chan when the Rogers first sent him to Vancouver. The two were wary of each other at first. When Lucas got the submersible it made him more of an asset than a rival. Fred introduced him to his uncle, who ran an import/export business, and they did some work together. After Lucas was transported, his Marsport base opened a new territory for Fred, and their partnership became even more fruitful.

Knowing Fred Chan was involved gave Lucas added confidence. Also it shone a light on Mia and Boris's relationship. Fred had a family but swung both ways, and when he visited Marsport he asked for male escorts.

Finding the kitchen fridge empty, Lucas contacted room service and got a recorded message. "The Black Pearl offers an extensive wine and liquor list, and a wide range of mood-altering drugs. Dine with us at our downstairs restaurant, or order here and receive meals via the dumbwaiter. Are you desirous of companionship? Choose males or females from Helena's most exclusive service."

When a young man appeared on the screen, Lucas placed an order for a bowl of clam chowder, a hot cheese sandwich, half a cantaloupe, and a large cup of hot chocolate. Afterward he took the phone to the living room.

He relaxed in an arm chair, and asked to see the female escorts. One by one, women's images passed across his screen. Most were beautiful, and exuded charm and personality. Although half-expected, one was stunning. "Hello, I'm Mia Zadora," she said.

"Show me shots from different angles." Yes, it was definitely her. Her black hair was severely pulled back, revealing a spare face with high cheek bones, wide, sensuous lips, and large brown eyes that had seen too much but still laughed. The clinging, violet-hued gown did little to hide the curves that flowed like romantic music, and fired the imagination of millions. While undeniably a sex symbol, she also spoke to a deeply troubled generation for whom love and beauty existed mainly in fleeting moments.

"Hello," he said. "Are you available?"

"You're inquiring about a special personality, who is separate from the regular escort service," a man's voice said. "An evening with Mia Zadora offers the chance to meet one of our premiere film goddesses, exactly as she was in her prime. Please note the baseline rules from the start, as they are strictly enforced. Mia Zadora accepts no behavior that strikes her as abusive, threatening, or disrespectful in any way. Should she decide to end things there is no recourse. The minimum fee for a visit with her is one thousand units, and no refunds are ever given. If you are unsure about any of these conditions, press zero now to return to the standard escort list. If you wish to continue press one."

After a long pause, he heard her voice. "Yes, can I help you?"

"It's me, Lucas, at the hotel. My apologies for the short notice, but I'd like very much to see you."

"What a nice surprise. I'll come right over."

A light knock on the door came as he was finishing the piece of cantaloupe. When he let her in, she smiled into his eyes, and gave him a quick hug. "It's good to see you again so soon," she said.

Boris brought in two small suitcases, and nodded to Lucas with a grin. He made a perfunctory search of the rooms, and left.

"I'm looking for something unusual," Lucas explained. "Watching you on the big screen in the old days, everything was so romantic, and as long as the show lasted it was like I was there with you in a different world. I'd like to get that feeling back."

Mia seemed to understand, and assumed her video persona.

CHAPTER 13

There was no air service for Cedar River on Sunday so we took the bus back, arriving at the dorm that evening, around seven. My guardian had left word that he wanted to see me. This was welcome news; we hadn't met for a long time.

At school on Monday there was a strong sense of disconnect, as everything was so different from up the coast. It took the whole day to readjust.

When I went back to the dorm room, Wang was lying on his bed. Assuming he was in one of his meditative states, I took a seat at my desk and prepared to review my notes from the day's classes.

Wang sighed deeply. "The world's been preparing the way for years, and we'd be among the first to live out the dream." He sat up and looked at me directly. "They made us a fantastic offer. We'll be like Adam and Eve, living in a perfect nature."

This struck me as highly amusing. "You've been dreaming of space since childhood. Remember?"

He gave a short mocking laugh. "Everything's dead out in space. On Earth we'll have forests like cathedrals, streams we can drink out of, and the oceans alive with fish and sea creatures. There'll be packs of wolves and big old bears--they'll be our brothers. On sunny mornings the chickadees and the chipmunks will come by to have some fun."

"I'm planning a minimum of twenty years in space," I said. "Aren't you?"

"As members of the Cedar River co-op we'd have families and a community. You'll have a wonderful life with Lisa Hays."

"Lisa Hays?"

Wang locked his hands behind his head. "My experience with Serena allows me to see women very clearly. Lisa is warm, loyal, and true. And she needs a partner. Can you imagine climbing into bed with her every night?"

Suddenly our room was flooded with soft music. Astra was on the phone. Her scalp was covered by a black cap, and her face seemed pale. Her blue eyes looked out at me in a concerned way. "Are you all right?" she asked.

I pulled my chair over in front of the screen. "Thanks for getting in touch. I've tried to call."

"Serena told me about the awful dead people on Red Sky Island. I'm worried about you."

"Never worry about me. Let's get together and we can talk."

"I'm free Wednesday evening. Maybe we could go for a walk along the water."

This phone call with Astra was brief but very absorbing to me. When she rang off, I turned to Wang and found he was gone.

I lay back on my bed, remembering every detail of the conversation. Her room basically looked the same as ours, but small changes, such as the blue blanket patterned with little gray owls which covered her chair, and the flowers on her desk, created a feminine atmosphere which was most alluring.

Then Zack pounded on the door. My freshman charge, Caplin Hanson, was in serious trouble. I got up immediately, and as we ran down the stairs Zack said that government security men were on the campus.

The students standing outside the lounge knew nothing. Zack and I went outside, where a police airship was parked on the grass near the entrance. We joined a group gathered around our principal, Mr. Rossiter. "Has there been an accident?" I asked one of the freshmen.

He shook his head. "Expulsion."

Everyone stepped back, as a campus policeman and a T-man administrator in a suit came through the door. They were followed by four officers in brown NAN uniforms. Two of them held Cap's arms. He had on his school shorts and T-shirt, and despite a ruffled look, did not appear fazed by the situation. When he saw me, he grinned sardonically. I gazed back as reassuringly as possible.

The NAN men took Cap into the airship, and almost immediately it rose and soared away.

"It's a sad day for the academy," Mr. Rossiter said coldly. "Some people don't know when they're well off." The other administrator beckoned from a nearby van, and the principal left to join him.

When Zack and I went inside, everyone was talking at once. "It's insane," a senior said, waving his hands. "A Resister, right here at STA."

"He's been agitating ever since he came to the school," a freshman said. "They should have caught him sooner."

Even Chico, one of our triathlon stars, got caught up in the hysteria. "The Resisters want to wipe us out."

I couldn't stand it, and went up to my room. "Make it dark in here," I told Charles. Feeling deeply depressed, I threw myself on the bed. As Cap's mentor it was my duty to help him. Instead I'd dealt with his problems in a superficial way. Apart from chiding him from time to time, I'd never involved myself deeply with him. I'd viewed him as an amusing character, even joked about him with the others.

Why had he grinned at me like that when going out? To demonstrate his unconcern in the face of any personal disaster? Or had he felt a real bond between the two of us?

There was a knock at the door. Plenso, my own mentor from freshman year, came in with his partner Cooper. I was relieved to see them, although their serious demeanor was not encouraging. Plenso commandeered Wang's desk chair, while Cooper sat on my bed.

Plenso was short and although quite athletic, one of the few at the school who could be called plump. "This situation goes beyond any individual cadet," he explained in his patient way. "It involves the entire academy."

"Especially if he'd blown us up." Cooper was a tall, thin man with somber dark eyes. He had a knack for getting on my nerves.

"As his mentor, you were familiar with his activities?" Plenso asked.

I made a grimace. "I found it difficult to deal with Cap. From the beginning he was very independent-minded, and argumentative. I felt that instead of accepting me as his mentor, he wanted to reverse the roles."

My painful admission drew a laugh from Cooper. The man always did have a strange sense of humor.

"The school was concerned about Cap's behavior, and they noticed he was using his chemistry periods to research explosives," Plenso said. "When they searched his room, they found the Resistance paraphernalia."

The information was sickening. "I never suspected anything like that."

"Understandable," Cooper said. "Cap's not an ordinary person."

They stood up. "Thanks for your time," Plenso said, shaking my hand. "You'll have to testify before the honor board, don't be too concerned."

After they left I just stood and stared out the window. Plenso was a steady presence for me throughout my freshman year, and remained solid and imperturbable in this present crisis. He always cared about me, and I knew whatever happened he'd be a lifelong friend.

How different was my relationship with Cap. The development made me wonder if my nature was deficient in the empathetic and nurturing strengths, and slanted too much toward selfishness. Would a more aware and caring personality have done a better job?

The next day was difficult to get through, as my esteem stock had dropped considerably in the school. Plenso's example helped me. I'd seen him sail through embarrassments that would sink a lesser man. Always phlegmatic, he outlasted temporary scorn and triumphed in the end.

At least the meeting with my guardian was something to look forward to. Shortly after three that afternoon I walked over to the transit loop. In a few minutes the Downtowner arrived, a lime green bus with large, light brown wheels. It was almost empty, and I had a seat by the window.

On leaving the neatly trimmed shrubs and extensive lawns of the campus area, we entered the forest. The woods were splendid in the spring sunshine, with new leaves bursting into life. Deer looked up from a sun-lit clearing. The bus went faster here, and soon we came to the city.

In late afternoon there was an easy, nonchalant air to the downtown streets and sidewalks. The traffic was not heavy, and pedestrians drifted across the streets when they felt like it. I got off in front of an outdoor café, where people sipped wine and listened to street musicians. Nearby a man in whiteface was doing mime.

In a few blocks, I came to the street of carefully preserved brick buildings where my guardian had his office. Then a siren sounded, very close by. A tall, fleshy man ran toward me, his face red and dripping with sweat. He came close, but although looking around frantically, did not appear to notice me. After glancing behind, he turned down a narrow lane.

He was followed almost immediately by a uniformed dromy, which loped gracefully down the middle of the street. The dromy's central compartment was shrunken for pursuit, and its springy, metallic legs were in the extended position. Its triangular head was held close to the ground, the large nose snuffing. In a few strides it pursued the man into the lane, and there was only the doleful rising and falling of its siren.

"Sin and you're out," an old lady murmured as we passed.

"Amen," I replied. We loved and admired the police for keeping our society clean. They did a necessary job well, tracking down the deviants who threatened our earthly paradise. Robotic officers were incorruptible, and implacable.

On the other side of the street, a small sign marked the entrance to

GERALD & AVERY
ATTORNEYS AT LAW

I went up a narrow staircase to the office and learned that my guardian, Mr. Gerald, was in court. His partner Mr. Avery was to join him, and I could go along.

Mr. Avery was a tall, slim man who favored loose fitting suits and longish hair. His humorous approach to life was attractive to me, and it was exhilarating to leave the office in his company.

Out on the sidewalk I told him about the dromy I'd seen chasing a man through this area. "Only an idiot runs from the police," Mr. Avery said. "It's almost impossible to get away, for one thing. Secondly it's viewed as an admission of guilt."

As we approached the sidewalk cafes, a trio of colorfully dressed performers danced around us, playing their flutes and drums. Mr. Avery gave them some money, and the gesture was acknowledged with bows and bright smiles.

At the next corner we turned south, and entered the administrative area. "You don't want to end up there," Mr. Avery said, nodding to the building across the street from us. The Cook Correctional Institution occupied two full city blocks. The wall facing us was a windowless, non-reflective black, and had a solid, gloomy look. It seemed the perfect place to house the criminals.

In the next block, we went into the courthouse, a glittering building with a fountain at the entrance. Making our way through the crowded hallways, we came to courtroom eleven, a large room where a dozen or so spectators sat watching a man in the truth booth, a glowing cage where both hands were inserted into metallic gloves and scanners slowly circled the head. Mr. Avery and I went to the front, and joined my guardian, Mr. Gerald, at a small table.

A broad, impassive man, Mr. Gerald had blond hair that fell to the shoulders of his blue suit. His wide face seemed impervious to the events around him, but he smiled when he saw me, and reached over to pat my shoulder.

Mr. Gerald's client was charged with buying poached game for his meat shop. The man's chances did not look good, but the crime was serious and it was difficult to feel much sympathy. He left with a guard, and Mr. Gerald turned to me. "Can you join Avery and me for dinner?"

The three of us went to a little restaurant a couple of blocks away. The hostess, a middle aged woman in a flowing blue gown, led us through the crowded dining room to a small table covered with a white cloth and set with silverware and drinking glasses.

A young woman in a short white dress came with a pitcher of water. On her right wrist she wore the silver docility bracelet. Her subdued and withdrawn demeanor showed the chemicals were working well, blocking any rebellious or aggressive impulses that might interfere with her work.

"Many thanks, my dear," Mr. Avery said when she finished filling our glasses.

She smiled dreamily. "You're welcome," she said in a childlike voice, and moved to the next table.

"I've never seen convict labor here," Mr. Gerald said. "The custom's spreading."

"At least here they'll get training; they won't sit uselessly in their cells," Mr. Avery said.

We had bowls of wonton soup, and chicken with rice. Used to eating in the cafeteria at school, I kept glancing around me. Many of the diners seemed to know each other; there was much laughing and joking back and forth between the different tables. The clientele was older and very well-dressed.

Several people made a point of exchanging a word with Mr. Gerald or Mr. Avery, and there were surreptitious glances at my uniform. A silver-haired man sitting nearby leaned over to shake hands. "We're all dependent on your courage as you extend Earth's rule into space."

"We'll do our best," I said.

His eyes glistened. "Earth rule forever," he said softly. "Forever." He sank back in his seat, and spoke to the other three men with him. They nodded and one called a toast to me.

Mr. Gerald smiled. "In that uniform, you'll always draw attention."

"I only hope to live up to everyone's expectations."

My guardian raised his glass of wine. "To the Space Training Academy." Then we heard repressed laughter a couple of tables away.

A balding man in a business suit held the water server's waist, while his other hand was underneath her skirt. I felt ashamed. The man's action was obscene, as the silver bracelet blocked the girl's feelings, and she had no way of resisting.

Mr. Gerald nodded to the side of the room, where a man in a red dinner jacket approached with cat-like stealth. He reminded me strongly of an athlete I admired. But how could this be? Getting behind the offensive diner, the man gripped the back of his neck. "Sorry," the diner yelled, jerking his hand away from the girl. "It won't happen again."

The convict girl took her water pitcher and walked off. The man in the dinner jacket ground his knuckles into the diner's scalp to make him grovel, while the other guests laughed and applauded.

I was staring, hardly able to realize he was really here. Handy Andy was one of my heroes. He'd taken a national team to the Olympics and shown we could play with the world's best.

The athlete arrived at our table. "Well look who's here," he said in a bass voice. "My favorite lawyers! Haven't seen you in a long time."

"It's been too long," Mr. Gerald said. "The wonton was delicious."

"That recipe's a good one. It's been in my family for generations, ever since my forefather married an illegal immigrant."

Mr. Gerald introduced me, and Handy shook my hand. "It's a pleasure to meet a future space man."

"I'm honored to meet you," I said, watching my right hand totally disappear in his grip.

"There was one occasion when it looked like I might end up on Mars myself. Happily I was connected with the best lawyer in Vancouver."

Mr. Gerald adopted his customary business appearance, a kind of stony blankness. "Had you not deserved to get off, I could not have saved you."

Handy chuckled. "This restaurant would not exist up there. No, I'd likely be in some other line of work." He punched my shoulder lightly. "Nice to meet you." He winked to Mr. Avery and ambled off to greet another table.

"My life is now complete," I said. "Thanks for introducing me."

"We see a lot of people in our business," Mr. Gerald said. "Of course, these situations can go either way. In your benefactor's case, we were not successful."

I was shocked. "What do you mean by that?"

"When I was first appointed your guardian, and charged with the administration of the Lupine fund which looks after your expenses, the principal behind it all asked that we never reveal his identity," Mr. Gerald said. "The situation has changed; he should be arriving here fairly soon. This is why I introduced you to Handy Andy, so you'll understand that not all those transported to Mars are bad people. In your benefactor's case, he was found guilty of bringing in illegal immigrants. Back in the old days this was considered a serious crime, as people were terrified of being over-run by the displaced millions. Today it's a different world."

"Your benefactor saved migrants from certain death," Mr. Avery said. "They look on him as a hero."

This remark struck me as irrelevant and dangerous. "Transported convicts are never to return. It's against the law."

"Your benefactor is old and sick," Mr. Gerald said. "He wants to see you before he dies. I'd say you owe him that much."

"It seems I owe him everything," I mumbled.

CHAPTER 14

In the morning, Mia donned a formless pink housecoat and became quite matronly. She never lost the glamour though, and for Lucas, the time with her was special. It was almost like he'd achieved a boyhood dream and joined her on the big screen.

She oversaw Lucas's haircut, his bath and Swedish massage, and insisted on both a pedicure and a manicure, while a tailor measured him for some clothes. Then Boris arrived, and they ordered a huge brunch.

A courier brought Lucas's birth certificate shortly after noon. Enclosed in the envelope was a note: "The second link is active till you say otherwise. Good luck with the loose ends." Lucas recognized Fred Chan's style.

When they set out to get his driver's license, he was wearing a fashionable brown suit, new boots, and a shoulder-length copper-red wig. His eyes were their natural green. Nobody mentioned money, but he knew the meter was running and the bill would be quite high. Seeing a currency exchange place, he asked them to hold the cab while he went in.

The office was very quiet. There was the scent of pine, and the carpet was thick underfoot. A slender young man with oiled black hair stood up to greet him, and Lucas explained his business. The clerk pulled back a beaded curtain and took him inside to a plain room with a black assay box mounted on the wall.

Lucas took off his jacket and opened his shirt. "It'll be good to lighten the load," he said, stripping off the money belt. He took out one of the small bars and handed it to the clerk.

The man looked closely at the inscription. "It's Russian. Three ounces." He put the bar into a slot in the assay box. "Three ounces platinum bullion, ninety-nine point nine five percent pure." He nodded to a flashing light on the wall. "Ninety-two hundred and thirty-five units an ounce."

"I'll change five," Lucas said.

"Certainly. First I'll need identification."

Lucas had no intention of leaving his name. "For platinum bullion?" he scowled. "It's as good as cash."

"No need to be upset," the clerk said. "We understand Helena attracts busy people, and we've set up a structure for this type of situation. For a straight transaction, twenty percent."

Lucas gave him a cold stare. "How stupid do you think I am? The standard rate, two and a half percent."

"I'll go to seven, no lower."

"Four and a half," Lucas said firmly. As he removed the remaining bars from the belt, he felt rock-like things in the seams. He remained expressionless, and said nothing.

The clerk went down to six percent, about eight-three thousand units. After seeing his money counted out, Lucas thought better and gave the man an even ten thousand units.

He joined Mia and Boris in the cab with his money folder stuffed with bills and the rest, a hundred and twenty thousand units, secured in the belt. His finances in order, he was eager to move on and get the license.

It was a lifetime since Lucas had looked at a driver's manual, but the "Rules of the Road" were still second nature, and he got eighty-three percent on the written test. The driver simulator put him through a variety of city and highway situations; here he made a perfect score.

Despite the advent of self-operating vehicles, humans were required in many situations. The United World States license allowed Lucas to drive in any country on Earth. More important for his present needs, getting the new license was proof the Outfit had successfully laundered his identity, and brought it out of Deep Freeze.

Back at the hotel, Mia and Boris came up for a drink. Lucas was to take them to the casino that night, but first he needed to have a nap. He expressed his gratitude for all their help and mentioned one more task. "It's best for me to leave town by car. Someone might have a vehicle to sell, and prefer to avoid the local dealerships."

Mia met his gaze. "With several weeks I might feel confident, but fewer?"

"You never know in a casino town. Ask around and we'll see what happens. Tonight let's have some fun."

After they left, Lucas slit the money belt seams over the kitchen counter. Squeezing the rock-like lumps into his hand, he gasped to see their fire. Several were colored with rich depths of blue, orange, and yellow. Two were red. He'd handled diamonds before, but nothing as fine as these.

While the discovery was exciting, it meant serious trouble. This was not some ordinary rich man's money belt. He had to expect a whole new crew would be looking for him now. Sliding the glittering rocks back into the belt, he locked it in the safe.

Hit by sudden paranoia, he scanned the news on the video, but found no mention of McCool's death or of himself. The newscasts were full of the devastation caused by nation-wide Resistance assaults; there were interviews with survivors and with the loved ones of the casualties.

Then his old partner appeared on the screen, introduced as the congressman from the West Coast. He'd grown a wide moustache and a pointed beard, but there was no mistaking Kenny Summers.

Kenny seemed perfectly at home with the woman who was interviewing him. Always well-spoken, his voice was now more resonant, with deeper tones that signaled maturity and self-assurance. "Make no mistake," he said. "The North American Nation stands united against the terrorists, and behind us is the unlimited power of the United World States. The Resistance is only a minor nuisance. Our dromies have the scent, and soon the enemy will all be captured." Kenny turned and looked directly out from the screen. "Resisters, we are on your trail. Give up and turn yourselves in now, while there's still time."

Lucas shut his eyes and burrowed into the side of the couch. He knew full well that Kenny had been in close contact with McCool and was one with the Resistance even as he stood with the NAN and the United World States. Kenny was playing both sides, and if anything he was even more slippery, devious, double-dealing, and self-serving than he'd been in the old days.

Kenny was one of the few who knew of Lucas's return to Earth. Kenny wanted him dead, and was powerful and accomplished enough to make that happen. His old partner was a menace, the worst threat he faced. *"I have a job for you,"* Lucas told Tomi.

"I'm happy to hear that, your honor. How may I help?"

"Use your satellite feeds to watch the places Kenny Summers frequents. He'll have homes in the Seattle area and also in the NAN capital, Winnipeg. The object is to kill him. I need to know every possible way of getting to him."

Before going out that evening, Lucas locked the Shiva gun in the safe along with his diamonds. He left Tomi as a lookout, stationing the varlet on the top of an armchair he'd shoved in front of the windows. From here Tomi could look through the suite to the entrance door. *"I'll be across the street at the casino,"* Lucas said. *"If anyone comes in, let me know."*

"Certainly, my lord," Tomi replied. *"Be careful over there."*

Mia and Boris watched the octopod change to a blue-green, and match the fabric of the chair. "Lovely," Mia said, stroking its back. "You're awesome, Tomi."

"How can I get one?" Boris asked as they left.

"The maker has to know you," Lucas said. "It's a lifetime commitment, Tomi will never serve anyone else."

It was warm out and the night seemed alive, charged with energy. The street was choked with traffic, many of the vehicles with their tops down. Lines of pedestrians were streaming into the casino.

"Tomi can be an asset to a gambler," Lucas said, as they approached the entranceway.

"Not in this place," Boris said. "It's against the rules."

"That's good to know."

Inside the card room the main casino's noise and garish lights were absent; here a hushed atmosphere similar to a library's enabled attention and concentration.

Deeply focused on the game, Lucas became separated from ordinary life. It was a night when he possessed anticipation for the cards and the other players; the resulting winning streak was pleasing, even though he was well aware of the temporary nature of such phenomena.

Not everyone in the room was a card player. Along the wall, individuals sat at video terminals playing the latest war game, General Chess. Boris was one of them.

Mia wandered in and out. Her laugh would ring out, he'd catch her perfume, and she'd be there. She'd bring him a drink or an especially tasty hors d'oeuvre, massage his shoulders and his scalp . . . a kiss on the cheek, and off she'd go.

Evening brought out a different side in Mia. While perfectly respectable, her sleeveless, thigh-length black dress revealed quite incredible curves. At the beginning, the others players couldn't keep their eyes off her. Now late in the game, most seemed resigned, accepting Lucas's possession of her as another aspect of his dominance.

The youngest player had difficulty with the situation. A thick-browed, brooding man, he'd bet irrationally all night, and was the table's biggest loser. From the sardonic looks and loud sighs he cast Mia, Lucas had the impression of an acquaintanceship between the two of them.

Was there a touch of malice in her disregard for the man? Lucas didn't know, and cared less. When she appeared again, Lucas leaned his head back against her bosom and grinned up at her. "You brought me good luck tonight."

"I have good news for you, too."

There was another loud sigh from across the table; the younger man folded his arms and turned away. "I came here to play cards, not look at some dirty whore wave her tits around."

Mia cried out in horror, and sank down against Lucas. "Sorry," he murmured, putting his arm around her.

"Damn it," the other man said loudly, slamming his fist on the table.

Boris approached with long strides. He yanked the offender out of his chair and, despite his struggles, removed him from the card room.

Lucas gathered up his markers, and nodded to the other players. "Thanks for the game, gentlemen. I enjoyed it this evening."

There were grins and brief salutes. "Different luck next time," someone said.

Outside it was a cool clear night, and a pale half-moon shone down. Mia and Lucas wandered past a fountain that sprayed water through colored lights into a dark pool. "What's the news you have for me?" he asked.

"A couple from India need to go home because of a death in the family. They've been traveling North America in a live-in camper, and they want to sell it."

"A camper? That might work for me."

Shortly before ten in the morning, a robocab picked up Mia and Lucas at the Black Pearl, and took them into the mountains.

Mia now wore a cream and tan suit, with a wide brown belt. While demure and self-possessed, her manner left no doubt she was all his. Lucas felt exceedingly fortunate to be sitting beside her in the back seat, and the idea of her as an escort was ever more repugnant.

They drove through a wooded section where campers were parked in small lots, and pulled up beside a towering, powder blue vehicle with wraparound windows and gray wings painted on the sides.

An Indian couple came down. They introduced themselves as Geeta and Jas Brar, and met Lucas as Bart Peters. A tall, relaxed, silver-haired man, Jas spoke slowly in accented English. "You'll like the *Freed Spirit*," he said. "We haven't had a single problem with it."

Geeta had long black hair and large dark eyes. "It's terrible to end this marvelous trip half way," she said. "Really there's no choice; our daughter-in-law passed away and our son is devastated, he needs us there."

A robot was waiting as they stepped up into the camper. A little under five feet tall, it had spindly arms and legs and a face that always smiled. "Manny goes with the camper," Jas said. "He's handy--a lot stronger than he looks and a good cook, too."

Mia and Geeta stayed in the lounge, while Lucas went back with Jas. "As you can see we're well stocked," Jas said as Lucas checked the kitchen cupboards and the fridge. "My work was mostly underwater, and it made me conscious of that kind of thing."

"Your place does remind me of a boat," Lucas said. "Were you a submariner?"

"Professional diver." He nodded to a couple of bicycles mounted on the wall. "Electro-assist, they're an easy ride. They fold up, too." Opening a closet filled with gear, he pulled out a gray-green garment. "This is a Shark, the smartest suit I've ever had. There's never any problem with the air supply, and plus it enhances your strength. You'll swim fast and far with the Shark."

Uncertain, Lucas touched the fabric. "Do the gills use water from forward motion?"

"No worries, you get a backup air tank for areas that are short of oxygen. The suit knows what to do." He looked Lucas over. "You look about my height."

The transaction was more complicated than Lucas expected. At Jas Brar's insistence, they went to an insurance office, where they showed identification and filled out detailed forms. Afterward he knew the clock was running; eventually the government clerks would make the connection with the hijacked airship. The Resistance might track it as well.

Returning to the hotel in the robocab, Lucas was elated. "It has a superb sound system, too," he told Mia. "You chose well."

"It was pure luck meeting them at the casino."

"The luck began when you showed up." Knowing that in a few days she'd be with someone else, Lucas sat back and looked at her. "Mia, why do you do this?"

"I'm a slave girl, till the debt's paid off."

"So tell me."

"Mother's only son, my brother Simon, was an architect and builder who planned a large development in Siberia. He only discovered halfway through that the guarantees he'd been given were bogus, and he'd built on toxic land. It was a horrendous loss and Simon was held fully responsible."

Lucas nodded. "I imagine your brother was using borrowed money?"

Mia sighed deeply. "When the backer, Mr. Tadjic, came up with the solution, Simon and my mother felt there was no other way but to agree. My four sister-clones and I were raised in Armenia, on the Tadjic estate."

"Did Tadjic give you a decent upbringing?"

"His goal was to recoup my brother's losses, and to make a profit on his investment in us. We were educated with the help of tutors, and we studied hard and learned as best we could. The main focus was mother's old films; we internalized each scene until Mia Zadora was second nature. Mr. Tadjic enjoyed us separately and together throughout our teenage years, and, at the age of eighteen, he sent us off to work. By then one of us had died and one ran off. My two sisters and I worked hard, and in another year or so we should have the debt paid off."

"How does Boris fit in?"

"Oh, he's in just as deep as me. Maybe more so."

Lucas closed his eyes. "Sorry, but I feel very tired right now. Wake me up when we get to the hotel."

Upstairs they found Tomi still in lookout mode on the arm chair. *"Any problems?"* Lucas asked.

"Nothing so far, your honor."

"I'm in the mood for a drink," Lucas said to Mia. "Maybe something with those fancy feel-good drugs."

"A drink and a sauna? We've never tried it."

Lucas had hardly noticed the sauna room; now reclining on a wide bench he was grateful for the heat. Space music poured from hidden speakers, reminding him of an infinity of blazing stars. Across the room from him, Mia, shrieking, rolled in a trough of powder snow. Lucas sipped more of the blue cocktail, letting the fruity flavors explode on his tongue. It was making him sportive but his mind was clear.

She climbed out and joined him on the bench, giggling uncontrollably. "I've never had so much fun in my life. Won't you try it?"

"It's more than enough fun just watching you."

"Alert!" Tomi cried suddenly. "Someone's at the door. Alert!"

Lucas got up. "Excuse me a minute," he said to Mia. He went outside to the living room.

There was a loud pounding at the front door. Then silence. *"They're working on the lock," Tomi said. "Room service is disconnected."*

Lucas rushed to the bedroom, got the Shiva gun, and hurried back out.

Mia opened the sauna room door. "Is something wrong?"

"Nothing's wrong," he snapped. "Go back to your sauna." Then he heard the outside door open.

"Two men in body armor are inside the foyer," Tomi said. "They've got boop guns." Lucas dived behind the couch.

"I'll look in here," an intruder said.

"One's gone to the bedroom, and the other is coming this way. Here he is."

A man holding a boop gun loomed over the couch. Lucas fired immediately, destroying the gun hand then taking out the front of the man's head. The armor was no protection against the Shiva.

"Judging from their clothes, a couple is staying here," the first intruder said, entering the living room. "Joe, what's happened?" he cried.

As the man bent over his partner, Lucas rose up and made the kill.

There was a sharp rapping at the front door. *"The grandmother from the airship has arrived," Tomi said.*

Keeping the Shiva gun pointed at the floor, Lucas went out to meet the large, orange-haired woman. "Why are you here?"

She looked at him sternly. "So it's you. I've come for my diamonds, why else?"

"Maybe we can make a deal," Lucas said. "How did you find me?"

"Do you think Russian platinum is so common here? You can't hide a transaction like that. What have you done with my security men?"

Lucas hung his head. "Sorry," he said, nodding to the living room.

"Oh, no," she screamed, staring at the bodies. As she staggered, apparently about to faint, her right hand went to her hair.

"Watch for the dart!"

Glimpsing a flash of silver, Lucas threw himself to the side and fired, severing most of her neck. He was trembling when he stood up; she'd almost got him.

The room lights began flashing. "We've had a temporary disruption in service," a voice said. "Service is now restored."

"Never mind that. I want privacy."

"Yes, sir. Your absolute privacy is guaranteed."

"Lucas, is everything all right?" Mia called.

"It's just hotel maintenance. I'll be there in a minute." He was thinking rapidly. It was almost certain the grandmother had paid to have the power interrupted while she broke in. Nobody would come to investigate.

As with McCool, there was hardly any blood. Standing over the woman's remains, he kept the gun on until nothing was left but spots of grease. Then he did the same to the two men. Wary of leaving traces on the floor, he called out the room's robotic cleaner.

Inside the sauna room, Mia was reclining on the bench, streams of sweat trickling down her torso. It was a relief to know she'd remained unaware. Kneeling beside her, Lucas kissed a perfect dimple in the middle of her knee. "You've made me so happy these last few days; I'd like to give you a tip."

Mia giggled. "Your tip?"

Lucas howled with laughter. "You're wonderful!" He danced out to the bedroom, and retrieving the money belt, squeezed some rocks out into his hand. The diamonds were fiery, alive. Were they worth it? Hell, yes! The grandmother was in the game just like anyone else. He'd join her soon enough; in the meantime he'd do his best to stay on top.

Mia was still lying on the bench, and he placed an orange diamond in her navel. "What is this?" She propped herself up to look.

Lucas examined her critically. "Hmm, I'm not sure." He placed two large blue ones farther down, and balanced two clear ones on her breasts. "Something for Boris, too."

Mia turned very pale. "This is more than I can even dream. Our freedom! But how can you afford to do this?"

"With the camper, what else do I need? Besides, I have more diamonds."

She stroked his face. "Out in the wilderness with that camper, who knows what might happen? I want you to be careful, and guard your wealth."

"I'm always careful."

"When I leave, these stones will be securely hidden." Mia pulled back the side of her mouth and tapped a molar.

Her dark eyes glowed when she said this, and Lucas felt a renewed sense of her film persona blending with his life. His special time with Mia was drawing to an end; soon he'd leave the theater. "Make me an appointment," he smiled.

CHAPTER 15

By seven thirty Wednesday morning Wang's bed was still unoccupied; he'd been gone all night. It seemed he was getting more and more erratic.

He came in just as I was leaving. He offered no explanation for his absence, just sat down at his desk and checked for messages. I was angry, but was not going to be the first to mention Serena. Instead I said something about our classes. Wang replied that he'd resigned from the college, and Serena was going with him.

The news was not a complete surprise, as he'd clearly been struggling. Still it was a heavy blow. We'd roomed together since our first day at the academy, and he was my best friend. "I have to run," I said. "Will you be around for a while?"

He shrugged and gestured to his things. "Yes, there's packing to do."

When I returned to the dorm for lunch, a Mandy's Foods truck was parked out front. The red and gold insignia produced the usual knee jerk reaction; the Yu family's high-end food marts were synonymous with gourmet dining worldwide. Wang once planned to extend their company off-world; maybe he'd found something better in Cedar River.

Wang was at a table by the side wall of the cafeteria, and he waved me over. The two men with him bore a close resemblance. I was not surprised to learn the older, heavier one was Max Yu, the head of their company. The other, wearing a red and gold uniform, was one of Wang's siblings, Dong.

The table was loaded with food. When I sat down, Max filled my plate from the different platters, and Wang poured me a large glass of red wine.

The Yus raised their glasses and I joined them in a toast. "To good times," Max said. Everyone laughed loudly. Apparently for them there was no sense of failure in Wang's dropping out.

"Wang told us you were a good friend to him," Max said. "That means a lot to us." He reached over and shook my hand.

"You're like a brother," Dong said, putting an arm around me.

"Thanks," I said. "You make me proud."

"It's the way of the Yu," Max said. "And there's no arguing with it, we just have to accept."

"The way of the Yu," Wang intoned in a deep voice. "Like the river moves to the sea, it finds its way regardless of any obstacles. The water flows around the sides, or over the top, or even underneath. If necessary it'll steam up to the clouds and arrive in the form of rain. But it'll get there."

Max put a hand on Wang's shoulder. "The world's oceans were sick for so many years, everyone thought seafood was dead. When Wang went north to do community service, he saw a different picture. He realized that the oceans will make a comeback. And you know what that means? Seafood is going to take off like crazy. Being a Yu, he didn't have to ask anyone's advice, or get permission. No, he is Mandy's Foods. Just like I am, and Dong too. We're of the same mind, and we think the same way."

Wang looked into my eyes. "The invitation's still open, if you decide to go with us. Ocean studies is an exciting field, and what we've learned at STA is fully applicable. We'll work closely with the T-men up there, and become fully transformed the same as we would here."

I smiled ruefully to the others. "I'm going to miss this man."

Then Zack came over. "What's this I hear about Wang leaving?" He pulled up a chair, and one by one the others in the cafeteria came over to say goodbye.

When I went upstairs Wang's things were gone, except for a painting over his bed. The Visitors showed people emerging from a landing craft on Mars's highest mountain, Olympus Mons. The work was by Peter Borodov, one of the first men to go there.

Wang left a note on my desk. "You are turning into a real spaceman, and this painting fits you. My future will be different, as Serena wants children. Life will be busy but should be fun, too. Let's keep in touch."

The place seemed barren without him, and I sat for a while and let the change sink in. For the first time in my life I'd have my own room, and, while it seemed lonely, there'd be increased freedom. Losing him hurt deeply, though.

Astra and her mother were shopping that day, and afterward she was to meet me at the Rosehip, a coffee shop in the old Kitsilano neighborhood on the city's west side.

I got a table in the outside section and sat looking across Cornwall Avenue and the small park to the sailboats out on English Bay. The place was not busy, and the server did not object to my waiting with a glass of water.

Astra arrived about ten minutes later. Casually dressed in shorts and a light sweat shirt, with only a small mauve logo to signify Old Lace, she had the relaxed look of a town girl. Straight blonde hair that fell loose around her shoulders completed the picture; while stunning, she clearly belonged here.

We ordered the Hippo, an amazing dessert of ice cream, raspberries, chocolate and whipped cream that was about as different from STA cafeteria food as thick slices of raw beef.

"Mother says hello," Astra said. "'A serious young man,' she says about you. Even if you were only ten."

"Ouch, I'm probably even worse now." I mentioned my latest failure as Cap's mentor, and she hadn't heard about it. That helped me put it into perspective; I was even able to laugh.

Our Hippos arrived, and Astra rolled her eyes. "I'll be paying for this in the gym."

"It doesn't have to be the gym," I said. "The ball's coming up."

Astra bit her lip. "I'm glad you asked me, and it's good to be with you now. You're one of my favorites in the whole school."

"Who are you going with?"

She looked away. "He's a senior--you know, George Damon?"

"Him!"

"Don't look so surprised," she laughed. "I've known George forever, it seems--not only here, but our families know each other. And he's on the executive, he needs a date."

"He may need a date, but it doesn't have to be you."

She looked at me searchingly. "Are you aware of the power the Damon family holds?"

"I heard they've got money."

Astra laughed. "That's the understatement of the year. They've got huge money and power--made a killing in the asteroid belt and never looked back. They're one of the founders of Luna Engineering."

"Interesting," I responded.

"Most people know my father's a vice president in Interplanetary Trading," she went on. "There's so much politics involved, in everything we do." She touched my arm again, and left her hand there slightly longer. "You don't seem very impressed by this."

"Maybe I'm not a very political person." I finished my Hippo, and waited till she was done with hers. "Let's get out of here."

It was warm out, and the air was still. We went down toward the water, and crossed over Cornwall Avenue to the little park of lawn and trees. People were sitting on blankets. Others danced to music from a harmonica and a set of drums. Farther down, a family gathered around a portable stove.

Astra linked her arm in mine, and swayed against me. With a laugh I seized her hand, and held it high. I was in the mood to do anything, and when she grinned it was like we were kids again, and she was daring me to go ahead.

We headed west along the seawall. At the base of the old Canadian missile station we went down the steps to the rocky beach, and strolled along the shore till we came to a patch of sand in between some huge boulders. Here we sat against a big log, the small waves coming in several meters from our feet.

It meant a lot to be alone with her in this type of situation; it hadn't happened since childhood, and the slightest touch and nuance of speech had overtones. I wanted to kiss her, but there was a gap to cross, even though she was resting partly on me.

As if unaware of my feelings, Astra continued our conversation. "Sometimes I wonder how it'll be when we're fully transformed," she said. "If people only communicate on the physical level they can't be very close. But if full mental communication comes, it might cause withdrawal in other ways."

"I've always felt close to you," I said, taking her hand.

"In what sense?"

I leaned over and did it. I missed at first--got her cheek--but she turned slightly and we came together. The touch of her lips was amazingly sweet and opened new worlds of meaning and delight. Eventually Astra pulled back. "I should get back, there's a lot of work to do." Then she threw herself on me, and we were together for a long time.

Leaving the beach, our hands found each other as if by instinct. Sometimes our arms swung in the air; then they hung straight down, allowing our sides to touch as we walked along. We laughed often and said the most serious things.

The bus was not crowded, and we got a seat to ourselves at the back. I put my arm around her and we were as free and natural as a couple of townies.

The tensions of ordinary life came back once we entered the campus. Our hands and arms no longer intertwined; we walked separately and made small talk about our classes. When we neared the Old Lace dormitory, Astra pulled me into a hidden niche between some bushes. Here she threw her arms around me and pressed her lips to mine. Then she hurried off.

Going back to the dorm, ordinary walking was too restrictive for me. Breaking into a run, I left the walkway for the grass, and after a few long strides, made a tremendous leap. The realization came that I loved Astra, and always had. There was nobody around to tell, so I shouted it to the winds.

But she was going to the ball with George Damon. She'd be in his arms, dancing to the music. And why? Money and power. The injustice of this was unbearable. The thought of Astra together with that reptile fired me, and brought me close to deadly rage.

It was me she'd kissed, though. Remembering how she'd held me and the sweetness of her voice, I knew she meant it. A surge of exultation had me skipping over the grass and speaking with the wind once more.

When I arrived at the dorm, Charles told me I'd have to appear before the honor board. The curt announcement was humiliating; I was not one to get into trouble.

At ten that evening a freshman in dress uniform brought me into a room on the top floor of the Polaris, where five seniors sat behind an oval conference table. Mr. Rossiter sat apart at the end. I stopped at the red line, a few feet away from the table. "I'm reporting as requested."

Plenso was in the middle, wearing the president's medallion. His head was thrust slightly forward, and his rotund form looked solid and immovable. "Now Dom, you must have some idea as to why we've called you here?" he asked, in his quiet, patient way.

I looked at him warily. "I expect it has to do with Cap's expulsion."

"The Caplin Hanson affair is one of the most significant in our academy's history," Plenso said. "At present Cap is still being questioned by NAN security. It's an open question as to how far he planned to go in the attempt to subvert our goals. He may have plotted a terrorist attack against us, using explosives."

"I feel considerable remorse over what's happened," I said.

Cooper leaned toward me. "As his mentor, you know him better than anyone. Did you see nothing that alarmed you?"

"It was difficult to get close to him," I said. "He was brusque and evaded my attempts at friendship. I failed to be alarmed by the situation. I saw him as a difficult personality, rather than a menace or a threat."

"I think we all did," Mr. Rossiter said. "In my opinion, the main weakness shown is in the screening process. He should not have been admitted in the first place."

"That doesn't excuse the middie's behavior," George Damon said from the other side of the table. "I've looked into this, and Caplin was notorious for extremist comments. It was up to the mentor to straighten the boy out."

"Did you make any effort to correct his ideas or his behavior?" Cooper asked me.

"Yes, I did."

"What were some of the ideas you tried to change?"

"Cap took the side of the old NAF, and continually advocated their values and beliefs."

"What's your position on these matters?" Plenso asked.

"I'm a believer in one world government, and in the re-creation of an earthly paradise through sound ecological principles, acting in accordance with the Great One. To me the NAF's greed and unrestrained growth was unsustainable, and eventually became disastrous."

"Did Cap ever indicate to you that he might be involved politically outside the campus?" Mr. Rossiter asked. "Specifically, did he ever mention groups that might support terrorism?"

"Of course not."

Plenso nodded. "That should wrap it up," he said. "Unless someone . . . "

"I see a pattern forming," George Damon said. Taller than the others, he sat well back in his chair and seemed relaxed. His long fingers were intertwined in front of him, and his thin lips held a cold smile. "Recently we've lost two candidates from the program. First the middie, Wang Yu, and now this freshman. What do the two losses have in common? He's standing before us!"

"Stick to the agenda at hand," Mr. Rossiter said strongly. "Now gentlemen, there's no need to cast blame internally over this matter. It's impossible to reason with some people, their minds are made up and their course of action set. Unfortunately Caplin was this type."

"Cap was stubborn," Plenso said. "I wouldn't be surprised if Mars is in his future--only not wearing a pro suit."

"It won't be the first time," the principal said. "You'll look down from your observation satellite and suddenly think, 'Don't I know that fellow?'"

The members shared a chuckle.

"We'll excuse you now, Dom," Plenso said. "Thanks for coming in."

"Wait a minute," George said. "I was afraid of this--Plenso is Dominic's mentor, and favoritism is creeping in. While I'm on this board there'll be no whitewash."

"There's no whitewash," Plenso said patiently. The others nodded.

"I agree," Mr. Rossiter said. "It's been open and fair."

George snorted. "We've got a real problem here. In failing to notice his freshman charge is a terrorist, Dominic shows very poor judgment of character. He should have tried much harder to straighten the boy out. Dominic may even be a terrorist sympathizer himself, as some of these scholarship types lean that way. Whichever way you look at it, the middie shows a fatal flaw for an administration candidate." He spread his hands, and nodded. "Yes, Dominic is flawed. That's my opinion and I want it on the record."

Mr. Rossiter shook his head. "This reflects more on you than on Dom."

"Sorry about this," Plenso said to me. "You can leave now."

They were still arguing when I walked out.

CHAPTER 16

The appointment with Mia's dentist cost Lucas hours of agony. He now had new upper and lower plates, with a full complement of molars. A large bony lump protruded from his palate, and two more jutted upward from the mandible close to the tongue. Yet another growth was just inside his lower lip. It was uncomfortable, but the dentist assured him it all looked natural, and he'd get used to it.

A couple of diamonds were left over, and Lucas offered them as payment for his and Mia's treatments. The stones were gratefully received.

Afterward he went to a sporting goods place and bought a pup tent, sleeping bag, camp stove, and survival rations, along with some prospecting gear. He was slipping back into the Bart Peters persona.

Lucas left Helena at dusk, heading west with winds gusting against the camper. Going through McDonald's Pass, he had a moon-lit overview of the mountainous terrain at the continental divide. Ahead, the road went downhill in wide curves. Their vehicle cruised along smoothly with Bob, the robot driver, in full control.

Manny cooked a large meal of cauliflower, curried corn and stuffed eggplants and brought it to the table in the lounge, where Lucas sat listening to music with the octopod at his side. "What's with these eggplants?" Lucas asked when he tried the food.

"I included bulgur, onions, olive, lemon and mashed nuts," Manny said.

"Well, it's delicious. Very good cooking."

"Your compliment is wasted on that thing," Tomi said. *"It's a simple machine, incapable of response."*

"Are you jealous? I'd train you to cook too, if you had more strength."

A loud beep sounded. The screen lit up on the dashboard, and showed an older man, with long white hair. "Hello the *Freed Spirit*," he said. "Bart Peters, are you there?"

Lucas was floored. "Yes, who's this?"

"I'm Paul Carson. Jas Brar mentioned you took his camper. I'm right behind you."

"Pleased to meet you," Lucas mumbled.

"We're members of the Association of Retired People, the Oldster Roadsters branch," Paul said. "As much as we enjoy the open road, it's always good to have a friend when we stop. Do you play cards? Missoula's just ahead, you know."

"It's not a pleasure trip for me; I've got things to do."

"Jas told me you're a prospector. It sounds fascinating."

Lucas was breathing hard when he got rid of Paul Carson. The ease with which the grandmother tracked him down for the diamonds was unnerving enough, now this.

"Your enemies cast a wide net, and they watch for the slightest anomaly," Tomi said. *"Paul Carson might report your deviant behavior."*

"I know that."

Lucas always felt it was foolhardy to go directly to Vancouver. If the Resisters followed it would ruin everything. He needed to stop the pursuit, and the best way to do that was kill off Bart Peters.

His mind awhirl, he went to the back of the camper where Jas Brar kept his gear. He dragged out air tanks, torches, tools, and a couple of underwater caches with homing signals. He tried on the Shark suit. The beginnings of a desperate plan came to him.

Returning to the lounge, Lucas had Bob call up a detailed map of the area. While several sites looked feasible, he decided on Dogwood Lake, in eastern British Columbia. It was a substantial body of water, in a mountainous area that was only sparsely populated. He found a small resort with an associated marina, and placed a reservation.

The beep sounded again. "Hello, *Freed Spirit.*"

Paul Carson's familiar, folksy tone infuriated Lucas. "I don't have time for this," he hissed to Bob. "Make some excuse--tell him I'm asleep."

As he left he heard Paul's reply. "That's why we have the Oldster Roadsters. Seniors are sleeping their time away when they could be living life to the fullest."

Nauseated, Lucas stomped off to work on the equipment. Underwater work was similar to space, in that survival depended on gear that always performed. He soon realized Jas Brar was meticulous; even so he double-checked everything. Once satisfied, he began to organize the underwater caches. He placed a folded bicycle in the first one, along with toilet articles, clothes, and a packaged meal. Into the second cache went the tent, sleeping bag, stove, and supplies for a couple of weeks.

He lay down for a few hours, and on awakening it was daylight. They'd arrived at their resort, the Kootenay Peace, on the eastern side of Dogwood Lake. The *Freed Spirit* was in a berth between some pine trees, with several other campers nearby.

Lucas stepped outside shortly after eight that morning and breathed deep of the mountain air. It was already warm. The main lodge was farther up the hillside, amid a wide expanse of lawn. He'd go and pay the rental fee after he found a decent boat.

Strolling down the driveway, he crossed a narrow road that ran along the bottom of the hillside. A picnic area overlooked the water. At this point the lake was a couple of miles wide, and the mountains on the western side fell steeply to a brief shoreline. He was close to the southern end; from here it ran north over sixty miles.

Going down a ramp to the marina, he paused and looked over the boats. An open motor boat would not do. While the ski boats looked interesting, he was drawn to an older, black-hulled cabin cruiser, the *Lucky Star,* which looked about twenty-five feet.

The marina office was just opening. Lucas told the attendant he was a prospector, and wanted a boat for a couple of weeks to look at some underwater sites. The man assured him that the *Lucky Star* would fit his needs.

The boat was clean, and had a comfortable feel. The automatic pilot, Trish, sounded cool and feminine. *"Can you control it?" Lucas asked Tomi.*

"The EXMIN series was standard on this size boat for over twenty years. It's a simple model, and should present no difficulties."

When they went to fuel up with hydrogen, Lucas learned that the storage tanks were underneath the afterdeck. The line ran to a fuel cell stack located amidships, next to the electric motor and the power pack. "I'm topping everything up," the attendant said. "If you run low, Trish will let you know."

Lucas borrowed the marina's hovercart, and with Manny's help brought clothes, gear, and food from the camper down to the boat. When the job was finished he had a last look around. He'd grown attached to the traveling home, and signs of his presence remained with clothes and toilet articles. He left Bart Peters's bead belt hanging in the closet. Lucas never met Bart's ex-wife, but always liked her for making that belt.

Taking his tool box with the Shiva gun and extra cartridges, he headed for the front door. "I'll be back in a couple of weeks," he told the robots. "If there's any trouble, contact the main lodge."

"Yes, we've already settled this with the resort," Bob said. "Have a good trip."

As the *Lucky Star* left the protected marina, Lucas felt a surge of exhilaration. Mountains all around, a blue sky, and setting out to explore a wondrous lake--it was to give thanks for.

He went north, scanning the eastern shore for a good spot to drop the first cache, which contained his getaway supplies. Lucas did not want to go too far, as it was already a long bicycle ride to the nearest town. After arriving at a small bay that looked deserted, he told Trish to keep the boat in place.

He got into the Shark suit. *"Will it be here when I come out?" he asked Tomi.*

"Certainly, your honor. Trish accepts me as its original manufacturer. I'm the god of the boat."

"We should be all right then." Lucas hung a rope ladder over the side, and took the cache into the water. Diving down with it, he swam along the bottom and anchored it against a rock about thirty feet deep. The beacon was set very low, at a frequency only Tomi would monitor.

Next, they crossed to the far side of the lake. Here the mountainside rose sharply from the shore, and there were no signs of human habitation. Lucas put out a couple of lines with buck tail flies, one shallow, one deep, and trolled slowly up the lake, looking at the shoreline. He was shocked to get a strike almost immediately: a two-pound rainbow that fought valiantly before he brought it on board. It was enough for Lucas's dinner; he removed the hooks while leaving the rods out for appearance.

A south wind had come up, and seemed to be getting stronger. Feeling it funnel through the narrow valley, Lucas could well believe the cautionary stories the marina attendant had told him about local storms.

Up ahead was an area where a landslide had hit. Much of the mountainside above was sheer cliff, and large boulders were strewn around the shore. A small creek came out here, too. When he got closer, he saw a heavy growth of trees and brush around the creek bed, and decided it would fit his purpose. He could hide out here for weeks, and no one would notice.

Substantial waves were slapping around the transom, but the *Lucky Star* rode well in the water. The sounder screen showed a rugged bottom, with what looked like deep spaces between the rocks. When Lucas said he was going down, Trish warned him that the storm was picking up. "Steer into the wind if you have to," he said, dragging out the second cache. "I won't stay long."

Down below he found a jumbled heap of rocks, with larger chunks that towered over ten feet high. Swimming through a narrow chasm, he came to a protected space between the boulders. Above was a ceiling formed by a granite slab which had fallen onto the other rocks. It was like being inside an ancient cathedral, the stone walls protecting a profound peace. While positioning the cache, he noticed a huge lake trout staring at him. "I'll visit you later." Doubting the beacon's effectiveness from here, he removed it from the cache and stuck it on top of the slab.

When he returned to the surface, it was very wavy. The boat was holding fairly well in place, and he swam over and grasped the rope ladder. Wind shrieked as he pulled himself on board; the Lucky Star bucked wildly. "I recommend we seek shelter from this storm," Trish said when he entered the cabin.

Having the Shark suit made Lucas indifferent to the weather. "We're going north. If there's a place along the way that has a bar you can stop there, I feel like having a drink."

Once they were under way, running before the wind, Trish sang an old sea shanty. Encouraged by Lucas's enthusiastic reaction, the pilot told a joke, of which it had a vast repertoire, including the bawdy variety. Only half listening to Trish, Lucas took the opportunity to service the Shiva gun.

The lake was deep here and he put the used canisters and power pack over the side. Afterward he brought out the money belt. It was crazy to keep anything linked to the grandmother. He used the Shiva gun to burn the belt and the old tool box.

In a couple of hours, they went down an inlet on the eastern side and arrived at Tracey Bay. The dock was crowded; they tied up alongside another boat.

It was past dinner time, and Lucas was starving. He boiled some vegetables and simmered his trout on the galley's little stove, while brewing a pot of coffee. He finished off with a piece of apple pie, and drank a cup of coffee. He poured the remainder into a thermos.

Settling back in his chair, he turned off the coffee maker and removed its plug from the socket. He opened a knife and stripped a section of the cord, exposing the wire.

"What are you doing?" Trish asked.

"Tell it I'm making some repairs," Lucas said to Tomi.

"I've overridden the pilot's objection. Now it thinks you're one of my technicians."

Lucas frayed the wire with his knife, plugged in the cord and got up. "I'll be back soon," he told the pilot. "Don't leave."

Strolling through the little town, he found three bars. The last one suited him best; it had only two customers, and no one seemed to mind him drinking quietly while he watched the video. This was pure Bart Peters. Alcohol was the thing; the presence of others was comforting at some level, but their conversation only a drone. By the end of the evening he'd nodded off. The bartender shook his shoulder. "Hey, wake up. Come on, it's closing time."

Lucas started. "Didn't realize it was that late." Getting up from the bar stool, he fell flat on his face.

Grabbing Lucas's upper arm, the man helped him up. "Let's go, on your feet. Keep walking, now, the door's straight ahead."

"I'm all right, just tired from being out on the water all day." After he got through the door, Lucas held out a hundred unit note. "Sorry for the trouble."

The bartender seized it, and barked a laugh. "No worries, come back any time." He gestured to the sky, which was ablaze with stars. "It's a lovely night isn't it?"

"Yes, lovely," Lucas said, walking away. *"Am I drunk?"* he asked Tomi.

"No, but the bartender will remember you drinking heavily."

"Good, it'll work out well."

Once on board the Lucky Star, they left immediately and headed for the main lake. Lucas stocked the Shark suit's backpack with tubes of high energy food and drink. The Shiva gun would fit in the pack too. He put a knife and a torch in sheaths at his waist.

The wind had died down, and Dogwood Lake was still. No other vessels were in sight. Trish opened the floor in the cabin, and Lucas looked down at the engine. "Stop the motor," he said. When everything was turned off, he set the Shiva gun to its narrowest focus and aimed it at the fuel line in front of the cell stack. There was a loud hissing sound, which soon quieted.

Donning the Shark suit, Lucas told Trish to take the boat north and wait for him at Johnson Bluff.

"The fuel cell system is not operating because of a leak," Trish said. "I'll use the auxiliary power pack to get to Johnson Bluff."

"Override that," Lucas told Tomi. *"Tell it to restart the fuel cell system and keep the floor open and the door and windows closed in the cabin."*

Going into the water, he stayed on the surface, lying on his back. There was no wind at all now, and an easy movement of his flippers carried him south at a good pace. Tomi stayed in touch with Trish the whole time, and when the pilot reported a heavy buildup of hydrogen in the cabin, Tomi instructed it to turn on the coffee maker.

There was a flash, and an explosion. Lucas went faster, using the full power of the suit. He wanted to reach the hiding place well before daybreak.

CHAPTER 17

STA students are required to have a hands-on acquaintance with the production of food, and Monday afternoon I was scheduled to supervise the freshmen on garden duty. Usually there were four freshmen on a crew, but since Cap was gone we only had three.

Garden duty was a chance to relax; everyone enjoyed it. The freshmen and I met in the lounge after lunch, and we headed over in the van. Percy and Samson were in the back. Gangly and long-limbed, with pale blue eyes and receding chins, they were cloned twins, sons of a well-known economist. Percy had a black nose stud, which was the only way to tell them apart.

Smokey, Wang's former charge, rode up front with me. A tall, dark, slender man with quick intelligence and an easy going, gregarious nature, Smokey was a natural athlete, his movements so fluid he drifted through our games with effortless grace. It was a big advantage to have him, and now that Wang was gone, I hoped to be Smokey's new mentor.

Soon the greenhouse loomed up before us. Larger than two football fields, its surface glittered with receptors. Years ago the STA engineers built it space style as a class project; it was made of insulating brick, nonconductive to heat.

Going down a ramp, we entered the loading area and left the van at the end of the dock. We walked over to the entrance, waving to a man who'd brought in a tanker truck of urine. "Eau de cadet," Smokey said as we went up the stairs. Everyone chuckled; we all contributed to the supply of perfect fertilizer. Urine is loaded with the three main plant foods, potassium, phosphorus, and nitrates. It's invaluable off-world.

Inside the main office, a clerk confirmed our produce requisition and issued a couple of wagons. We headed out to work.

Most of us were awed by the STA greenhouse. There's an innate grandeur in the spaciousness of the place, with its high ceilings and soft light that radiates throughout. It's always warm inside, and the breeze is heavy with the odors given off by the plants.

Plants vary in their need for temperature, moisture, and nutrition, and we passed through an array of different worlds as we started down the corridor with our wagons. Between the hanging walls on one side were pumpkins, squash, and melons; on the other side, bananas, date palms, figs, pomegranates, and persimmons.

A couple of STA botanists were down on their hands and knees in a cabbage patch, but seeing them deep in concentration, we didn't stop to chat. Their expertise is highly valued off-world; plants need nurturing to survive out there.

After the cabbage patch was an intersection with another corridor. Here I split up the team, sending the twins for a load of potatoes and carrots while Smokey and I went to pick some raspberries, peas, and beans.

The raspberry bushes were loaded, and Smokey and I ate plenty. While I avoided prying into the freshmen's backgrounds, it was a relief to hear he was not a clone. "I'll be the first of my family to go into space," he said. "And, the first to become a T-man." As we talked, his hands stripped off the red berries and plopped them into the container strapped around his neck. He worked like he played sports, relaxed and efficient. When we moved on to the legumes, I learned he'd grown up in a town in northern Manitoba where his father was a dentist, his mother a teacher. He'd done well enough in school to earn a scholarship.

"If a man really wants space, nothing gets in the way," I said. "It depends on who you are." Smokey's eyes met mine, and there was a sense of recognition.

The twins were already out in the hallway with a big load of potatoes and carrots, and we got the produce to the kitchen ahead of schedule. This was a solid achievement for our pared-down unit. We'd performed in a smooth, problem-free manner; best of all, there was no bickering.

My confidence renewed, I took the freshmen out for a run. We cut through the forest toward town, and came out in a neighborhood park that bordered a shopping center. The men ran easily, and reminded me of a pack of healthy young wolves, ready for anything. It was in my mind to treat them to a drink or an ice cream.

A breeze came up, and we ran through the pink snow from a line of ornamental cherry trees. Some older people were walking ahead of us, and I set up the chant. "Training for space," I called.

"Training for space," the freshmen yelled. "STA! STA!"

The older group moved to the side to let us run by. Several of them applauded, and one lady made a V sign with her fingers.

All of a sudden rain came, beating down with fat drops. We dashed into a roofed picnic spot and stood looking out at the downpour.

Over at the shopping center, most of the shoppers had gone inside the low-lying buildings. Two men carrying sports bags stayed outside. Swarthy and vigorous looking, with closely trimmed dark hair, they looked to be in their late twenties or early thirties. Although their light shirts and slacks were getting soaked, the men did not seem to notice the weather. They just stood there chatting. The taller one laughed often, showing white teeth.

The two strolled over to the side wall of the small bank. The taller one took a gray, fat-bodied gun from his bag and pointed the weapon at the wall of the bank. Darkness came from the gun, and part of the wall disappeared. The men went through the hole.

Reporting the robbery on my emergency phone, I told the operator it was a Shiva gun. "Stand by," she said tonelessly. "Help is on the way." In the distance a siren sounded.

Percy pointed to a sleek black airship slowly descending into the courtyard beside the bank. "That ship must be for their getaway."

The rain was falling even harder, big drops that spattered when they hit. The police were nowhere in sight. "We need to intervene," I said, gazing around at my crew.

"Not against that ray gun," Samson said.

"They might not notice us," Percy said, gesturing to the rain. "We could make a sneak attack."

"Let's see how things look when the robbers leave," I said.

The cloudburst got even stronger; the rainfall was so thick that we could barely see the bandits when they came out through the hole. Laughing and shouting protests about the downpour, we pretended to make a run for the shopping center.

The robbers ignored us and ran for the airship, holding their sports bags close. The taller one still wielded his Shiva gun. Samson and I jumped the gunman from behind, while Smokey and Percy took the other one.

My main concern was the gun; I snatched it before the bandit could react. He came at me strongly, punching and swinging the sports bag, but failed to land a blow. When he turned to run, Samson tackled him, and we soon had him on the ground. Throughout the struggle he kept a tight grip on his sports bag.

Glancing over at Smokey and Percy, I saw their robber was also subdued, and apparently unconscious. Then blackness covered Smokey's leg, and he cried out in an awful way. He never stopped screaming, and he was writhing in pain. Percy tried to embrace him while still sitting on the robber, the other sports bag partly open on his lap.

On the entrance ramp of the airship, a relaxed looking man with a dark moustache was looking for another shot. I sighted at him and held down the trigger. Blackness spread over the airship entrance, and the robber disappeared. The ship glowed for an instant, and then exploded. Flames burst forth amidst dense smoke.

"You've killed Jorge," our bandit shouted, pulling himself upright. I smashed him over the head with the gun, and he went flat. Samson crouched above him, ready to strike. When the robber lay still, Samson sat back, and smoothed his limp blond hair away from his eyes.

The rain stopped as suddenly as it came. Emergency vehicles and police dromies arrived with blaring sirens. Four policemen with drawn guns surrounded Samson and me, which was confusing. When they ordered me to drop the Shiva gun, I understood and was happy to comply.

The bandit we'd captured was already known to the police, and they immediately took him into custody. Our STA uniforms were not a sure pass, because the possibility of disguise had to be ruled out. Once the officers ascertained that I'd called and reported the robbery initially, they told us not to leave, and moved on.

No one else approached us, and I went over to where people in white uniforms were lifting Smokey onto a stretcher. He was badly hurt, his right leg gone halfway down the thigh. Anguished for his loss, I touched his cheek but he didn't recognize me. They put him in an ambulance and left immediately, with the siren blaring.

An airship marked MEDIA ONE hovered overhead, a camera protruding from its belly. When it landed, a middle aged man wearing a NEWS cap emerged, and started talking to a couple of policemen. A woman in a purple suit went to where the twins were sitting on a curb.

I wandered back to where two fire trucks were parked alongside the airship. Firemen in hazard gear were flooding the wreckage with water hoses. Part of the ship's sheathing was burnt away, exposing the passenger compartment where seats were jumbled about. More firemen were inside the compartment, examining burnt fabric that looked like clothing.

The reporter in the purple suit stood beside me. "How do you feel at this moment?"

She made me think. "Saddened, mainly," I said.

"The man who brought down the Mendez airship is mainly sad. What about before you fired? Did you know the power of the Shiva gun?" She gestured to the wreckage.

A heavy man in a loose brown suit came up and flashed a badge. "You'll have to come down to the station to answer some questions." He helped me into the back of a large police van, where I sat on a bench across from the twins. An officer tossed in some towels, and we got dried off and wrapped ourselves in gray blankets. I closed my eyes, and we rode in silence. I kept seeing Jorge, standing at the entrance of the airship. His unconcern in the face of death was beautiful to me.

We stopped in a dimly-lit underground parking area. Keeping our blankets, we followed the man in the brown suit into an elevator. We went up several floors to a quiet, high-ceilinged hallway, and he showed us into a small gray room. "If you want the washroom or something to drink, just ask."

"I do have to go," Samson said.

"It's over here, sir," the room's voice said. One of the panels slid open, revealing a restroom. Samson went inside.

Percy gave a high-pitched laugh, and turned to me. "You can't blow up an airship and expect nothing to happen," he said. "What about the people who fried inside it?"

"Somebody had to stop those robbers."

Samson came out of the bathroom. "Us two were following orders," he said, taking a chair beside his brother.

The door opened quietly beside us, and Mr. Rossiter came in, followed by a bulky, middle aged man in a blue suit. "I came as soon as I heard," Mr. Rossiter said. "What an ordeal for you boys." He gestured to the other man. "This is Chief Williams."

The police chief stepped forward. "Boys, you went beyond the call of duty today. Which one of you is Dom?"

I stood up and he took my hand. "Son, do you realize what you did today? We've been after the Mendez gang for years. Jorge Mendez has wiped out whole villages all by himself. And you got him with one blast!" He shook hands with the twins. "Well done. Good work."

"We were scared we might be in trouble," Percy said.

The chief shook his head. "No, you saved society from some very dangerous men. It's frightening they got hold of Shiva guns; there might be a connection with the Resistance. I've already spoken with the governor, and she's delighted. There's no question you're eligible for the reward."

The twins straightened up. "How much is the reward?" Samson asked.

"Two hundred thousand units," the chief said. "Fifty thousand for each of you."

"That'll be a help," Mr. Rossiter said.

"Oh yes," Percy said.

Depressed by the day's events, I remained silent. The talk of reward money only made me bitter.

An STA van was waiting outside. After we got in, Mr. Rossiter swiveled his seat around to face us. "You've all gone through a traumatic experience. I've booked you into the university hospital for the night, so the psychologists can debrief you."

None of us objected. I was aware that the day's excitement had left me drained; the growing darkness was a comfort. A glance at the twins showed they too must be tired. Percy was staring out the window, while his brother's eyes were closed.

At the hospital, an orderly showed us to a room with four beds separated by sliding curtains. We used the shower and put on hospital gowns.

Samson pointed to the large video screen at the front. "We might be on." The video came to life, and showed a duck swimming frantically across a pond, pursued by a fox in a helicopter.

"No news tonight," a man in a white nurse's uniform said, coming in with a cart. He gave us each a small glass of thick brown liquid. "Drink this down, it's anti-stress." The stuff was powerful; I watched the cartoon for a few minutes and passed out.

"Wake up," a woman said, shaking my shoulder.

Feeling groggy, I staggered getting up, and she held my arm until we got to Dr. Penner's waiting room. The rounded, encircling chair was very comfortable. I was on the verge of going back to sleep, when Dr. Penner came in and took my hands. "Dom, I'm so sorry for this. I came as soon as I heard."

It was the first time I'd seen her without the hospital garb. Slim and dead sure in a black evening dress and silver skullcap, it was clear she was far above my station on the social scale. "Sorry to interrupt your evening," I mumbled, getting to my feet.

"No, no. Treatment is crucial after such trauma."

Following her into the other room, I doubted the session could do much. This site of transformation, once charged with excitement and hope, was now only another place. Everything was ruined; my previous life was history to me. I stretched out on the couch, and she took a seat beside me. "Have you felt disturbed by what happened?"

"I acted without thinking," I said in a bleak tone. Then the words started pouring out of me. "It wasn't just me. I dragged the others in too, and now Smokey's lost his leg. After the man on the airship shot at us, I fired back and the whole ship blew up. All the people inside are dead." The anguish grew within me and burst out in harsh sobs. I hadn't cried much since childhood, and it was ugly and painful.

"I'm informing you now that you did exactly the right thing," Dr. Penner said, wiping my cheeks with a tissue. "It's all been worked over by the police and the school--and my department, too." She brought a headset down from the wall. "In situations like this we address both the intellectual and the emotional. In your case there is no conflict. Your training and instincts served you well, and the airship carried no one but hardened criminals. Additional data will improve your rational understanding of events. Thanks to the progress you've made with your implants, I'm also able to assist your emotional recovery."

She fitted the headset on me, and everything went dark. "A career criminal, Jorge Mendez robbed, raped, and killed all over the NAN," a deep voice said. The man I'd seen on the airship's entrance ramp was at a sidewalk table with a group of men, all wearing casual summer clothes. Jorge Mendez looked utterly relaxed, as he laughed with his friends and drank from a bottle of beer.

The scene shifted to some woods by a stream. Two boys lay sprawled on a blanket, covered with blood. Jorge Mendez squatted beside them, eating a chicken leg from an open picnic basket. On another blanket a girl of about seventeen was being raped by a fat man with a long moustache, who'd shoved his pants down to his knees. Mendez tossed the bones from his chicken leg into the bushes, and opened a long bladed knife. He stared into the girl's eyes and slashed her throat. He laughed uproariously as the rapist continued to have sex with the girl's twisting body.

I was shocked and afraid. My feelings changed to cold disgust as I witnessed more of Mendez's murders. "Killing was his sport," the deep voice said. "It was his fun, and he was good at it."

"Now we're changing over to schematic," Dr. Penner's voice said from far off. "Do you see?" There was a blank whiteness, and the shopping center buildings took shape.

"It's all here," I said, as the airship come down. Two black stick men came jerkily out of the bank, while four red ones entered the scene from the side. As the blacks moved slowly toward the ship, the reds tackled them from behind. A figure in the airship's doorway was illuminated.

"He only fired once," Dr. Penner said. "Can you think why?"

"He was afraid of hitting his own men."

The bags of loot the bandits had carried were now highlighted; one on Percy's lap, the other beside the robber, close to me and Samson. "If he'd blasted you he would have destroyed what he came for."

"Maybe I could have bargained with him," I said.

"Jorge Mendez despised deals. He preferred to wipe the slate clean and kill the witnesses."

The schematic became more lifelike, and I felt a growing anxiety. The rain beat down heavily, and I was on the ground, lying behind the bandit. I fired at Mendez, saw him disappear and the airship exploded.

At this moment a wave of elation and triumph hit me that was higher than anything I'd ever experienced. Part of me knew the headgear was stimulating my emotions, but it didn't matter. My doubt was washed away.

Next day I visited Smokey at Vancouver General, in a bright, spacious ward on the fourth floor. He was half sitting up in a bed by the window. Clear tubing was connected to his left arm; other lines ran underneath the sheet that covered his lower body. He was watching a video screen that hung from the ceiling and, despite everything, retained his athletic air.

Two older women had beds close by, and one of them beckoned to me. "The nurses were saying he's a hero."

"That's right," I said. "Smokey lost his leg in a shootout with some bandits."

I pulled up a chair and sat close to his bed. "How're you doing?"

He glanced my way. "There's not much pain," he said listlessly.

"It's a huge loss to have you out of the program. I'd looked forward to working with you."

Smokey gave a cynical little laugh. "You'll go on from this, but I'm through. No taking orders from some bonehead, out to pull a grandstand move. I'll use the reward money to find a different school, and another line of work."

His coldness confused me; I did not know how to respond. "We took down Jorge Mendez," I said. "You're a hero, Smokey."

"Everyone says that. It's a lot of crap--the truth is, I was just there at the wrong time."

Leaving the room, I wore a fixed smile to mask the pain his rejection and disrespect caused me. Outside, the realization came that any one of us could have been hurt. I bore no guilt.

What he said about the reward money changing his life was interesting. Fifty thousand units was a lot, it was the first time I'd had anything like that. "Fifty thousand units," I said aloud. The words had a ring.

Back at the school, I had a sandwich and gulped some juice. Today's physical education class was in the dojo beside the gym.

Only a few other students were present when I got there. I did some stretching exercises, and moved on to a few of our basic patterns. Astra grinned at me in the mirror and aimed her foot at the back of my head. When I turned with a sidekick to her waist, she moved in with a quick punch to my abdomen. "Saw you in the news," she said, stepping back.

"How was it?" I asked, making a grab for her.

With a quick twist she sent me to the mat. "You looked pretty good," she said, laughing down at me.

"What are you up to this weekend?"

"Going home, as usual. What about you?"

"Schoolwork." The thought came that fifty thousand units might open up other possibilities, but I couldn't imagine what.

There was a loud clapping from Cooper, our attending senior. "Let's get started."

Astra left me on the floor. I scrambled to my feet and lined up behind Zack.

CHAPTER 18

"We're arriving in Chilliwack," the bus driver announced. "You'll have a half hour rest stop here. We'll be in Vancouver before midnight."

Lucas remained on the bus, and told Tomi to bring him the local news. One of the stories, "Space Cadets to Split Mendez Reward," showed a picture of his boy. Tomi brought up the available information, and Lucas learned that Dom's group had destroyed a notorious criminal gang. The story disturbed him, because things could easily have gone wrong.

Lucas had kept track of Dom's development over the years through the lawyers. He'd seen pictures, and heard recorded conversations. Meeting him for the first time on the verge of adulthood was not good; the years had slipped by too fast. There was a lot to make up for.

He drifted off and woke to see an illuminated sign, WELCOME TO VANCOUVER. It was misty out, and the lights had a diffused glow. Following tree-lined Granville Street, they passed palatial homes, and came to an area of theaters and restaurants. Lucas was glued to the window. He'd dined here and seen the shows. Continuing on, they went down the hill toward False Creek and entered the downtown tunnel. In a few minutes they reached the main Vancouver bus depot.

When he left the bus, his only luggage was a backpack with a change of clothes and toilet stuff. He cleaned up inside the spacious washroom, and went to the street level restaurant.

The booths were crowded, and baggage was stacked in the aisles. The servers waddled and bobbed to the simple, incessant beat of an Earth song about a flock of ducks. Lucas sat at the lunch counter, soaking up the atmosphere.

Before leaving the camp site he'd used the Shiva gun to get rid of his garbage and most of the gear. It was still dark when he retrieved the escape cache on the other side of the lake. He took out the bicycle, and had some breakfast. Then he used the Shiva again, destroying even the Shark suit. His last swim was in the nude; he took the Shiva gun into deep water, dismantled it, and let it go. When he came to shore, Bart Peters was gone for good.

It was difficult to part with the most powerful weapon he'd ever had, but given the security scanners on the public transportation lines, it was the only thing to do. Now he was just another nondescript traveler. This was exactly how he wanted things.

After a large cheese omelet and several cups of strong, sweet tea, his energy came back. A line of cabs was waiting when he left the depot, but Lucas preferred to walk.

The dilapidated office buildings and department stores in this part of town were old when he was young, and little had changed in his absence. Doubtless these buildings and streets would be here long after his death.

Ahead were the bright lights of Granville Street's downtown section. Pausing at the intersection, he gazed at the revelers thronging the casinos, strip shows, and bars. There was more action than he remembered. Making its way through the crowds was a uniformed dromy. Not wanting to encounter the police, Lucas waved down a passing robocab.

As they left the downtown area, Lucas spotted a family of raccoons sneaking past the entrance to an apartment building. *"You don't see those bandits up on Mars."* There was little traffic, but at Lucas's request the cab drove slowly.

Closer to the water, they encountered patches of fog. The drifting mist transformed everything and caused nostalgia in Lucas. When they approached the beach, he paid his fare and got out. Crossing the almost deserted road, he stood and stared out over the water.

The apartment towers rising from Needles Island made an impressive sight. While he vaguely remembered the plan to have the complex change color with the weather, he could not have pictured this image of shimmering pink. And the bridge, arching over from the dark forest of Stanley Park. This was like a dream--real fairy tale stuff.

"You're pleased then, your honor?"

"I'm delighted. It's the perfect place to bring the boy."

In the old days, the rising seas threatened to engulf parts of Vancouver. The "Not One Inch" movement promoted the idea of aggressively moving into the ocean's space by creating a new island, and Lucas was one of the first to choose an apartment and make a down payment. He watched for months, as the cooker devoured loads of rock and piped lava to the ocean floor.

Lucas was transported to Mars well before the project was finished, but in his absence the lawyers rented out the apartment and the mortgage was paid down. Now he had a place to come home to.

Feeling at peace with the world, Lucas strolled along the beach front and entered Stanley Park. This place of trees, beds of flowers, and extensive lawns was the jewel of the city, where countless generations came to relax in natural surroundings. He chuckled to see the fenced-off lawn bowling section, on the other side of the road. The sport might be worth a try.

The mist was thick here. Up ahead, the steady blinking of a red traffic light marked an intersection. This would be the entrance to the Needles Island Bridge; he was getting close to home.

Shouts and shrill laughter came from farther on; it sounded like possible trouble. Whatever it was, he had no intention of getting involved.

The noisy bunch came into view as he got to the intersection. Men in shorts and light shirts were rolling a large trash container down the middle of the road. A man with long black ringlets kept balanced on top of the can with easy grace, while a large, round-faced man wearing a red headband waddled alongside, applauding the can dancer with hands held high. Suddenly the container struck the curb, spun around and came to a stop.

The can dancer jumped free. The container lid flew off and a girl with metal studs in her lower lip crawled out. She staggered off to the bushes and got sick, while the others laughed and cheered. "Next victim," someone yelled.

When Lucas walked by, they fell silent and stared. "Hey," the fat man called in a high-pitched voice. "Do you want to go for a ride?"

"No thanks," Lucas said. "I'm too old, my bones are brittle now."

"Brittle bones," one of the rollers said. "That's the worst excuse I've ever heard, even from an elder."

"No excuses are accepted from elders," another said.

Shaking his head, Lucas kept on toward the bridge. "Stop!" a man yelled.

Lucas turned to meet them. "Stand back," Lucas bellowed. "I did you no harm. Now leave me alone, and let me go in peace." They seemed abashed, and he walked on.

Then something struck his left shoulder. They'd hit him with a rock. Infuriated, he picked it up and turned back to the gang. In that moment the man with the black ringlets ran by to stand between him and the bridge.

The fat man laughed. "Now the Can Dancer has you trapped. You don't leave without permission."

"Screw your permission," Lucas replied carelessly. "I am not getting into that can." Throwing the rock as hard as he could, he just missed the fat man's head. Barking an angry curse, he moved toward the Can Dancer. "Get out of my way, Dancer. I don't have time for this."

Screaming curses, the others rushed him from behind. He fought back hard, landing several solid punches, but they soon got him down. The fat man pointed a small white canister at him. "Nighty night," he grinned, and shot a perfumed spray into Lucas's face.

Lucas lost his strength, and went limp. The attackers shoved him into the container and put the lid on. It was totally black inside. *This looks bad.*

"Your best chance may be to stay in place," Tomi said. *"The can offers some protection."*

"Which way?" somebody asked.

"Over the bridge," the fat man said. "The elder wants to go home, so let's take him there."

Lucas's can began rolling, faster and faster. It was like being inside a cement mixer. Rendered limp and unable to brace himself, his body rose and fell with each spin. Almost immediately he struck his nose. He knew it was bleeding, but couldn't tell how badly. Outside were shouts and excited laughter. There was a rhythmic banging, and he thought the dancer must have jumped on top again.

A horn blared and an amplified voice called "Clear the road." The can stopped moving. "This game interferes with traffic," the voice continued. "I have to report you." Tires squealed as the vehicle sped away.

"I'll report you too," Lucas shouted. "The whole pathetic bunch of you mutant perverts will be transported to Mars."

"You call us pathetic? And you plan to report us?" The fat man's voice was unmistakable. "Put the elder over the side, that'll shut him up."

"Where are we, on the bridge above the water?" Lucas asked Tomi.

"I don't know. The bridge extends over shoreline before it crosses the water."

"Don't do this," Lucas cried. "You'll rot in jail forever!"

Their container swiveled around and turned a few times before colliding with a fixed structure. Several people laughed. "This thing weighs a ton," someone groaned.

"Are they lifting us up?" Lucas asked.

"I think they are."

"Come on, we're almost there," a man said. "Everybody lift at once."

Lucas heard cheers, and knew he was airborne. After an awful, stomach turning drop, the bottom end of the container hit something hard with a horrendous jolt. The can spun, fell, and struck again. They went end over end and landed with a tremendous crash.

Cold water lapped against Lucas's cheek. The top was off the can, and he could see dark waves running over black rocks. *"How long was I unconscious?"*

"You were out at least five minutes, your honor. I'm happy to have you back."

He needed to get out of here, but could not seem to move his arms or legs. There was an awful pain in the back of his neck. *"I must be paralyzed."*

"That's very likely. It was a hard landing."

A larger wave washed in, and he sputtered. *"I don't know if the tide's coming in or going out, but we could die here. Contact Grace Hospital, and notify Dr. Nils Johansen that Lucas the Ferryman has had an accident. I'm paralyzed from the neck down and need an ambulance badly. I'm on the rocks underneath the Needles Island Bridge at the park end."*

"Right away, your honor."

Lucas heard voices and saw a small beam of light moving around. "I wonder if he's alive?" someone asked.

"It doesn't matter much with elders," a high-pitched voice replied.

"Don't have an argument," Tomi said. *"This person is crazy; he might do something even worse."*

"I won't say one word."

Taking hold of Lucas's shoulders, the men hauled him out of the trash container and onto a large rock. Lucas saw three people. A black man, with a lime green Mohawk, put a hand on his chest. "He's still breathing," the green-lover said, close enough that Lucas caught a heavy mint smell on his breath.

"The man upstairs is looking after him." This joker had spiky blond hair; his arms were peeling from sunburn.

They emptied Lucas's backpack and threw it to the side. The fat man searched Lucas's pockets, sprinkling drops of perspiration from his flushed face. "A billfold. Just as I thought, the elder's got a few units."

"I can't get the ring off," the black man said.

"Hold the finger steady, I'll cut it," the blond said. Lucas was aware of them removing his finger, but felt no pain.

"No reaction to the knife," the black man said. "He's hurt bad."

They took off his shoes and searched the rest of his body. The fat man started giggling. "Look at this squid on his back. What a find--this makes my night complete." Then he screamed. "The filthy thing gave me a shock! Help me put it in a bag."

"Master, they're taking me," Tomi called. "Should I contact the police?"

"No police. I'll try and catch up with you later. Don't give the robbers any information. Nothing at all."

"I won't. Good luck, your honor."

Before leaving, the fat man bent down to Lucas. "The tide's coming in, so you won't have much time left. Remember this. Your own awful mouth did you in, not us. We're only harmless pranksters."

Lucas kept his eyes closed, and remained quiet.

The men left laughing as they jumped from rock to rock. Lucas heard a splash and curses from the fat man. Then there was silence, except for the waves.

The relief Lucas felt when his attackers left quickly turned to dread. A quadriplegic, without his varlet or his casting ring, he was helpless as a baby and very close to death. He must be bleeding where they'd amputated his finger, but with no feeling in his hands, and unable to move, he could not assess the wound. Unable to escape the horror, his mind retreated to a space where he was oblivious to the surroundings. He lost awareness of the passage of time.

At last lights shone and a woman came to Lucas's side. "My dear ferryman, are you all right?" Although her hand was on his brow, her voice seemed far away.

"Still alive," he muttered. "I'm paralyzed, and my finger is lost somewhere."

"Hurry with that stretcher," she called.

He awoke to bright light; even the air was shimmering. Looking up, he recognized a tall blond man dressed in hospital whites. "Hello, Doc," he said.

Nils Johansen smiled down at him. "Thank God you're here."

"So he's awake," a young Filipina woman exclaimed, coming to stand next to Dr. Johansen.

Lucas stared at her, striving to understand. She was the one who'd rescued him from the rocks; also she reminded him of someone he'd known years ago. "Her daughter?"

She laughed. "It's me, Bibi! We'll catch up on the news later. The main thing now is to help you get better."

"Two of your neck vertebrae are fractured, and the spinal cord was severed," Dr. Johansen said. "Your pelvis is fractured. Also the cancer has spread throughout your body. You need a total treatment."

"Back to the womb," Bibi said. "You'll emerge a new man."

"I'd like to get my finger back," Lucas said.

"We found it," Bibi said. "Hopefully it'll reattach; if not, you'll grow a new one."

CHAPTER 19

After the award ceremony, everyone wanted to shake my hand. Even George Damon clapped me on the back, and said, "Well done," in a gruff voice. The recognition was sweet but soon died off.

Receiving the fifty thousand units was more tangible. The reward money would end the dependence on my convict benefactor. Once he arrived, I'd let him know that his help was no longer needed. The Lupine scholarship almost certainly arose from the proceeds of crime, and I wanted no part of it.

I was putting long sessions on the multivox these days, partly because within the world of music, confusions and upsets were managed and resolved. Despite this release, the anxiety mounted. Then came the message I'd expected; my guardian wanted to see me.

Mr. Gerald was in his shirtsleeves, sitting behind his large desk. Behind him the windows were open, but the room remained shadowy; the dark walls, with their paintings of war ships, and shelves that held ancient leather-covered law books, seemed to absorb the light. I took the chair across the desk from him.

"Congratulations on the award," he said, shaking my hand. "It's a big advantage to have that on your record."

"The money's good to have, too. I'll be independent of my benefactor."

Mr. Gerald smiled and stood up. "I have a special wine that's been waiting for a moment like this." Opening a cabinet below the bookcase, he brought two goblets over to the desk and poured clear amber liquid form a fat dark bottle. "It's from the Turkish renaissance, almost seventy-five years old." He touched his glass to mine.

The wine was sweetish, loaded with complex flavors. It helped relax and open my mind, and I somehow felt in touch with the past ages, in which similar interviews had played out.

Leaning back in his chair, Mr. Gerald looked at me for a long time. "You're a man now, and it's time to hear the rest of your history."

"Is there much more?"

Mr. Gerald chuckled. "As it turns out, I needn't have mentioned the previous nonsense. Lucas Rivera's conviction was for a minor offense, and he was transported by the NAF regime in chaotic times. Our office made a thorough search, and there's no record the incident even took place. Today's NAN authorities have no reason to bother him."

I toasted him with my glass. "Hopefully Lucas Rivera can live his remaining time in peace."

"All right then." Mr. Gerald made a fist and opened it again. "To start with the why of it, Lucas wanted you to grow up free from the kind of negative influences he felt dragged him down and ruined his life. Avery and I also believe that while genetics may partly determine a man's development, environment and upbringing are more dominant. Having you in the crèche was not a perfect situation, but we kept an eye on things, and made sure you had good teachers, and went to the best schools. We welcomed you here at the office, and looked on you as one of our own."

"You were here for me," I admitted.

Mr. Gerald sipped some wine. "I don't know quite how to tell you this," he muttered. Then his wide face assumed its customary business appearance. "Dom, you were not conceived as someone's love child. You are Lucas's clone."

This was unimaginable. I sat up straight and gaped wordlessly.

"It was difficult to conceal the truth from you, but the result was highly successful. You turned out an admirable young man, one who personifies the virtues aimed for by every space cadet. Dom, you are noble, honest, brave, and true. Avery and I are extremely proud of how you turned out."

Anger grew in me as I realized the extent of their deceit and betrayal. "When can I talk with Lucas?"

"He's asleep now, but you can see him at Grace Hospital, out in Surrey. They'll be expecting you."

Back outside, I hailed a passing robocab. As we drove off, my thoughts were clear and cold. Despite my protected upbringing, I was no hothouse flower. My training had prepared me to recognize danger and to deal with it.

Without question, the man's appearance was a threat to me. As a child of the crèche I'd had to try harder, and prove myself on every occasion. But a convict's clone? That did not go well. I'd make him understand. As a space cadet, my duty came first. No sense of family obligation, or gratitude for his paying my tuition could outweigh that.

After crossing the Fraser River, the robocab exited the highway and passed a business district before turning down a long, straight road through some farmland. Coming to a high fence of close growing cedars, we entered a driveway.

Grace Hospital was a large, two-story building, surrounded by lawns and flower gardens where people strolled and sat on benches. The entrance area was congested with limos and other cabs. "Shall I wait, sir?" my robot driver asked.

The charge was already over forty units, but I was in no mood to quibble. "Yes, wait," I replied. "It'll only be a short visit."

Inside I went to a reception desk, where a man in a dark jacket took my identification. "You're expected," he said. "Wait here, Dr. Santos will be down shortly."

In a few minutes a slender, dark-haired young woman in a white hospital uniform came up to me. "I'm Bibi," she said with a bright smile. "I'll take you to see Lucas Rivera."

As we walked down a ramp to the floor below, she kept looking at me. "You're so tall and straight, just like him. You're twenty, aren't you? He was twenty-five when we first met."

"You must have been a child."

"Here at Grace Hospital, we specialize in rejuvenation. I'm older than I look."

At the bottom of the ramp, we went through an area where technicians monitored screens and did lab work. Farther along was a nurses' station. Down a gray hallway, we passed the rooms where patients stayed. "Your parent is in here," Bibi said, opening a door.

Inside the room were four tall glass tanks, each with a patient suspended inside. I recognized Lucas immediately on the far right. It was shocking, but his figure drew me and I went up to the glass. His green eyes were open but seemed vacant; he remained motionless.

I'd always been slim, but he looked dangerously thin. His ribs stuck out, and his abdomen was almost nonexistent. It shrank back toward his spine except for the navel, where a gray umbilical tube was attached. The muscles in his legs were long and sinewy. He was completely hairless.

Conscious of a steady pulsing sound, I looked at Bibi. "Am I hearing his heart?"

"Our hospital control has taken over his circulation. Nanobots are destroying the diseased cells, while fresh stem cells are moving in. If all goes well, he'll come out of here in full remission."

His member stirred. It enlarged and became erect.

Bibi giggled. "That's normal, he's probably dreaming again."

I glanced up at the lacy, metallic skull piece covering his scalp. "Maybe he's dreaming he's not here."

"Let's leave him now." She led me to a nearby waiting room, where we had tea at a small table. "Has anyone explained your connection to this hospital?" she asked.

I had no idea what she meant.

"It was important to Lucas to preserve his lineage, and before he was transported, we made some clones and froze the embryos. When the time was right for him, about twenty-one years ago, he instructed us to create you."

The information was sickening. "It's hard to imagine some convict wanting to preserve his lineage."

"Lucas comes from an ancient noble line. He'll tell you more about your family background when you have a chance to speak with him."

I'd never pictured myself coming from a noble line. "It seems you've done a lot for us."

Bibi poured more tea. "My family owes your parent a huge debt. If not for our ferryman we might not have survived." She showed me a crystal, with a picture of Lucas standing at the bow of his submersible. A bull of a man wearing only shorts, his wavy, red-gold hair was shoulder-length, and he had a handlebar moustache. He wielded an automatic rifle, and a black cigar was clenched in his teeth. Bibi turned the crystal, and I saw a young woman in a white dress and wide-brimmed white hat, standing in a green launch.

"Hundreds of thousands came to Luzon from the low-lying islands menaced by the rising seas," she said. "Manila was a hell, as armed gangs fought for a space to live. The criminals found out we were planning to leave, and tried to force us to take them along. Lucas was so stern and cool headed."

"And the woman in the white dress--is she your mother?"

"It's me."

"Impossible," I laughed. "You look about eighteen."

"I'm almost the same age as Lucas. This hospital is a special place, and I've been able to reclaim my youth. We're hoping Lucas will do that too."

This sounded nonsensical to me. "Your tank treatment must do wonders," I said sarcastically.

Bibi smiled enigmatically. "Lucas loves you, you know. After he instructed us to go ahead, we found a young psychology student, with a strong interest in human development, for your surrogate mother. Lucas paid her handsomely, and after the delivery she stayed and nursed you for almost three years at the Mountain Spirit Crèche. It was like a practicum for her. As you know, this crèche is world class, and staffed only with professionals."

"There were lots of mothers there. I can't remember the first one."

"Today she's a professor at the University of Toronto. She became fully transformed."

"It must be true that Lucas paid for my upbringing and education. Still it's difficult for me to accept a man I've never met as my parent, or even as an identical twin. Everything I know about epigenetics tells me that his life in a radically different environment will have fashioned a very different person from me. Once he recovers, I suppose I'll find out more."

Bibi gave me another smile. "You'll be pleasantly surprised."

CHAPTER 20

End of term was getting closer, and each of my instructors was gripped by the same compulsion; to get as much done as possible in the time we had left.

Monday night after dinner I joined some students huddled in front of the notice board and saw my name posted for next year's executive nominations. Percy shook my hand. "Good going." Then Cooper slapped me on the back. These nominations were among the highest awards the faculty handed out, and having my name there was a real boost for my self-esteem.

Zack came to my room later that evening and congratulated me. "Did you hear Astra got nominated too?"

The news made me smile. "I hadn't heard, but it'd be natural for her. Serena would be good, too."

Zack frowned. "It makes me furious, thinking of how Wang screwed up. You'll never see me give up my career for a woman."

A couple of nights later, I received a message from Astra's mother. "Hello, Dom," Mrs. Allison said in a low voice. "We haven't seen much of you lately, why don't you come out for the weekend? Astra and Bruce will both be home. Pack some clothes and we'll see you Friday."

Closing my eyes, I fell back on the bed. It was the first time I'd heard from her since coming to STA, and her voice was exciting to me. As a child, the invitations to the farm were a huge part of my life. Now that Astra and I were grown up, the possibilities were endless.

Friday night I went downtown and got a bus that went east along the Fraser River. It let me out at the little town of Pitt Meadows; from there a robocab took me north toward the mountains. We passed through flat farmlands and came to a place of mansions and large estates. Shortly after ten, the cab stopped at the arched gateway to Allison Farms.

I tapped the knocker at the side, and light flooded from the arch above. Feminine laughter rang out, and Astra smiled at me from the screen. "Come on in, I'll pick you up." The barred gate swung open, and I walked down the little entrance road. The warm night was rich with the smell of close-growing trees and bushes. Night birds swooped after swarms of tiny insects.

In a few minutes a curious pattering sound came toward me, and a headlight appeared. As it got closer, I realized it was a train with several cars, but without tracks or wheels. Each car had short, stout, springy legs, all working in unison. It stopped beside me, and Astra leaned out a window in the front car. She had on long blonde hair, and a striped engineer's cap was tilted over her eyes. "Need a lift, stranger?"

I just stood there and stared. "You never told me about this."

"Come on, get in."

A door opened on the side, and I climbed a couple of steps to a little coach, illuminated by a pumpkin glow from the walls. Astra was at a table in the front, by the window. Her light jacket was unfastened, and I was awed by the freedom with which she'd dressed: halter top, bare midriff, and thin, white pants. She gave a throaty little laugh. "It's good you came."

"I'm happy to be here," I said, taking a seat beside her.

"Mother wants to see you, too. Let's go home."

Astra's house was a two-story hacienda style structure, with a central courtyard. Its low pitched roof overhung second floor balconies, and an encircling ground floor verandah. When I was a child, it seemed an enchanted fairyland, and now it drew me again.

A couple of big dogs came and nuzzled us as we approached the door. "Stay out," Astra said firmly, pushing them away.

"Dogs, go back." Mrs. Allison's imperious tone hadn't changed. A slight blonde woman in a rose-colored robe, she came out of the shadowy verandah and shook my hand. "Welcome, Dom. Come in, we'll have a bite to eat." We followed her to the kitchen. "Milk and cookies, Dinah," she said, clapping her hands.

"Yes, ma'am." Plump and bosomy, wearing a long brown dress, Dinah filled glasses with frothy white liquid from the fridge, then moved to the counter and piled gingersnaps onto a plate.

A door slammed; I heard some whistling and Astra's brother came in. Seven years older than his sister, Bruce was a dwarf, with a large head, a normal torso and short arms and legs. There were white streaks in the dark hair that swept back from his bulging forehead, and deep facial lines drew his lips down. He was an accomplished engineer, and I admired him a lot. "Hot tea, Dinah," he said as he came in. "Put some lemon in it." Bruce kissed his mother on the cheek, and sat down with us at the table.

"You remember Dom don't you?" Astra asked.

"The man who took down the Mendez gang." Bruce reached over to shake hands. "Excellent. I'm glad you came to visit."

"You've made some changes," I said. "There was no train the last time I was here."

"Are we colonizing space, or is it the reverse?" Mrs. Allison asked.

It was an old joke, but we laughed. "As long as Earth remains in charge," Bruce said. He stretched his arms. "Dom, I'll look forward to showing you the farm."

After our snack, Mrs. Allison went off to bed, and Astra showed me to my room. "We don't have guests very often," she said, as we went up the dark, creaky staircase.

"I always liked this place."

At the top, she led me into a spacious bedroom. The windows were wide open, and white curtains on the sides moved gently in the air currents. "I aired out the room and put fresh sheets on the bed, so you should be all right. Don't mind the spiders, they're well-mannered." When I pulled her to me, she turned away. "Mother gets upset so easily, I can't disturb her."

After she left, I went out onto the balcony. There was no moon, and the stars were very bright. The light breeze was warm, and laden with perfume.

No one was around when I went downstairs in the morning, so I went into the kitchen and said hello to Dinah. Grandmother Allison came in while I was having scrambled eggs. She wore a pink padded dressing gown, and her black hair was tied up in a knot. Dinah gave her a glass of grapefruit juice, and she watched me eat. Her face and hands were wrinkled and deeply tanned. "You're sweet on her, aren't you?" she asked.

Her sharp tone made me remember that the women of the household, including Astra, were not above making cruel fun of me. "How could I not be?" I asked.

She smiled. "We've been proud of you, Dom. I'm happy that you're becoming friends with Astra again. The years have gone by very fast, and it gives me confidence knowing you'll be out there in space with her."

It was a surprise to hear she might be on my side. "Space is a big territory. We don't know where we'll be posted."

"We're not without influence. My son has a lot of pull." This way of thinking was new to me, and I remained silent. "You and Astra have to be careful out there in the radiation. Never forget what happened with Bruce."

Her choice of subject matter definitely felt disturbing. "Our school provides excellent training," I said, finishing off my eggs. "Astra and I are going to be real high flyers."

Her mouth quivered. "Dinah, get Dom some more coffee."

"No thanks," I said, getting up. "Bruce promised to show me the farm, I shouldn't keep him waiting."

Outside the kitchen door, the sunshine was filtered by big maple trees that lined the driveway. The two dogs I'd met the night before were lying near a tall black dromy that stood against the garage. The dogs came up and I rubbed their scalps. "I'm Dom," I told the dromy.

"Yes, Master Dom," it said. "I'm to take you to the workshop. Won't you come in?" Its holding compartment expanded, and the side opened up. I took a seat and we started off.

The path we took brought back more childhood memories as it wound through the garden, offering glimpses of secluded arbors, bursts of colorful blossoms, and, at one point, a tile chessboard with large men carved from stone. I'd played hide-and-seek behind these fountains, stared into dark pools where goldfish lurked, and searched for candy eggs at Easter time.

Ahead as we came out onto the main driveway, Mr. Allison's rocket plane stood poised as if ready to take off. While it would never fly again, it remained a magnificent symbol of power and achievement. Across from it was the workshop, a large brown building.

When I went inside, Bruce shouted a welcome and beckoned me over. One of the centipede cars was suspended in midair, and Bruce and two men in white coveralls were underneath working on its legs. "It's good you can see this," he said, coming out. "The old people smothered too much of our world with concrete and blacktop, and now we're taking it back. If you pave the ground, nothing can grow underneath, so let's give the soil a chance to breathe again. Off-road and off track, that's the best future for Earth."

"Are these centipedes related to the dromy?" I asked.

"They're a spin-off. The centipedes are a tougher sell here on Earth because of our gravity, but we're looking at extreme lightweight construction for the cars and stronger legs."

"Your centipede train is fun to ride in," I said.

Bruce laughed loudly. "Fun's a good selling point. Everybody loves fun, and fun's going to make me very wealthy. Come here, I have something else to show you."

We set off in a two-seat carriage that was propelled by four legs. It was similar to the dromies, but with a wider platform. Down the road from the workshop, we passed some smaller houses, set amongst flowering fruit trees and neatly kept gardens. At the last house, a young woman in a broad-brimmed yellow sunhat waved to Bruce and blew him a kiss. "My sister-in-law," Bruce said. "I know what you're thinking--droit de seigneur."

"I never thought that. Now that you mention it though, is there anything in it?"

"We joke about that kind of thing here," Bruce said with a laugh. "I have to admit the situation here at the farm is somewhat medieval. There's a lot of work, and it's not possible to do it all myself."

We continued on, past a stable and a barn, and along a tree-lined trail. On either side were pastures where animals grazed, and fields prepared for cultivation. Bruce kept a fast pace, and we neared a bamboo fence at the end of the property.

Entering a glade of trees, we stopped at a gazebo beside a small pool where water poured from the mouth of a dark stone frog. "Dad likes to come out here when he visits." I got out and leaned against the table, while Bruce, standing on the carriage, filled some bird feeders that dangled from the trees. "Oh, good," he exclaimed, as a hummingbird went by and hovered against a cylinder filled with red liquid.

"Is Mr. Allison still posted at Ganymede?" I asked.

"He's back on Mars now. I think he'll call us tonight."

After lunch Astra and I went outside to the garden, and she led me to an old wooden bench under a willow tree. The two dogs followed, panting loudly. "It's good to get away from schoolwork for a while," Astra said. "The engineering problem I'm working on is a nasty, snarled-up thing, all stresses, and strains."

"In contrast to your own perfect form."

Astra laughed, and slapped my arm. Stretching out on the bench, she put her head in my lap. "Here's a comfortable spot." One of the dogs licked her face, and she pushed it away. "Not for you."

I ran my forefinger down her nose and around her mouth then traced her neck and the top of her gray dress. "Did you bring your telecap? I'll let you know my thoughts."

Astra frowned. "Speaking is enough for now." She sat up and looked at me levelly. "Do you realize we'll both be on the executive next year?"

"Well, maybe. People haven't voted yet."

"It's a sure thing for both of us. Our senior year's going to be dominated by that." Knowing she'd figured things out that far ahead made me feel slow. For an instant she reminded me of her grandmother. "We should discuss it while you're here," she said, getting up. "I have to get back, there's a lot of work to do."

Upstairs in my room, I went out on the balcony and looked over the garden to the fields and the mountains beyond. As a child visiting Allison Farms, I never thought to estimate the size or value of the estate. Would a relationship with Astra also involve the farm? Such thoughts were new to me; in truth though, Astra's connection to her family was much more solid than the transitory school situation.

Before dinner, Bruce brought me into his office at the back of the house. It was a large room, cluttered with diagrams and models of legs, and different types of robots. Waving me to a sofa, he stood on a chair and took a slender green bottle from a cupboard. "Garden Elixir," he said, holding it high. He got down and poured a small glass for each of us.

The green liquid was syrupy, with a sweet mint taste. "Interesting," I said, rolling it around in my mouth. Soon my vision became clearer, and I sensed a growing energy.

"I envy you and Astra going into space. The doctors tell me to avoid it, my being conceived there already created enough problems." Sensing my protest, he shook his head. "No complaints on my part. My life is here, but it's undeniable that the future is up there. Dad made a terrific career of it, and Astra's following in his footsteps." He poured more drinks.

"You Allisons make me feel simple."

"I'd never call you simple," Bruce said. "If you're loyal and dependable, that can take you further than the schemers that are so common in today's business world. Eventually Dad will retire, and I'll lose the one totally trustworthy connection I have for the kind of opportunity that's given me first chance on the centipedes. There's nothing like real family. Hopefully Astra will be there to take his place. And you'll be there, too."

"You make a good point," I said. We smiled at each other and shook hands.

That night we ate in the main dining room, next to the kitchen. Smaller than I remembered, the light gray room had an oval wooden table in the middle, and heavy, old-fashioned chairs. There were several family pictures on the walls. At the back was a large painting of Mr. and Mrs. Allison on a bench under a willow tree. It was the bench Astra took me to earlier, in their garden.

Dinner was roast lamb from their own flock; the vegetables were also from the farm. Dinah kept refilling our glasses with a dry red wine, and everyone was in high spirits. The family's attention was on Bruce's two sons, who were drawn up to the table in high chairs, and their mother Sarah, who was helping them eat. The boys reminded me of their father, boisterous and voluble, but with Astra next to me it was difficult to follow the conversation. Her tight gray dress made her look years older, and was a real distraction.

After dinner we lingered over coffee, until Dinah announced that Mr. Allison was on the line. Everyone left the table and filed down the hallway. Astra and I followed, holding hands. "I've never seen you look so good," I said.

She pulled me into a doorway, and we kissed. "Let's go out after this," she murmured. "We can practice with our telecaps."

We found the others in a small room, gathered around a platform where Mr. Allison was standing in hologram form. Despite his gray hair I recognized him immediately. He projected the same energy, kindness, enjoyment, and tremendous interest in his surroundings that I remembered from childhood.

It was a good night for communicating with Mars; the delay was only six minutes, which was nothing for the Allisons. One by one they went to the platform, received their message, and spoke to Mr. Allison. When

Astra's turn came she mentioned me, and called me up. I hadn't expected this, and only blurted out that I was happy to see him and it was exciting to speak to him on Mars.

Twelve minutes later a reply came. "It's good to see you again, Dom," Mr. Allison called, waving. "There's a place for you out here. We always need leadership."

When it ended the two toddlers were crying, and everyone started talking at once. Thrilled that Mr. Allison recognized me, I hardly noticed. Then Astra mentioned that we were going out to Ronny's Roadhouse. "Be careful," her mother told her. She lifted the silver pendant from around Astra's neck. "This is not something to wear to Ronny's Roadhouse."

It was dark when we went outside. The dromy expanded its compartment, and we stepped in. "We're off to Ronny's," Astra told it. She sat close to me, and propped her feet on the other seat.

Earth music was throbbing as we stopped in front of a square building lit by a pink sign, RONNY's. Inside the music was much louder. The entrance hallway was covered with pictures of glitzy roadsters from before the turn of the century, when the car as an art form reached its peak. Inside the lobby was a full-size model of the Mercedes Aero, one of the old people's plane-cars. "Beautiful, isn't it?" Astra asked, stroking its wing.

"The ultimate in luxury," I said. "And in waste."

A doorman in a black tuxedo came up, and Astra handed him some money. He took us through a lounge to a small table overlooking the next level. Arms on the railing, we looked down on a stage where musicians dressed like farmers performed Earth music for the fifty or sixty people crowding the dance floor.

A screen lit up on the table. "What can we get you?" a woman asked.

"I'd like a Saturn screw, they're good here," Astra said.

"Two Saturns," I said.

"Astra," a deep voice said from behind me. A well-dressed man with longish black hair leaned down to her. "We've got some catching up to do. Let's go down and give it a whirl."

Astra got up. "Excuse me, Dom," she said, touching my shoulder lightly. The two went off toward the staircase.

A server in a low-cut dress brought two tall glasses that tinkled with ice. Fumes rose as I put the drink to my lips. It tasted of pineapple, with a lime background. After a few sips a numbness spread over me.

Astra came back, cheeks flushed and her eyes lively and bright. "That was so much fun," she laughed. She toasted me with her glass and drank deep. Then a large blond man appeared and she was gone again. "Sorry," she said when she returned. "Some of these people I haven't seen for years."

"Mind if I grab a dance while there's a chance?"

"Of course." She drained her glass and led me over to the staircase, where we descended into a pit that was jammed with jerking bodies. We danced for a long time, and ended by behaving like a couple of foolish chimpanzees. "That was hilarious," Astra laughed, as we came back upstairs.

"Good practice for the Grand Ball," I said, sitting down. "Will you save me a dance if you can get away from George?"

"Don't worry, I'm only going with him out of duty." A short, very erect man with a wispy dark beard approached our table. "Paul," Astra cried. She got up and threw her arms around him.

It was after two o'clock when we finally went outside. Astra whistled, and our dromy came over. "We'll take our time getting back," she said, sitting close beside me. "I've been looking forward to this all night."

"Looking forward to what?"

"Telecaps." Laughing, she put hers on. After I did likewise, she slid her lips against mine. We kissed for a long time, our bodies slowly moving on each other. Her thoughts were not formed in words, but I experienced her feelings and knew she experienced mine. Suddenly she pulled away. "Oh, no." Sitting up she ripped the telecap off her head. "I'm just not ready for this."

I removed my telecap too. "Maybe it's those Saturn screws."

"It's our chemistry," she sighed, and moved away. "Look," she said coolly. "If we're both on the executive, there'll be all kinds of things we can do as a couple. It'll make our senior year." Her ideas struck me as highly amusing but I didn't reveal this out of fear of spoiling the moment. "I wouldn't go with you just for that reason," she said. "But it would be so perfect! We'd be like the king and queen of the whole academy."

This time I had to laugh. "The king?"

"You'll be in charge, telling everyone what to do." She sounded amazingly sure, like she had a new suit of clothes ready for me to step into.

"Can I tell you what to do too?"

"We'll talk about things. What do you wish for?"

"Another kiss."

Astra stayed in my arms until we got back to the house.

CHAPTER 21

Lucas woke up in a bed with rails along the sides. A nearby table held a fluted vase of pale daffodils. There was an empty bed alongside his; he was alone in the room. The ceiling and walls were white, and it was quiet except for a faint humming sound.

"How do I get out of here?" he asked. Then he remembered he'd lost Tomi. There'd be no peace till he got his varlet back.

He reached over and shoved the side rail but it didn't move. *No pain. Interesting.* Throwing aside his top sheet, he palpated his torso and nether regions. Again, there was no pain. Had he totally recovered? He tried sitting up and raised his arms above his head. His head swam, and he let himself fall back. What about the replacement finger, though? He wiggled them all and touched them to each other. They had feeling; he was a lucky man.

"I see you're awake," Bibi said, coming into the room. Smiling warmly, she approached the bed and took his hand. "Don't look so puzzled, I am her. Also I'm me."

"Talk sense, I'm not in the mood for games."

Then Dr. Johansen arrived. "I see our ferryman is awake. Welcome back, old friend."

Lucas smiled up at him. "It's good to see you again, Doc. You're looking well. Who's the young lady?"

"My beloved bride you rescued years ago."

Lucas gave Bibi a long, deep look. "This is hard to believe," he said. "You haven't aged one bit."

"Bibi and I have made remarkable achievements in the last thirty years," Dr. Johansen said. "We've turned Grace Hospital into a center for rejuvenation therapy. Did you review the information we sent you?"

"It's why I came here. The doctors on Mars advised me to make my peace and prepare to die."

Dr. Johansen shook his head vigorously. "No, no. You responded well to your treatment in the tank, and as of today you can look forward to many years of productive life. But as the brochure says, this is only a first step. At present you're a healthy man in his fifties. Grace Hospital can take you to the next level, and give you back your youth."

Lucas looked to Bibi. "Was it difficult for you?"

"More wondrous than difficult for me," she shrugged. "Having a clone was like a normal pregnancy, except that my husband had no part in the baby. Ever since Cici's birth, we've been loving and of one mind. Cici knew from an early age that I planned to transfer myself into her brain, and the prospect was exciting to her. She looked forward eagerly to an early step into adulthood and a chance to be even closer to me. The merger offered big advantages for both of us, so it's been highly successful."

Lucas turned to Dr. Johansen. "What about you?"

"I remain undecided. My own clone is studying medicine over in Switzerland, and doing very well. He wants to become a T-man, and this is a route I've never cared to follow. Also I've never been afraid of growing old in the usual way. In the meantime, I'm very happy with my lovely wife."

Bibi slung an arm around her husband and smiled up at him. "Cici adores you too. The merger was fulfilling for both of us, in that sense."

"I'm very interested in this," Lucas said. "I'll have my boy come in, and you can explain things."

"Dom visited once when you were in the tank," Bibi said. "You need to spend as much time as possible with him. It's crucial that you get to know each other before the merger. As an older, well established man you have a lot to offer. In time Dom should realize our procedure is a win-win for both parties."

162

"Much of the preparatory work is completed," Dr. Johansen said. "We surveyed your Martian brain implant, and our computers have made the adjustment. Secondly, we wormed your brain; you relived much of your life while in the tank. Also, we captured your rich dream life. The fourth point has to do with your life from here on. We've left sensors throughout your cerebral cortex, to analyze your thought processes."

Lucas had a sinking feeling. "I don't have any secrets left."

"Yes you do," Bibi cried.

"Your privacy is sacrosanct," Dr. Johansen said. "The data goes only to the machine, and it's automatically erased once the transfer takes place."

"I trust you," Lucas growled.

"Dom is a perfect recipient, because his brain transformation is almost to the T-man level. The main thing missing now is Tomi. Your varlet was close to you for many years and holds much of your information."

"I mean to get Tomi back." Turning onto his side, Lucas held the edge of the bed's railing and looked up at them. "These mergers don't come cheap, and I'm not one to ask for charity."

They laughed. "We did some dental work on you," Bibi said. She showed Lucas a small pouch filled with fiery stones. "You haven't come here empty-handed."

"They've been assessed at over five million units," Dr. Johansen said. "Say the word and we'll sell the diamonds. Our procedure won't cost more than a million, even considering the Martian technology."

"I agree with one condition," Lucas said. "Your wife chooses one of these stones for herself."

Bibi gasped. "They are gorgeous. A blue one?" She put her hand on Lucas's brow. "Ferryman, it won't be long till you start your second life."

After Lucas started eating normally again his strength returned, and in a few days he felt ready to take charge of his affairs. On the afternoon of his lawyer's appointment, a nurse-robot took him down the hall to a small conference room.

Mr. Gerald arrived accompanied by a younger, dark-haired man. "I'm glad to see you out of that damn tank," Mr. Gerald said as they came in. "You look well."

Lucas laughed, and took the lawyer's hand in his. "I don't think you've changed one bit. You're even wearing the same suit."

"It's probably the same tailor, but it's not the same suit." He brought the other man forward. "This is Rod Campbell, from the Hong Kong Bank." The two shook hands. "You did well on the diamond sale; they went for five million, four hundred thousand units."

Lucas made a low whistle. "That's very good."

They took chairs around a black table. "Rod's an expert on handling this kind of transaction," Mr. Gerald said.

"The Hong Kong Bank is very pleased to have your business," Rod said.

"It's good to talk with an expert," Lucas said. "I imagine five million will provide some income?"

"Our basic savings rate today is three and a half percent," Rod said. "If you lock in for different time periods it goes up; right now we offer four and a half percent on the ten year guaranteed income option." Opening his briefcase, he handed Lucas a pamphlet. "These are the bonds we have available. Our clients also like to invest in equities, especially when dividends are involved."

Lucas glanced through the pamphlet and put it in his pocket. "If you can give me three and a half percent on basic savings, it'll yield one hundred and seventy-five thousand units a year. That's enough for now. I'll look through these other options, and decide later. I don't plan to stay in Vancouver forever."

"Very good," Rod said. "I'm always available if you want to discuss investments." He brought out some documents. "I'll ask you to sign these papers."

Lucas began scrawling his signatures. "At the moment I'm totally broke," he muttered.

"Some clients use a prepaid thumb chip, would you like that?"

"Yes, I would."

Three days later, Lucas left the hospital. Bibi accompanied him in the robocab to make sure he got settled in at his new place. It had rained that morning, and now in the early afternoon, the sky was clear. They got through the city in good time and paused at English Bay to look over the water at Lucas's new home. The towers were a light gold color today. Within the sea and mountains setting, the complex had a striking beauty.

Bibi wore a long, light blue dress, and her face was shaded by a black and white baseball cap. "I wonder if you have food up there?" she asked.

"It wouldn't hurt to pick something up."

They stopped at a nearby fruit stand, and Lucas looked wonderingly at the array of produce. "This'd be priceless up on Mars," he said, choosing a bunch of black grapes. "And these," he sighed, grabbing some fat pears. "Oh, look at the bananas."

Holding a large bag clutched to his chest, he followed Bibi into a delicatessen. There he bought a loaf of rye bread, some sliced meat, a large slice of cheddar cheese, and a bottle of dill pickles. "Would you like dessert?" Bibi asked. Lucas nodded to a peach pie.

The robocab continued on above the Seawall, and drove past the lawn bowling green. Coming to the place where the muggers jumped him, Lucas went cold. "They took Tomi," he said. "I need to find them."

Turning toward the water, they drove onto the narrow arched bridge that led to Needles Island. The complex had three apartment towers that shared a central courtyard. Coming down off the bridge, the robocab circled the outer drive, and they got out at the back entrance of Lucas's building.

A stiff breeze blew Lucas and Bibi toward the entranceway. Water gushed from a fountain on the left side; standing in a shallow pool was an immense statue of a logger holding a double-bitted axe. Sinewy and robust, shirt half open to expose a brawny chest, the rough-hewn figure was the embodiment of virile purpose. "A figure from a different time," Bibi said.

"There's still plenty of his kind around--up on Mars."

Bibi grinned. "It might be fun to visit."

"You wouldn't get lonely."

At the door he went to the speaker panel at the side. "I'm Lucas Rivera, an owner," he said loudly. He touched the fingerprint scanner.

"Welcome, Master Lucas," a voice said. The door slid open, and they entered a deserted, high-ceilinged foyer.

The elevator took them to the sixty-third floor, and they went down a quiet hallway to the end. Here Lucas stopped before a recessed door decorated by a circlet of small red roses. He looked into the circlet at the iris scanner; there was a sharp "click" and the door swung open.

Inside the place was still and quiet. They brought the food into the kitchen and put the bags on the table.

A little robot rolled out from beside the fridge. Dressed in a white skirt and a black top, it had a pleasant humanoid face, with red hair done up in pig tails. "Welcome home, Master Lucas," it said in a high-pitched voice. "I'm Maude, your cook."

"I'm happy to meet you, Maude," Lucas said. "This is my friend, Bibi. Is there anything to drink around here?"

"The kitchen is fully stocked, as per the instructions."

"I'd like a large Wild Grouse and water, and then you can make some lunch. Bibi?"

"A glass of white wine would be nice."

They took the drinks through the living room and went out onto the balcony. The apartment was a northwest corner unit that overlooked the entrance to the harbor; to the west, they saw Vancouver Island. Below them a huge freighter was coming in, loaded with containers. "I'll be spending some time out here," Lucas said.

"People say these buildings sway in the winds," Bibi said.

"They sing, too," Lucas said. "Imagine when a big storm comes in and all the buildings are swaying and singing, and changing color."

Bibi laughed. "Along with thunder and lightning, and the roar of the waves--you'll be in your element."

She followed him back inside and sat on the couch as he examined the massive table in the dining room and the paintings on the walls. He stopped before a picture of his old submersible, the *Seashell*. "Do you remember this?"

"How could I forget the vessel that saved my family?"

"Yes, it was a good ship," Bibi growled. Then she made a girlish giggle, and slapped herself hard on the wrist. "Cici!"

"A fine time was had by all," the low, guttural voice continued.

"This is embarrassing," Bibi laughed. "Cici knows you're the only man I've slept with beside Nils, and she's excited."

"I'm irrepressible," her low voice said.

"Nils started on Cici long before the merger, and she feels we owe her. We joke that she's taken over our id."

"The id?" Lucas asked.

"Freud divides the psyche into id, the ego and superego," Bibi said. "By id he means partly the subconscious."

"I'm the primitive id," Cici said. "An eternal 'I want,' which seldom listens to reason. I'm the Dionysian side, ready to strip off my clothes and run wild through the forest, or dance under the full moon; Bibi's the Apollonian, always keeping me in check."

"Cici loves to overstate her case," Bibi said, laughing. "We do have a good time, it's a lot of fun being together. Years from now, when Didi joins us, it'll be even more interesting. Cici will move up to the ego spot, and I'll take over the superego."

Lucas shook his head. "You'll be a formidable combination." He drank some bourbon. Muttering, "I haven't seen the bedroom yet," he went to the doorway and looked over the wide bed.

"I want to show you something," Bibi said, standing beside him. Unbuttoning the top of her dress, she pulled out a silver necklace with a fiery blue stone. "Isn't it something? Oh, Lucas. Only you would bring me such a gift." She kissed it then made a running jump onto the bed and sat down against the headboard, stretching out her legs.

"It's like you haven't changed at all," Lucas said.

Bibi grinned up at him with perfect white teeth. "It's a joy to be eighteen again, and experience this avid hunger for life."

"By the two moons--I want the same thing." Throwing himself on to the bed, Lucas drew her close, and pressed his lips to her neck. "Your skin is unbelievably silky smooth," he murmured. "You never lost the glow of youth. Everything about you is so young."

"I seem young because I am," Cici said. "If you want to make love to her, the only way is through me. And I'm no bystander."

"We're definitely two in one," Bibi laughed. "Cici likes you, Lucas, otherwise we wouldn't be here."

"I'm crazy for the both of you," Lucas said. "You're driving me wild."

Bibi left Lucas tired in a wonderful way, as if they were a couple of kids who'd never left the *Seashell*. It was years since the "Once is Not Enough" club. His sensitivity was back, too. He felt things.

There was no doubt the time in the hospital tank had put him into full remission. But he remained a man in his fifties, with old age around the next corner. His chance for true salvation rested with the boy. As with Bibi, a successful merger would give him a second life.

CHAPTER 22

On his first day home, Lucas woke up early and stayed in bed for a while. The apartment was very quiet. It felt good to be out of hospital, but he wanted Tomi back. He found a dressing gown in the closet, and went out to say hello to Maude.

While delivering the weather report, which promised clear skies, the robot squeezed some orange juice and brewed a carafe of coffee.

Lucas picked up the phone. While connected, it lacked the encrypted Universal Post service he needed. He called up the company, and they agreed to send somebody over. Then he downed his orange juice and took a cup of coffee onto the balcony.

It was only seven, but Vancouver's port was already busy. Lucas watched a loaded grain ship leave, and two container ships come in. The spectacle stirred him deeply; he'd loved the freedom of the seas. His submersible might still be out there somewhere. The government took it after his conviction, and that was the last he heard about it.

The episode was still incredible to him. Deep down he did not see humans as much different from other life forms such as fish, birds, or butterflies, which crossed borders as if they did not exist. When armed bands of men conquered a piece of land, the first thing they did was establish boundaries, like dogs that peed around their territory. Force of arms backed up the theft; there was no real justice behind it.

He'd never regret using the *Seashell* to rescue people and bring them in. If not for him, Bibi and her family would all be dead. And look at the achievements they'd made here, extending the human lifespan at Grace

Hospital! To him one Bibi was worth all the slime sucking politicians and swelled up generals who ever lived. Not to mention the border guards, who strutted around like armed penguins and defined territories throughout the world.

Up on Mars, when he first heard about the United World States taking over, it raised hopes that universal justice might finally prevail. Then when the T-men arrived at Marsport, his illusions were soon shattered. The new administrators were no different from the old ones. If anything they were more efficient in levying their damn taxes.

Humans were meant to be free. But there was a never ending fight between ordinary people and the greedy, power hungry bastards who wanted to enslave them and keep them penned up. He'd fought that war all his life, because it was unavoidable. He remained at war today because of his loved ones trapped on Mars. It was despicable to see their movements regulated by the clowns here on Earth. There was no reason whatsoever why his people should be treated as less than fully human. Lucas vowed the day would come when all the Martians traveled freely between Earth and Mars, just like he'd done.

That morning around ten, two Universal Post men showed up with his new phone. Before activating it, they swept his place for bugs. "We can't be too sure," one of them said. "Encryption is not much use if everything you send and receive is being monitored here at home."

After they left he immediately tried to reach his varlet, but there was no answer. He left a message, asking Tomi to reply as soon as possible.

Next, he placed a call to his wife Lena. He knew she was worried about him and being able to report good news about his health was gratifying. Before he left Mars, they'd looked over the Grace Hospital brochure together and joked about his returning with a new body. After seeing Bibi, Lucas was convinced. "I might actually do this," he told Lena. "The ones who undergo the procedure seem happy."

His call to Rosie had a darker tone; she needed to know Tomi was stolen. Varlets had been broken before. Everything they'd worked for was in jeopardy until he got Tomi back.

In a little over half an hour Rosie replied from the office at work. She was very concerned about Tomi's loss and suggested he get help from their Earth-based contacts.

Lucas phoned back immediately. "Don't tell anyone, we can't show weakness to those people. I'll handle this myself."

He waited over an hour for Lena, but her return call never came. Assuming she must be out, he ordered a robocab to take him downtown.

It was clear and warm outside, and he sat in front with the window open. As they crossed the bridge from Needles Island, he told the cab to stop for a moment at the far end. Getting out, he looked over the side to the seawall and the rocks below. He'd fallen a long way; it was a miracle he was still alive.

A high-pitched voice came back to him strongly; Lucas relived the horror of lying helpless on the rock, with the fat man's perspiration raining onto his face. A black man with a green Mohawk had put a hand on Lucas's chest to feel for breathing. "Hold his finger, I'll cut it," said the man with the bad case of sunburn, and spiky blond hair. Lucas thought of the Can Dancer, too. That one moved with exceptional grace, his long black ringlets flowing.

Despite the evil they'd done to him, revenge was not a priority. Getting Tomi back was all that mattered; he'd pay a ransom and not even think twice.

As the cab left the bridge, Lucas began sending out his thought voice. "*Tomi are you there? Talk to me, old friend. Talk to me.*" Lucas's range was not far, but the varlet was very sensitive. If Tomi caught even a hint, he would respond.

The apartment blocks in this area housed one of the densest populations on Earth, and it seemed possible the gang might live close by. The cab went through slowly, but there was nothing from Tomi.

Going up the shop-lined Robson Street hill, they came to a main drag, Burrard Street. As they crossed over False Creek the wind came in strong from the water, buffeting the pedestrians and hard-driving cyclists, and Lucas glimpsed sail boats out on the bay. He continued south to Twelfth Avenue, and turned west.

They were heading toward the university area now. It wasn't long before the houses looked larger, and the private vehicles more expensive. When Lucas sighted a couple of T-men standing in a driveway, it was time to turn back. He couldn't picture the gang members living in this kind of neighborhood.

Speeding back the other way, the cab crossed Burrard Street and continued east past the hospital and biotech complex. Farther along, they came to other residential areas.

Some of the pedestrians struck Lucas as roughhewn, and this aroused his interest. He instructed the cab to go north along a narrow side street, and they came to blocks of houses that were boarded up. He'd never seen that in Vancouver.

"This place is not good," the cab said. "We must use caution."

"Keep going," Lucas said.

Despite the closed-down buildings, people were out on the street, drifting around like leaves. Lucas was reminded of his childhood back in Tacoma, when men and women without purpose or hope thronged some neighborhoods. This type of situation produced gangs, and Tomi might be nearby. Imprisonment in a Faraday cage would prevent him from sending or receiving messages.

Farther down the road, grass grew in the middle of the street, and children were out playing ball hockey. Lucas's vehicle drove up to one of their goals, a space between two rocks. The kids did not interrupt their game. After watching a while, Lucas told the cab to turn around.

They traveled north on a major route, Knight Street. Stuck behind a slow-moving truck convoy, the robocab told Lucas that unemployment in Vancouver was close to thirty percent. Despite the guaranteed income provided to citizens, sections of the city remained blighted. The information confirmed Lucas's worst suspicions. The United World States' pretensions were wildly exaggerated; the new regime was rotten at the core. Wealth and power gravitated to the T-man rulers, and ordinary people were screwed into the ground.

Lucas followed the big trucks to the waterfront area, where they spread out to the different container yards. His senses were on full alert. He remembered this part of the city as vigorous and vibrant; ships loaded day and night, and the bars and restaurants stayed open twenty-four hours to service the seamen and port workers. Lucas had worked on the docks at Tacoma while still a boy, and although his former contacts were dead or gone now, he always felt at home in this part of Vancouver.

He needed a short-term team to help locate the muggers and get Tomi back. The waterfront was the perfect place to find such people, people who did not mind tough jobs in rugged conditions if the pay was high.

His boy should be involved too. It was time for Dom to find out who he was. The school seemed a good safe place for a kid to grow up, but he had to join the real world eventually.

Spotting a familiar sign, EDMONDO's, he decided to have a drink and a bite to eat. He stopped the cab and paid it off with his new thumbnail chip.

It was getting dark when he returned home, and as he passed the lawn bowling green and the place where the gang jumped him, he felt a sense of dread. The punks might hang around here all the time, looking for more victims. He'd been easy pickings for them once, and if they saw him again he'd be a goner. Approaching Needles Island he kept his eyes open, but the area looked clear. When he got inside the building lobby, he felt safe; they had no way of knowing his address or apartment number.

Ascending in the elevator, he realized he'd made progress in his day outside. Going into Edmondo's was a good move. He didn't recognize anyone, but the main thing was showing he belonged.

When he entered the apartment, Maude greeted him warmly and poured a tall glass of Wild Grouse and water. The robot came into the bedroom with him and helped put his purchases away. He'd brought home two shopping bags full of new clothes.

When they went back to the living room the message display was blinking on the phone. It was not Tomi; this call had come from Mars.

His wife Lena sat upright in her favorite white armchair. Her tall, slim form was wrapped in a light blue robe, and her light brown hair was tied back in a loose bun, revealing a mobile, expressive face, devoid of makeup. "Lucas my love, it's a joy to hear from you," she said. "You look so well! Yes, I remember laughing at the thought of you returning in a new body. Believe me, I'm not laughing now. You are a great soul, capable of overcoming any obstacle. But I'm in love with your inner self, not your body. I don't care what body you return in, as long as you come back.

"Things are going well here in Marsport. The community is coming together for our arts center project. As you know, I'm on the board. The new facility will be a place where artists of all types can work together. We're blessed with a lot of talent here, and I'm looking forward to seeing a real surge in growth once we get this set up.

"Well, I don't have much more to say. I love you Lucas, and always will. I look forward to having you back home soon."

Lucas watched Lena's message several times, letting her voice fill him. When he went to sleep it was as if he were safely back at home and she still held him in her arms.

CHAPTER 23

Lucas did not spend much time resting up after leaving the hospital. He had many things to do, and plunged right in. Meeting with me was high on the list.

He called me Monday evening after I returned from Allison Farms. I was not enthusiastic about seeing him, but did not see any way out of it. Incapable of gratitude, I at least had to show respect. He'd given me a good education; to this extent he'd done his duty. Could I do less? Another factor was that after seeing him in the hospital, I thought about him a lot. He was the only family member I'd encountered, and for good or bad I needed to find out more about him.

Edmondo's, the place where Lucas and I were to meet, was close to the docks where ocean ships came in loaded with goods. Above the restaurant a stripper bar was blaring music. As I approached the entrance, a couple of aging townies in brown military fatigues looked me over. The one in front was tall and gaunt with shoulder-length black hair, and a thin moustache that drooped past the corners of his mouth. His partner was compact, and had neatly trimmed light brown hair. "Want to get high?" the long haired man asked in a low, hoarse voice.

I shook my head, and went down some stairs that smelled of urine.

On the next level was a dark, cavernous restaurant, most of its tables taken. Lucas waved to me languidly from a booth across the room. He was wearing a white suit with a pink carnation in his lapel, and had on a wide-brimmed hat. Despite his incongruous appearance I had the same unsettling impression as when he was in the tank, that he was another version of me. I slid onto the padded seat across from him.

He sat forward, his green eyes burning. "Look, Dom. I saw on the news how you attacked those outlaws, and it scared the life out of me."

"It wasn't planned," I said. "The situation came up, and we reacted as we've been trained."

"Learn to use your brains, not just act like some robot." Removing his hat he tossed it to the edge of the table and rubbed his head. Reddish stubble was growing on his scalp, and I knew it must be itchy. "Men die so easily; their lives are gone in a flash. It was none of your business anyway, you shouldn't have interfered."

Then his whole being seemed to relax and he smiled. "I'm happy to see you. All those years on Mars--I can't tell you how often I've looked into the night sky and thought of you. My prayers were always with you, even if I couldn't be here." He took my hands in his. "I must say, you look good. That uniform suits you. I'm proud of you."

An older man wearing a black suit and red tie came by with a tray and gave us some coffee and ice water. "What looks good today, Joe?" Lucas asked.

"We've got sole, also live crab."

"We'll have the sole. And clam chowder." He glanced at me. "Okay with you?"

His manner was irritating, but I only shrugged. "It sounds fine."

"Ah, what a day," he sighed, sitting back and throwing an arm along the top of the booth. "I spent a whole hour this morning, just watching the waves roll in and the clouds drift by. By the two moons--much as I love Mars, and the life up there, there's nothing like Mother Earth."

Joe came back to our table and put out bowls of soup and covered plates. Lucas broke some crackers into his soup, and I did the same. "It's good to be with you, after all those years," Lucas said. "Has the shock worn off?"

"The shock?"

He smiled knowingly. "I knew it would be difficult when you found out your secret benefactor was a convict."

This was the first time we'd spoken, yet he saw to my very core. I glanced around to make sure no one could overhear us. "No matter what your crime, you paid a terrible price."

"There was no crime in any real sense. It's the same for lots of transports; they run afoul of ill-conceived, unjust laws made up by idiots."

It seemed useless to argue. "I wonder where they farmed the sole."

"Farmed?" he asked. "This is real fish, from the depths of the ocean. They charge a fortune, but it's worth it."

"So the lunch was poached. How could I be so stupid?" When I lifted the cover from my plate, the tantalizing aroma reminded me of Dorothy's rock cod in Cedar River. One day all the oceans would be brought back. I began to eat. "In answer to your question, yes the initial shock's worn off. I must say, though, you're a different kind of person."

"They transported me before the conquest. I never lived under your Nanny state." He stirred sugar into his coffee. "My way of looking at things was formed by long experience. Wisdom grows over the years." Then he frowned. "When those punks beat me up they stole my varlet and my casting ring. I need to get them back."

"Have you spoken to the police? Well, probably not."

"I had connections in the old days, but not today."

"Pawn shops, or second hand stores?"

"Hmm," Lucas said with a smile. "I'm not sure they're dumb enough to pawn stolen goods, but you never know. We're in the right neighborhood to find them."

As we left the restaurant, the townies were still in the doorway of the upstairs bar. "Want to get high?" the long-haired one asked again, raising his arm. He seemed rusty, like a machine left too long in the rain.

Lucas paused. "What have you got?"

"They're military issue," the shorter one said, staring at us with glazed, pale blue eyes. "Warrior Ace gets you fully awake and ready to do battle. Valhalla is to celebrate your success."

"Have you used it yourself?"

"Many times. We're retired soldiers, who served the United World States for years. We don't usually sell our drugs, but it's a long wait for the pension."

"I'll buy some on one condition," Lucas said. "You take a break and have some lunch. The food downstairs is very good."

The soldiers laughed, and we shook hands. The long-haired one said his name was Bear Claw; his partner, an Inuit, was Curtis.

Bear Claw took a couple of packets from his pocket. "The base price is a hundred each."

Lucas counted out ten twenties, and added two more for their lunch. "There's better work than this for military men. Maybe we can talk business later on?"

"We're open," Bear Claw said, handing him a card.

Lucas started down the street; I accompanied him in morose silence. "I've never tried Warrior Ace before, have you?" he asked.

"The day I need drugs to wake up, it'll be time to take off this uniform."

Lucas laughed. "That school must keep you fairly keyed up."

"How could you think of taking that stuff? Military issue! For all you know it's mixed with rat poison."

"They'd lose a lot of customers that way," Lucas said, glancing in a window where open drums of ice cream were on display. Suddenly he stopped. "You're looking fine," he said to two women coming toward us.

I moved to the side, as they cooed over him. Their skirts, too short for their long legs, and the low-cut tops that barely covered their extensive bosoms, left little doubt as to their occupation. Lucas seemed pleased by their attentions, and promised to get in touch.

"Syphilis is making a comeback," I said as we walked away. "Open sores, and pustules. It's really gross."

"It must be risky for the younger crowd. I like the look of those two ladies, though. And that scent! Tiger lily is my guess." Then he pointed across the street. "Look, a pawn shop."

We looked through three pawn shops before finding the ring. Musical instruments, household utensils, sporting goods, tools, and jewelry were all on sale.

I'd almost given up hope when we spotted a shop called

ANTIQUES & CURIOSITIES

The ring was in the front window, placed between a trumpet and an ancient rifle with an attached bayonet. The door made a tinkling sound as we went inside. Lucas beckoned to the short, white-haired man behind the counter. "The ring in the window," he said. "I believe it's mine."

"I paid fair value for it, and at present it's my property," the shopkeeper said, getting up. "We'll have a look."

"There'll be two moons inscribed on the inside."

The man removed the ring from the window space and examined it with a jeweler's glass. "It might be the one."

"Don't worry, if it's mine I'll give you back whatever you paid." Lucas held it up to the light and immediately pressed it to his lips. "This makes me very happy," he said with a chuckle, slipping it on his finger. Taking a card from a stack on the counter, he handed me one. "Stand here, and hold this up." He moved back to the doorway. With no further warning, he snatched the card from my hand. I hardly felt it go.

"The spaceman's ring," the shopkeeper said. "You shoot an almost invisible thread, that's strong enough to bear your weight. I paid two hundred units for it."

Lucas drew me aside. "Let's split up now," he said quietly. "I've got more business, and I know you're busy too."

The abrupt way he dismissed me was insulting, and I left the shop without a word, closing the door quietly behind me. The bus to take me back to the school stopped a couple of blocks away. Walking up there was wasted time, as was the bus trip. The more I thought about it, the more irritated I got.

The years on Mars had clearly done little for the old man's rehabilitation. Even in decline, he showed an alarming taste for drugs, whores, and poached game. I'd never met anyone with so little respect for the law. If word leaked out that he was my sponsor, my career would be ruined. Luckily he showed no interest in making things public.

The shopkeeper closed the shade on the door and led Lucas to a back office, where he accepted two hundred and fifty units for the ring.

"I only saw the robbers briefly, on a dark night," Lucas said. "One had spiky blond hair, the second was a black man with a Mohawk. The third was quite heavy, and wore a red sweatband."

The shopkeeper held up three fingers, and watched as Lucas put the money on the table. "One of the men who gave me the ring had blond spiky hair. The other was fat, and wore a sweat band. They were here before, and another customer referred to them as Beach Lords. They left an address, but it's not likely to be correct."

"Was the ring all they had to sell? They took my varlet too. A little octopod."

The shopkeeper raised an eyebrow. "An interesting item, perhaps too much for my shop. There was no mention of it."

Lucas nodded, and put another two hundred units on the table. "I'm new in town and need something for self-defense, but there's no need for useless paperwork. Can you sell me a weapon?"

"It seems wise, under the circumstances." Swiveling around in his chair, the shopkeeper pulled out a shelf on the wall behind him, revealing an array of guns on a floor of black velvet. "The boop gun is my most popular weapon these days. Even a hit to a limb will cause incapacitating pain."

"Let me see that pistol," Lucas said, pointing.

Leaving the shop with the casting ring on his finger, and a Smith & Wesson in a shoulder holster, Lucas felt like his old self. Even better, he'd met prospects for his team. The two prostitutes struck him as real possibilities. They seemed intelligent and were sure to hear things out on the street. Obviously in need of money, they'd sell whatever information they had. He planned to talk more with them.

Dom's idea about the pawn shop was a good one, but their brief meeting was enough to cut him from the team. His whole being radiated space cadet; he did not belong in Edmondo's or even this part of town.

Their encounter with the two drug dealers struck Lucas as highly for-
tuitous. The Beach Lords were a mean, nasty bunch, and he'd need backup
when he dealt with them.

When he arrived at Edmondo's the soldiers were finishing lunch, and
they greeted him like old friends. He slid into the booth beside Curtis. Joe
the waiter came over, and they ordered a round of drinks.

"My job involves a delicate situation," Lucas told them.

"What do you mean?" Bear Claw asked.

"The other night I was walking through Stanley Park and some mutant perverts jumped me. They stuffed me in a trash can, and threw it off
the Needles Island Bridge. Then they robbed me and left me for dead."

"That's ugly," Curtis said. "Did you contact the police?"

Lucas shook his head. "What's happening with you two?"

"We fought twelve years for the UWS," Curtis said. "Now they've
downsized the forces."

"We're headed down to Patagonia, picking up jobs along the way,"
Bear Claw said. "You might call us soldiers of fortune."

"What they stole that night is very precious to me," Lucas said. "The
last thing I want is trouble. Likely they'll want a ransom, and I'm willing
to negotiate. But I need someone on my side, backing me up." He signaled
to Joe for another round. "I'll pay well for your support, and start things
off with a decent retainer fee in advance." The soldiers smiled and nodded.
"Are you armed?" Lucas asked them.

They laughed. "We have more firepower than your local gangsters
would imagine," Bear Claw said.

"What did they steal?" Curtis asked.

"A little octopod. My varlet, and my best friend. I've called and called
but there's no reply. Likely he's trapped in a Faraday cage, unable to trans-
mit or receive."

CHAPTER 24

In May the seniors underwent their final transformation; the thought transmitters were set into their skulls, and activated. After lunch on Wednesday a group of us middies sat talking in the cafeteria when five of them came in, all wearing white skull caps to cover the dressings. Although their gestures implied communication, not a word was spoken.

It gave me an eerie feeling, and the other middies were impressed, too. "Full telepaths," Zack said. "It's something, isn't it?"

Up in my room, I'd put the telecap on for a music intake when Plenso entered my mind. *"Hello there, Dom. This is a real awakening for me. I've met so many amazing people all over the world. For the first time in my life I'm free."*

Cooper appeared beside him, his dark eyes ablaze with excitement. "Come on," he cried to Plenso. "They're waiting for us."

"I'll talk to you soon, Dom," Plenso said. Then he was gone.

It was a thrill to see them go flying around the world in thought. There was sadness too in being left behind; for the first time since entering the school I felt real doubt about my ability to succeed.

I hadn't talked with Astra since Monday. When I contacted her room, she was working at her desk, and seemed to hardly recognize me. Breaking in on her concentration made me feel terrible. "Sorry for interrupting," I said.

"No, I'm glad to hear from you," she said, sitting up. "What's going on?"

"Oh, nothing much. It's a little depressing to watch the seniors take flight, when I'm such a groundling."

She smiled into my eyes. "Telepathy is not a strong point with me either, and I'm counting on your help. Have you forgotten about you and I going together for our senior year?"

"Of course not. I'm with you all the way."

"Let's hope so. I had to get an extension for my physics project, and it'll take all weekend to finish. After that, we can get down to serious stuff."

The graduation ceremony was held early Friday afternoon in the domed assembly hall at the center of the STA complex. Everyone attended. It was one of the few times our five schools got together, and it was impressive to see all twelve hundred cadets in dress uniform, sitting in rows in the hall.

Up on the stage were dignitaries in loose white robes, the ceremonial dress of the T-men. The five principals were all there, including Mr. Rossiter. Dr. Sumner, president of our parent school, UBC, sat in the center. He wore a black headband, signifying he was a commander, the highest rank in the T-man hierarchy. STA's controller, Vince Lalonde, was in the back.

Vince Lalonde spoke first, and was greeted with warm applause. An accountant, Mr. Lalonde had served for several years at Marsport, overseeing the taxation of exports and imports. "Welcome to our graduation day," he said. While his voice seemed diffident, it easily reached throughout the hall. "This spring we've got a highly successful senior class, an eighty-four percent success rate. That's as good as it gets. To each of you, our congratulations. Today you enter the fellowship of the T-men, and, from now on, you'll find yourselves in demand. Many of you will now move into the public service, either in space or here on Earth. Others will continue with higher education before taking a job. Whatever path you decide to take, the admittance you gain today almost guarantees your future success. Once again, congratulations."

Dr. Sumner came forward next. Tall and lean, with a long white mane, he had a presence that while amiable, commanded our total attention. "As some of you may know, I'm a biologist by trade. There was never any expectation I'd become the president of a university. It's surprising how many of us have that in common. We planned careers in science, engineering, or technology, not in administration or government.

"While outlining this talk I did a thought program, and looked back to different historical periods. Do you know how unusual it was for someone like me to play any part in government? It rarely happened. Throughout most of history, power went to men who dominated through force of arms. When fortunate, artists and intellectuals found patrons amongst the kings and nobles. Even after the industrial revolution and the rise of the great democracies, scientists played little part in public life.

"Today's technocracy did not arise because scientists lusted to take power; we were forced to take control because of a total collapse in the world's environment. Luckily there'd been a huge step forward in artificial intelligence with the Great One, Raina, as humans alone were not capable of dealing with the situation.

"By this time technologies in many fields, including the military, had advanced to the point where we were the only ones who understood how things worked. Throughout the world, the transformed ones talked things over in their private language of thought. When we made our move it was swift, lethal, and effective. And today we remain in full control.

"It's ironic, really, considering that we never wanted that. Our love is still to the truth, and to efficiency, and to the larger good. I ask you today, in this congratulatory moment, to keep things in perspective and never lose your common sense.

"Never forget, the geniuses of the past were not transformed. Just think of Sir Isaac Newton, or Benjamin Franklin, or Albert Einstein. While we try to bring the world's best and the brightest into our ranks, it does not always happen.

"The situation of being in power must not lead us to become blind or arrogant. Power is seductive, and the ever-present menace is that power corrupts. I ask you today, always be vigilant. Never cease to guard against this evil.

"The old people's desire for growth was so extreme as to become malignant. Funneled off-world, this drive can be highly positive. While here on Earth we're now committed to healing and sustainability, off-world growth is accepted as one of our main hopes. The colonies are important generators of new sources of wealth.

"In the outer solar system, taking big risks for the chance of huge rewards is something we admire. Some have succeeded. Some succeed often. Despite our differences, we T-men do not shun them. They need us, and we need them.

"STA grads sometimes find themselves in frontier situations, which appear the antithesis of today's Earth. It's difficult, but remember you are not going alone. You have access to a vast resource center, allowing you access to any expert on any subject you want.

"Think of us, and we will be there."

Vince Lalonde came back out to call the roll, and one by one the seniors came up on stage and were embraced by the T-men. We clapped hard for every one of them. They'd toughed it out over a long, rough road to get there.

That evening I worked late with the telecap, and shortly after twelve Plenso appeared in my mind again. I'd never seen him so pale and agitated.

"Dom, this is an amazing day. I've learned so much. And I've fallen in love."

"I'm delighted to hear that," I replied.

The image he sent then was of a dark-haired woman who looked to be in her late twenties. Slim and graceful, she wore a full-length white robe and a diamond tiara. Her large eyes were expressive of endless compassion; her full lips seemed sensuous.

Stunned, I could only ask, "Is this Raina?"

"In truth. I'll serve her all my life and afterwards I'll be with her forever."

I heard strong winds and saw a mountain meadow with jagged peaks in the background. It seemed like the Himalayas, although I couldn't tell for sure. The meadow was blanketed with high grass and white and yellow flowers, and the wind that rippled through it had a music.

Plenso and Raina danced there, hand in hand. The choreography looked quite advanced but judging from Plenso's enraptured look, I reckoned he'd got the hang of it.

The vision lasted only a minute or so and Plenso was gone. In our two years together this was the deepest I'd seen into him. There seemed little doubt that what he'd said was true, and he was sworn to her forever.

CHAPTER 25

It was Saturday afternoon. Stretched out on his living room couch, Lucas watched a news program that showed the West Coast congressman, Kenny Summers, inspect a state-run Seattle nursery. This part of the nursery was all windows; the sun shone on a long, narrow wading pool where women dipped their offspring. Apparently the young mothers still found Kenny attractive; they were all smiles, holding up their babies to be kissed. "Enjoy it while it lasts," Lucas murmured to Kenny. "I'm coming for you."

The bell sounded at the door and he let in the two streetwalkers. They'd toned down their appearance since he met them. Gone were the exaggerated breasts and ultra-short skirts; they now wore slacks and pullovers. Also missing was the heavy scent that reminded him of tiger lilies.

The blonde, Sasha, kicked off her shoes and dropped two inches or so in height. "I love your place," she said in a strong Slavic accent. "Thanks for having us up."

"Here's a present," Monique said, handing him a slender box wrapped in white. Her straight black hair was tied back, revealing a pale, youthful face with direct dark eyes. Her wide mouth was accentuated with dark red lipstick.

"Thanks, I like presents," Lucas said.

He led them into the living room, where the video now showed a big parade, with a marching band. The people lining the streets roared appreciation for the center float, which carried five young women in brown uniforms, dancing amidst masses of flowers. "Have one for the state," the women chanted, in time with the music.

"Carnival time starts tomorrow," Sasha said, sitting on the couch beside Monique.

Lucas turned off the video. "Would you like some wine?"

"Something on the sweet side goes well with the Sinful Delights," Monique said.

"Oh, really?' Lucas opened the narrow box and tried one of the soft dark chocolates. "Mm, cherries." He told Maude to bring in some tawny port, and had another chocolate. "Are you looking forward to carnival?"

"Hopefully we'll see some of the races," Monique said. "I enjoy that."

"I'll want you both for the week," Lucas said.

The women looked at each other. "Carnival's our busy time," Sasha said.

"You'll be much better off with me," Lucas said. "I'll take you to those track and field events, and whatever else is available." He produced a wad of bills from the pocket of his dressing gown. "Let's start off with an advance."

When Monique went to the washroom he moved next to Sasha. "I'm feeling strongly about you."

She put a hand on his knee. "You've already had two chocolates. Usually one's enough."

"One for each woman," Lucas said. "Come on, I'll show you the bedroom."

Later, reclining between the two of them on the large bed, Lucas felt at ease with the world. His wife loved women too, and the honesty with which Monique and Sasha showed their feelings for each other was delightful to him.

He sat up, and leaned back against the headboard. "There's some advantage to being an older man," he mused. "While younger men are godlike in their powers, they often can't appreciate a woman for who she really is. Sasha, you're perfect in every way, beautiful to the core. Monique, you're a being of pure loveliness. I'm grateful to you both."

"I've been in love with Sasha ever since we met," Monique said. "The killer nurse from Tomsk--she's not only divine, she's a real celebrity."

"Tell me," Lucas said. "Are you really from Tomsk?"

"My first job was there," Sasha said. "Alone in the city, I went out a few times with a young doctor from the same hospital. It seemed all right at first, he was on the shy side but good looking and interesting to talk to. The main difference was that he was a T-man, as were all the higher-ups at that hospital. His friends had their own way of communicating that left me out. The relationship ended over comments from these others, obscure jokes and references that made me realize he'd shared our most intimate moments. I could not stand to see him after that."

"Understandable," Lucas said. "What assholes."

"For him a relationship still existed," Sasha said. "He sent notes swearing eternal love, while at work his black looks spoke of resentment and anger. One day, the head of the department called me in. She said I'd ruined this man's life. By then I loathed the sight of him."

"Is that how you got your name?"

"I got my name over a mix-up with the medications that caused the death of forty-two patients. One of my jobs was to give out the pills, and they pinned the accident on me. It was nonsense. Everything was automated and color-coded, so it was impossible to get confused. The mistake happened back in China, when they were mixing ingredients, and putting the pills into the containers. The Chinese administrators were T-men too, and they worked with my bosses to cover things up. That's how I achieved infamy, reviled all over Russia."

"People like you often get sent to Mars," Lucas said.

"The nurses union had the charges thrown out, but by that time I'd lost my job and was labeled a troublemaker."

"I'm on your side," Lucas said. "The Tees are another form of tyranny, and it's right to stand up against them. What are your plans? Are you going to stay in the sex worker profession?"

"There's no future in this," Sasha said. "We want to open a clothing shop in Europe."

"I can help you get there," Lucas said. "When I hired you, it was not only for your looks. I need to find the ones that beat me and left me for dead. Have you heard of the Beach Lords?"

"Yes, we've encountered those abusers," Sasha said.

"The only one who still goes with them is Ellie," Monique said. "She has no self-esteem."

Tremendously pleased, Lucas brought them back to the living room, where Maude served coffee and cinnamon rolls. "Who are these Beach Lords?" Lucas asked.

"Nobody, really," Monique said. "Or, very ordinary men who work at ordinary jobs and gather to make trouble at sporting events, or get drunk on weekends and beat people up. The only one of distinction is Jeffrey."

"The famous Jeffrey," Sasha said. "He achieved the dream of all Beach Lords and solved the Super Eighty." Seeing Lucas's questioning look, she laughed. "Jeffrey picked the winners of eighty sporting events all over North America and became an instant multi-millionaire."

"Is he fat?"

"Disgustingly obese," Sasha said. "With his money, it's inexcusable."

Monique had Ellie on the phone: a slip of a girl with straight sandy hair, a coral nose ring and three silvery studs in her lower lip. Lucas knew her from the night the Beach Lords attacked him. She'd been in the garbage container before him. "What's up?" Ellie asked in a flat Australian drawl.

"It's your lucky day," Monique said. "Sasha and I are here in the Needles, and a man wants to meet you."

"Everybody's going to Jeffrey's to see the pictures," Ellie said. "Awesome scenes of space and Mars. Scary killings, sex--"

"Come here first, as soon as you can. He's an older gentleman, and very generous." The screen went blank and Lucas, horrified, sank into his chair and closed his eyes. The thought of them accessing Tomi's information made him feel weak and sick. His worst fears were realized, but he had to stay calm and handle things properly. "This changes things," he said finally. "These Beach Lords threaten my loved ones and everything I hold dear. I need to get those pictures back."

"Monique and I don't want serious trouble," Sasha said. "You should call the police."

"I'd rather hurt myself than see an injury come to you two," Lucas replied. "The police are out. As a retired businessman with a lot of experience, I'll do a better job than the authorities in this situation. My problem is I need a temporary team. I like you both, so let's raise the stakes. The main difference is the large upside in your pay. Work with me, and by the end of the week you'll have your shop in Europe."

Sarah stared at him, her eyes intent. "Do you know how much a shop like that costs? Half a million units, at least."

Lucas held her gaze. "This is the real deal," he said firmly. "You're saying two hundred and fifty thousand each. I've seen that much on the turn of a card. So go ahead, it's yours for the taking. In return I ask for your silence forever. At the end of the week, you leave Vancouver and never return."

"Let's talk about this," Monique broke in, taking Sasha's hands. She smiled at Lucas and led her friend into the bedroom. There was laughter and some sobbing. After a few minutes, they came back out. "We'll do it," Monique said.

"I couldn't ask for better partners. Do you think Ellie might join us? With that kind of money she can go where she wants."

"Maybe," Monique said. "She's different, so it's hard to say."

"She has to understand," Sasha said.

Ellie arrived wearing a short yellow dress, with large brown buttons down the front, and a matching sunhat. "Nice place," she said. Monique brought her into the living room where Lucas waited in his arm chair. "Is this my man?" Ellie asked with a grin. Then she froze. "No," she moaned, looking to Sasha and Monique.

"There's nothing to fear," Sasha said softly.

"Take off that hat," Lucas said. "It's you, isn't it?"

"It's true I was there," she said. "But I'd never do you any harm. It's not my nature to hurt anyone."

"I know that. Like me, you were a victim. And now there's a chance to turn your life around." He turned to Sasha. "Can you talk with her?"

The women went into the bedroom for a long time. When they came out Ellie threw her arms around Lucas. "It's like a fairy tale. Thank you so much."

Lucas tousled her hair. "Welcome to the team."

Monique gave Ellie a big hug. "You're a true friend, and I'm glad you're with us. When we're over in Europe, Sasha and I will take you out and choose a new wardrobe. Afterward we'll go to some fancy restaurant, and let them pamper us. Ellie, you'll be a princess. Stay with us over there or go home to Australia. You'll be a well-off lady, whatever you do."

Leaning back in his arm chair, Lucas watched them without expression. "Ladies, here's our plan for the evening."

By eleven that night, fog had blanketed the city. Lucas's long black van cruised slowly down a dark, misty street, and paused at the bottom of Jeffrey's driveway. The property was cut off from its neighbors by a high fence. A faint glow came from the lights of the house at the top of the rise.

They'd turned off the robot driver, and Bear Claw was behind the wheel, with Lucas beside him in the front seat, and Curtis sitting behind. Wearing orange coveralls and light gray gloves, they looked like a crew of movers.

Ellie was still inside the house, and Lucas was getting edgy. The girl's instructions were simple and clear: stay until the guests arrived, mark them, and leave. They'd fixed nanocloud patches on the back of her hands; all she had to do was scratch. The invisible gas would identify anyone present for hours.

There were only two ways to leave Jeffrey's house. Sasha was stationed on the street in front of the driveway; Monique was in back, in the alley. Both women had their robocabs in turtle mode so nobody could see in. Their job was to use the special Rad glasses to watch for people marked by Ellie and photograph them.

Their van continued on and turned right, up the hill. "I fought for the United World States and the NAN most of my life," Curtis said. "Now I'm working for a Martian."

"Money's money, Juice," Bear Claw laughed. "The bonus will get us down to Patagonia."

They went down the alley toward the back of Jeffrey's house. "How did you get the name Juice?" Lucas asked the Inuit.

"He earned that name," Bear Claw said. "Back in the old days, some of the settlers couldn't knuckle under to the world government; they remained loyal to the NAF. Our job was to put them down, and we'd go through their towns with huge machines. In the morning the cleanup crews went in, and Curtis's work reminded them of squashed tomatoes. Flattened houses and a lot of red seeping out. Some say it's his German grandfather that makes him so efficient."

"I never did like the settlers," Curtis said. "Before the big warm-up, that land was ours."

"Blubbering again, blubbering again," Bear Claw said. "After the warm-up the Northlands became desirable real estate."

A bell tinkled and Sasha appeared on the phone. "Someone's coming," she said. "He's glowing green."

"Two more greenies coming my way," Monique said.

"Good work," Lucas said. "Take some pictures."

"What happened to the girl?" Bear Claw asked.

"She might have switched sides," Lucas said. "Put on your Rad glasses, we need to pick up the three who left." They exited the alley, and went back to the main street. At the end of the block was a pedestrian who glowed green.

Bear Claw stopped the van ahead of the pedestrian. Lucas, Bear Claw and Curtis got out and opened the van's back door. The man striding down the sidewalk towards them had long, thin arms and legs, and looked to be about six and a half feet tall. Bear Claw shot him as he went by. They caught him while he was still upright and bundled him into the back of the van where they'd placed a tarp.

When they returned to the alley, the other targets were out of sight. "Did you see which way they went?" Lucas asked Monique.

"It's hard to tell much in this fog, but they headed west, and I think they went as far as the next street."

Pausing at the corner, Bear Claw nosed the van into the street, straining to see. "Try going left up the hill," Lucas said. No other vehicles were around, and they sped almost blind through the mist. Spotting a green glow on the right, Bear Claw slowed down.

Both the walkers wore shorts and sweat shirts. As the van pulled closer, Lucas recognized the first man's long black ringlets. He moved with easy grace, in contrast to the spiky-haired blond man strutting beside him. Lucas was ecstatic; he had the Can Dancer and the Finger Cutter both at once! Reaching back, he opened the van's side door. Curtis turned his ray gun on the two Beach Lords.

The bodies were heavy, and by the time they shoved them in the back with the first one, Lucas was breathing hard. "I'm not getting any younger," he muttered as they drove off.

"Next time leave the lifting to us," Bear Claw said.

Curtis guffawed. "Take the rest of the night off."

Driving back down the hill, they stopped beside a vacant lot to put on their hazard suits. Curtis handed Lucas a Warrior Ace pill. "Bear Claw and I will do the killing. You find that varlet of yours."

After swallowing his pill, Lucas held up his fist. "For Mars!"

The soldiers touched their fists to his. "It's righteous and I like it," Curtis said.

The fog was even thicker now, reflecting back the glare from their headlights. As Bear Claw drove up the driveway to Jeffrey's place, he turned the lights off.

They knew from Ellie that the Beach Lords had a gym in the basement. On the main floor was a big living room, with music and video equipment. The bedrooms were upstairs.

"We'll fire gas shells into all three levels," Bear Claw said. "The gas kills on contact, so keep your hazard suit on. Once we're in, Curtis will check the main floor and make sure everyone's dead. After that we'll do the basement, and then the upstairs. You should stay outside until we've cleaned the place."

Lucas could feel the battle drug working to heighten and clarify his concentration. He imagined if someone shot an arrow at him he'd see it coming and pluck it out of the air. "I'm comfortable inside," he said. "I have my pistol."

"It's best you stay and watch the door for a while," Curtis said. "You never know with gas, somebody might survive."

"Good point," Lucas said. "Once we're sure, I'll go and find my varlet."

As the van neared the house, they saw four or five men outside on the dark steps, passing around a lighted smoke. The van slowed, and the left side door slid open. Curtis's ray gun played over them, and they curled spasmodically like ants on a log thrust into a bonfire.

Bear Claw stepped outside with a fat-barreled gas gun. The house windows shattered as the gun coughed over and over. He shoved the gas gun back inside the van. "We're going in." The two soldiers rushed the house.

Lucas stayed in the front seat of the van, his ears straining and the pistol ready. All was quiet. He got out, and went over to the bodies lying on the steps. He checked for signs of life, and found nothing. On the top step sprawled against the wall was the black man with the green Mohawk. Lucas could still remember the man's mint-scented breath in his face as he lay paralyzed on the seawall. This one would never rob another elder.

"Master, is it you?" Tomi called faintly. "Please help, I'm badly hurt."

"I'll be right there."

Lucas could wait no longer. If anyone else left, Monique and Sasha would spot them and let him know.

Entering the house, he passed through a short hallway and into the living room. Corpses were everywhere here.

The place had a lot of video equipment, and screens on the wall played scenes from Lucas's past life. There he was on the dock of the Marsport space station, with a couple of huge freighters alongside. Another screen showed him down on Mars, the space elevator in the distance rising into the sky. Still another view was of Lucas at home in his apartment, relaxing on the couch while his wife Lena played music in the background.

"Is this a dagger which I see before me, the handle toward my hand?" Tomi cried. *"Come, let me clutch thee:--"*

"We'll need more than a dagger tonight," Lucas said grimly.

Hurried footsteps sounded in the hallway. "Going downstairs," Bear Claw called.

"Got you," Lucas replied.

At the back of the living room was a wire mesh cage, its door ajar, with two more bodies just inside. Lucas approached and gaped in disbelief. A high table held an illuminated glass container; Tomi rested on a ledge in the center, encircled by a grid of colored light which danced and blinked all around. The octopod was cut in two. Several arms also had parts missing. *"My dear Tomi. What have they done?"*

"They did and did, sliced and diced. Sushi for Jeffrey, they said."

"The damn, wicked butchers." His gaze followed the dancing lights up glass rods to a metallic disc. *"Where are your missing parts?"*

"Somewhere close by. They call to me constantly."

Lucas opened the table drawers and found a small box with slices of Tomi's arms. He put the box in his pocket. *"I'll have you back together, I promise you that."*

"I have thee not, and yet I see thee still," Tomi intoned. *"Art thou not, fatal vision, sensible to feeling as to sight?"*

"All Marsport went to see MacBeth that week," Lucas said. *"We put on a damn good show."* There was a power box outside the cage against the wall. Lucas pushed the button and the dancing lights went out. Taking the top off Tomi's container, he put it on the floor and took hold of the octopod's body.

"Be careful," Tomi said. *"The probes went deep inside me."*

Lucas lifted Tomi's nearest half straight up, freeing it from an array of metallic bristles. "We're going upstairs," Bear Claw called from the living room door.

"Was Ellie down in the basement?" Lucas asked.

"No women so far."

Lucas knew she must be dead, but there was nothing he could do about it. He freed the octopod's other part, and put both pieces in his pocket with the box. Then he took the disc down. *"Are there any more of these?"*

"Not as far as I know," Tomi said.

Shaking in anger and disgust, Lucas used a chair to smash the glass rods, and the container they'd used to hold Tomi. Nothing else was breakable, so he pushed over the table. Feeling somewhat calmed, he went upstairs to join the soldiers.

The first bedroom Lucas came to was quite spacious. The bed was at the end, partly curtained off. Jeffrey was on a recliner, in front of a large video screen that still played the Martian pictures. He was wearing only shorts, and his mass of white flesh was suggestive of a giant fungus. Two more dead men were on the couch.

Bear Claw shouted from the second bedroom, and Lucas joined him. Ellie was there, her arms around a tall, skinny man with long brown hair. She looked peaceful and happy, as if she'd only fallen asleep.

Opening a closet, Bear Claw showed Lucas some martial arts gear on the inside of the door. He grabbed a throwing star and held it ready. "Wicked." Next he brought out a black belt that had a wide buckle with a red spider embossed on the front.

"That's a gang sign," Lucas said, taking the belt. He removed the center part of the buckle and pushed the spider with his thumb so it shot out a slim, glass-like blade. Grabbing a cushion from the bed, he threw it high and sliced it as it fell. He handed the belt back to Bear Claw. "No souvenirs, it's too risky."

"Yes, sir," Bear Claw said, reassembling the buckle.

"I checked everywhere, nobody's alive," Curtis said from the doorway. "I'm going out to the van for the fire accelerant." Lucas followed him downstairs.

Using a tubular dispenser, Lucas helped spread the clear gel throughout the house. "Even the metal has to burn." Afterward they returned to the van, and opened the hoods on the hazard suits. Lucas got Sasha and Monique on the phone. "It's over, you can leave," he said. "I'll see you at the meeting place."

"It's Valhalla time," Bear Claw said, breaking a capsule under Lucas's nose.

There was a shock of extreme pleasure; Lucas was filled with elation and the glow of triumph. "Yes we did it," he cried. "Good job, good job."

Bear Claw backed the van up to the front steps. Curtis opened the back door and pulled out the Can Dancer. He and Bear Claw dragged the corpse over to the other bodies.

Glad to let them do the heavy lifting, Lucas leaned against the back of the van and watched. To his surprise, Bear Claw had the Asian gang belt fastened around his waist. "I told you to leave that upstairs."

Bear Claw grinned. "I never thought you meant it seriously." He shot the blade out and showed it to Curtis. "Isn't it something?"

"We killed a lot of people for you tonight," Curtis told Lucas. "Don't screw us around."

The soldiers were icy cold; he was the one who'd gone wrong. Not wanting things to spiral out of control, Lucas held up his hands. "Gentlemen, don't misunderstand me. You've done a fine job and I think the world of you. To prove it I'll throw in a bonus. Fifty thousand more, which makes two hundred thousand for each of you. Will that make things right?"

The soldiers laughed. "That should do it," Curtis said.

When they came for the Finger Cutter's body, Bear Claw lifted Lucas's pistol from the holster and stuck it in his new gang belt. "No disrespect sir, but I'm going to keep hold of this till we get paid."

Lucas felt like he'd been kicked in the gut. Taking his gun was unforgivable. He shoved the third man's long, skinny legs aside and sat down in the end of the van. "I'm too tired to worry about anything," he said in a dull voice.

"Yes, it's been a long night," Bear Claw said. He and his partner tossed the corpse high onto the steps.

"You take it easy, sir," Curtis said coming back. "We'll look after everything." He grabbed the tall man's legs and pulled him out. Bear Claw put his hands under the arms.

When they neared the steps, Lucas used his ring and snatched the pistol back. He fired immediately, hitting both men in the back before they could react. Curtis lay still but Bear Claw cursed and twisted, and Lucas rushed up to shoot him in the head. He gave the coup de grace to Curtis also, just in case.

Fury growing in him, he tore the belt from Bear Claw's waist and threw it onto the corpses. He spat on the soldier's body. "You're an idiot."

Working quickly, Lucas took the rest of the gear out of the van and put it on the steps. He spread the last of the fire accelerant over the bodies. Then he got into the van, activated the self-cleaning mechanism, and drove back down the driveway.

A couple of blocks away, he pulled over and signaled the detonator. There were several sharp blasts, and flames shot up. The job finished, Lucas reactivated the robot driver, and the van took him through the murky streets to a small park.

Sasha and Monique had sent one of the robocabs away, and were waiting there in turtle mode. Lucas dismissed his van, and approached the cab. Clearly relieved to see him, the women got out and hugged him tightly. "What happened to Ellie?" Sasha asked as they drove off.

"She changed her mind," Lucas said. He cracked a Valhalla capsule for Sasha and another for Monique. "Ladies, you did wonderfully well. Just think, in a few days you'll be off to Europe."

"It's a shame Ellie won't be with us," Monique said. "Europe has to be better than Vancouver."

"Everyone makes choices." Lucas slid an arm around each of them. "Your happiness is very important to me. Some night after you're established over there, you can look up at the stars and remember your old spaceman."

They both pressed against him. "We will."

Once back home, Lucas took a large whiskey and lay back on the couch. He placed the octopod's parts on his stomach. *"You're safe now, nothing like this will ever happen again."*

"The square of the length of the hypotenuse of a right triangle is equal to the sum of the squares of the lengths of the other sides," Tomi said.

"Don't worry," Lucas said. "We stopped the leak, and the perpetrators are all dead."

"The circumference of a circle is pi times the diameter. The area of a circle is pi times the square of the radius."

"Bibi will see you at Grace Hospital," Lucas said. "After that we'll make a decision. It might be best to send you back to Mars."

"A Martian trip involves high risk for dubious rewards," Tomi said. "The best option may be to terminate me."

CHAPTER 26

The announcement of Plenso's death came over our school's public address system on Monday morning, just at the start of history class. Mr. Rossiter said we'd lost a fine young man, who was only starting his career. Plenso died at the carnival, but there was no information as to the circumstances or the cause.

A murmur of disbelief ran through the classroom, and we looked at each other with amazement. Our solid and stolid Plenso was the most unlikely candidate for such a fate. How could it be? The morning had turned ugly, and I wanted to leave and come to grips with the situation. Then Mr. Beebe walked in and began talking about nineteenth century imperialism. I'd intaken considerable information about this period, and became caught up in the discussion.

When I went in for lunch, there was a swirl of malicious gossip in the cafeteria. Some of my classmates heard for the first time that Plenso was homosexual. His memory came to me strongly, and I showed no reaction to their hateful remarks.

Always phlegmatic, Plenso had a skin like a rhinoceros. He was a master at not letting things get to him. On the occasion of his death, I'd learn from him once more.

I noticed Cooper at the lunch counter and went up to give my condolences. He took me over to the wall, so we could talk. "I should have gone with him," he said tonelessly. "Nobody was watching his back, and now he's gone."

"For me he was the perfect mentor. I'll never forget him."

He locked onto my eyes with a powerful gaze. "I'm going to tell you something important. Plenso and I weren't in contact when he went out to the carnival; we'd had a little spat. Later that night, he came and said goodbye to me; it must have been right after that bastard slit his throat. But it didn't feel the way our standard telepathy feels. This was different. His whole self was there, and then he was gone. This is strange coming from a T-man, because I know full well there's no telepathy for us without the implants. But I still believe in the human soul." Seeing Mr. Rossiter enter the cafeteria, Cooper broke things off. "Excuse me; I have to talk to him."

Surrounded by excited students, Mr. Rossiter stopped and held up his hands. "All of you settle down. I have some information, but not everything." His lips pursed, he waited until there was calm. "From what's been gathered, Plenso's death was the result of a dispute that occurred on a night when there was thick fog. The evidence shows at least two other men present. The investigation remains on-going."

After Mr. Rossiter's statement, everyone was silent. From their expressions, I understood the seniors were communicating in thought. I left the cafeteria.

Hearing shouts from the lounge, I went inside and joined the group watching the video. The screen showed a small crowd gathered around an airship parked next to Stanley Stadium. A somber dirge played softly. Nearby, people were lined up to get inside for the track and field events.

A door opened in the wall of the stadium, and six men in white robes carried a white coffin covered with flowers toward the airship in time with the slow, mournful music. "Thick fog played a role in the deadly encounter between a space cadet and two other men," the announcer said. "Plenso, so recently accepted as a T-man, will now travel to India and be with the Great One forever."

"Blame it on the fog," a man said as the video went dead. "The night was so black, Plenso couldn't tell the boys from the girls."

The remark brought a few chuckles. "Make sure I'm in the right hole, darling," someone said, mimicking Plenso's voice. "Otherwise pregnancy will not result."

"It's the only hole I've got," a large freshman said in a resounding voice.

This was pushing me toward the edge. "You've got a big mouth," I told him. "Does that count as another hole?"

"You should know--he was your mentor, wasn't he?"

In a flash I grabbed his throat and slowly pushed him backward onto the couch. "Do you have anything else to say?"

He stayed very still. "It's my mistake, I apologize."

As I walked away, another man stopped me by pulling at my shoulder. "We all miss Plenso, and it's a damn shame he had to go like this. It's not like he's really dead, though. In a few hours he'll be part of the Great One."

"Are you crazy?" I cried. "Preserving his personality inside a quantum computer is not Plenso living out his life in the real world."

"He might continue by seeing through your eyes and all the other T-men. We won't know until it's our turn to join Raina."

This idea was too much for me to deal with. Although close to tears, I started laughing uncontrollably and hurried away.

Late that evening, Lucas left a message that he wanted to see me. The next day after lunch I took the bus into town, and walked over the bridge that led to Needles Island.

I'd often seen Needles Island from afar, and it was awesome to get close and look up at the towers. This island was one of the last major works completed by the old people in our city.

Lucas's door was opened by a young, dark-haired woman in a short-sleeved white blouse and green slacks. "You must be Dom," she said. "I'm Monique. Come on in, your father is in the living room with Sasha."

Following her inside, I found Lucas in an arm chair, holding a drink. "It's good to see you, my boy," he said.

A blonde woman in a light gray dress got up from the couch. Although she wore almost no makeup, I recognized her from the day on the street with Lucas. "Welcome," she said in a Russian accent. "Monique and I wanted very much to meet you."

"They prefer the younger version," Lucas said to me.

The women laughed. "No, you are the beauty," Sasha said. "But what a son! Identical, except for the shaved head." Taking my arm, she pulled me to the couch. "Come and sit down, I want to hear everything about you. Monique, can you get him some wine?"

I had no intention of getting involved with the two streetwalkers. "Not for me thanks, it's the middle of the day and I have a lot of work to do. Lucas said there's something important to tell me."

"I can't remember ever being that busy," he said. "Have one of these chocolates, it'll sweeten you up."

"No chocolates, thanks."

Lucas frowned, and looked to the women. "Maybe do some shopping. Call me later, we'll go out for dinner and see a show." He closed his eyes as Sasha and Monique gathered a few things, gave him a kiss on the cheek, and left. Then he emitted a loud groan. "This is carnival week, and I thought you'd like some action. Do you prefer boys?"

"Of course not. I'm in love."

"Love? I'd like to meet her."

This encounter struck me as something to avoid at all costs. "She's busy too, there's a big project she's trying to finish off for school. We don't have a lot of free time."

"I can understand that," Lucas said. He touched the small control panel on the side of his armchair, and a classical guitar began to play. "I asked you up here because it's time you learned something of our family's history. It's a glorious past, and you come from a line of kings."

His revelation was not a total shock, as Bibi had prepared me when I first saw him in the hospital. So far, what I'd seen of the old man was not glorious. Besides, it was not easy to impress me. I'd been raised in the crèche, and had to fight hard every inch of the way to succeed as a space cadet. I made no reply, just gazed at him in sullen silence.

"Maude," he called. "Bring more wine, and a glass for the boy."

A red-haired robot in a white skirt and black top wheeled in with a large bottle, and poured some dark red wine. The drink had a brownish hue, and a fragrance like ancient flowers. I touched it to my lips and experienced deep richness and a growing calmness.

Lucas downed his wine, and the robot refilled his glass. "Almost a thousand years ago a noble warrior, born in Mongolia, built an incredible empire that encompassed almost all of Asia. His name was Genghis Khan."

"You don't look much like a Mongol."

"That's a misconception," Lucas said with a grin. "Genghis Khan was a redhead."

"Were you raised in a wealthy home, then?"

"Pops came over to the United States as a Turkistan trade representative. Times were tough, there was a lot of turmoil, but adversity never bothered Pops. He was a true warrior; the main problem for us was he had to be away a lot."

"What was mother like?"

"An angel, I've never met a better person. Her family was Spanish originally, high-born grandees who'd fallen on difficult times. She was meant for better things, and getting married to Pops was incredibly bad luck for her. The turning point came when Pops was called back to his homeland. We learned he had another wife and more children over there. Mama was furious, and she couldn't forgive his betrayal. So we left him."

"It sounds like you never had a real home, either."

"That 'real home' talk is overdone; the main thing is standing on your own two feet. I learned young because mama was working two jobs to survive, and when I came home from Catholic school nobody was there. A local gang, the Rogers, kept an eye on things in the neighborhood, and I went there sometimes for milk and cookies. When mama died they took me in."

"Maybe the Rogers thought another Genghis Khan would fit well with their gang."

He shook his head. "I wasn't stupid enough to tell people that. You won't either. Listen to me, now. When they transported me, I was still a young man, not even close to settling down. Up on Mars it was a good ten years before I established myself, and by that time I'd been poisoned by radiation, and it was too late to have a family in the normal way. You were my only hope. Here on Earth you got an education and a chance for a better life."

"Well, I'm grateful for the education. I'm looking forward to my career in space."

"That'll make me happy, too. I'm terrifically proud of the way you turned out." He heaved a deep sigh. "All of a sudden I feel tired, probably from too many late nights. I hired those girls for an entire week."

"If you need a rest, go ahead. I'll come back another time."

Walking back from Lucas's place to catch the bus, I was deep in thought. While the information about the past was disturbing, I could not allow it to affect my life unduly. My personality was set. I'd become myself long before meeting Lucas.

Sasha and Monique assumed that because Lucas was older he must be a father to me. That was nonsense. As Lucas's clone my father and mother were the same as his, Pops and Mama. Both were long dead, I'd never meet them.

The truest thing Lucas said was the importance of self-reliance. I'd been on my own from the very start, and the best break I had was him being cloned before he was poisoned by radiation. Blessed with good health and a clear mind, I'd make my way.

This question of our breeding might prove difficult; like a growing whirlpool at the base of things, it looked dangerous but also drew me. It could not be ignored. Lucas clearly felt a strong connection with Genghis Khan, and the more I learned about the ancient warrior, the more I'd understand myself.

CHAPTER 27

While there was a lot on the news about the destruction of the Beach Lords, Lucas thought that skulking in the shadows would arouse more suspicion than being in the open, especially during carnival time. Sasha and Monique were busy preparing to leave for Europe, but they still made time for him. They adored dressing up, and Lucas enjoyed the street dances and sporting events at the stadium with them on his arms.

The main person missing was Dom. The women both liked him and offered a perfect chance for the men to bond in an important way. Lucas understood that Dom was in love with one of his classmates, but it was difficult for him to accept emotionally. At Dom's age, he'd never been in love. Life with the Rogers offered him many sexual opportunities, and, after losing his virginity at fourteen, he'd taken full advantage. Dom's rejecting the chance with Sasha and Monique was disturbing to him. It made him wonder if clones were really the same.

On Lucas's last evening with Sasha and Monique, their laughter was even giddier, and they plied him with chocolates. He sensed they were afraid he'd kill them. Unable to assuage their fears, he went along with their Arabian Nights type defense of being ever more tantalizing and alluring. Back at his place it all came true; they led him into an amazing world.

In the morning he ordered a robocab, and helped the women with their luggage. As they neared the airport, Lucas cracked Valhalla capsules for each of them. "Ladies, this is it. Enjoy Europe to the fullest."

The women kissed his cheek. "We will."

After they boarded, Lucas had a drink in the lounge and watched the airship. As much as he liked Sasha and Monique, they were major loose ends that needed to be tied up. When the ship lifted off he left immediately, his focus already shifted to what to do about Tomi. Outside the depot, he took another robocab to Grace Hospital.

Bibi was busy when he got there, and the receptionist showed him to a small waiting area, where the works of art on the walls came to life. The images showed the progression of man from infancy to old age; instead of succumbing to weakness, though, people threw away their crutches, arose from their sick beds, and regained youth and vitality. Lucas was spellbound and moved by the theme of rejuvenation.

Hearing laughter, he sat up and looked to the hall. Bibi was at the doorway, talking to a girl with blonde pigtails and a brawny young giant with shoulder-length brown hair. Although it seemed impossible, Lucas felt he recognized the young woman from thirty years ago. She looked like Edna Halley, the heiress to the Comet food chain who'd gained notoriety in her teens by appearing in a sex video. After that, there'd been other minor acting roles and several marriages. Shortly before being transported, Lucas heard she'd taken charge of Comet and was opening restaurants in the high Arctic.

After seeing them off, Bibi came to get him. "Sorry about that." They took an elevator to the basement, and Bibi explained that Ms. Halley was another patient who'd reclaimed her youth. When they got to the bottom floor she stopped and looked into his eyes. "We retrieved what we could of your data from the octopod. The disc you brought was helpful too. We're ready for the transplant whenever you are."

"And my varlet?" he asked. "Is there any chance you can help him here."

"I doubt anyone on Earth has the expertise. It might be possible on Mars."

"I can't risk Tomi falling into the wrong hands," Lucas said.

"The alternative is to destroy Tomi. I know it's hard." She unlocked a nearby closet and handed Lucas a small box.

He took it into the hallway and opened the top. The octopod was resting on a white pad, and seemed intact. *"Are you feeling better?"* he asked Tomi.

"Sadly, no."

"And the data?"

"Transferred, your honor. As you commanded, I let them have it all."

Bibi led the way down the hallway.

"I'll never forget the day you purchased me," Tomi said. "From the moment of my creation I hungered to know life, and you indulged me fully. You've shown me so much."

"You taught me a lot too," Lucas said. "I was like a Mongol getting his first colt, thrilled and awed. A man on horseback can conquer the world, on foot he won't get very far. You've been the ideal partner for me, and more than that, my best friend."

A locked door at the end of the hallway was opened by a smallish robot in a white smock. It ushered them through a store room, into a brightly lit laboratory.

"Where are we now?" Tomi asked.

"We're still in the hospital," Lucas said.

Bibi went to a large metal structure on the side, and pulled out a tray.

"Is this the end?"

"I'm afraid so, my dear. I'll always miss you. I love you."

Bibi took the box from Lucas and placed it on the tray. She slid it inside. Sickened, Lucas took a chair and hung his head.

Bibi stroked his neck. "This oven is a release and a gateway," she said. "Lots of times embryos are forgotten or unwanted and they end up here. To me they're all little angels."

"Tomi was the closest thing to an angel I'll ever know."

Bibi took a seat beside him. "I know how you must feel, I cremated my own sister." Lucas looked at her questioningly. "Not exactly like this," she said. "After my merger with Cici I'd planned to destroy my old body, but she was still the same person, and I was incapable of harming her. We have a large home, and I wanted her with us always. Then one day I went to her room and found her unresponsive in her chair, looking out the window at her beloved garden. She'd suffered cardiac arrest; the dispenser she'd used was on the floor beside her."

Lucas shook his head. "Sometimes this is an ugly world."

"Goodbye forever," Tomi howled.

Lucas collapsed in tears, and Bibi held him to her breast.

CHAPTER 28

Back at the school I intook a huge batch of information on Genghis Khan, and the period in which he lived. That night I dreamed of warfare against an army that left its walled city to meet us. I led my horsemen toward the enemy at top speed, and thousands fell under our arrows. The city opened its gates to us and we made our entrance. Many of the locals were huddled within the central palace, and they quailed as I rode into the hall and took the throne. The king begged for mercy, but as he'd made trouble for us by resisting, I slashed his throat open and kicked him away. With that, my soldiers began killing in earnest. Every man had to go. This whole city was to be burned to the ground, everything of value looted, and the women and children taken as slaves.

Someone brought me a flagon of wine, and I drank deep. When the nobles were dead, my officers began raping the court women. Beckoning to a couple of generals, I went back to the king's quarters to view his wives and concubines. The serving girls prepared us a banquet to celebrate victory's sweetest moment.

When I woke up in the morning, the front of my pajama bottoms was stiff with dried ejaculate, and I remembered vividly how it was to overrun the city, slay the king, and enjoy his wives. Throwing on a robe, I went down the hall for a shower. The usually pleasant sensation of water beating down on me was a torment; nothing would be the same again. Genghis Khan was one of the worst men who'd ever lived.

The development was horrific, something to be buried deep and never exposed. All day long, though, the information surfaced. Genghis

Khan's mother was a kidnapped bride. As a child Genghis Khan had an older half-brother who threatened to dominate him, so he murdered the boy. Being ruthless he employed fiendishly ingenious tactics, such as herding peasants into moats in order to climb over their bodies. Again and again, he ordered total massacre of those who refused to surrender.

The histories showed that the Mongol empire brought in progressive reforms in several areas. Promotion was based strictly on merit. The new legal system was applied fairly, and everyone was treated the same. All religions were accepted; there was no discrimination or bigotry.

Praise for the Mongols left me cold; good could not come from such evil. Genghis Khan's claim that God had sent him struck me as the worst hypocrisy. The atrocities he committed could never be justified.

After two days of inner struggle, a message came that Lucas wanted to see me again. This was welcome news, as there were questions only he could answer.

Lucas wanted to get outside for the afternoon, so I went down to Needles Island and picked him up at the apartment. He was already dressed in shorts and walking shoes, and had packed a sports bag with sandwiches and a light jacket in case of rain.

Neither of us said much at first. "I haven't been this way since I arrived," he remarked to me as we headed north along the seawall. He set a good pace; it was clear he'd been looking forward to the walk.

A wind came in from the west, stiff enough to create white caps on the water. Overhead was an ever changing array of white cumulus clouds; the weather forecast called for possible showers.

"Pops took me to Alaska once," Lucas said. "We saw Mount Denali."

"Did he communicate with the mountain's spirit?"

Lucas gave me a sharp glance. "Not audibly." Then he chuckled. "I wouldn't put it past him; that kind of thing runs in the family. One of the things I noticed on Mars, is the mountains have a different feel about them. You sense they are not used to people."

A group of joggers came up behind, and we stood aside to let them pass.

"Is Pops still alive?" I asked as we walked on.

Lucas shook his head. "He died when I was eight years old."

"What about mother's side of the family?"

"The Riveras? Well, I never saw much of them, either. When Mama ran off with Pops it was a sudden departure, kind of an elopement. She planned to look them up, but never did before she passed away."

Some drops of rain fell; the clouds had darkened. Lucas got the jacket out of his bag and put it on. My uniform was all-weather, so I wasn't worried.

"The Rogers are gone now, too," Lucas said. "There's a lot riding on your shoulders; you might have to start a dynasty."

This struck me as hilarious. "There are some big steps to take before that comes up."

"I'll back you," he said.

Coming to a stairway, Lucas recognized some buildings. "I know this place, let's go up."

There was a strong gust of wind, and a cloudburst started just as we got to the top. We went inside a ground-level bar and took a table beside the window. The room was long and narrow, and had an unlit gas fireplace at the far end. There was only a few other customers.

"I haven't been here for thirty years," Lucas said. "It seems slower here now."

An older woman in a black uniform smiled as she came over, and I figured she'd noticed the family resemblance. Lucas ordered Wild Grouse and water for both of us.

"I intook some information on Genghis Khan," I told him when the waitress left.

"You intook some information?" he asked, looking at me thoughtfully. "Well, I wanted you to know what Pops said, even though I never accepted the idea of a personality being passed down. A thousand years is a long time. And don't forget Mama's side of the family. We've probably got some Aztec, and whatever else was mixed in over the centuries."

Our drinks arrived, and Lucas touched his glass to mine. "I'm glad we can have this little talk."

I took a sip and nodded. "Good stuff."

"Environment and education are more important than genetics," Lucas said. "My whole life I never stopped learning."

"Hopefully it'll be the same for me, especially when I go off-world."

"I want that for you too," Lucas said. "Your being a space cadet makes me very proud, and Pops and Mama would feel the same." Then he grinned. "We have to get that dynasty happening. I want to meet your young lady."

I could feel myself blush, and didn't like it. "I already said, we're both really busy. Besides, it's nowhere near that stage.'"

"Sorry, I don't mean to pry," Lucas said with another smile. He looked out the window and finished his drink. "It looks like the rain has stopped. Are you ready to move on?"

In a couple of hours we finished our walk, and parted ways. Returning to the school after this visit, I sensed a growing closeness with the old man and felt much better about things. Lucas was undeniably a real character, who'd made some mistakes in the old days. Since then, he'd gained a lot of wisdom and become a different person. I was thankful he'd come back to Earth to connect me with my roots.

CHAPTER 29

Committed to recapturing his youth, Lucas resigned himself to spending up to a year on a charm offensive with Dom. The young man had a mind of his own, and dreams, and a full life; the merger procedure could not be rushed. Dom was sure to see the benefits of merging eventually, but one year was the deadline. Next spring, Dom was scheduled to become a T-man. If that happened, he'd be lost forever.

The main threat left was Kenny Summers. Kenny's betrayal could never be forgotten, and given the chance he would finish Lucas. Lucas had to act first. Once Kenny was out of the way, Lucas would enjoy his stay on Earth in complete security.

Kenny's Seattle base was well protected; targeting him was a formidable challenge. Tomi left several scenarios, but Lucas wanted to go there and look around before deciding the best way to do the job. One possibility was a Swedish long gun he'd left under a fig tree in the Rogers backyard. The gun was carefully wrapped.

Poison was another approach. Ever since the dragonfly guided him to the Helena safe house, he'd been playing with different possibilities. He called his old friend Fred Chan and they talked about these matters.

A forty-year-old technician came to his place three days later. Amy Lim's briefcase held samples of miniature surveillance and attack bots. She was prepared to arm the bots with incapacitating and lethal drugs, and equally powerful biological weapons.

Lucas ordered two types: fleas, that moved by hopping, and bees, which flew. The fleas required physical contact with the target. A handshake or an embrace provided the opportunity to get onto someone's clothes; after that, the bot worked its way through to bare flesh. The bees could strike from a distance, but they worked best when an enemy was isolated. In a crowded situation, the swarm could get confused.

Amy coordinated the control systems with Lucas's Martian implants, and made several visits to help him guide his tiny force with thought. Once Lucas had the bots under control, Amy armed them. The bees got a drug which caused sudden paralysis and, shortly thereafter, cardiac arrest. The fleas carried a deadly virus which dated from pre-conquest times, a product of the secret warfare between corporations. The bots' containers fit inside the cuffs of Lucas's jacket. At the end of his mission, Lucas was to soak the sleeves. The inserts and the bots would self-destruct, and the poison be rendered harmless.

Lucas left for Seattle Sunday afternoon on the Speed train he used years ago when the Rogers first sent him to Vancouver. The seats were large and comfortably built, and the windows dimmed on command. The main difference was that many of the seats were empty. In the old days, this train was jammed.

The train left the station at four PM; they entered the tunnel and the outside walls became a blur. Then it was bright outside. The Speed was now elevated, and protected by translucent walls that could withstand the strongest winds.

Lucas had a similar sense of security in the submersible. He'd never trained as a sailor, and the wild Pacific Ocean could be a real challenge. When he sank below the surface, the storms were powerless to reach his vessel.

Without Kenny as his partner, he'd never have gotten the boat. The Rogers invested because they trusted Kenny to handle the business end, the same as when they bought the West Seattle bar, The Cedars. In those days Lucas trusted Kenny totally; they were as close as brothers.

With McCool gone and Kenny soon to join him, Lucas would be the last surviving Roger. The prospect was depressing, but also clean. Yes, there'd be justice and a final accounting for past misdeeds.

He got off the train in Seattle's underground station. As he neared the escalator, a wall lit up with a mural that showed the Earth's president, Ranjit Kumar, standing beside a fountain with his arms outstretched to the heavens. The image infuriated Lucas, but he smiled when a group of children in yellow uniforms ran up. "Praise Amma," they cried to him.

"Praise Amma," he replied, putting some coins into their baskets.

When he got to the exit it was windy outside, and pouring with rain. Lucas donned a light raincoat from his grip and headed into the weather.

This was the heart of Seattle, rebuilt when he was a boy. While Vancouverites fought bitterly against the rising seas, contesting every inch with their Seawalls and dikes, Seattle chose a different strategy. Low-lying areas were razed, and written off. The city was reconstructed on safe land, in modern triumphal style. Using the ultra-strong, ultra-light materials developed in building the space elevator, architects built what they wanted, as high as they pleased.

The years before the conquest were chaotic but it was also a time of peak energy, when mankind did amazing things. Looking up at the buildings all around, Lucas felt pride in being part of this period, when the men of Earth were still giants. It was all in the past now. The strong men--the good ones--lived on Mars.

Lucas made his way to Fifth Avenue, where he'd reserved a suite on the eighty-fifth floor of one of Seattle's tallest buildings, the Galaxy Hotel. The rooms looked across the street to the Rupert Building, where according to Tomi's report, Kenny Summers had a multi-floor residence at the top.

Established in his new place, he ordered a bottle of Wild Grouse and a Cajun style chicken dinner from room service. He ate outside in the glassed-in balcony, and was pleased to find himself slightly higher than the other building's roof. Tomi had done well.

The Rupert Building was worth a fortune, and Kenny owned a big chunk. About two thirds of the way down, a section of the building pulsated a deep red. This was the Ruby, a combination restaurant and night club. Kenny frequented the place with a blonde female companion.

Lucas long suspected that much of the Rogers' great wealth was now in Kenny's hands, but Tomi found no traces of how this came to be. Kenny's record was spotless; no connection was evident between him and the Rogers. Nor was there information on Kenny's father Matt, the gang's president. According to Kenny's official biography, Matt was a barman who managed The Cedars. Lucas remembered having him on the payroll, but Matt never worked there. He only visited the bar once, to have a look.

Lucas stayed on the balcony the whole evening, sipping bourbon. Lights were on in Kenny's place but the windows were shielded. Three times during the night, an airship landed on top of the building and let out visitors. Shortly after midnight, the sky cleared and two couples went onto the balcony and looked up at the moon. The taller, bearded man was Kenny Summers. Seeing him there, Lucas almost stopped breathing.

After Kenny's party left the balcony, Lucas went inside and sat on the couch to think. Shooting Kenny from the hotel looked feasible, with the right weapon. He'd go back to the Rogers club house. After thirty years there'd be changes, but the cache might still be there. His long gun would be effective and untraceable. The gold coins would help out, too.

The next morning Lucas got up around seven-thirty. After a light breakfast in the hotel cafeteria, he went out into the rain and grabbed a robocab. The cab was a larger vehicle, with a rounded front and back, and looked plush and comfortable. Getting into the back seat, a hint of fragrance made him remember that as a young man from Tacoma, he'd viewed Seattle women as exotic and sophisticated.

Rain came down in force as the cab approached the highway; huge drops pounded on the roof and bounced off the pavement ahead. Interstate 5 took control in the entrance lane, and they rocketed ahead to merge with the speeding traffic.

South of Seattle it stopped raining, and the clouds broke up. Ahead, Lucas glimpsed Mount Rainier; a trick of light made it seem almost right above him. It was as if the mountain's spirit recognized him after his long absence from the planet. "Hello, Rainier," he murmured in his deepest voice. Then the clouds moved in again, and the moment was gone.

When the Tacoma docks came into view, he told the cab to pull over, and he got out to gaze down at the Alaska ferry landing, where he'd worked as a boy. Several vehicles were lined up to board, but it was nothing like before, when masses of people came through on their way north. In those days, there was always a full-sized ship in each of the three berths, and schedules were tight, with rapid turnovers. The little vessel in there now was nothing like the ones he remembered. The container yards were cut back, too.

Returning to the cab, Lucas gave the address where he and his mother lived before he moved to the Rogers house. "That address does not exist," the robot driver said.

"What are you talking about?" Lucas said. "It's right at the top of the Twenty-Fifth Street Hill. Display a map and I'll show you." When the screen came down he stared at it in disbelief. Tacoma as he'd known it no longer existed; the entire hilltop section was colored green, and marked Environmental Reclamation. The old Rogers place was wiped out too. "We'll go and have a look," he growled.

They took the low road along the water, and headed up the hill. Lucas remembered this area as a place of crowded tenements, where people screamed at each other through the floors. The old apartment buildings had been replaced by houses, with carefully tended lawns and ornate, semi-tropical plants.

At the top of the hill the road ended at a force fence that ran outside an unbroken line of coniferous trees. The cab stopped before an information kiosk, and Lucas got out. "I need to go inside," he said. "This park is built on a neighborhood where I lived as a child, and there might be remains of the old buildings."

"Humans are not allowed to enter," the kiosk said. "It's not a park as such."

"There must be exceptions. Who's in charge?"

"The Ministry of the Environment has reserved this area for the non-human species. There are no exceptions."

Engulfed by a sense of loss, Lucas went to the fence and stared in at the trees. Even though the old neighborhood was crowded and run down, wonderful people lived here. Now he was forbidden to go inside and see what was left.

Recovering the cache after more than thirty years away was always unlikely. It was hard to let go of it, though, because the long gun would suit the job. His old Seattle contacts were gone, and getting another gun would be very difficult. He was forced to use the bots, which required direct contact with Kenny.

Another storm hit as he returned to Seattle. Gusting winds coated the windows of his Galaxy Hotel suite with rain.

Lucas spent the rest of the day renewing his acquaintanceship with the robotic fleas and bees. He let them crawl all over him, so they'd never forget where home was. Amy Lim promised they'd never attack him, but he needed to erase even a hint of mistrust.

He drilled them endlessly with thought commands, sending the bees up to the ceiling, over to the windows, and back. He had the fleas hop underneath the bed, come to the other side, and jump up again. They could hop four feet, which he considered good enough. Both types had chameleon capacity, which, combined with their tiny size, made them almost invisible.

Around four, Lucas poured a drink and went out to the balcony. Across the street, Kenny's building looked solid and formidable. The coming mission was one of the most dangerous of his life, and he missed Tomi very much. The fleas and bees were a solid backup, but they could never replace his varlet. Tomi was like a second self.

Lucas was strongly tempted to give up, and return to Vancouver. But then he'd live in fear. Kenny could find him out at any time, and come to kill him.

After dark he dressed for dinner and went to the lower level, where a passageway under the street took him to the Rupert Building. Waiting for the elevator was a small group who could have passed for Martian overlords on a night out. They wore skullcaps and iridescent unisex evening suits, and while no one spoke, it was apparent from their stance and facial expressions that communication was taking place. Showing nothing of his discomfort at being trapped with a bunch of Tees, Lucas followed them into the elevator.

The Ruby's restaurant level, the twenty-sixth floor, was a place of dark reds, interspersed with black and silver. The effect was dramatic, and Lucas thought Kenny probably had a hand in it. Kenny had artistic talent and was very detail conscious. When they bought The Cedars in West Seattle, the renovations occupied them for months.

The Tees marched straight through the entrance foyer to a desk at the end, not looking at the people already waiting. A red-turbaned attendant greeted them warmly, and showed them inside.

Trailing behind, Lucas passed the doorman a substantial tip and was asked to have a seat. In half an hour, a woman in a crimson dress led him through a maze of rooms to a quiet area where several other singles were dining. He read the menu thoroughly, and came across dishes he hadn't tried in years. He decided on lasagna.

In the course of the dinner, he realized that things were close to perfect here. Not just the food, but the table cloth, the cutlery, the furniture, and the lighting. Each detail was carefully chosen, and everything fit together. Mars had nothing like this. Not yet, maybe not for fifty years.

After dinner, Lucas went down a hallway to the recreation area. Feeling slightly disoriented, he followed some Tees into a theatre. Inside, the atmosphere was electric; the audience's attention was fixed on a bare stage where two actors with shaved heads sat at a table in absolute silence. Realizing that everyone here must be telepathic, he left.

At the end of the hallway was a large, crowded gambling area, with wheels, card games, and video terminals. In the old days Kenny never gambled, but in thirty years there'd be changes. Lucas spent close to an hour in this section, studying the action. Once he started to play people watched him too, and he disregarded their attention. He was not here to sneak around.

A wide staircase led him up to the next level. It was quieter here, and he noticed several interesting pubs and lounges. If Kenny was in the mood for a nightcap, this would be the spot.

Farther on, the lighting dimmed. Perfumed mist rose from a darkened window, and he heard female giggles. Animated signs beckoned him to massage parlors; a statue of the Roman god Priapus stood outside the SATYR'S BATHS. At the end of the corridor was a TRAVELER'S REST sign. Standing next to the window a scantily clad, buxom robot waved wildly and blew him a kiss.

The scene struck Lucas as overly raunchy for Kenny. There was little chance of finding the congressman here.

After a couple of drinks in a piano bar, Lucas decided it was time to leave. Walking along the underground corridor to the hotel, he felt his opening to the dangerous game was at least acceptable. Hopefully an encounter with Kenny would come soon.

CHAPTER 30

While Astra claimed it was totally normal for us to spend a week in the mountains, we did not travel there together. I was to meet her at the Elephant Bar in Whistler Village, wearing townie clothes and a wig.

A fast-talking Vancouver sales clerk outfitted me in red and yellow sports gear, and bushy, light brown curls that added a couple of inches to my height. I left the store with the new look; I'd stuffed the school uniform in my bag.

It was five thirty and still bright out when the limo dropped me in the Village, outside the Elephant Bar. The large, dimly lit tavern was almost deserted. No one here looked like Astra, so I got a glass of cider and sat at a small table by the door to wait. A woman at the bar kept eyeing me and I was about to speak with her when Astra strode through the door, wearing a white cap atop long black hair, and a green townie outfit that looked sprayed on. She knew me immediately, and sat down at the table. "Been waiting long?" she asked.

I couldn't stop grinning. "You look good."

Astra laughed. "I get so damn tired of wearing the same uniforms every day. This time with you is special to me." She leaned over and, although our lips only touched lightly, the power that flowed between us seemed unlimited. Her eyes widened, and she sat back in her seat. "Have you checked out our place yet?"

I shook my head, and held up my drink. "Want some?" She took a swallow, and handed it back to me to finish off.

222

Outside the bar people were wandering the narrow streets, going in and out of the shops and restaurants. We hailed a passing dromy, and for a couple of units, it took us away from the village, through a wooded area to some cottages. Our place, the Eros Chalet, was isolated from the others by trees and bushes. It had steep roofs and a covered verandah.

The interior was huge, with two large bedrooms, a monstrous living room, a well-appointed kitchen, and a luxurious bathroom. As the name suggested, an erotic theme ruled throughout, expressed in paintings and sculptures. The bedrooms were equipped with massage oils and sex toys. I noticed boxes of the Sinful Delight chocolates Lucas had at his place.

Watching Astra prowl around and examine everything, I was glad we'd decided to come here. It wasn't easy, as although the Eros Chalet was the first choice for both of us, neither wanted to appear overly eager, or act pushy.

Suddenly she picked up a huge dildo and threw it into the top drawer of a dresser. "I'm not looking at this garbage all week. When they said Eros Chalet I expected something lovely and romantic, not this. Maybe we should demand a refund."

This was scary but it was easy to see her point. I helped her put the stuff away. "I had no idea," I said. "It's my first time here." She was crying now, and I put my arms around her. "Sorry," I said, holding her tightly.

We sat down on the sofa and had a talk. I learned that her anger at George was uppermost; the sex toys reminded her of him. She'd become very dissatisfied with their relationship.

The Damons lived just a few miles from Allison Farms, and the two space families often socialized. Astra grew up knowing that George, a year and a half older, was a realistic candidate for marriage. On Astra's side, though, things had cooled. "Last week he was bragging about his conquests at the carnival. According to him he seduced three townie girls."

I shook my head. "George's an idiot."

After hearing her story I told her things nobody else knew. Growing up in the crèche, contact with the outside world was restricted, and childhood innocence never violated. At thirteen I was sent to St. David's school in Toronto, where the older boys created a ribald atmosphere. My roommate Rajinder, also a scholarship student, was even more shocked than me so we kept apart from the others. After I turned sixteen, an art teacher, Ms. Rita McDonald, asked me to her office to discuss my work and showed me some of her own paintings. She was working on a series about ancient Greek and Roman gods, and invited me to pose for her. This led to an affair that was the main sexual experience of my life.

"Did you love the art teacher?" Astra asked.

"My feelings were mixed up. She always remained the all-powerful teacher, and I resented being dominated like that."

"I can understand that," Astra said. "One reason I like being with you is we're both middies. George was always a step ahead of me. Sometimes it was comforting to be looked after, but I felt stifled. When I got my telecap, the difference was even worse. Mentally he's stronger and more advanced, and he did things in my mind that I couldn't allow."

"At least here in the chalet our privacy is guaranteed," I said. "It has the T-man seal."

"We have to make the most of this time," Astra said. "I've heard real horror stories about people who never mastered their defense systems, and shared the most intimate details of their lives with thousands of total strangers. I am determined not to let that happen. You and I will communicate on a private level, and we'll bring in others or screen them out at will. Mental strength is another priority. Powerful telepaths can dominate or overwhelm the weak. We must work hard and ensure that we're above that."

Astra's concerns about the telecap went beyond what I'd considered, and made me realize the Old Lace women were ahead in this area. Having her as a partner would be a big advantage.

After our talk I felt closer to Astra than ever before. There'd always been gladness at being with her, and this was deepening. It was clear we were on the same wavelength and that we'd embarked on an important journey together.

A screen in the chalet living room displayed a detailed map of the area, including a list of "secluded spots for lovers," kept separate from regular vacation sites. We were especially drawn to a spot where a mountain stream formed a small pool in the upper woods before flowing into a valley. We booked it for the next day.

The whole evening was ahead. After dinner in the village, we explored the bars and nightclubs. Back at the chalet there was a wide selection of the pure fun type movies that were seldom seen at STA. Neither of us was ready for porno, but we readily became absorbed in old people era comedy and adventure stories. Close to two in the morning we were watching a thriller set in Brazil, about a detective trying to catch a serial killer whose murders became more and more grotesque. The underlying samba beat was hypnotic, and exotic dance scenes were interspaced throughout.

Suddenly Astra got to her feet, and started dancing along with the women on the screen. I knew her athletic prowess from school but she'd never shown such a controlled use of energy and power. The rhythms were fast paced, and Astra never missed a beat. And her butt! Without ever glancing at me, she came closer and closer, bringing me into a deeply erotic experience.

Finally the music stopped. She turned and stretched like a lioness, and gave me a crooked grin. "Well, I'm going to call it a night," she said.

In the morning we walked into the village and picked up some Mexican food. A dromy took us up through the mountains to the stream, and followed a path along the bank to where large rocks constricted the water's flow and created the pool.

The area had a wild, untrammeled feel, with substantial firs that stretched skyward, while the huge chunks of granite at the base of the pool cut off the outside world. Choosing a sunny patch of grass, we spread a blanket and had our lunch.

The surrounding trees made it private so we took off our clothes and went in. It was surprisingly cold and Astra, laughing, stood up in the waist-deep water. In that moment she could have posed as the ancients' love goddess Aphrodite. I lacked the skill to paint her, but a melody began in my mind. This was something new for me, as before I'd only played the compositions of others. I sang it for her, and she was pleased.

Back at the village we listened to a group of Russian singers in a wine bar, and had dinner in a Vietnamese restaurant. After returning to the chalet we drank more wine, eventually falling asleep on the couch.

Awakening hours later, I found Astra still snuggled against me. She pressed her lips to mine, and went to the bathroom. I heard the shower running, and she came back wearing a silky beige nightgown. She took my hand and led me into her bedroom.

CHAPTER 31

Lucas awoke early Tuesday morning after an awful dream. He hadn't had a nightmare like this since childhood: the sense that someone had come in his room while he was helpless, incapable of reacting in any way.

The feeling was so strong he had to wonder if anything real had occurred. It was only four-thirty, not yet time for him to wake up, but he climbed out of bed grimly and went out to the living room to look around. The door seemed properly locked, and there were no signs that anything had been disturbed. His wallet and keys were beside the bed on the night table where he'd left them. The fleas and bees were still in place in his jacket.

The Galaxy was a five-star hotel, one of the best in Seattle, so his fears were almost certainly unfounded. Even if someone had come in, there was nothing for them to see. It was not as if he'd recovered the cache from underneath the fig tree.

If only Tomi was here! With the varlet as lookout, he never had to worry. There might be a way to use the bees, but Amy Lim never mentioned it. They had no judgment whatsoever; he couldn't trust them unless he was fully in charge.

Later in the day, he had another scare. The glands in his neck were becoming swollen, and in the course of the afternoon he developed a bit of a sore throat. He had to wonder if his fleas had made a slipup and infected him.

By evening his nose was dripping, and he was able to relax. The virus carried by the fleas was originally derived from yellow fever, which was transmitted by mosquitoes. This version was engineered to die with its target; there'd be no sneezing or other nasal problems which might spread the infection to others.

He hadn't had many colds in his time away. Once in a while a visitor would carry something in and everyone got sick, but not often. Coming back to Earth was a real challenge for his immune system, as it involved a reengagement with trillions of microbes, many of which had no doubt evolved considerably during his absence.

He could well afford to be philosophical about this new encounter and welcome the visitors into his body. The shop in the hotel lobby had some pills designed to subdue the symptoms of cold and flu, and he swallowed a couple before setting off.

Lucas arrived at the Ruby for dinner at eight o'clock. Perhaps in recognition of his healthy tipping the doorman greeted him like an old friend, and the server helped him choose dishes that were especially good. Afterward, he gambled in the games room and drank in the upstairs lounges. As there was still no sign of Kenny, he decided to visit the Traveler's Rest.

The scantily clad wench in the window waved as frantically as before, and this time she hit her mark. Inside, Lucas bought a silver room key and slung the chain around his neck. He'd sometimes found Traveler's Rest to be the perfect solution. The robots looked and felt like real women, and were eager to please. There was zero risk of pregnancy, disease, or emotional entanglement. The franchise was popular with spacemen across the solar system, with Marsport no exception.

Several of the rooms were darkened, meaning they were engaged. Coming to a live window, Lucas joined a small group of men looking in at a slender, dark-haired woman in a light brown leotard, who was on her hands and knees, arching her back. She went down on her stomach, and slowly raised her head and shoulders.

A burly man with a thick black beard came up. "Excuse me, gentlemen," he said. "This robot is a master." He turned his key in the lock and went inside. The window went dark.

"Is it permitted to observe?" a white-haired man asked.

Lucas pointed to the red "X" on the eyeball above the window. "No peeking." Lucas strolled off down the hallway. The next window showed an Arabian Nights fantasy: an entire harem in silk pajamas, watched over by a powerfully built eunuch with a scimitar in his belt. Wandering on, Lucas passed a Japanese geisha in traditional garb, blonde twins romping in an alpine meadow, and an Amazonian warrior princess.

Any of these rooms would have offered a memorable encounter, but he was looking for something special. And there she was: Elsa, the waitress at the corner Deli, working behind the lunch counter. She hadn't changed since he saw her up in Marsport. Forever eighteen, her sweet smile, and laughing blue eyes would never fade.

Slipping the key in the lock, Lucas entered the restaurant. Elsa looked up with a smile. "Oh, a customer. How are you?"

On leaving the Traveler's Rest, there was a new lightness in Lucas's step. While not deep, an encounter with Elsa always left him smiling. For a moment he'd connected with his younger self, when life was simpler and he was strong and good.

On the fourth night, he lost over eighty thousand units on the roulette wheel. He went upstairs in a state of shock, and came to THE HITCHING POST, a bar he hadn't noticed before.

Pushing through swinging doors, he found a barn of a place with saw-dust floors. He stood there a moment and adjusted to the semidarkness. To his right were tables, and on the left a long bar, tended by servers in ten-gallon hats. Farther down the room, a crowd danced to old-time western music played by a band on a stage. At the very end were bucking bronco rides and a horseshoe pit.

Lucas was about to head for the bar when two large men in business suits came up. "Secret Service," the first said, holding out a badge. "We need to check you out."

Lucas's first thought was for his attack bots. *Take cover,* he told them. *"Bees to the ceiling, fleas to the floor."* He smiled to the two officers. "You won't find much of interest in me. I'm a retired visitor on a permanent vacation."

"We'll be the judge of that." Grasping his arms, they took him back against the wall. One kept hold of his arm, while the other ran a scanner over him. Afterward, they examined his identification.

In this long moment, things hung in the balance. If the men rousted him out, the bees could bring them immediate death. "Well, everything seems in order," one said, handing back the ID.

"The Hitching Post looks like a nice place," Lucas said. "Are you expecting trouble?"

"This is standard procedure, we're not expecting anything." They walked away.

Lucas remained motionless, and called to his bots. *"Fleas, hop back on my pant legs. Bees, fly to my shoulders."* One of the officers looked back at him as he went to the bar.

After a quick whiskey for his nerves, Lucas ordered a Western Sunrise, an energy enhancer recommended as a wakeup. The drink was orange in color and came in a tall glass, tinkling with ice. He tried a sip as he walked toward the dance floor. It had a fruity taste and was not overly sweet.

The musicians were frantic, sawing their fiddles and stomping their boots, while the lanky cowboy singer remained cool, delivering his ballad of love betrayed in a steady nasal twang. Lucas stopped to watch them.

Catching a flash in the corner of his eye, he looked over at the horseshoe pitch and saw the scoreboard lit up. Someone had made a ringer! Then he froze. The winner was Kenny Summers.

Kenny shook hands with a couple of other men and left the pitch area for a nearby table, where a blonde woman in a black suit was sitting with a group of Tees. When Kenny got there, the woman stood up and embraced him. Everyone at the table was laughing. Seeing Kenny play the politician, Lucas wanted to vomit. The man had no principles whatsoever.

It was odd that Kenny would take up this particular sport. The Rogers brought horseshoes home once after a raid on a Texan caravan, and set up a pitch in the backyard. He and McCool played enough to get good at it, but there was no memory of Kenny being there. Kenny had more important things to do.

Lucas sat down at an empty table. A girl wearing blue jeans, a short-sleeved plaid shirt, and a cowboy hat asked if he wanted anything and he shook his head. Halfway through the glass of Western Sunrise, the drink was working well; his head was as clear as it had ever been. From this table he could reach Kenny with the bees, but he chose not to. Far better to get closer and use the fleas, then he'd be absolutely sure of getting the right target. Later, when death came, there'd be no sign of his involvement.

Amidst more laughter at Kenny's table, the blonde woman pulled two of the Tees to their feet and led them off to the dance floor. The others watched wistfully as the trio walked away holding hands.

Thinking it was a good time to make contact, Lucas opened a napkin from a holder on the table and wrote a message. "A friendly challenge! Horseshoes--you name the stakes." He beckoned the waitress in the cowboy hat.

The server handed Kenny the note. When Kenny turned and stared, Lucas made the secret Rogers sign, slowly waggling his crossed middle and index fingers. Kenny seemed to sink in his chair, as if shrinking in size. Then he stood up.

"The target is approaching," Lucas said to the bots. *"Bees remain in place. Fleas move to my forearms, prepare to board."*

"You're crazy to come here like this," Kenny said, looming over the table.

One of the secret service men hurried to his side. "Is everything all right, sir?" he asked, giving Lucas a cold look.

"Yes, thank you," Kenny said. "He's an old acquaintance I haven't seen in years." When the officer left, he turned back to Lucas. "What the hell do you want?"

"I come in peace," Lucas said, spreading his open hands. "There's not much time left for me since I'm terminal, and there was a powerful instinct to come back home. I'd like to make amends and go out in a good way."

"McCool mentioned you're terminal," Kenny said, stroking his beard. Then his dark eyes snapped and he straightened. "How could you do that to McCool, after he took you in? What happened there?"

"He invited me to stay and help him on the farm, but I couldn't do it. After he left I snuck out in the middle of the night. It was rude but I needed to get away."

Kenny stared at him. "McCool has disappeared. Everyone thought you must have killed him."

"How could they think that? He was my brother." Lucas shook his head, as if bewildered. "I'm real sorry to hear he disappeared. It was a pleasure to spend time with him after all those years, just as it is to see you again. It's a shame you've gone downhill physically, but some deterioration is probably natural."

Kenny made a short laugh. "Deterioration. You're the one to talk."

"Even after thirty years on Mars, I'll kick your butt--if you have the guts to try."

"There's no time for this shit. Don't you know who I am?" Then he sighed. "We'll have one game, just for fun. The first man to make fifteen points is the winner." He strode off toward the horseshoe pit.

Lucas took his Western Sunrise and followed Kenney. *"Boarding is impossible at present,"* he told the bots. *"Return to secure traveling positions."*

Kenny was by the nearest stake, a golden horseshoe in hand. "Throw for first," he said.

Seeing Kenny's long, lean body poised with serious intent, Lucas had to smile. He'd never known Kenny to possess any athletic prowess; it would be a sad day when Lucas couldn't beat the club lawyer at horseshoes. "It'll be a minute--I have to choose my shoes," he said, going to the rack.

Kenny scowled as Lucas hefted the different horseshoes, and felt the cleats. "You don't look all that bad, are you sure you're terminal?"

"Everyone's terminal, there's no way out." He was looking for the shoe that fit his hand, and none of them felt exactly right. The realization came that the years of exile off-world had drastically changed his body. The game would be tougher than he'd imagined. "Martians can live an extended lifetime in the low gravity, but I took a heavy dose of radiation." Grasping a green colored horseshoe in each hand, he held them high.

"Let's go, then." Kenny stepped forward with a careless toss that rang off the far post.

As he came to the pitching box, Lucas moved the shoe around in his hand, trying the weight in different positions as he tried to remember what kind of spin he wanted. He and McCool spent hours figuring it all out. Now his mind was blank, he'd have to go by instinct. He swung his arm and let the horseshoe go, only to see it fall way short. Ignoring Kenny's laughter, Lucas picked up the other shoe. "I haven't done this in years; that first one doesn't count." His second toss hit Kenny's, and bounced away. "Enough practice, I'm first," Kenny said, going to the other end. He retrieved his horseshoes and assumed his stance without looking at Lucas. Using the same fluid delivery as before, he scored a ringer and hit the next one off the post.

"Been practicing?" Lucas asked.

"Maybe I want revenge for those times in the backyard."

"There is no backyard left," Lucas said. "I went to look and everything's gone." He hit the post with the first shot and sailed the next one over the top.

"I've got three, you've got one," Kenny said. "The world we had back then is gone, like it never existed. You shouldn't have come, there's nothing for you here." Settling into his stance he threw one ringer, then another.

"Damn straight, things have changed. Before I left, this was our world, everything was for the humans. Now the old neighborhood is given over to the rabbits and the deer, and you're sucking around with a bunch of Tees. It can't be easy, ruled over by foreigners." Lucas's first shot was long; trying to correct with the second, he came up short. "Nine to one. Ouch."

Kenny just stood and stared at him. "You're such a loser," he said. "Look, nobody rules over us. We're part of the world government like everyone else. As congressman, I'm the voice of the West Coast. Everyone speaks through me and that includes our Tees. Believe it or not, they're humans too." Stepping up, he pitched one wide. "Damn." He let go a hard shot that hit the post and bounced back out of scoring range.

Lucas grinned. "I knew you'd fade." Grasping his horseshoe in the middle, he stepped forward and made a ringer.

"That's a pussy toss!"

"You think I care?" Lucas threw another ringer. "The Rogers were not saints but they fought for what was theirs, like all the forefathers had to do from the beginning. If humans built that Hindu computer they can destroy it, just like they did to every other challenger that came along. Destruction's in our genes."

"The Great One is committed to bringing back our planet. It's in everyone's interest to have her continue."

"Do the Resisters know how you feel?"

Kenny smiled and patted Lucas on the head. "The Resisters manifest emotions and impulses that are still present in this constituency. But they're nightclub cowboys living an illusion."

As if admitting defeat, Lucas hung his head and stared at the floor. "Like you say, the old world is gone. Since I'm terminal I wanted to make amends and live in peace for whatever time is left."

"I'm not so sure," Kenny said. "According to McCool you had a crazy idea about me setting you up. You think I'm to blame for you getting transported to Mars."

For Lucas these words stopped time; his head swam and he looked at Kenny from a long way off. "It's true, I thought that. My fate was so cruel, I needed an explanation."

"Try looking in the mirror," Kenny said. "I advised you over and over to give up bringing in illegal immigrants. The feelings of the time were too strong against it. But you were young and bullheaded. You saw big money and didn't mind the risks." He raised his hands. "Lucas, nobody set you up. You set yourself up."

"Is that the truth, then?"

Kenny grinned. "Yes, that's the truth."

"Fleas, get ready to board." Lucas made two throws wide of the target, and turned to Kenny. "You win. Good game."

Kenny shook Lucas's hand. "It's been a pleasure," he laughed. "Enjoy your time, I won't bother you."

Holding Kenny's right hand tight, Lucas pulled him in for a quick hug. *"Board, fleas, board!"* He patted Kenny on the back. "It's so good to see you again."

Kenny remained very stiff. "Look after yourself," he said in an impersonal tone.

Lucas released his grip and stepped back. "Thanks for the game," he said.

Over at Kenny's table, the blonde woman was looking at them. When Kenny walked that way she rose to meet him.

"We've found bare flesh," the fleas reported.

"Strike deep, my hearties! Now your task is done, hop down from his body. Find your way home to me." Lucas recovered his almost finished Western Sunrise drink and went over to the dance floor. A group of female musicians was playing now, and Lucas stopped to watch while the fleas caught up to him. Kenny's party was gone now. Once the bots were back inside his cuffs, Lucas went to the bar and had a large whiskey.

As Lucas walked along the passageway to the hotel, he thought of Kenny's coming death and smiled. At least he'd done something right.

CHAPTER 32

Astra was frank about her main objectives in our week away. First she wanted to cement her relationship with the designated boyfriend--me--for the coming senior year. Secondly, said boyfriend was to help her master the telecap.

We made a good start after she invited me to her bed. Certain that my love and tenderness would erase whatever impact the boorish George had left, I employed gentle words and gentler caresses. Our physical union took place at daybreak, and was perfect and ecstatic.

The next day, after a late breakfast in the chalet kitchen, we took our coffee into the living room. Astra wore only her nightie and I hoped she'd settle next to me on the couch, but she grabbed her telecap and sat in an armchair. I went and got mine too.

She smiled when I came back in. *"Is it too soon?"*

Her thought voice was cool and clear in my mind, and had musical overtones; awareness also came that she liked my wearing only shorts. I flopped onto the couch and grinned over at her. *"I like it."*

"There'll be no secrets left, by the end of the week."

"Like you say, there's probably ways to hold back sensitive information."

While considering this, Astra moved her position and crossed her legs. My mind immediately changed gears, switching from logical thought to this new view of her upper thighs. Astra blushed, sat up straight, and smoothed down her nightgown. We looked at each other and burst out laughing.

"This is a good example," Astra said. *"Working with real Tees, they're right on top of that kind of slip. Things happen when they choose, and never otherwise."*

"Wang used to talk like that about Buddhism. Mindfulness he called it."

"Wearing the telecap is even more powerful. You'll know whatever happens in my mind, and the same with me about you. The feedback will put us on a fast track to absolute control."

"I'll be back in a minute." Draining the last of my coffee I went off to the bathroom. The flow of urine soon started.

"I always wondered what it's like to be a man," Astra laughed.

The surprise interruption squeezed off my pipeline, and I went back out.

She grinned at me. *"Serena and I went over this same situation, it's all predictable. By the end of this senior year I mean to be fully transformed, with no doubts about my competency or control. I want to find and fix any weak spots now. Working off-world, ignorance and naiveté are not an advantage."*

"You strike me as highly sagacious and ahead of the game."

"We have massage cream here. If it's all right I'll put it on you. Go over you inch by inch and experience all your sensations. You can do a similar thing with me."

"I'm up for that."

"We'll make love with the telecaps on too. I want to know everything you think and feel while it happens."

Astra's ideas struck me as bold and exciting, and I was eager to give them a try. Once inside the bedroom, though, there was no rush to put on the telecap. Instead, she sat in front of the mirrored dresser and tried on a new wig. A curly red one this time. "How does it look?" she asked with a smile.

"Very cute. An attractive woman like you makes me wonder. What is she really thinking about?"

"Right now I've never felt so shy," Astra said. "It's like walking into a room where everybody is dressed up except for me who went nude for the occasion. After this week you'll know everything about me. What if you don't like what you see?"

Getting up from the bed I nuzzled her neck and cheek. "I love you and always have. Nothing can change that."

Astra stood up and took my shoulders in an iron grip. "I want you to swear," she said sternly. "Our time here is only between you and me."

"Cross my heart," I said, not flinching from her gaze. "The blood oath."

When we fell back onto the bed with the telecaps on there was a whole kaleidoscope of impressions, as her feelings and sensations entered my consciousness equally with my own and even dominated at times. The experience of her delighting in my body as I did hers was overwhelming. I ravaged her, driving to a climax while realizing she'd been left behind. The release was ecstatic and triumphant. It left me quivering. *"Sorry," I said.*

Astra sat up and removed her telecap. "Don't apologize for being yourself, Genghis Khan."

"How did you pick that up?"

"There are no secrets here. I sensed something last night, but still it's a surprise."

Sitting up, I tried to pull her to me but she edged away. "Look, Astra," I said. "While that lineage apparently forms some part of me, it's not all there is. Many strains merge together in the formation of an individual. Thanks to our training I'm more self-aware than most people and consider myself a work in progress, not the finished article. I strive every day to become a better person and a large part of that is encouraging my empathetic and caring sides. This relationship with you has already helped me."

Astra did not make much of a response to my heartfelt statement, just left and took a long shower.

Truth telling is a trying process, and it was a relief to put on our wigs and townie clothes. The curly red hair seemed to bring out a vivacious side in Astra; she started talking nonstop, telling me about her life in a woman's dormitory. Carrying a picnic basket with our telecaps and a blanket, we strolled down to the village and picked up some take-out food. A dromy took us back in the mountains, to the pool we'd bathed in before.

The sun was now high in the cloudless sky and the air still. Spreading our blanket on our sheltered patch of grass, we had a light lunch. It was getting warm now, so we went for a swim. Afterward we decided to soak up some sunshine.

Giving me a deep look, Astra took off her wig and reached for her telecap. I did the same. We lay there side by side, on our backs.

"I love feeling the sun beat down on your chest but we shouldn't do it too long," Astra said. *"There's sun block in the basket."*

"I'll put it on you."

"No I thought of it first."

Bending over me she rubbed it on my chest and arms, then my stomach, and moved to my lower legs, slowly working her way up. I enjoyed the way it felt and knew she was cataloguing my reactions, creating a sensory map of my body.

When she started on my genitalia I caught a clear image of her as a young teen, giving George a hand job. She sat very straight, as if this was a serious task for her. The picture seemed so ridiculous I couldn't help laughing.

"He called it taming his wild beast. Back then going out with George Damon made me feel important."

"He does manage to carry off a kind of image. Maybe it's all that family money and power."

Then she gave me another picture, of George deliberately striking her across the face. *"I'm sick of you,"* he shouted. *"You cold bitch--you're frigid!"*

This put me close to tears. I pulled her to me, and cradled her in my arms. *"Astra, you are not frigid. The one with a problem is George. It's tough to feel much warmth for a reptile like that."*

"The truth is I never had an orgasm in the normal way."

I could not pretend to be more experienced, and showed myself posing naked on a blanket for my art teacher. Ms. McDonald, an older, dark-haired woman, left her easel and came to fondle me, so I'd be erect.

Astra laughed. "What were you posing as, Priapus?"

"No, Hermes. He's the messenger of the gods, young and fast moving, and revered by thieves and athletes. Originally the Greeks showed him with an erection.

My art teacher wanted to get back to that early style, because she said it created a more godlike look."

Later in the session Ms. McDonald removed her black slacks and joined me on the blanket. *Slim, with hollow cheeks and a prominent bosom, she never disrobed from the waist up.*

"What a creepy lady," Astra said. *"It's like if she had spurs she'd use them on you."* She took off her telecap. "I can't handle too much of this at one go. What say we have another swim?"

She was right; it was a relief to dive into the coolness of the pond and splash around. We stood up in the middle and kissed. Everything was clean and perfect. Running my hand down her back to her rump, though, I missed not knowing her sensations. It was then I realized telepathy is as seductive as any drug. Maybe more so.

Back at our place we continued with Astra's plan, using the massage creams to systematically map our bodies. Genghis Khan was now laid to rest. This was about the two of us, and we were both part geek. Our brain implants were a big advantage, providing a photographic memory for information we chose to keep.

The hours I spent slowly going over Astra's awesome body were highly pleasurable to me. I'd intaken quite a lot of poetry recently, and now Andrew Marvell's To His Coy Mistress came to mind.

> *An hundred years should go to praise*
> *Thine eyes, and on thy forehead gaze;*
> *Two hundred to adore each breast*
> *But thirty thousand to the rest;*

"I know that poem too," Astra said. "For me the ending is too much from the masculine point of view. Listen to this:

> *Let us roll all our strength, and all*
> *Our sweetness, up into one ball,*
> *And tear our pleasures with rough strife*
> *Through the iron gates of life.*

"Do you see what I mean?" she asked. "When you start tearing your pleasures with rough strife I get left behind. My nature is gentle, not rough. Plus I'm just slower with that kind of thing."

"My deepest desire is to be there for you," I said. "We'll learn the rhythms and harmonies that are right for both of us." I hummed the song I'd made for her the first time we went to the mountain pond, and she moved to it.

This is how our romantic art first developed, that was created by us, and that utilized the map of each other's sensations. The goal was not to orgasm, and get things over with. Rather it was approaching the edge, and staying there in bliss. Astra then banished the idea that she was frigid. No, she was multi-orgasmic.

Thus with the telecaps time seemed to slow down, and we never wanted our stay at the chalet to end. The week did pass though.

On our last evening it was on the news that Congressman Kenny Summers had come down with an exotic virus and collapsed while working out in his gym. This was a blow to both of us, as the congressman had been part of our government forever. He was like a father figure. It looked as if he would pull through, thanks to a couple of T-man physicians who happened to be exercising alongside him.

The video showed the congressman in his hospital bed. He seemed to perk up as the interview progressed. "According to the doctors, this sickness is no accident," he said. The video showed his face close up, and his dark eyes gazed out solemnly. "Let me assure you, this cowardly attack changes nothing. My voice cannot be stilled, and my work on behalf of the West Coast region continues without letup."

Astra shut down the video and reached for the Sinful Delights. It was past time for dinner; we'd been lazy about leaving the bedroom. Her chocolate-smeared lips were tempting, and I soon forgot all else.

CHAPTER 33

Exhausted after returning from Seattle, Lucas slept for twelve hours straight. On awakening it was a warm spring day, and he set up a recliner chair on the balcony. He got Maude to brew some tea, and took a cup outside.

Here, sitting in the sunshine, the knowledge he was free from his nemesis finally took hold. He'd done it, he'd turned the corner. Relaxation was never easy for him, danger usually lurked somewhere. With Kenny gone, this was over. He'd watch the mountains and the ships and not worry about anything.

Amazingly, he drifted off again. When he woke up, the sun was high in the sky and a strong wind was coming in. His tea was cold. Deciding to go inside, he got up and almost blacked out. He stood there and held onto the back of the chair until his strength came back.

This was not like him. Maybe it had something to do with that cold he picked up down in Seattle. The pills seemed to knock it out to some degree; the sniffles were gone, even though his glands were still swollen. Could it be lack of exercise? He'd been complacent since getting out of the hospital.

He told Maude to rustle up a decent breakfast of pancakes, bacon, and eggs. While waiting he had a big glass of freshly squeezed orange juice. Smelling the cooking food, he was sure it would help a lot. Once it was in his stomach he'd go for a walk along the water, and maybe try his hand at lawn bowling.

After two bites of the pancakes, he had to run for the bathroom. Bending over the toilet, he vomited out the contents of his stomach in wrenching spasms. When he washed his face his eyes were bleary, and he was awfully pale. A deep enervation pervaded his entire being. He called Grace Hospital, and they told him to come in right away.

A robocab took him to the emergency entrance. Two hospital attendants in white uniforms brought him inside the entranceway on a gurney. Then an alarm sounded and they both left. "Come back," Lucas called, propping himself up. They made no reply, but walked rapidly away.

In a few minutes a man in hazard gear approached, accompanied by a nurse-robot. "Don't be alarmed," the man said. "You're an unusual case, and as a precaution we're taking you to isolation." They quickly wheeled him down a hallway and into a small room, where they transferred him to the bed.

"I was just here for a full treatment," Lucas said. "My problem shouldn't be anything major--it might be some kind of bug."

"Yes, I'm Dr. Carney, one of the interns who looked after you. One thing that strikes me is your appearance. It looks as if you're aging."

"Aging," Lucas said. "Well, that sounds natural."

"Not in Grace Hospital." Dr. Carney inserted a needle, and began drawing blood from Lucas's arm. "We'll run some tests and find out exactly what's going on. In the meantime we need to keep you quarantined, in case you're infectious."

The time in the isolation room seemed interminable. The video was a welcome distraction until a public affairs program showed Kenny Summers sitting up in a hospital bed, assuring a reporter he'd be back soon.

According to the program's host, an attempt had been made to assassinate Kenny with a biological weapon. A physician recognized the specially designed virus as similar to the pre-conquest handiwork of an Egyptian scientist, and the man was contacted. While not admitting responsibility, the scientist provided some drugs that saved the congressman.

This was the worst news for Lucas, and it pitched him into a deep despondency. If only he'd used the bees and made sure.

Then Bibi appeared on the video screen. "Hello, Lucas," she said. "They've updated me on your case. The lab's finished your analysis, and we've set up a treatment plan for you. You'll be started on that tonight. I'll come in to see you as soon as possible."

"All right," Lucas muttered, waving his hand.

The screen went blank, and Dr. Carney came in. "Whoever set this up is laughing at us," he said. "Do you have enemies?"

"Not that I know of."

"The lab results show a perverse alteration of standard gene therapy. Several viruses are active in you, each targeting a different group of cells. They're working as vectors, to alter your DNA. But instead of disabling defective genes and bringing in the normal, they've done the reverse: they've deliberately established defective genes. This is what's caused the rapid aging I noticed in your appearance. You've developed Werner's syndrome."

"Is it the same rapid aging as what children get?"

"No, yours is different from childhood progeria," Dr. Carney said. "Tonight our first priority is to attack the viruses. You'll get a cocktail of several drugs through the intravenous line. Later on we'll attempt to return your DNA to its normal state."

After Dr. Carney left Lucas's mind worked coldly, sorting through the events of the recent past. Not for the first time, he'd badly underestimated Kenny Summers. A man like Kenny probably had ring after ring of defenses guarding his home base. They might have spotted him on the Speed. Maybe the Galaxy Hotel noticed he fit a profile.

He'd eaten at the Ruby night after night, relishing the pastas and pastries, and lingering over coffee and liqueurs. After dinner he gambled and spent time in the clubs and lounges, never going home till he was half drunk. A poisoner had countless opportunities. Kenny could have got to him through Elsa, at the Traveler's Rest. A robot was a robot; it had no loyalties or feelings.

The cruelty of the fate Kenny had chosen for him made a period of observation highly probable. He'd come out of the treatment in Grace

Hospital's tank a new man, and relished every minute of his newfound strength, vigor and virility. Someone like Kenny would not celebrate that with him, not for a moment. Kenny was a jealous rival, who'd enjoy taking these gifts away from him.

The flush of a second youth was only a memory now. Reality was a rapidly decaying body, stuck in this hospital bed. If he made it out of here alive, the future looked bleak. The diminished energy, wrinkled skin, flaccid muscles, and stooped posture common among most old people would come to him at an accelerated pace.

Luckily there was a washroom attached to his room. Not bothering to buzz the attendant he climbed out of bed and went in there, taking his intravenous line along. He could see new wrinkles in the mirror, but overall he didn't look too bad. Could the intern be exaggerating the situation? Finding some toilet articles on a shelf he took a comb and ran it through his hair, only to have a bunch come right out. This was monstrous.

It was three days before Bibi and Dr. Johansen appeared, and by this time Dr. Carney and the others were coming into his room without hazard suits. The viruses were under control; there was no risk he would infect others through casual contact.

"How are you feeling?" Bibi asked, smiling down at him.

"Not too bad, considering," Lucas replied. "Is there any decision about my case?"

"We've consulted with specialists worldwide," Dr. Johansen said. "There's no doubt about how to attempt a cure, but the problem is the time frame. We might lose you before we eradicate the viruses and bring back your DNA."

"Your immune system is compromised," Bibi said. "You're exposed to opportunistic infections, which increases the risk."

"Do you want my judgment of your best course of action?" Dr. Johansen asked. He looked into Lucas's eyes. "Do the merger with your clone."

"I'll try," Lucas said hoarsely.

"There's one more issue," Dr. Johansen said. "I think it's pretty clear the filthy bastards made a criminal attack against you. Really our authorities should be called in."

Lucas closed his eyes. "It would create more trouble than it's worth," he said finally. "I have a good idea who's responsible, but there's no hatred in my heart. My wish is to keep the police out of this, and just concentrate on getting better."

"You're one of our dearest friends," Bibi said. She looked to her husband.

Dr. Johansen put an arm around her and smiled down at Lucas. "Don't worry, you'll have your wish."

CHAPTER 34

Although not considered contagious, Lucas was kept confined to his own room. He suspected this was to avoid scaring the other patients. In Grace Hospital, it was not good to age rapidly by the day.

His main hope was the merger with Dom, and he thought endlessly about how best to convince the boy. When Bibi came in, he gazed up at her from his couch, and admitted that Dom scared him. "The loss of his autonomy will be a big stumbling block. He'll hate being dominated."

"You're talking about issues I deal with every day," Bibi said, taking a seat beside him. "These same concerns crop up with every merger."

"So how do you convince a person to do this when they're still young, and just starting their own life?"

"They come to understand that it's not a loss of autonomy, it's a loss of isolation and separateness. A merger creates a larger, more complex, sophisticated, and much more powerful being, that pools the knowledge and experience of both parties, and makes the most of their resources. A good merger opens the door to rapid success in every undertaking."

"Dom will never rule over me, I promise you that."

Bibi nodded. "I make sure the dominance issue is resolved during the procedure. But it is not a simple matter of you running everything. Once you and your clone unite, his concerns hold equal weight with your own, and you find ways to accommodate each other."

"The experience will be a real education for me."

"Nobody realizes how wonderful it is until they get there." Then she frowned. "You and Dom need to spend a lot more time together."

"I planned to do it this year," Lucas said. "Getting sick was a bad break."

"It's a tricky situation, and we're entering new territory with your case. Just be brave, as you were thirty years ago when you rescued my family. While I'm in charge here your precious life will not slip away."

Grace Hospital contacted me late Thursday morning. It was a shock to hear Lucas was sick again; he'd looked so well when he first got out of the hospital.

Not much was going on around campus, because it was our break time. Most of the students, including Astra, were at home; for me the dormitory was my home. I was part of a skeleton crew, still hanging around. I'd planned to go over to the Polaris after lunch and play some music. Saturday night was the Grand Ball, and in another week I'd start classes as a senior.

I ordered a cab and left the school as soon as possible. It was a gray day, with constant drizzle. I hardly noticed the other vehicles as we sped along.

When I arrived, it was close to two o'clock in the afternoon. Bibi met me at the reception desk, and we walked down the ramp to the lower level. "Thank you for coming," she said. "Lucas wants very much to see you."

She stopped me as we went by the room where I'd seen him in the tank. "Someone else wants to meet you," she said. "Let's break for a minute." She took me into the waiting room.

I sat at the little table, and Bibi poured tea, and offered me a plate of cookies. "It's been hectic here today," she said with a sigh, sitting down. "This hospital is a madhouse sometimes."

"What's happened to Lucas?" I asked. "He looked so well before."

Bibi shook her head. "Everyone has ups and downs. Nothing's for sure in this life of ours."

Then she took a deep breath and smiled. "I've never met a space cadet before," she said. Her voice struck me as markedly different. Pitched slightly lower, it sounded younger, and lacked her usual practiced, stylized quality. "I'm Cici," she said, offering her small hand.

She was most engaging, and I couldn't help grinning. "It's good to meet you," I said, taking her hand in mine. "I'm Dom."

"Yes, I've met your older twin. Lucas is a very nice man and I'm sorry he's taken ill again."

"Shouldn't you be in school?"

"You're not the first to ask me that," Cici said. "If I return to school it'll be for postdoctoral studies; Bibi and I are the same, and what she knows, I know. The merging experience was incredible, because my brain was fairly pristine until it was flooded by my sister's information. I have plenty of room left, especially with my implants, so there's potential for lots more growth."

"You two are the same? And yet you have a different personality from Bibi."

"She handles the work, and I take care of the fun."

She slapped her wrist, and Bibi's laugh rang out. "It's true, we have a division of labor," Bibi said. "One advantage for a busy health care professional is that Cici keeps me from turning into a machine. She's strongly caring and human, even when I'm most rushed. But that's us. Other merged clones have their own concerns, and do what's right for them."

When we finished our tea, Bibi took me down the hall to the very last door. She knocked softly, and opened it. "Dom's here," she called to Lucas. I went inside, and she left.

The room was fairly large, with a bed against the window, and a sitting area by the door where I came in. Lucas was in a reclining chair, watching a game show. He shut the video down and swiveled to face me. "Dom, I'm glad you came."

"It's good to see you," I said, taking a place on the couch close to him.

Lucas appeared tired. While his green eyes still conveyed their focus and intensity, he was pale and his body seemed to lack the vigor and force which impressed me when he first came home from the tank.

"They've had me locked up here," he said. "I'm not contagious, so there's no risk, but they're afraid of bad publicity. The look of old age is a disaster for them."

This did not seem likely, and I wondered if senility had set in. "It's raining today," I said. "Otherwise we could sit outside."

"I don't plan to stay here much longer," Lucas said. "When I'm back home at the Needles you and I will walk in the park, or along the seawall."

"I'll look forward to that."

"You're one of the main reasons I returned to Earth," Lucas said. "I wanted to hook you up with the family tree."

"Learning about our family was crucial for me," I said. "Meeting someone who looks like me is a relief too."

Lucas started to cough. Grabbing a tissue, he hacked up some sputum. "Sorry," he said, tossing the wad into a nearby basket. "They put me on drugs for the viruses, but I'm still not clear." Leaning forward, he held onto the arm of his chair, planted his feet on the floor, and stood for a moment. Then he went over to the window. "You're right, it's raining." He turned to face me. "Mars doesn't have rain anymore. Nobody's ruled out bringing it back; we've seen so much change, and gone so far. They tell me Earth's new quantum computer, the Great One, has done away with death for the T-men."

The sudden way he brought in the subject made me laugh. "The T-men work closely with Raina, and when someone dies she recreates their personalities. From what I can tell it's not doing away with death, it's creating an artificial life form which mimics a former person. The Great One is very social, and enjoys being part of the T-man community, both while they're alive and then in this after-life, she's created."

"Still it's a major advance. Here at Grace Hospital they've gone even farther. They're altering people's life spans by merging clones. You know Bibi, don't you?"

I flushed. "Yes, and I met Cici. It's like they've gone back into the ancient times and resurrected the system of serfs and slaves. How monstrous for that girl, never to know the basic freedoms and delights of being an independent person! Bibi abused her all-powerful position in the lieu of motherhood, and took full advantage of her. People are not trees that you can graft another shoot onto. What Bibi's done is a gross violation of human rights."

Lucas scowled, and clenched his fists. "Bibi is special to me, and I never saw her that way. Cici's a sweetheart too. She and Bibi are of one mind."

"Being in love has made me more understanding of women," I said. "Astra is a person in her own right. She's nobody's sweetheart, in the sense of being self-effacing."

The old man smiled, and went back to his chair. "I look forward to meeting Astra. She might be the queen who can recreate our dynasty."

Again he touched a nerve, and it made me most uncomfortable. "That kind of talk is out of line. Nothing's for sure at this point."

Lucas sighed, and his head lolled. "All of a sudden I'm exhausted. Thank you for coming."

Seeing his eyes close, I touched my lips to his forehead and left the room. Bibi was nowhere in sight. I went down the hallway, and up the ramp to the exit door, without speaking to anyone. My cab was there waiting.

During the drive back to the school, I was lost in thought. Meetings with Lucas were intense, and they often disturbed me.

His sudden change from robust good health to a more fragile condition was difficult to understand. Clearly he was in danger. Yet given his age, and all he'd gone through, his present condition might be normal.

Luckily, he was in good hands. Grace Hospital was a world-class geriatrics center. If the worst ever happened, I could be sure that Bibi and her colleagues would arrange for the best palliative care available.

While deeply concerned, I did not feel sorry for him. His life was full to overflowing with adventures and rich experiences most could only dream of, and he'd developed into a real character. After such a career, death was a normal part of the human condition and could not be seen as a tragedy.

I couldn't help thinking of a comment Mr. Beebe made once in history class. We were discussing the convicts Britain transported to Australia, and Mr. Beebe said "In those times, resolution was often found at the end of a rope." Would things ever change much for an unrepentant reprobate like Lucas?

Bibi showed Lucas the video of his visit with Dom, and they discussed it in detail. "I'm seeing empathy and compassion," she said. "He's developed strong feelings for you." She stopped the video when Dom was about to leave, and kissed Lucas on the forehead. "That's a powerful statement of filial concern."

"I've often felt fatherly toward Dom."

Bibi backed the video to where Dom's face twisted, and his voice dripped with contempt. "How monstrous for that girl, never to know the basic freedoms and delights of being an independent person!"

"We see these concerns over and over again with mergers," Bibi said. "It's a major stumbling block."

"Dom does not understand merging," Cici said. "Bibi and I are contemplating a life span of four to five times the average person's. There's plenty of time for me to wear the captain's hat, especially after Didi joins us. Our mission is to help others, and we dream of doing this on a grand scale, as saviors and benefactors."

Bibi sighed deeply. She nodded firmly and hugged herself, then straightened. "Lucas, I'd love to see you and Dom with many more months together full of quality time, before we do this merger. Unfortunately, because of your rapid aging, our window of opportunity is shrinking fast. The procedure can be demanding and quite intense. I'll need you to be alert and awake, and capable of performing an active role. The hospital has a time slot open Saturday night, and I say we start the operation then."

Lucas felt weak. "What if the boy says no?"

"Never forget, we're doing the right thing. Your life is precious, and that comes first. The merger with you will prove a huge gain for Dom; resistance on his part is mainly the result of ignorance. And he is your clone. It's not like you're strangers. He's another version of your own self. So stay strong, and don't doubt me. Rejection is normal; I deal with it all the time, and we have procedures in place."

"How will it work?" Lucas asked.

"Saturday night we'll complete the transfer of your information. Everything's ready, so it should go easily. Once that's done, we'll enter the stage which I term the period of difficulty. I'll work closely with you and Dom for weeks. The final synthesis will depend on both of you recognizing rival needs, making conscious the differences in beliefs, and ultimately rising to a higher level where a new, fully integrated being is born."

Tired from the visits, Lucas relaxed and closed his eyes. The state of reverie was quite pleasant until a memory from childhood came strongly to him. As often happened, his parents were screaming and cursing each other, and this time the argument turned serious. When his father knocked his mother to the floor, Lucas went to his room for the hunting rifle. The horrendous yelling never stopped, and now his father was kicking her. Lucas took careful aim and fired. The blast was loud in the little room. His father's rant was cut short; spinning, he gave Lucas one last crazed grin.

Then he fell.

Lucas didn't like calling himself a patricide, but he was one. When his father came over from Turkistan, he lied about his marital status to win a new wife, and kept up the pretense throughout Lucas's childhood. The truth came out when he had to return home. The thought of joining the other family was too much for Lucas's mother to accept, and open warfare erupted, ended only by Lucas's bullet.

The two of them fled New York and began a new life on the West Coast, in Tacoma. This was the happiest time Lucas had ever known, until she was murdered on her way home from work and the Rogers took him in.

Leaning back in the hospital chair, Lucas's thoughts turned to Dom. He had the same bad blood as Lucas, and was likely a cold, black hearted schemer, just like their father.

Bibi had to be warned that Dom's nature was dangerous, and devious. The boy was not to be trusted, and she needed to watch him carefully.

CHAPTER 35

The Grand Ball at the end of term was one of the few times STA students got together for a real party. The dance was held in the assembly hall at the center of the complex.

We had wine that night for dinner, and upstairs in the dorm the atmosphere was wild. Studies forgotten, everyone was in the mood for a blowout. Men ran back and forth from room to room.

I'd taken a shower and was in my bathrobe, sipping from a bottle of old bourbon Wang had sent as a present. Pleasant flavors spread on my tongue, and I felt a growing warmth. The drink was conducive to meditation, and it struck me that although Wang was my best friend, his departure hadn't changed my life much. I'd continued on, seldom giving any thought to the past. This evening I wanted very much to speak with him, and I asked Charles to get in touch.

The video lit up, and Wang grinned at me. "Hello. It's good to hear from you." He looked lean and fit and he sported a moustache. I recognized the bunk beds from Nora's guest room in the background.

"How are things going?" I asked.

"It's coming together. The co-op gave us some land, and today we poured the foundation for our house. It'll be a big place, Serena wants about ten children. Our wedding's next month, will you be there?"

"I wouldn't miss it." I held up the bottle. "Thanks for the present."

"I knew you'd be celebrating, the night of the Grand Ball. Tonight's the full moon. Magic, romance . . . "

I grimaced. "It might be a long night for me, watching Astra with George Damon. I'll get through it, though."

"Now you're talking." Wang held up a clenched fist. "STA!" Then he was gone.

There was a pounding on the door and more friends burst in, led by Zack. "Thought so," Zack cried, when he saw the bottle. "Smelt it all the way down the hall."

"Help yourself, gentlemen," I said. "If you don't mind the lack of glasses."

Zack held the bottle to his lips and swallowed. "Whoa, good stuff." He passed it on to the next man.

When it was time to go we put on our dress uniforms. Laughing and joking, six of us started off toward the assembly hall. "STA," Zack hollered.

We all joined in. "STA! Training for space! STA!"

After walking to the end of our field we passed through the Old Lace campus. Music was coming from the assembly hall up ahead. Men and women in dress uniforms streamed toward the entrance.

A huge black limousine was parked on a side street. "Someone important must have come," Zack said. We eyed the car curiously as we got closer.

A tinted window slid slowly down. Lucas, dressed in formal evening wear, pointed to me and beckoned. A sinking feeling overcame me. "I'll catch up with you later," I told the others.

They walked on, and I went up to the car. "What's going on?" I asked. The back door opened, and Lucas told me to get in. When I sat down beside him, the door slammed shut and we pulled away. The side walls emitted a low glow, but I could see nothing of the front. "Why the limo?" I asked sharply. "And why are you dressed like that?" We were speeding up. "You couldn't have picked a worse night."

"Sorry to interrupt." His voice was quiet and sounded as if it was an effort to speak, but he gripped my knee with surprising strength. "I've had an awful setback, a severe turn for the worse." We turned a sharp corner, and he fell against me. A flash of light from outside showed we were traveling at high speed. "Damn this sickness. There's so much I wanted to speak to you about, to prepare you for the transition."

This sounded like inheritance talk, and it made me queasy. "I couldn't touch the proceeds of crime."

Leaning against me, he spoke into my ear. "There's a higher law than you've known at the academy, and there are issues which far outweigh your individual life or mine. Have you heard of the Universal Church?"

"Yes, but only in passing."

"Before getting transported I was a tough nut, but on Mars my hard shell got pared away. I made a living as a stevedore, loading and unloading the freighters at the top of the space elevator, and every shift I faced the blazing stars and the vastness of the universe. Can you imagine how small that makes you feel? Dom, I was less than a bug."

"That's interesting," I said. "At my school they prepare us for life off-world through intakes. We see through the eyes of T-men working out there, and we feel what they feel. The information is all job related though, there's nothing about their personal lives."

"In my case there was an accident. I was trapped out in the open, and took a huge dose of radiation. Down in Marsport people had pity in their eyes, as if I was finished. Then one day I wandered into the Universal Church. It was a small place on the corner; I'd hardly noticed it before. But when I listened to what the pastor was saying and met the others, I found they understood. They'd all gone through similar experiences to mine. That was the beginning of a major realignment in my thought. It resulted in me becoming a real Martian."

"You're talking about something deep," I said. "The T-men never cut their ties to Earth, their minds are still hooked up."

"They're the administrators, and we're the colonists. The Martians aim to change the situation, and we've already made considerable progress."

Lucas lapsed into silence. I made a comment about religion, hoping to draw more out of him, but there was no response. He'd fallen asleep.

The car came to a stop underneath an awning, in the lighted entranceway to Grace Hospital. Lucas stirred. "Let's go," he said. "They're expecting us."

Inside, a stocky man with bristly white hair stood behind the reception desk. His short-sleeved blue shirt revealed anchor tattoos on both forearms. "Welcome Mr. Ferryman," he said. "Dr. Johansen will be out in a minute."

The man pointed us to a nearby waiting room. When we sat down on one of the couches, music began and the images on the wall lit up, showing man's progress from infancy to age. "Thanks to today's medical science, people are free to reject old age and reclaim their youth," a voice said softly. "Speak to your Grace Hospital adviser." The images on the wall showed people rising from their sick beds. They smashed their wheel chairs, and danced around.

Lucas had fallen asleep again and was snoring softly. I was shocked to see how he'd gone downhill. The vitality and youthful glow were absent; he seemed shrunken, and weakened. His skin was wrinkled, his hair graying. In contrast to his physical condition, his clothing was top-drawer: an iridescent evening suit, and sparkling cuff links which looked to be diamonds.

It was difficult to be stuck here on the night of the Grand Ball, but my duty was clear. Lucas's sickness was not something to walk away from. Closing my eyes, I pictured Astra twirling to the music, and sent her a thought of love. "I'll be there soon, that's a promise from my heart."

"You must be Dom." A tall blond man in a white doctor's uniform came in, a robot-nurse at his side. "I'm Dr. Johansen," he said, shaking hands with me. "Is Lucas all right?"

"I'm awake," Lucas growled, sitting up.

"Let's be off, then." Dr. Johansen took Lucas's right arm, and the robot-nurse the left.

Lucas soon shrugged off their grip, and we followed Dr. Johansen down a beige colored hallway that reminded me of a rest home. Glancing into a dining room, I recognized Buck Havoc, the famous action star. In his late seventies now, Buck's face was lined. His companion at the table looked like a clone in his twenties.

"Quite a few actors come here for rejuvenation," Dr. Johansen said, dropping back to my side. "We're especially honored to have Thailand's royal family." He nodded to a group of Asians clustered around two tables pushed together. "Yes, we're working with the king. Over at the far table, the client is an Arab sheikh."

Fearing Lucas might slip, I kept an eye on him, but he managed the walk perfectly well. The flash of his diamond cuff links seemed bizarre, as ostentation was useless here. Sickness dragging him down, he may have wanted to make a statement with his appearance, that he was a nobleman, a descendant of Genghis Khan, a Martian, and a Roger. Realistically though, who could he impress in this wealthy private hospital?

When we entered an elevator, Lucas stood against the wall and groaned. "How are we doing?" Dr. Johansen asked, taking his arm again.

"A touch of pain in the chest," Lucas said, leaning against him. "I'll be all right."

On the next floor soft music played, and I smelled lavender. The hallway was deserted except for a child with a shaved head approaching in a stretcher bed, guided by a robotic attendant. "How are you, Helen?" Dr. Johansen asked, patting her thin cheek. The girl did not reply, but hummed tunelessly.

"Here's the office," Dr. Johansen said. He opened a door to a light brown room where Bibi sat behind a curved pink desk. She wore hospital whites and had on dark red lipstick.

"Come in," she said in a husky voice. "Lucas and Dom, it's marvelous to see you together."

Bibi had me sit in the chair next to Lucas. The top of her desk lit up and a picture appeared that had been widely circulated in the media, of me standing beside the wreckage of the Mendez airship. Beside it was a shot of the young Lucas on the deck of his submersible, the day he rescued Bibi's family from Manila. "Two men," Bibi said. "Both are heroes. These unique Individuals are nevertheless one and the same."

The still pictures were replaced by images of Lucas and me sitting at Bibi's desk, captured by some hidden camera. "Two halves of a whole," Bibi said. "One is a man of wealth and power, with huge life experience and accumulated wisdom. The other's a student, just embarking on life's journey. They are drawn to each other for different reasons and in different ways. One has much to give and to pass on; the other needs a helping hand from a teacher and a mentor. The time they spend together is invaluable, for it completes them both."

Her desk went dark again. She clasped her hands together and gazed at Lucas and me. "Life is transformation, and change," she said. "Nothing stays the same, not even stone. Lucas, are you prepared for this step forward?"

Lucas scowled. "The familiarization process was supposed to take at least a year, but I don't have that kind of time."

"We'll just have to do our best," Dr. Johansen said firmly.

Bibi smiled to me. "Dom, you've been able to spend some time with Lucas? You've gotten to know him?"

"We've had some good talks," I said warily.

"Do you experience a sense of closeness with him? A kinship?"

"I do feel something like that," I admitted. "I was an institutional kid and he's the only contact with my real family there's been."

Bibi reached over and took my hand. "Dom, as Lucas's clone he is everything to you. Your father-brother--a second self, really. And now you'll be even closer."

"Look, kid," Lucas said. "I've often regretted not being a better father, or mother, to you. It was hard not being there when you were growing up. But I loved you from afar and made sure your needs were looked after." He made a sniffling sound and used a handkerchief to blow his nose. "I didn't want this merger to be too much of a surprise."

"Merger?" Anger rose in me such that I'd never known. Springing to my feet I kicked away the chair. "Are you out of your mind?" I shouted.

"I'm not you, or anything like you. You're a criminal, and everything I hate!" A needle jabbed my upper arm. Turning I saw it was the robot-nurse. Then everything went black.

When I awoke Bibi hovered over me in a control booth. We were in a walled-off section of a large, brightly lit room, and Lucas and I were side-by-side in recliners with elevated sides. I was strapped in. He wasn't, and was snoring loudly. He and Bibi wore bulky black head pieces, and it felt like I had one on too. The robot-nurse stood with arms folded a few feet from our recliners, a flicker in its black eyes the only movement.

"Are you awake, lover boy?" Bibi's *thought voice was lower than her usual tone, and had a sultry quality that alarmed me.* "Cici thinks you're hot, and I have to agree."

"Don't talk like that," I told her. *"This is worse than kidnapping, you can't force a person."*

"I'm sorry if it appears that way. It's only a communication problem; let's not start off on the wrong foot. I want to explain some things to you, will you listen? If not I'll put you back to sleep, and we can talk later."

"Don't put me to sleep, I'll listen."

"An adequate merger can usually be accomplished in three to four weeks. In Lucas's case the time line has to be extended, as the preparation stage was poorly done, and you are showing strong signs of rejection."

"Signs of rejection? You're not discussing an organ transplant; it's the rape of my very soul."

"Calm yourself," Bibi said sternly. *"My drugs can counteract and subdue the worst rejection, and I'll start you on them right now."*

"No, don't. Sorry, I do want to know what's going to happen."

"No worries. When we work as a team these mergers are positive for every-one. Thanks to your T-man quality implants, I see no technical difficulties. We'll make good use of your memory capacity and readiness of access tonight, as our control center stands ready to transfer Lucas's information."

"What type of information are you talking about?"

"Everything. The information constitutes a complete record of the adult Lucas, including his memories and dreams."

I was starting to feel sleepy. "This alone won't transfer Lucas's mind to my body, will it?"

"Tonight we'll work in fast time and you won't be conscious of any of the new material. The actual awakening won't come until later. The three of us will enjoy many hours of quality time together, reliving the experiences that helped form both you and Lucas. Toward the end, Lucas will begin to take control of your body in simple actions. By then you'll accept him totally and welcome his dominance."

What she said did not seem right, but I could no longer keep my eyes open.

When I woke up Bibi and Dr. Johansen were talking with Lucas, who was sitting up in his recliner. The robot-nurse was by the door.

Glancing my way, Bibi laughed and came to remove my headset. "You did well."

"It's the night of the Grand Ball. I need to get out of here!"

"I'm so sorry," she said, making a sad face. "The ball must be over, it's almost two in the morning."

It only felt like a short nap, and I looked at her uncertainly. "As I said before, I'm not going through with this. You have to call it off."

"Quiet," Lucas shouted. He got to his feet and looked down at me coldly. "You'll have to accept the inevitable. The merger was supposed to not happen until a year from now, but things changed. Now, do you understand?"

"You are crazy," I yelled, pushing against the restraints. "Absolutely insane. I want out of here!"

Dr. Johansen chuckled. "The young man has spirit. He must come from good stock."

Lucas grinned, and gripped my biceps. "See the lightning flash in his eyes." He howled with laughter. "This is one of the happiest moments of my life." He planted a kiss full on my lips.

The touch of those cold, dead lips was unbearable to me. "Aargh!" I screamed, a wave of loathing rising up. Twisting violently, I tipped the recliner over and fell sideways onto the floor. The impact tore out the top restraints, and freed my chest.

"Stop, you idiot," Lucas shouted, kicking at me.

He connected with my shoulder but I caught his leg and got him down, lunging partly on top of him. My legs were still trapped and he kneed me in the groin, causing sickening pain. Then he did it again. With a shriek of agony I twisted away. Reaching under his back I pulled him up half sitting, and slammed him down. His head made an awful smack on the floor and he lay still.

Still in a lot of pain, I freed my legs from the restraints and stood up, only to see the robot-nurse rushing toward me. Picking up the main body of the recliner, I shoved it at the robot and knocked it flat. As its arm still reached toward me, needle in hand, I made a wide swing with the recliner and sent its head askew.

"It was a mistake to rush things," Bibi sobbed. "I said so from the beginning."

Dr. Johansen knelt over Lucas, who was on his back, his mouth sagging open. "You've killed him," he hissed at me. "You're a monster."

Overcome by the need to get away, I hardly heard, and they did not try to stop me from leaving. Outside in the hallway an alarm rang shrilly, and the lights blinked on and off. One last strap from the recliner still clung to me; I ripped it off and threw it away. At the end of the hallway a STAIRS sign flashed with the other lights.

I went into the stairwell just as the white-haired man from the reception desk was coming up. "Stop right there," he said, raising a stun gun. Leaping instantly, I kicked his chest and he fell backward down the stairs.

I entered the ground floor hallway. The alarm was loud here too, and people in pajamas were coming out of their rooms. "Nothing's wrong, it's a false alarm," I said loudly. No one replied; they all stared as I ran quickly to the front exit.

Outside, Lucas's limo remained parked under the awning. I hurried past. Farther down the driveway, I started to run.

The full moon was out, and the road ahead was easy to see. A couple of horses stood silently in the pasture to my left, across the road. Time was the crucial factor now. If I could make it back to the school before daybreak, nobody would notice my absence.

My dress shoes were not designed for running, but I made myself ignore the growing pain. Up ahead was an intersection, and a transit shelter. "North to Vancouver," I cried, going inside.

"The next Vancouver bus will arrive in eight minutes."

Hoping to be back at school well before dawn, I sat on the bench and closed my eyes. Then an eerie, high-pitched siren cut the stillness. I was the logical prey, and it filled me with horror.

The surrounding area was all flat farmland, but somewhere there must be a place to hide. I hurried off, and once away from the intersection, waded through high grass and climbed the fence to the field.

This section had recently been plowed, and the earth was exposed in rounded furrows. Running hard, I slipped and fell in the dirt. The siren was ever closer and I raced on, desperation growing in me.

Ahead was a large greenhouse, glittering in the moonlight. The ground was hard here. I stole past, and spying a small shed, crept through the partly opened door. Tools were propped up against the walls, and there was a big pile of sacks in the middle of the floor. I pulled the door shut and covered myself with the sacks.

Outside there was a loud snuffling, as if from a large animal. I stayed silent, hardly daring to breathe.

The door to the shed burst open and someone came inside. "Do you see anything?" a woman asked.

"Maybe under here," another one said. My sacks were thrown off, and a light shone in my face. "Get out of there."

The two policewomen seemed quite young. One pointed a gun at me, while the other held the light. "You're under arrest by the laws of the North American Nation," said the one with the flashlight. "Everything you say will be recorded, and can be used against you in a court of law. You're advised to remain silent until you speak with your lawyer."

They took me outside to a waiting dromy and we got into the lighted interior where I sat facing the officers. One was tall and thin with dark hair; the other was a short, heavy-set blonde. "We're ready to go," the dark-haired one called.

"Yes, ma'am," the dromy replied. Our compartment dimmed. Shortly after we started off, a bulky woman in dark clothing darted out and waved a stick. "What are you doing on my property?"

"A criminal was hiding in your shed," the dromy said.

"Of all things!"

"Don't be alarmed, this one is apprehended."

It was bizarre, insane even, to be called a criminal. "I'm a space cadet," I told the officers when the dromy moved on. "We fight for justice and the right."

The women stared back at me, expressionless under their uniform hats. "I told you before, you're advised to remain silent," the tough looking blonde said curtly.

After this I shut up. Mr. Gerald knew everything about the law, and I planned to contact him as soon as possible.

Leaving the farm, the dromy went down a dark narrow roadway and leaped a fence that crossed the end. Out on the street it trotted along at a fast pace, using the siren when it crossed intersections or encountered traffic. We came to a business area and passed a fire hall.

The police station was a low-lying building with several vans parked out front. At the entranceway, the dromy stopped and opened the compartment. The blonde took me inside.

The room we went to was noisy, and seemed chaotic. Keeping a firm grip on my arm, the officer marched me through to a lineup waiting in front of a desk, where an older, heavy set policeman was stationed. People stared and there were derisory comments about my uniform. My shame was intense.

When it was my turn, the white-haired, ruddy-faced policeman looked at my soiled uniform and smiled knowingly. "I've had STA men here before, around the end of term," he said. "Did he disturb the peace?"

"It's murder, sir," my officer said. "We were called to Grace Hospital at two fifteen this morning, at which time we saw the victim, an older man named Lucas Rivera. Two witnesses, Dr. Nils Johansen and his wife, Dr. Bibi Santos, said that the perpetrator, Dominic Tessier, assaulted Lucas

Rivera and killed him. Next he attacked a security man in a stairwell, causing severe injury. Our dromy took the scent, and we followed the perpetrator to Columbus Avenue. We found him hiding in a farmer's tool shed."

The policeman stared into his video screen. "Here's the initial complaint, reported from Grace Hospital." He turned his eyes on me. "You're Dominic Tessier?"

"Yes, sir," I said, meeting his gaze. "There was no murder, though."

The policeman looked back at the screen, and scratched his head. "Well, I'm instructed to hold you. You'll have a chance to explain things to the justice."

I was ready to explode. "This is all crazy. I'm not a criminal. I need to get back to my school!"

"There's nothing I can do about that," the policeman said. "Speak to your lawyer, if you have one."

A guard took me to into an office, where I was fitted with a neck chain that held an identification tag. Another guard took my personal effects, and put them in a storage bag. They advised me again of my right to contact an attorney.

As Mr. Gerald did not accept calls after office hours, I left a message explaining what had happened. Then the guard brought me to one of the holding cells, where I was to spend the night.

CHAPTER 36

There were ten of us in the cell that night, sprawled out on perforated benches. My rest was taken in snatches, as men cried out in sleep, or got up to use the urinal. Close to daybreak I entered a true sleep, but that ended early with a banging on the bars. Two attendants brought in our breakfast of fried egg sandwiches and strong, sweet tea.

After breakfast someone left, and I got his spot where the end of the bench met the wall. It was more comfortable here and I soon went back to sleep.

"Hello, Dom." Awake immediately, I sprang to my feet. My guardian's partner, Mr. Avery, looked in at me. His tall form was relaxed as always, and his casual style made an elegant contrast to the prison situation. I went to him gladly, and a guard opened the door to let me out.

"Was the night too terrible?" Mr. Avery asked as we shook hands.

Relieved to be with him, I laughed loudly. "It was not as pleasant as going to the ball."

"I can imagine." He took me past more cells to a small conference room. The place was quiet, with light brown walls and comfortable furniture. I went inside the adjoining washroom and got cleaned up, relishing the hot water on my face and hands.

When I came out, Mr. Avery had some apple juice for me on the round table where he was sitting. I gulped it down and went to the dispenser for another glass. "Tell me what happened," he said.

"I was on my way to the ball when Lucas arrived in a limo. He'd suffered some kind of relapse, and wanted me with him at Grace Hospital.

After we got there, it turned out he planned to merge with me! A couple of doctors there were helping him. They drugged me, but it wore off enough that I was able break free. Lucas died in the struggle. I never meant to do it, it was a terrible accident."

"Merge, you say? Were they planning to use your body for spare parts--a replacement heart, for instance?"

"No, he intended to transfer his mind into my brain and take control."

Mr. Avery shuddered. "How ghastly."

"After escaping from the hospital I ran down the road, but a police dromy was soon on my trail. I guess it was a bad mistake to run away."

"People often act strangely in difficult situations," Mr. Avery said. "Don't be too hard on yourself."

A buzzer sounded. "Dominic Tessier, report to the justice."

One floor down we entered a dark, narrow room and stood before a blond-haired clerk who sat behind an illuminated gray desk. The man touched my identification tag with a scanner. "Dominic Tessier," he said.

The back wall lit up to show an outline of a human in black robes. The image's eyes were dark holes that seemed to draw everything in. "You've been busy, Mr. Tessier," it said in a melodious tenor. "You finished off the Mendez gang almost single-handedly, and now another is dead and one more injured. How do you explain yourself?"

I looked to Mr. Avery. "Well," I began.

The lawyer touched a finger to his lip. "Mr. Justice. If I may speak on my client's behalf?"

"Go ahead."

"What happened last night was purely self-defense," Mr. Avery said. "My client had been kidnapped and was restrained by force. Lucas Rivera planned to use his body for a mind transplant."

The justice turned my way. "Is this true?"

"Yes, sir."

"Very properly my client resisted, and fled the scene. Lucas's death was unintended, a chance accident that occurred as my client broke free."

"A situation like this requires an investigation."

"Mr. Justice," Mr. Avery said. "We'll cooperate fully with anything you say. But my client's a student at the Space Training Academy. We ask release under security for the sake of his studies."

"I'm not authorized to grant release to suspects who are potentially dangerous to society." The image began to fade. "Dominic Tessier will remain in custody until the investigation is complete."

"No," I cried. "Wait, don't do this!" The wall was blank; I hung my head despairingly.

"That's the decision," the clerk said. "It looks like they'll hold you at the Cook."

"This will be straightened out before too long," Mr. Avery said as we left. "It's only bureaucracy making a mess of things."

His reasoned approach was not what I wanted to hear. "I have to get back to school."

"We all want that for you," Mr. Avery said, putting a hand on my shoulder. "Don't forget, you have one of Vancouver's best law firms working on your behalf."

After lunch a guard took me behind the building, and I got into the back of a windowless van with three other prisoners. "You'll arrive at the regional corrections facility in approximately twenty minutes," a voice said. "Remember, you are being monitored at all times. Anything you say or do can be used against you." A classical piano began to play Bach fugues.

The Cook was in downtown Vancouver not far from the courthouse. I knew the general route, but lost my sense of direction once the van got underway. Everyone remained silent; there was only the music.

The van came to a stop and we waited for a long time. Then a uniformed man opened the side door. "Everybody out, ladies," he yelled. "Obey the robots."

We exited onto an underground loading dock where other trucks and vans were lined up. "This way, this way," a guard robot called from an entranceway.

"Smash the robots," a disheveled young man said in an undertone as we went down a long, drab corridor. His eyes were reddened, as if he'd been crying.

"I'm Dom, what's your name?"

"Nevil."

"Go on, keep moving," the guard bellowed from behind us.

Another guard was stationed at the entrance to a large, two-level hall. The entrance area was separated into lanes, by wire meshing. I followed Nevil into a middle lane, where he leaned back against the mesh.

"Welcome to the Cook Correctional Facility," said an amplified female voice. "You'll be processed as quickly as possible. Act calmly and politely, because your behavior is monitored at all times. Disturbances are not permitted here and offences are dealt with immediately. Thank you for your cooperation."

"Welcome to the Cook," Nevil mimicked. "We look forward to roasting you up for dinner."

CHAPTER 37

The new quarters were more comfortable than I'd expected. The inmates in this section were only under investigation, and the prevailing mood was of fairly relaxed optimism. Our uniforms were bright orange.

My room was larger than the one at school, and had its own washroom. I shared with Phil, an accountant who'd been falsely accused of embezzlement by jealous co-workers. Convinced the truth would come out eventually, he passed his time playing cards.

I expected to return to school before long, and was determined not to waste my time. The Cook (or "Cookie" as we called the prison's motherly sounding voice) refused to hook up my school assignments but allowed library access, and I found material that fit well with my studies.

On the second day I was in the common room watching Phil play cards, when someone put their hands across my eyes. It was Astra. With a laugh I seized her hands and held her close. Then Zack gave me a hug. When I saw tears in his eyes it almost made me cry, too. They looked wonderfully healthy and strong in their uniforms, and I knew we were one. I was an STA man to the core, nothing could change that.

Back in my room, Zack took a seat at the table while I sat with Astra on the couch. "Nobody can believe this," Zack said. "Assuming you're cleared in time, you're sure to win the election."

"You were kidnapped," Astra said. "You did what you had to do."

"Absolutely," Zack said. "The world's depending on us, and all the stuff they preach. But when you use your training they jump on you."

"You're giving me ideas for my speech," I said.

When it was time to leave, Zack went outside and Astra and I embraced. "I miss you so much," she said.

"Me too," I mumbled. Glued together, we fell back onto the couch.

Astra straddled my torso and looked fiercely into my eyes. "There is so much I want to do with you. You have to come back." After a long kiss she got up and went to the door. "Come back soon," she said, going out.

That night it was difficult to fall asleep. Events had gone by so fast, it left little time to think much. Ever since the night of the Grand Ball my life had been a nightmare. Being attacked in the hospital was overwhelming, as was the aftermath.

Lucas asked too much of me. My life was just starting to take shape. I was on the verge of achieving things, and he'd have taken it all away.

I'd come to accept being his clone. But what did that mean? All I had to do was lift my hand to know I was my own man. I had my own life, my own will, my thoughts and my purpose, just as Lucas had his. We were different people, with little in common.

The memory of his poor body lying helpless on the hospital floor came to me then, and I was seized by a powerful sense of remorse. It was a shame he had to die.

It was impossible to change things now. The best I could do was to make a good job of my own life and make that his memorial.

Mr. Gerald came to my room Wednesday morning, shortly after ten. As long as I could remember he'd been the one constant person in my life, and it was a huge relief to see his solid form in the comfortable blue suit. He greeted me in the familiar, caring way he always had. On shaking hands, though, his grasp was cold and limp.

"Quite the place, isn't it, sir?" I asked, ushering him in. "You just missed my cellmate, Phil."

"Is he a decent sort?" Mr. Gerald asked, sitting at the table.

I nodded to the stack of cards on the table. "He's showing me a lot."

Mr. Gerald picked up the deck and started shuffling, the cards moving snakelike in his hands. "I'm afraid there's no way out of your situation. The authorities have decided to continue with your case, and you'll have to stand trial."

"Trial." Numbness overcame me, as I realized my life at STA, and my whole career were threatened.

"Someone's released information about Lucas's past. The investigators know he's a convicted transport who returned from Mars, and that I defended him originally."

"As a returned transport, Lucas had no rights. He could be killed on sight."

"It's not that straightforward. The prosecution has referred me to the Bad Breed law, which enabled the World Court to shut down a European genetic engineering company's plan to recreate monsters like Adolf Hitler and Vlad the Impaler. In my opinion the Bad Breed law was always deeply flawed, because a person's character depends much more on upbringing and environment than it does genetics. Human beings are not pit bulls. But in some jurisdictions the precedent's been cited when trying clones of psychopaths, pedophiles, and career criminals."

After Mr. Gerald left, my mind was in a whirlwind, my life's certainties swept away. Every hope and dream I had was threatened.

Over and over I looked back on things, but found no way to change the course of events once they'd trapped me at the hospital. What was I to do, just lie there and let them steal my body? After again concluding I was in the right, I found a modicum of inner peace.

If the prosecution planned to twist things, Mr. Gerald was the one to handle the trial. He was one of the best lawyers in Vancouver, a man of wisdom and huge experience. I'd put my trust in him, and hopefully justice would be done.

Shortly after Mr. Gerald left, Cookie announced that I was charged with manslaughter, and had to move to a different section. "Act calmly and politely at all times," the prison's voice reminded me. I got washed up, and wrote a note to Phil. Then a guard arrived to escort me.

CHAPTER 38

The clerks at the processing desk had better things to do than look after me, and I waited in silence for a long time. At last a man glanced up in a bored, sardonic way. After scanning my identification tag, he glanced at his screen and whistled loudly. "There's not much doubt about this case. Convict's clone." The others looked me over, and laughed.

An attendant had me disrobe and pass through a shower room. I was issued a gray uniform, and another guard took charge of me.

My new room reeked of body odor. A large, long-haired man lay on the bottom bunk with his shirt off. "Jake this is Dom, your new cellmate," the guard said. Jake made a grunting sound and turned toward the wall. "Call if you have any questions," the guard said, and left.

Seeing a screen at the end of the room, I sat down at the table to watch. The video showed a line of cyclists winding through a mountain crevice, heading for a tunnel. An Asian in black skin-tight garb, her damp face taut with effort, pulled out and pumped for the lead.

"I never told you to sit in my chair." Jake towered over me, hairy belly hanging over his gray pants. "Am I talking to the wall? Move, sucker." He cuffed me across the ear.

It was too much. Springing to my feet I made a quick fake and cuffed his ear in return.

"You little punk," he gasped. An intent look came over him and he set on me, flailing his arms.

"No fighting allowed." Cookie said loudly. "No fighting allowed."

There was no time to listen; the anger surging in me was a huge relief. I stepped forward and hammered my fists deep into Jake's gut. He reached for me and I stepped back, then moved in again. Jake went down.

The door burst open, and three guards rushed in. They shoved me against the wall and pushed me to the floor. I did not resist, but lay still. One of them lifted my head with his foot. Taller and older than the other two, he had pale blue eyes that seemed amused. "The convict's clone," he drawled. "Already fighting, displaying his true animal nature."

Jake spat out some blood. "Convict's clone," he said. "No wonder he laid me out."

"Let him up," the head guard said. The others relaxed their hold and I got to my feet. "Dominic Tessier, you're a violent boy. You've got a true predisposition for it and I'm thinking silver in your case."

His words were terrifying. If they put the silver bracelet on me I'd be a zombie-like creature, incapable of resistance.

They took me down the hall, and into a corner office. A woman wearing a brown uniform like the others was there alone, working at a desk. Dark complexioned, with high cheekbones, her black hair was knotted tightly with a wide red ribbon at the top of her head. "What's the problem, Mason?" she asked, turning her large dark eyes on me.

"He's acting up," the head guard said. "He needs to be fixed."

When the woman scanned my identification tag, I noticed her nails were short and ragged, as if they'd been bitten down. "Dominic Tessier is in serious trouble," she said, looking at her screen. "He's difficult here as well?"

"He beat his cellmate half to death."

"A pattern of violence in the past, and he's up to the same thing here. Well, we've got the solution." She went to a cabinet on the wall. Her waist was slim in the tightly cut brown uniform, with wide hips and breasts like heavy melons. She took out a length of silver fabric and held it up to me. "Attractive, isn't it?" Wordlessly, I shrank back. "The bracelet won't be on forever," she said softly. "It'll cut down your libido, do you care?"

"Why, Mona, you interested?" Mason asked.

"I've had it with you," Mona shrieked. "Shut up!"

"Relax, I'm only joking," Mason muttered.

Mason steadied my arm, while Mona fitted the fabric to my wrist. After the ends coalesced she held the bracelet under an intense white light, and the whole thing glowed. The light changed to orange, then red and turned off. "It'll take a while before the chemicals take effect," Mona said. "I'll examine you later and see if we need further adjustments."

Back at the room Mason gave me a shove and I stumbled in. Jake helped me sit down at the table. "It was a set up," he said, staring at the bracelet. "I'm a strike two, so I have to stay on their good side."

"Why would they want to get me?" I asked.

"They never said."

The bracelet felt constricting at first but this passed and there was a sense of contentment, and of being insulated from my surroundings. Jake encouraged me to lie down on the couch and have a cup of tea. His conversation was understandable, but seemed to come from far off.

Now Mason was there. I didn't know how he'd come into the room, but it was good to see him. Mason pinched my cheek. "Are you feeling more relaxed now?"

"Yes, very much so," I said, pleased by his attention.

He pinched me again. "When I tell you to do something, you say 'Yes, Mr. Mason.' Got that?"

The request seemed most reasonable. "Yes, Mr. Mason," I said, making a little wiggle.

He pulled my arm until I got up. "The guards are holding a competition for you bracelet boys," he said as we went down the hallway. "Ever do much racing?"

"We have races sometimes at the school." From up ahead came cheers, and shouting. Around the corner, a crowd of guards and prisoners was gathered in a large room where tables and benches had been pushed over to the far wall, creating an open space.

Mr. Mason shoved me to the front, where three half-naked inmates were sprinting furiously. It was very noisy; spectators screamed their lungs out. The runners finished and collapsed, sweat running down their bodies.

"Get out of that shirt," Mr. Mason said, pulling at the buttons. "My money's on the convict's clone!" He positioned me behind a chalk line, beside two others wearing silver bracelets "Go as fast as you can," he said urgently, his breath hot in my ear. "I want to win this race."

"Yes, Mr. Mason." Filled with purpose, I took some deep breaths.

A guard with a flushed face stood at the line. "Get ready," he shouted, holding up his hand. "On your marks. Get set. Go!"

I sped off in a burst of pure energy. Touching the far wall I spun around and started back, aware the man in the middle was ahead of me. Although I tried my best, my body could not seem to close the gap. Then he wasn't there anymore, and I charged ahead.

Something hit my legs, and I fell flat. "Get up!" "Go!" people screamed. I started running again, and when another tried to trip me I jumped over his leg and kept going. The man in the far lane came first; I was close behind.

Exhausted and dizzy, I went to the sidelines. Men were shouting all around, and money changed hands. "Turkey race," someone called out.

"Turkey race," the others yelled.

Four new prisoners lined up and went on their hands and knees. "You turkeys gobble as loud as you can," the guard said. "Let me hear you."

A cool hand touched my forehead. "I have to run some tests," Mona said. She helped find my shirt and I put it on. "Did it disturb you when he made you run?" she asked as we left.

"No, Miss Mona." Well aware of her importance and beauty, I was grateful she was holding my hand.

"The staff runs things at the Cook, sometimes I wish there was more oversight. Mason thinks he's instilling discipline but I say it's his dark side coming out."

Inside the guard station she had me sit at the table, while she measured my pulse and pressure and drew a blood sample. "We'll do this several times over the next few days, to make sure our chemistry's properly balanced." She put my silver bracelet under the intense light again and gazed at her screen. "I never planned on becoming a guard; my intention was to be a real nurse. But, here I am. It's not so bad. In fact I like working with men who have the bracelet." The light turned red and went out. "There, that's done. The only thing left is the urine test."

She handed me a sample bottle, and I went into the bathroom. "Good boy," she said when I brought it out. "Don't forget to wash your hands."

CHAPTER 39

The news media ran high-profile stories about Lucas's conviction thirty years ago, and his subsequent return from Mars. This was previously thought impossible, and caused widespread fear and anger. Watching the broadcasts, I knew his notoriety would undercut my situation. The silver bracelet kept my emotional responses well subdued, though. I felt relaxed, and enjoyed very deep sleeps.

On the morning of the trial, an older guard, Jim, escorted me to the Cook's subbasement, where a carriage ran through an underground passageway to the courthouse. An elevator took us to the second floor.

Stepping out into the wide courthouse hallways gave a wondrous sense of freedom. Unfortunately people shied away from our prison dress, even though Jim and I were no threat.

My trial was held in one of the larger rooms, because of the public interest. A group of men stood at the entrance, and as we approached I recognized the congressman, Kenny Summers. He stared at me, and stroked his beard. Jim took me in through a different door, and I missed the chance to say hello.

We entered the courtroom at the front; across from here spectators were sitting in rows that sloped up to the back wall. Mr. Gerald came to meet me. He took me to the defendant's table, and Mr. Avery got up to shake my hand.

"All rise," a man in a red uniform boomed out.

Everyone stood and faced the front, which was draped with UWS and NAN flags. A slim, balding man in black robes came out from the side and stepped up on the dais. Taking a seat behind a table, he rapped sharply with a gavel. "The court is now in session." He turned to the man in red. "Summon our higher authority."

The man in the red uniform bent down to a protuberance in the floor that was covered by a gray cloth. "The court requests attendance of the Chief Justice," he said loudly, pulling back the cloth. An immense head rose slowly out of the floor. Wide-browed and bearded, with huge gray eyes, it resembled the ancient Greek god Zeus. A ripple of applause spread through the gallery.

The judge rapped his gavel, and everyone sat down. "Today we open proceedings on a manslaughter case," he said. "This case is complex, and the implications far-reaching, so I appreciate the presence of the higher authority. The Chief Justice brings the total body of NAN and UWS law to the courtroom, and interprets the law in accordance with current policies and directives, in a way no human can. There is no appeal from this court."

"No appeal for a Martian transport," a man said loudly. "They're gone for good." Laughter and jeers rang through the courtroom.

The judge hammered his gavel furiously, and the room was suddenly silent. "You're in contempt, mister. Think I won't charge you? I'll clear this whole room." He stared around at the gallery then smiled coldly. "Let's continue by reviewing the circumstances. This court is in possession of records from the time of the North American Federation, that document Lucas Rivera's conviction for defying their special prohibition against immigration, and using a submersible to smuggle people into the country. We were unable to obtain the actual NAF records on this case; apparently some data was lost in the collapse of that government. However, a thorough search turned up the entire transcript of the case right here in Vancouver. There's plenty of corroboration in the local media files, as the case was covered both in Seattle and Vancouver. The NAF court judgment was that Lucas Rivera be transported to Mars, never to return under penalty of death." The judge looked to the table across the room from us. "Any argument on this?"

A long-limbed woman with short-cropped blonde hair stood up, and pressed her hands together. "No argument, your honor," she said. "I've seen the transcript."

"We call her the Mantis," Mr. Gerald whispered to me. "It may look like she's praying, but she's usually preying."

"Does the defense agree also?" the judge asked.

"Definitely," Mr. Avery replied. "Our firm also has these records, because we defended Lucas Rivera thirty years ago."

"Today you defend his murderer," the prosecutor said. "Isn't that a conflict?"

"Not at all," Mr. Avery said. "Lucas Rivera was a hero, who defied the genocidal laws enacted by an outlaw regime; his clone Dom is of the same stock, upright and true." He got to his feet. "Your honor, I ask that Dominic Tessier be released immediately. As a returned transport, Lucas had no rights in the North American Nation and could be killed on sight. No crime was committed, and there's no reason to hold my client."

"This trial must continue," the prosecutor burst out, striding to the front. "The 'killed on sight' clause was never meant to excuse a son murdering his father, or a daughter her mother." The black-clad woman paced back and forth, glancing at me periodically. This angel of justice was thrilling to watch, and I felt considerable sympathy for her. "Dominic's killing of his only parent, Lucas Rivera, is so unnatural, and so horrendous, we must turn to the Bad Breed act for protection. I intend to prove that Dominic's abnormal propensity for violence is a danger to society. Furthermore, the killing happened in a hospital setting in the midst of an important and delicate operation. The law must make an example of this case."

"The prosecution's characterization is wildly erroneous," Mr. Avery said. "Lucas Rivera was not convicted of a violent crime. He saved people from certain death, people who today are exemplary citizens. Nor is Dominic by nature a violent individual. The Bad Breed act was not meant for this type of person, nor should it be invoked here."

The judge frowned. "Well, the prosecution makes some good points. If there's a bad breed type before us, I need to ensure the safety of the public. Defense will have ample opportunity to show otherwise in the course of the trial." He turned to the higher authority. "Anything to add, Chief Justice?"

"No, nothing at present," it said in a low-pitched, cultured voice. "Proceed with the trial, it's all very interesting."

The lights dimmed, and screens at the front of the room and on the table in front of us showed the Vancouver Police Department insignia. "The events portrayed were seen through the eyes of Officer Six Zero Seven," said a dispassionate voice that I remembered well. "It was the evening of May twenty-seventh, twenty-one hundred and forty-three." The dromy appeared with its head turned, and nostrils flared. "At nine forty-five I received an urgent call to report to Surrey's Grace Hospital. Police officers Carla Sanchez and Vivian Henderson accompanied me."

Red Exit signs flashed on and off, and an alarm rang shrilly, as the scene moved swiftly up a hallway. A robot-nurse waved from a doorway. "In here."

Inside, Lucas lay on his back, arms outstretched, and lips parted. The two policewomen took photographs and made notes.

"Dominic Tessier did it," Dr. Johansen said. "He's the twenty-year-old clone of the deceased."

Bibi pointed to an overturned recliner. "This is where he sat."

The dromy snuffled loudly. "I have the scent."

Red splotches appeared, a visible spoor. My scent was everywhere; on the overturned recliner, the restraint straps, the floor where I'd walked, and the door handle where I'd gone out. It continued down the hallway to the stairs, and through the lobby. Outside there was no darkness, and the red was marked all along the street where I ran.

The dromy tracked me to the farm and found the tool shed. It stopped at the doorway, and the policewomen went inside. When they brought me out, there were cries of scorn from the gallery. "Coward," a man shouted.

These video testimonials continued for the rest of the day. A man from Grace Hospital told how they transplanted one of Lucas's clone embryos into a surrogate mother. Mr. Gerald testified that he oversaw my upbringing in the crèche and later education. Dr. Penner, my psychologist at UBC, explained how the transformation process that was preparing me to become a T-man made me capable of receiving Lucas's personal information in a merger.

In the afternoon, a man from the coroner's office discussed the results of the autopsy. Lucas's death was caused by a brain hemorrhage that occurred during a violent struggle.

After this, the white-haired security man I'd kicked down the stairs was shown lying in a hospital bed, with a brace around his neck. Dr. Johansen promised that Grace Hospital would spare no effort, and the man would walk again.

"A sad situation," the prosecutor said. "We're seeing clear evidence of the unrestrained violence this perpetrator is capable of."

"The defendant regrets this unintended injury very much," Mr. Avery said. "Kidnapped and held against his will, he only wanted to get free."

When the guard returned me to the Cook, Jake greeted me with a handshake and a grin. He looked clean, and the smell was gone from the room. "My lawyer says I'll be out of here tomorrow," he said as we sat down at the table.

"I'm happy for you."

"I was scared, I didn't want to face Mars. It was good to meet you, though. I shared a cell with the Convict's Clone. Not many men can say that."

His comment seemed so strange I did not reply.

"There was more on the news about your old man. It's like I thought. Lucas Rivera was a big time gangster."

"He's everything I hate."

CHAPTER 40

In the morning, Bibi entered the glowing witness cage, and put her hands in the gloves. There were disbelieving murmurs when she was sworn in, apparently because of the contrast between her fresh-faced, youthful look, and her title as doctor and head of Grace Hospital's rejuvenation program.

Her emotions chart showed only shades of blue; she was clearly at ease. "Yes it's me," she said with a broad grin. "Forty-nine-year-old Bibi, together with my second self, eighteen-year-old Cici."

"Dr. Santos," the prosecutor said, pressing her hands together. "When you merged with your clone, was there any struggle involved? Was it difficult to unite?"

"It's similar to a good marriage, where the partners contribute wholeheartedly. The union made a much more perfect being."

"What about the personality of the clone, has it survived in you?"

"Thankfully yes."

"Consider for a moment, possible resistance to the merger. Were there struggles for dominance, fear of losing control, or resentments on either side?"

"We'd always loved each other and felt unity. The older version had experience, position, and wealth which the younger self lacked. Advancing age brought difficulties which health of youth, bursting with vitality and passion, could overcome. We offer everything to the other. No loss is involved, only gain. There's deep gratitude on both sides."

"Knowing all this, how do you react to a clone that rejects the merger?"

For the first time, Bibi darted a glance at me. Yellow and orange crept into her chart. "This failure was terrible for me. We knew it would be difficult, because they hadn't spent enough time together. Lucas was very sick, and the procedure offered his best chance to survive, otherwise we wouldn't have gone ahead at this point."

"Information was transferred into the clone, though?"

Bibi sobbed briefly and shook her head. "Sorry, this is so difficult. With a miscarriage like this, there's no predicting the outcome, but I don't see how Lucas's personality can emerge and dominate in the usual way. Perhaps some kind of chimera, a travesty of what should have been, will arise. Nothing like this disaster has happened in my entire career, so I can't guess what the final outcome will be for Dominic. But Lucas is dead. There's no bringing him back."

"Dominic resisted the procedure in the most violent way possible," the prosecutor said. "Was it inevitable, given the two parties involved?"

Bibi shook her head vehemently. "I heard what was said before, and to me the Bad Breed theory is a lot of nonsense, because personalities depend so much on environment and upbringing. Lucas was a marvelous gentleman, and will always be a hero in my eyes for rescuing my family from certain death, whereas Dominic is an ungrateful little swine who refused to help save his only parent's life. There's no Bad Breed about it."

"Thanks for your opinion," the prosecutor said hastily. "No further questions."

Mr. Avery approached the witness box. "Dr. Santos, the relationship with your Cici is most admirable. You raised her well. But what if she'd grown up separate, and only met you a few days before the proposed merger? Would it have been so easy for her to surrender her independence?"

"Of course not."

After Bibi stepped down, the prosecutor addressed the judge. "Your honor, Dr. Santos is a true role model, and her clone is also to be commended. What a contrast to Dominic's lack of gratitude! Lucas Rivera lived for this boy. Working in conditions unimaginable to us here on Earth, he always supported the child he'd never met. Dominic lacked for nothing. He went to the best schools and enjoyed every comfort and advantage. And how did he repay his benefactor? With the foulest rebellion imaginable. Dominic Tessier had the chance to save the one who embodied both his father and mother; instead he coldly snuffed him out. His crime is no ordinary murder."

Mr. Avery leaped to his feet. "I object. The crime committed that night was the assault on Dominic Tessier. An attempt was made to force the merger of a criminal's mind into his. It would have been a nightmare, the shackling of one of our healthiest youths to a dissolute convict. Dominic was well within his rights to break free."

That evening I relived the day's events over and over. Bibi's relationship with Cici interested me deeply, and helped me understand that the meetings with Lucas were always meant to prepare me for a merger. None of them saw me as a real person. From the start, they planned to have Lucas take control of my body and dominate me totally.

Bibi's calling me an ungrateful, murdering little swine did hurt. The prosecutor also calling me ungrateful, made me think perhaps I was. Lucas did a lot for me; I'd always wondered about my unknown benefactor.

When the prosecutor spoke of the foulest rebellion possible, it reminded me of teachers back in the crèche, when they told us about Satan rebelling against God and being thrown down from heaven to the fiery pit. Rebellion was the worst of crimes. Children were always to respect authority, and strive to become trustworthy members of society. There was no mention of a situation where the authority is a criminal.

In considering these issues, I realized that life had put me in a box with no exit. I had as much control of my destiny as a piece of driftwood caught in a raging torrent.

And what of Bibi's saying that the information she'd put into my mind from Lucas would eventually change me in an unknown way? That I'd become a chimera, some kind of travesty? Clearly, this was a real threat. In the intakes I'd undergone at STA, there was no suggestion that information could ever be removed.

There was a soft knock at the door, and Mona came in. She needed to check my chemicals before going home. "Are you suffering any anxiety about the trial?" she asked as we went down the hallway.

"No, Miss Mona. I think a lot, now that the day's over."

"That's normal." As we turned the corner, she stopped me. "Cookie can't hear now, it's one of our private spots." She smiled, and stroked my face. "I've been thinking about you all day. You're a very nice person, and I'm sorry you have to go through this."

"At the trial they say I'm a monster."

"It's not true." She glanced around, and we walked slowly on. "We're having a hall talk now. Never tell anyone about this."

"I won't, Miss Mona."

"I really am a frustrated nurse, who mothers the inmates. To me the prison is not for punishment, but a place where someone can get treatment, and return to the world a better person. I see something special in you, and want to help."

"I've never known a mother."

Now her eyes swam. "My own son might say the same. I was pregnant at nineteen and had a lovely boy, who I loved very much. The authorities persuaded me the state would give him better care, and after a year we parted, never to meet again. Today I'm thirty-seven, and will never have another child."

Not knowing what to say, I patted her arm.

She stopped and held my shoulders. "It's difficult to betray my job, but my feelings for you override that," she whispered. "I want you to know your trial is mainly for show. Everyone goes through the motions, but it's sure they're going to convict you."

I remained perfectly still, as my mind began recalculating things. "How do you know?"

"The fight with Jake was set up, they never do that otherwise. In their way of thinking, you're guilty of being the clone of a transported convict."

"The Bad Breed act. My lawyers are fighting it."

"The media campaign is another sign. The ones at the top are furious that Lucas escaped from Mars. They can't punish him any longer, but they can hit at you."

If she was right and the trial was just for show, my world was over.

"I'm going to ease your chemicals a little. Not so much that they'll notice, but enough to help you wake up. I want you to be aware, and inwardly prepared. Know something else: going to Mars is not a terrible fate. It's alive there. People do things that are no longer possible here on Earth."

CHAPTER 41

Mona's assessment of my trial had the ring of truth, and I awoke in the morning feeling like the goat in some age-old ritual, destined to be sacrificed. When my guard Jim came to get me, I fell in step as usual, as there seemed no choice.

Our walks tended to be quiet, but this morning I asked Jim a few questions, and he told me about his plans to travel after retirement. When we got to the subbasement, it hit me that I might strangle him and escape up through the courthouse. The thought was soon squelched. I would not give them an excuse to shoot me down.

The courtroom was jammed when we got there; people were standing in the back. As Jim and I entered, an extraordinary murmuring sound rose up from the crowd. It was powerful, and I was relieved to find Mr. Avery and Mr. Gerald imperturbable as ever.

"I'd like to consider once more the character of the accused," the prosecutor said. She pressed her hands together while bent slightly forward, looking to the judge, and I saw her as if for the first time. Mr. Gerald's likening her to a praying mantis was not far off the mark.

The lights dimmed, and the courtroom screens showed a silent video of me in the prison room, punching Jake until he went down. Gasps and whistles came from the galley. "Like father like clone," a man said in a western twang. When I turned to look, a short, balding man stretched out his arm at me as if leveling a rifle. He was in the second row from the top, sitting close to Congressman Kenny Summers.

"Dominic found entry to our best schools," the Mantis said. "This is why I've called the next witness. George Damon is a recent STA graduate who's known the defendant for years, and can give a true assessment of his character."

Wearing a dark blue jacket, wine striped tie, and white skullcap, George strode toward the witness cage, his head thrust forward, and his face expressionless. His voice was clear and unemotional, as he swore to tell the truth.

Mr. Gerald put his hand on my arm. "What's the main issue between you two?"

"I've been seeing another cadet, Astra Allison. She used to go with George."

"Did you have to deal with the accused as part of your honor board duties?" the Mantis asked George.

"Yes, and I'll never forget it," George said. "Cap Hanson, a first year student Dom Tessier was mentoring, got expelled because he was involved with terrorist activities. The board cleared Dom of any blame, but I entered a dissenting opinion."

"What is this opinion?"

"In my judgment, Dom failed both Cap Hanson and the academy. Cap was very confused, and needed strong guidance to straighten him out. He was desperate for help, but got nothing from his mentor. I looked at Dom's case closely and saw only two possible conclusions. Either he's too involved with his own self to ever make a good leader. Or the second possibility is that Dom himself has terrorist sympathies. In either case, he's unfit to be a space cadet."

"What else about Dominic do you remember that might give insight into his character?"

"Well, there was the famous take down of the Mendez gang that was all over the news. Everyone forgot that one of Dom's men lost a leg and had to drop out of school."

The Mantis pressed her hands together. "What did this incident tell you?"

"Dom will act without thinking things through. He's got wildness in him, and can be vicious. Once in physical education class, when we were introducing the middies to the pro suit, he attacked me like an animal. That's why I'm not surprised to see him charged. I always thought he had a criminal nature."

The Mantis nodded and turned to our table. "Your witness."

Mr. Avery stood up. "Your honor, I do have some questions for this witness, but I'd like to pause for a recess."

"And why this interruption?" the judge asked.

"What the witness has said about Dominic's character is very important, and I need to review this."

The judge looked at the clock on the wall. "The question of the defendant's character is pivotal to this trial. Take all the time you need. Let's call this recess our lunch, and meet back here in half an hour."

Out in the entrance hall, the lawyers questioned me in detail about my relationship with Astra. Then Jim took me to the prisoner's canteen.

When we returned, the courtroom was mostly empty. I was standing behind my chair waiting, when a man sauntered over. I'd seen him earlier sitting with Congressman Summers' group, pretending to point a rifle at me. Below average height, he wore a western suit with a bolo tie, brown cowboy boots, and a black slouch hat.

His large gray eyes were the coldest I'd ever encountered. "Your old man killed the best friend I ever had," he said in a quiet voice. "I miss him a lot. A war hero and a patriot, he was a real prince. I was tracking Lucas, but you got to him first. Otherwise he wouldn't have had an easy death."

I had nothing to say, and just looked at the floor.

"Lucas was a Martian, and had no place here on Earth. And you're one of them, too. Soon you'll get sent where you belong, and that'll be the end of it."

Mr. Gerald was back in the room. The short man's cold gray eyes flicked over me once more, and he walked away.

When George Damon returned to the witness cage, Mr. Avery went up to him then hurried back to our table and referred to some notes he'd jotted down. He strode toward the cage, stopped once more, and consulted with Mr. Gerald. George glowered at us.

"Sorry for the delay, Mr. Damon," Mr. Avery said. "I needed to refresh my memory. Correct me if I'm wrong, but as a senior at the Space Training Academy you'd come to know Dominic Tessier fairly well?"

"It's a small school, and the seniors get to know the underclassmen thoroughly."

Mr. Avery moved closer to the box, standing in his loose-limbed, very relaxed manner. "Well, then," he said with a puzzled expression. "The other members of the honor board made submission that Dom Tessier is of good character, and that he has the school's support. Yet you are saying the opposite."

"That's my view," George said. "Right from the start I doubted his character, and now there's proof of it."

"Dom Tessier was nominated for next year's executive. This is one of the highest honors the school can confer."

"Mistakes happen," George said.

With a wan smile, Mr. Avery spread his arms to the courtroom. "Mistakes happen." He straightened and turned back to George. "I suggest you're here not out of duty but from rivalry," he snapped. "You like Astra Allison, and you're afraid she has feelings for Dom."

"Objection," the Mantis said. "The witness's personal love life is not relevant."

"Overruled," the judge said.

"Are you in love with Astra Allison?" Mr. Avery said.

"Well, I--she's my fiancée," George said.

George's chart colors were changing rapidly, going through the whole spectrum.

"But Astra's in love with Dom," Mr. Avery said. "That's why you're here, isn't it? You have a strong interest in discrediting Dom and, if possible, you want to destroy him."

"No," George cried. "I have no personal interest."

The emotion chart flashed off and on, and the LIAR sign lit up in bright orange. The gallery erupted with hoots and laughter. Scowling, George left the courtroom.

"Avery did well with that witness," Mr. Gerald said.

Struggling to accept that George and Astra were to be married, I barely heard him. Behind me, the audience hushed. A woman sighed loudly. Another one giggled.

Zack strode up to the front. I could see no softness in his face or body. He looked fine in the STA uniform. Zack nodded to me before going to the witness booth.

"Mr. Cameron, I notice you're wearing the Space Training Academy uniform," Mr. Avery said. "Are you proud to be a student there?"

"Yes, sir," Zack said. "It's an honor to wear the uniform."

"In your two year association with Dom Tessier, was there any indication he engaged in improper or illegal activities?"

"Of course not," Zack said. "Dom's always been honest and trustworthy. He's one of the finest men I've ever met."

"Dom was called a hero for his actions in taking down the Mendez gang," Mr. Avery said. "Are there other sides to his character you'd like to mention?"

"After the Vancouver Island earthquake, we were assigned community service duty at Cedar River. They needed a multivox player to accompany the singer, Milly Tall, and Dom stepped in. He handled it coolly and the performance was a success."

"I think that says it all," Mr. Avery said. "Unless the prosecution has something."

"I do have one or two questions," the Mantis said. She approached the witness cage, and Mr. Avery returned to our table. "Your honor, at this point I'd like to read something from the court that sentenced Lucas to be transported to Mars. This material taken from the transcript of that trial has bearing on faults in the defendant's character which I believe are innate and that threaten our society."

As the Mantis read from her hand-held device, the words appeared on the courtroom screens. "Lucas has broken from normal human conduct and behaved with extreme violence." She turned to Zack. "Do you recognize this sort of tendency in Dominic?"

Zack remained expressionless but his graph began to move. "I'm a wrestler. If it's a crime to achieve ends through violence, than lock me up too, along with most of our school."

"My understanding of sport is that you keep within certain rules, or limits," the Mantis said. "There's a difference between organized wrestling, and acting in an unpredictable and dangerous fashion that might injure or destroy your opponent."

Zack shrugged. "What's your point?"

"We've seen Dominic Tessier use extreme violence in the takedown of the Mendez gang," the Mantis said. "This was viewed as heroic, because it resulted in the destruction of wanted criminals. Are you aware of Dominic displaying this kind of behavior in circumstances that did not involve an attack on criminals?"

"No, of course not." Zack's graph surged up and down, and the LIAR sign flickered.

"You might want to rethink that answer," the judge said.

Zack paused. "There was some talk going around, but I didn't see anything myself."

"What is it?" the Mantis asked. "You can't hold things back in this courtroom."

"When Dom's mentor Plenso was killed, some of the men joked about his being homosexual. Dom grabbed one of them by the throat and could have easily killed him. The ones who saw it were afraid of Dom."

"No more questions," the Mantis said.

Zack gave me a mournful look and left the courtroom.

"Your honor that last statement is pure hearsay," Mr. Avery said. "I'd like to see it stricken from the record."

"What about this?" the Mantis said. "Is this hearsay?" The video of me punching Jake came on the screen. The gallery spectators howled and jeered.

Back at my room in the prison, I got a drink of juice and told Cookie to find some news on the video. The screen showed the entrance to the Vancouver courthouse, where Congressman Kenny Summers was being interviewed. I'd seen him in the same brown suit and striped tie, less than an hour ago.

"There's big trouble in the Space Training Academy," Kenny Summers said in a measured way. "This school is not a liberal institution; it's at the center of the ultra-conservative pole. Graduates embody principles of Earth superiority, and justify Earth rule. Morally, intellectually and even physically they're expected to be among the very best.

"Lucas Rivera, a convicted gangster who recently escaped from Mars, struck at the heart of our system with the help of his clone, Dominic Tessier. Recently Dominic was nominated for the executive at STA, just before receiving a mind transplant from his parent. The clone, now with the mind and purpose of a master criminal, was close to becoming student president. At the end of the senior year, he'd be fully transformed. Then the entire T-man hierarchy would be wide open to him. It's only by accident that the plot was foiled."

Summers's face became larger on the screen. "I'm keeping a close eye on the situation, and I'm optimistic that justice will be done."

These hateful comments were so twisted as to be ludicrous. Yet I had no way to answer him.

That night I dreamed of Genghis Khan in modern times. My troops marched through the streets of Vancouver in endless columns, backed by dromies and huge war machines. Buildings collapsed, and flames and smoke rose everywhere.

Then I was on Mars, where my ships attacked the space station. After it blew up, my dromies pursued a centipede train across the desert. Wang was to my left, and Zack was on the right. Kenny Summers was driving the centipede train. George Damon, dressed in a pro suit, was there with him.

When I woke up it was half past three in the morning. The bed clothes were a tangled mess; I'd been tossing around.

Today was the final day of my trial, and my whole life hung in the balance. It was healthy and good that I was dreaming. A dream like this showed Mona's readjustment of my chemicals was having a real impact.

In thinking over the dream, I realized that the injustice of my trial had shattered my faith in Earth's one-world government. I now doubted if T-man rule was much better than the systems that had come before. This was a major departure, as I never questioned the established order while growing up.

But what would this mean for my future? After seeing the damage caused by the Resisters, and their indifference to the lives of others, I could never stand with them. Nor did Lucas's obscure references to some kind of higher concerns mean anything to me. The man was a criminal; because of him my expectation of a life with solid foundations had been totally swept away. The only certainty for me now was that major changes lay ahead.

Getting kicked out of school and sent to prison was an awful experience. The main thing I'd salvaged from the mess was in waking up more. After this I could never slip back into complacency, or trust others to handle things properly. I'd remain on guard, try to keep learning, and become a true individual.

Another huge gain was in humility. In my fool's paradise days I'd grown conceited, and newly expanded consciousness was no occasion for pride. If not for Mona adjusting my chemicals, I'd still be half asleep.

CHAPTER 42

Jim and I were old friends now, and as we rode through the passage to the courthouse, I asked if he planned to visit the off-world colonies when he retired.

He smiled, and rubbed his head. "The journey would be difficult for my wife. Otherwise I'd like to go. I know quite a few people up there." The carriage came to the end of the line, and we got out and called the elevator. "It's hard to believe it's your last day," he said. "These trials are getting shorter and shorter."

"Do many people get off?"

"Once in a while." The door opened, and we stepped inside. "When you work here over the years, the system starts to look like a conveyor belt. The off-world colonies need manpower, and we supply it."

"At least it's not the death penalty."

"Most of the cases wouldn't warrant that. People resort to poaching or thievery because of economic hardship."

When we arrived at the courtroom, Mr. Gerald came and took my arm. "I hope it hasn't been too much of an ordeal?"

"I'm grateful for what you've done."

As we approached the defendant's table, Mr. Avery grasped my hand with both of his. "It's good to see you, Dom."

I grinned at him and took my seat. Hope arose within me. Was it possible that my luck would turn around and things return to normal?

The judge went to the dais, and rapped his gavel. His face looked gray and his eyes were glassy. "Well, we've had a long haul, and it's been a complicated business. Luckily the Chief Justice is here, to ease the burden from my all too human shoulders."

The room lights dimmed. The Chief Justice's head was spotlighted, and it made a revolution, looking out at everyone. "Thank you for receiving me in your courtroom," it said. "This case is not a simple one; there are arguments on both sides that have considerable merit. Nor does my decision concern only this one man, Dominic Tessier. Prosecution is persuasive in characterizing the case as a medical emergency. The raising of clones for mind transplants extends the human lifespan beyond one generation. Since Lucas was near to death, a merger with Dominic was the only chance he had to live on. An analogy is made with the lifeboat situation. Would Dominic extend a helping hand to his parent, or allow him to perish? Lucas's doctors clearly felt the situation was desperate, and Dominic's refusal of the merger was tantamount to murder.

"There are also issues of civil rights here. Clones are common in today's world, and nowhere are they treated as less than normal human beings. I have no wish to set a precedent that would undermine the freedom of choice for clones in general. Nor would I interfere with a technology which lets humans transcend the limits of one lifetime.

"Dominic's being the clone of a transported criminal sets his case aside from the normal. His existence questions the efficacy of the transport program. When the NAF court ordered Lucas removed, it did not contemplate him leaving a copy of himself behind.

"I find that in this situation, the Bad Breed Act supersedes the arguments of the defense. Prosecution's demonstration that Lucas's propensity toward violence lives on in his clone was telling for me. As Justice, one of my principal mandates is to protect society against this type.

"After duly considering all aspects of the case then, I find the accused guilty of manslaughter, with the recommendation he choose between indefinite confinement here on Earth, or Martian exile under the condition he never return." The Chief Justice turned its gaze toward the judge. "Thank you for having me here, it's been interesting."

"We are grateful to receive your decision," the judge replied. The audience applauded loudly as the man in the red uniform draped a cloth over the Justice's head, and it sank beneath the floor.

Back at the prison I lay down and closed my eyes, remembering the curious, eager way the spectators had stared at me, and their jeers and whistles when the verdict was given. The people had spoken; they hated me, and now I was to be sent away.

When I woke up, the room was very quiet. I felt rested and at peace, as if the past no longer existed and I was floating above things. "Cookie, what time is it?"

"It's five o'clock, Dom. In another half hour it'll be dinner time."

By the time I got to the dining room, people were already eating. A tall man in a white hat was behind the counter. "We've got a special tonight," he said. "Baked trout, straight from the farm. The men who come here, sometimes it's their last night on Earth. We hope you all enjoy your meal."

Taking my tray, I found a space at a nearby table. The men there nodded to me as I sat down. "How's your trial going?" the one across from me asked. He was quite thin, with curly, reddish-blond hair and a moustache.

"Convicted," I said. "Sentenced to Mars."

"The same as me, even though I did nothing wrong."

There was a chicken-like clucking from the table next to us; a dark-haired young bracelet wearer made the sounds as he licked up pieces of bread that were lined up along the table top. Three older men at the table watched him with big grins.

Recognizing Nevil from when we first came to the Cook, I called him over. He came immediately, without looking at his tormentors. "How are you?" I asked as he sat down next to me.

"It's over, I'm off to Mars," he said in the slow speech of the heavily sedated. He still had reddened eyes, as if he'd been rubbing them, or crying.

"Here's a whole table of chickens." The three older men stood over us.

A stocky, bearded man came up behind them. "Be careful who you mess with," he said in deep, resonant tones. It was Gern! The castaway from Red Sky Island scowled at the older men. "Next time it might be you wearing the silver bracelet." They moved off, and he shook my hand. "I wish you luck on Mars."

"Luck to you too, Freeman," I said. "I always wondered what happened."

"Freedom's a state of mind," Gern said. "Though I'm happy to say I'll be back on the water in a month or so." He made a humorous salute, and walked away.

"What did they charge you with?" I asked Nevil.

"Mother and I argued, and she hit her head. Matricide, they called it. They said I'm a monster, not fit to live on Earth."

"That's over now," the redhead said. "Whatever they call us, thieves, murderers or rapists, when we go to Mars we start clean. It's a new life."

"As long as we can make a living," a tall, bald man beside him said. "It has to be better than what we've got here." He raised his glass of juice to us. "Here's to Mars."

We held up our glasses in the toast. "To Mars."

Later Mr. Gerald came to my door with a burly man who carried a large metallic case.

"Would you like something to drink?" I asked.

Mr. Gerald shook his head. "There's business to do." He handed me a card. "Go visit Lydia McPherson's office in Marsport after you're settled in. She's handling Lucas's estate, and they'll look out for you, just as our office has done here."

"Will my reward money be there too?"

"Unfortunately the government's had your award rescinded. We've launched an appeal, and intend to fight the injustice vigorously. Now, a couple more details. Did you ever notice a lumitoo on Lucas's left shoulder?"

I nodded. "A dagger in a rose."

"Before all this happened, Lucas requested us to put the same mark on you. The request still stands, and it's paid for. You'll be going into rough territory, and this will help protect you."

Mr. Gerald helped me out of my shirt, and the other man, Graham, swabbed my upper arm. Then they had me lie down on the couch. Graham worked with a quick sureness; soon light shone through wild roses, and leaves and petals rippled when I moved.

There was a gobbling sound from outside, and a loud knock on the door. "Turkey race," Mason shouted, coming inside. "Where's that convict's clone?" He stopped short when he saw the other men.

Mr. Gerald stood up. "I'll have your balls for this," he said menacingly.

"No need," Mason replied, backing to the door.

"Don't try that again." The door slammed shut. Returning to the couch, Mr. Gerald watched the haft of the dagger take shape. "When Graham is finished he'll take a tissue sample for Grace Hospital."

"How could I ever trust them?"

"Bibi wants you to know she's sorry. She's a person of strong passions, and was carried away by frustration and anger. She thinks you are a strong-willed person, as Lucas was himself. You're all that's left of Lucas now, and Grace Hospital is there for you if you ever need help."

"If I decide to have a clone will you be its guardian too?"

"Yes, I'll be proud to. Avery and I will make sure he gets the best of care."

When they left I was about to get ready for bed, when there was another knock on the door. I opened it part way and saw Mona. "You have a visitor," she said, bringing Astra forward. Stunned, I stepped aside and they came in.

Astra was bundled up in a long blue coat with shiny buttons and a brown headscarf. She carried a large black bag. Realizing she'd disguised herself to enter this part of the prison, shame mixed with the gladness I felt at seeing her.

"I understand how important this is for you," Mona said to me. "The room's now set for a conjugal visit, so you'll have privacy. It's only until six; then she'll have to leave."

"Thank you," Astra said quietly.

Mona nodded. "Good night," she said, and left.

Astra and I stared at each other. "I've missed you so much," she murmured. Putting her bag down, she took off the coat and kerchief. Her short gray dress was tight and clingy; I couldn't take my eyes off her. "I'm sorry for not going to the trial. The situation was unbearable. From the beginning they created a huge circus, making up all kinds of frauds and lies. It's been monstrous for everyone who knows you."

"The trial was not my finest hour, and it's good that you weren't there."

Astra took my hand and examined the bracelet. "It's unimaginable to see this on you," she said, stroking my wrist. "These jailers are rotten."

"George said at the trial you're to marry him," I blurted out.

"He actually said that?" Astra asked with a short laugh. "Well, we're nowhere near that stage. It looks like I'll be working with the Damons, once I get out of school. As you know they're entrepreneurs, and I'll have the chance to build things off-world. My brother wants to be involved too, but he can't go into space. My father will retire soon, and there'll be more responsibility on my shoulders."

Her logic struck me as somewhat evasive. "Isn't marriage different from business?"

"You and I can discuss this better in thought than words," Astra said. She opened her bag and brought out two telecaps. "Dr. Penner let me take yours for the visit."

"Amazing it's not recycled yet." I took a place on the couch, and Astra sat next to me. We put on our telecaps.

Astra rested her head on my shoulder, and I put my arm around her. A maelstrom threatened to erupt. However, space cadets practice strict control over inchoate emotions. Awareness grew of a strong sense of yearning, as well as the anxiety in both of us.

"I'll never have this with anyone else," Astra said. "You are so special to me."

"I'll love you till the day I die."

"I can't follow you to Martian exile," Astra said. "I need to become a Tee, and go off-world and create the structures I dreamt of. As much as my heart cries out for you, I can't follow my heart's desire."

She started to cry, and I held her tight to me. "It's all right, I wouldn't want the guilt of dragging you down. We'll both survive, and I'm grateful for what we shared. Most will never know this level of happiness."

I hummed the music I'd composed for her, and Astra smiled. Our lips met and we kissed deeply. Ever so slowly we came together, until we were making love.

Six o'clock came early, and Astra left, taking my telecap with her. She was the love of my life, and now we'd said goodbye.

After breakfast, a guard took me down to the processing area. I went through a shower room and donned a different uniform, the black and white stripes of the condemned convict.

At the exit desk, a clerk with a shaved head removed the identification tag from the chain around my neck, and scanned it. "You're Dominic Tessier?"

"That's right."

"Sin and you're out." He put the tag in a slot, and there was an intense light. "Under the privacy act, the data about your past crimes is now erased from this tag; only personal information is encoded here." He reattached it to my necklace. "You begin your exile with a clean slate."

The guard took me outside. It was sunny, and I blinked in the unaccustomed glare. A bus was parked against the curb, and men in black and white striped uniforms were boarding.

I breathed deep of the fresh air and looked around, thinking Zack and Wang might have come to see me off. Nobody was there.

End

CPSIA information can be obtained
at www.ICGtesting.com
Printed in the USA
LVOW04s1351151116

512916LV00024B/482/P